A
TRUTH
FOR
A
TRUTH

Comedies:

Life Swap
Take a Chance on Me
What Happens in France
Suddenly Single

A
TRUTH
FOR
A
TRUTH

Detective Kate Young series

CAROL WYER

THOMAS & MERCER

Published by Thomas & Mercer, Seattle

www.apub.com

Amazon, the Amazon logo, and Thomas & Mercer are trademarks of Amazon.com, Inc., or its affiliates.

ISBN-13: 9781662506130
eISBN: 9781662506123

Cover design by Whitefox, Dominic Forbes
Cover image: ©Aline Sprauel / Arcangel

Printed in the United States of America

A
TRUTH
FOR
A
TRUTH

CHAPTER ONE

SEPTEMBER 2022

The night cloaked Kate's movements, allowing her to walk unobserved among the shadows – unobserved and undisturbed. She crept alongside the hedgerow, prepared to secrete herself in the undergrowth should a vehicle pass by. Her senses were on full alert, her nerves coiled, her mind calculating. Exactly like a killer's.

The killer she had become.

The events of the last hour were crystal clear in Kate's mind. Every word, gesture and detail of her confrontation with Superintendent John Dickson beside the dark waters of Blithfield Reservoir was now stamped into her memory.

The admission that Dickson had been responsible for hiring the hitman who had murdered her husband was a hollow victory, even though it was what she had been seeking for months after discovering evidence of Dickson's corruption.

Kate had hoped he would tell her the truth about the death of her husband, Chris. And, in that respect at least, she had got her wish. She could not, however, have anticipated what would happen after the confession . . .

◆ ◆ ◆

'The wheels to bring you down are already in motion. The Gazette *is running an exposé. They're in possession of the footage from the Maddox Club as well as all the information I dug up on you. You're right, I don't give in. I've been digging since the beginning, building my case against you. Your lies and corruption will be plastered all over the papers. It won't be long before the nationals take up the story and, as the saying goes, mud sticks. You will face charges and you will be brought to justice. I'm not my father. I can't be bullied.'*

Dickson breathes heavily, shoulders rising and falling, then smiles.

'Kate. I warned everyone you were taking on too much.' He tuts. 'You were brave to come back so soon after Chris's death. Everyone could see the effect the pressure was having on you – the pills, the talking to yourself and then that mini breakdown on the train when you almost attacked that passenger. And you've poured yourself back into work, relentlessly, day after day. There's been the intense pressure of not one but three heavy investigations all to be handled by a small team. Little wonder you were showing signs again of cracking. You've been burning yourself out. It's clear from your weight loss and your appearance.' He tuts again. 'It won't come as a shock to people when they discover you ended it all here.'

When he finishes, he withdraws a gun from his pocket. Kate has little time to react and throws herself to one side. The bullet whizzes past her to bury itself into the bank. She scrambles to her feet and hurls herself at him, knocking the gun out of his hand. It spins off and she reaches for his arm to wrench it behind him. He kicks out, twists away and hunts for the gun. Kate can't see the weapon, only Dickson's snarling face as he pushes her into the ground. She bucks her hips, causing him to tumble, then boots him with both feet, using all the force she can muster. He falls on to his back but quickly recovers and rolls away. She spies the gun, now in his hand and launches again for him, hands fumbling to take it from his grip. She feels cold metal, grabs for the handle. She feels rather than hears the shot. The impact punches her

2

in the ribs, winding her. She feels the weight of the man as he slumps against her chest and slides down the length of her body.

She drops beside him. An artery has been punctured and blood is pumping out. She needs to pack the wound. She pulls off her top, rolls it into a ball and presses it hard into his chest. He groans.

She doesn't have her phone. Maybe Dickson has one. She pats his pockets gently. Nothing. It could be in his car. If she doesn't keep up the pressure on the wound, he will die. If she doesn't phone an ambulance, he will die.

His lips move. 'I ordered the hit on Chris. Happy now? I'm not the only one. There are others, worse than me. You're a lone soldier, Kate. You can never beat us all.'

'Shut up. I need to get you help.' She races to his car, yanks open the door and begins searching for a phone. There is one in the glove box, and she tears back with it in her hand. Before she can dial for emergency services, she knows it is already too late.

She walks to the edge of the reservoir, looks across the water where a shaft of moonlight places a spotlight on the female swan gliding alone.

'Fuck, Kate. What have you done?' *The imagined voice of her dead husband, Chris, is loud in her ears. Ever since his death, she has been reliant on hearing it. Chris has guided her as she has struggled to find proof that Dickson is corrupt. He has been her support, her confidant and reason she wanted to expose the man she believed to be behind her husband's death.*

'Chris? Is that you? I found out what happened. He admitted the hitman was his idea. I got you justice.'

'Justice? This isn't justice. Not the justice I wanted. You've screwed up, Kate. You've totally screwed up. What are you going to do now?'

The anger in his voice chills her. He's never used that tone of voice with her before. She has no answer for him. She has killed Dickson, albeit out of self-defence.

Yet she can't admit it was an accident and ring the police. Dickson told her there were others ready to replace him. Those same people are dangerous. Like Dickson, they will have reach. Given Dickson's ability to cover up murders, she has no qualms in believing these same people would rig evidence to prove she murdered Dickson in cold blood. Especially if they believe her to be a threat to them.

Every code hard-wired into her soul screams she should call this in and yet the idea that there are officers worse than Dickson, operating outside of the law, means she must box clever. The only way is to ensure that no suspicion can possibly fall on her. She's up for promotion, a role that will enable her to expose these individuals. What's more important: coming clean and hopefully being exonerated, but allowing the syndicate to continue in their nefarious activities, or continuing her quest until every single one of them is caught out?

A gentle breeze blows against her cheeks.

The swan dips her elegant neck and head underwater to feed.

Kate pockets the gun, her mind spinning.

There is a way out of this.

But if she takes it, she will never be the same person again.

She broke away from her reverie. What was done was done. Dickson was dead. It was time for action. First things first, she needed to find the device, no larger than a paper clip, she had used to record Dickson's confession. Somehow, in the scuffle, she had dropped it.

'Well?'

She paused for just a moment. It wasn't like she was unused to hearing unexpected voices. Chris had made a habit of popping up inside her brain when she least expected it.

But this voice didn't belong to Chris. The timbre was lower. Was that . . . ?

Was that . . . ?

Dickson?

'You'll never find it. Not in the dark. Give yourself up.'

It was Dickson who was now taunting her.

She ignored the voice, focussing instead on unscrewing the light from her bike and using it to check the ground. The device was the proof she required to attest to Dickson's frame of mind: that he had tipped over the edge. It would substantiate her claim that he had attacked her. She would be exonerated, wouldn't she?

The device had an operational range of about fifty feet indoors, which would have been enough to pick up every word of their conversation. However, here, beside open waters, the stiff breeze might have snatched or masked his words.

Everything now hinged on the quality of the recording. How else could she explain why she'd rung Dickson from a burner phone and lured him to this out-of-the-way location?

'Face facts. You didn't really choose the right device for the job. You were more focussed on hearing him confess.' Chris's voice in her head was solemn.

'Chris. Thank goodness. I thought . . . I was sure I heard Dickson.'

She heard a low laugh. It didn't belong to Chris. Was Dickson trying to replace her dead husband's voice? The thought chilled her. She spoke aloud, hoping by speaking directly to her husband, she'd keep his voice foremost in her head.

'Chris, I've got to find it. It might provide another way out of this mess.'

She panned the beam left to right, trying to keep calm, using a grid search pattern like she was forensically examining a crime scene. The beam picked up small stones and even a tiny piece of foil, but there was no sign of the device. She directed the beam further.

The miniscule device was small, black, designed to blend in. In all likelihood, only a proper forensic search would unearth it. Kate didn't have the luxury of the time needed to find it. A decision had to be made and sharpish. The wind chilled her skin, yet she felt no discomfort. Blood coursing through her veins kept her warm.

Where was it? Had Dickson grabbed hold of it? Was it in his cold, dead hands? She didn't want to shine a light on his body or ghoulish face. For the time being she had to remain focussed. The device was the only thing that could objectively prove her version of events.

Chris's voice was back. *'You're clutching at straws. They're going to question why you phoned him and arranged to meet here by the reservoir, rather than in his office, or why you didn't take your suspicion higher up the chain of command. Even if you find the recorder, it might not be clear who is actually talking on it. And, as to why Dickson was carrying a gun? Well, it could be argued you were carrying an illegal weapon and he attempted to snatch it from you. Face it, Kate. This looks suspicious. I can't see how you can justify what has transpired. How do you explain your decision to park your car and arrive here on bike?'*

'You know why. I attached the recorder to the handlebars. I guessed he wouldn't trust me and would want me to prove I wasn't wearing a wire. The bike was the perfect hiding place. I needed him to confess to your murder!' she gasped.

'And who on earth will believe that after you killed him?'

She stood stock still. Chris had always been the voice of reason, yet he was being more negative than usual. Ordinarily, he'd have been supportive or offered solutions. And his voice. It was changing. Little by little. It was dropping in timbre and there was an edge to it she recognised as Dickson's.

Chris's voice continued.

Or was it really Chris's voice?

There was someone else talking at the same time – was that Dickson's voice? It was like two tracks playing at the same time, ever so slightly out of synch. *'If there's no recording device, you have nothing to support your reasons for meeting him here.'*

'He was corrupt!' she said.

'Kate, everything you had to prove how rotten he was you gave to the journalist, Dan Corrance. I grant you that's something, but not enough for Dickson to come to the meeting with the intention of shooting you. And nobody will believe that Dickson was behind hiring a hitman to kill me. Your accusations will be dismissed as the deluded ramblings of somebody who is still struggling to come to terms with her loss. It'll backfire. Questions about your state of mind will be raised. Lawyers will flag that, following my death, you were on medication and that you committed a grave error when you thought an innocent member of the public was a gun-wielding hitman and almost attacked him. They'll even say that Dickson prevented you from killing the man. And you aren't in any position to convince them otherwise, not without solid evidence. A half-arsed recording isn't going to cut the mustard.'

The voice droned on. Unfriendly, unhelpful, not like Chris at all. The voice underneath Chris's was becoming stronger. Was Dickson taking over?

She tried to block it from her mind, and just when she was ready to scream, she discovered the black plastic device. She crouched to retrieve it with a groan. It had shattered into fragments during the scuffle. Whatever conversation it might have picked up was now superfluous. It had been rendered useless. It had been stupid to remove it from the bike to show Dickson he'd been caught out. That move had cost her.

She swore loudly. This changed everything. Now she had nothing to confirm what had transpired here. Moreover, she'd rung Dickson from a pay-as-you-go phone, the SIM card purchased using false ID, which would be construed as suspicious if anyone found out. In fact, everything she'd done to entrap him had now conspired to entrap her instead.

To cap it all, Chris – or Dickson – was right about her state of mind. From the outside, her actions over the last few months would appear to be those of someone losing their grip.

'You've fucked up big time. You better call this in. Explain it was self-defence.'

'No.'

'What do you mean, no? You've killed a human being. It doesn't matter what you think he was guilty of, you were still responsible for his death.'

'That's not true. *He* brought the gun here. He intended to kill *me*. I wanted to bring him to justice, according to the law.'

'Like hell you did! If that had been your real intention, you'd have done it ages ago, when you first knew he was implicated in the death of that young boy at the Maddox Club.'

The voice was now distinct.

Harsher.

Colder.

Dickson's.

'Give yourself up, Kate. Everyone knows you've been under a huge amount of strain since Chris was murdered.'

'Shut the fuck up!' She strode a few paces from the body, made sure no cars were in sight. Even if they were, they wouldn't have a view of Dickson's Mercedes, parked down the lane by the reservoir, or of her. Nevertheless, she was taking no chances. She checked the road to the left and right. There wasn't a sound. No traffic.

She needed help. The only person she could turn to was her friend, mentor and boss: DCI William Chase.

William had been her father's best friend. After he'd passed away, William had stepped into the role of surrogate father.

William would help her through this, like he'd helped her through her father's and then Chris's death. Tears welled in her eyes.

William was safe – somebody who would protect her, argue that this had been an accident. She'd call him. Tell him what happened.

The thought calmed her, until Dickson spoke again.

'He was my friend too. He'll never believe I would turn on you. He knows that your mind is fragile. He knows you've had a grudge against me ever since I had you put on sick leave. He won't believe your version of events.'

Did she really want to lose the special bond she shared with William? If he saw her in a different light, everything between them would change.

An angry sob escaped her throat. There had to be another way. She turned back, took in the scene as best she could: the crumpled body in a heap on the dirt track. Her mind turned cartwheels. If she didn't confess, then she had to cover this up. Forensic evidence – blood, DNA, footprints, etc. – always led to suspects, but if nobody knew that Dickson had died here, this area wouldn't even be examined. She snapped off the light and crouched in the darkness to think her idea through.

Her car was parked a good mile away. In hindsight, the decision to leave it there would save her from being immediately implicated in his death, and had given her space to work out a plan. There were no CCTV cameras along this road. There'd been no other vehicles the entire time she'd been here. It was remote.

Could she pull it off?

'You're not tough enough. You'll cave in at the first hurdle.'

She shook her head, desperate to rid herself of Dickson's voice. Chris had abandoned her before, when she had taken steps that he hadn't approved of. She willed his voice to return.

'Chris,' she said, 'I won't do anything without your consent. I won't go through with this if you think it's wrong. I can't lose you again.'

'Forget him. Chris has gone!'

She tapped her knuckles against her head. She couldn't live with Dickson's voice. All the while, it continued to mock her.

'Why are you even considering this option? Face it, Kate, it would make more sense to try to pass off your self-defence version of events than to attempt to hide my body and pretend you know nothing about it.'

'Your cohorts will fix it somehow, so I get charged with your murder. Paperwork or some other proof showing I owned the gun will magically appear. Maybe some gangster will come forward to claim they sold it to me. Then it'll be claimed I deliberately lured you here with the intention of killing you.'

'Ha! Even though I'm dead, you are still afraid of my reach.'

'I'm not frightened of any of you! I'm just not risking getting caught. If I hand myself in, your syndicate will find a way to ensure I get sent down for killing you – and I won't stand a chance in prison any more than Cooper Monroe did after you paid the guard to murder him and make it look like suicide so he couldn't talk to me. This way I won't have your *mates* baying for my blood.'

'Come on, Kate. You're not capable of this level of subterfuge. You can't manage it alone, and there's nobody in their right mind who would be prepared to help you do your dirty work. Especially given the consequences of getting caught. Because you will get caught. I had influence. You don't. You're a lone wolf.'

She mulled over his words, then picked up his mobile from where she'd left it while searching for the recording device. Her heart urged her to call William. Her head told her not to take the chance.

There was somebody else. Somebody who would be prepared to get his hands dirty and who would keep a secret. Bradley Chapman hated Dickson as much as she did, and with good reason: Cooper Monroe had been Bradley's best friend. Using the phone would leave a trace, but given she would be ringing a prepaid phone, that wouldn't matter. Even if he refused to help her, Bradley would not drop her in it.

She tried to activate the mobile and cursed again. The wretched thing was protected by a biometric print.

Dickson gave a quiet chuckle.

She knew what she had to do. She didn't have to like it.

She marched up and down, then returned to his body, where she hesitated before stepping away once more.

'Come on, you can do it!' she told herself.

'You haven't got the guts.' This time Dickson's laugh was louder.

She approached him again but spun on her heel for a second time. Bile rose in her throat. This was so wrong. Besides, using the phone could get her into serious trouble.

'You could leave behind an imprint of your voice, DNA—'

She pushed the voice away. 'Come on!' she urged herself. 'You're already in the shit. There is no other way.'

Psyching herself up, she returned to the cadaver, where she took a deep breath and, trying not to look at his face, pressed Dickson's forefinger against the screen. The phone lit up. She released his hand and stepped away. Still there were no cars. The cool wind slapped her semi-naked torso and, with shaking hands, she dialled the number she had recently memorised.

'I need help. Usual place. Urgent.' She ended the call.

Bradley Chapman was already assisting Kate by guarding Stanka – an underage sex-worker who Dickson had been searching for for the last few months, hoping to silence her. Stanka not only knew about Dickson's involvement in covering up a murder, but possessed evidence: a video that, only the day before, she had given to Kate, who in turn had passed it immediately to journalist Dan

11

Corrance. Having been rescued from Blackpool the day before, the girl was currently hiding out at Bradley's house.

Kate reasoned that the number of the burner phone Bradley had given her for emergencies would work in her favour. Even though it would appear on Dickson's call log, it wouldn't be traced back to Bradley. He'd dispose of it straight away. Bradley could be trusted. An ex-SAS serviceman with as great a reason as Kate to want Dickson dead, he was the sole human she could rely on to keep his mouth shut.

She marvelled at the fact she was now being so cool-headed. Her mind was surprisingly focussed, her heartbeat steady. Moreover, there was no remorse.

Dickson spoke. *'You believe you are thinking straight and making sensible choices now but later you'll discover you messed up in some way.'*

She scrolled through the call log, spotted nothing suspicious, although every text message had been erased. This didn't surprise her. Dickson would be stupid to keep anything incriminating on his phone and he was anything but.

She returned to the body, and, looking closer, saw that its mouth was agape, as if he'd really been speaking to her, and wasn't just a voice in her head. The idea made her shudder.

There was still time to change her mind. She could ring William. Tell him what had happened. She longed to be comforted in his arms, told everything would be alright and for all of this to go away, yet deep down she knew she couldn't. With his dying breath Dickson had confirmed there were other officers in the force who had to be rooted out.

If Kate didn't resolve to uncover them, there would be more victims like Stanka, and her friend Rosa who had been murdered, more wasted lives. Dickson had warned her there were worse people than him. It was down to her to do something about them. A job she could only do if his death was covered up.

'Chris? I am doing the right thing, aren't I?'

'Of course not. Your self-righteousness will be your downfall. I look forward to watching you fail.'

Dickson's voice!

She stared again at his face, this time with less trepidation. She reminded herself that he'd been rotten to the core. Moreover, he could no longer harm her. To that end, she would deal with his asides and comments in her head. He hadn't beaten her when he was alive and certainly wouldn't now that he was dead.

'Don't you feel a shred of guilt?'

'No. Now shut up.'

CHAPTER TWO

DAY ONE – TUESDAY MORNING

The alarm on Kate's mobile punctured her dreamless sleep, rousing her. With her mind sluggish and her mouth dry, she wondered if she was suffering a hangover, then a sharp snort of derision jolted her awake.

'How are you going to play this one, DI Young?'

The sneering voice was Dickson's. She sat bolt upright, struggling to open her sticky eyes and block out the mocking voice that taunted her.

'I don't think you can pull it off. Last night you were full of adrenalin. You felt invincible. It'll be a different story today, especially at work. Once your colleagues begin probing into my disappearance, they'll see right through you. Mark my words. You won't get away with this.'

'Chris!' she gasped, hoping her dead husband's voice would emerge and obliterate the one now making her heart beat a rapid *rat-a-tat-tat*. The reassurance she needed from him wasn't forthcoming. 'Chris, please. Help me!'

As she threw off the covers, it struck her that Dickson was the reason that she could no longer hear Chris. Maybe Chris was gone for good, leaving her to face life alone. Deep down, she'd always suspected that once she'd accomplished her mission, she'd lose that connection with him. The one thing she hadn't banked on was Dickson's voice taking over.

'You fucker. It's your fault he's gone!'

'Tut, tut, Kate. He left because he's had enough. Done. Dusted. Given up on you. After all, you are a criminal now. He doesn't want to be associated with the callous, bad Kate.'

'You're the reason. You're to blame. Not me!'

'Now, now, getting emotional will lead to mistakes. Hmm . . . as it happens, you've already made a few of those in trying to cover up my death.'

She tossed the duvet on to the floor and stood up. 'No!'

Her head spun, forcing her to rest a hand against the smooth pine wardrobe to steady herself. 'Dickson's wrong. You covered all bases. Keep your cool,' she told herself.

'Keep your cool! So that's going to be your mantra to get you through this? Good luck with that.'

'Shut up! Shut the fuck up!' The sudden outburst frightened her. She needed to regain control. She breathed in and out several times, before walking as calmly as she could to the bathroom. There she splashed cold water on to her face, then went through the practised routine of dabbing moisturiser and patting it into her skin. When she looked in the mirror, she was heartened to see her own reflection, and no sign of Dickson. She daubed concealer on to the dark circles under her eyes and got ready for work. She had covered all the bases.

Hadn't she?

Dimmed headlights bounce along the track towards her. Bradley has arrived in his Land Rover. The breeze has picked up in the short time since she rang him. The top she used to try to stem the blood flow is

still in place on Dickson's chest, leaving her in only a training bra and cycling shorts. Her exposed flesh is icy cold, yet she feels little discomfort. Her mind has been churning over all the possibilities and outcomes of her actions and now she's satisfied with the course of action she's about to embark upon. It is risky. It is bold. But if she holds her nerve and Bradley plays his part, it should work. No, it will work. She's thought through her plan, and it is foolproof.

◆ ◆ ◆

The door to the office clattered open. DS Emma Donaldson strode in. She tossed the copy of the *Gazette* on to Kate's desk before sitting on the edge of the one next to it, leaning forward, eyes burning brightly. 'I couldn't believe it. My brother, Greg, spotted it. Front-page news.'

Kate picked up the paper. Although she was fully aware of what the article would contain, she feigned first puzzlement, then shock.

Dan, the reporter to whom she'd fed the information, had done her proud. A photograph of Dickson in full police regalia at a charity function took up much of the front page, along with the headline, 'Senior Police Officer's Secret Sex Scandal'. It appeared they'd gone with the sensational angle that Dickson had been one of several men to pay for the services of underage sex-workers at an exclusive gentlemen's club. The article alluded to his involvement in withholding evidence regarding a murder there and promised more to come over the following days.

Kate slapped the paper on to the desk. 'I don't know what to say.'

'That's our investigation they mention – the Maddox Club,' Emma said. 'I remember he admitted being there the night of the boy's murder, but he didn't say anything about being with an underage sex-worker. Do you think there's any truth to that?'

'If there is, it's not for us to investigate. They'll hold some sort of internal investigation. It might simply be speculative nonsense.'

'Says they have proof of its validity,' said Emma, eyes widening even further.

Kate continued to play it cool. Pulling a face, she said, 'Best not to jump to any conclusions. After all, he—' The word 'was' had almost escaped her lips, but with a quick throat clear to cover up the pause, she moved on smoothly with, 'He is our boss.'

The door banged open again. This time DS Morgan Meredith marched in, a takeaway coffee in one hand and a paper bag in the other. 'What's going on? I just got stopped by a reporter who asked me if I knew anything about Superintendent Dickson.'

Emma handed him the paper and watched his face for a reaction.

'Fuck me! You reckon this is true?'

Emma shrugged. 'The journalist certainly has a lot of information. They wouldn't dare print anything like that unless they had proof. Dickson's lawyers would chew them up and spit them out if they got a single fact wrong.'

Kate marvelled at her own ability to feign as much surprise as her officers at the sudden appearance of this story.

But she had to be careful not to overplay it.

Morgan, seemingly satisfied they'd finished talking about the scandal, pulled a roll from the bag, peeling back the two halves to reveal crispy bacon. Kate found herself watching him, even though she couldn't say why. He took a packet of ketchup and squirted red sauce liberally over the meat.

Kate blinked away a vision of blood seeping from the bullet hole in Dickson's chest. She reminded herself she was in control. *Keep your cool. It's all taken care of.*

She methodically recapped the events of the night before to convince herself she had nothing to worry about. She'd used the firepit in her back garden to dispose of her blood-splattered clothing. She could still feel the warmth from the flames as they leapt in front of her eyes, reducing the fabric to nothing but a handful of ashes.

But not everything had been disposed of. At first, Bradley had taken Dickson's handgun. It wasn't a police-issue weapon. Probably illegal. She could see it clearly in her mind's eye, the dark brown handle with its small star identifier, Baikal, etched on the barrel.

◆ ◆ ◆

'Dickson most likely obtained it via one of his nefarious contacts, or even the dark web.' Bradley turns it over one last time in his wide hands before slipping it into his coat pocket. He cocks his head, eyes narrowing as he stares at the lifeless form.

'Only one place to dispose of him – Grange Farm. Leave him to me.'

The pig farm is one of the largest in the area. There is something in his tone that suggests this isn't the first time he's been asked to dispose of a body. Kate catches his eye and nods. Some things are best not probed.

'You sure about that? Do pigs really eat everything?'

A ghost of a smile flickers. 'Trust me. There won't be a morsel left. They're a hungry bunch. Better take that, though.' He crouches down to fumble with Dickson's left hand. A sliver of moonlight illuminates the object: a ring. He drops it into her open palm. 'Might be useful to you.'

It seems odd to her that Dickson has continued to wear his wedding band, even though he and Elaine separated earlier in the year. She doesn't look at it, merely shoves it in her pocket, at the same time pushing away any thoughts of those who will mourn Dickson. If she lets her mind wander in that direction, her resolve will crumble, and she will give herself up.

She focusses instead on all the wrongdoings Dickson has committed, the people who have died at his hands.

She'll place the ring in the glove box of his vehicle. When it is found it will add weight to the theory Dickson has done a runner. This is her plan. There will be no body and therefore no death to investigate. That way, there'll be no chance of her being found out. Once the newspaper story about his corruption breaks, it will be assumed he has gone into hiding.

◆ ◆ ◆

'Shouldn't we speak to DCI Chase? Kate!'

Emma's voice brought her back into the room. Emma was looking at her strangely. Did she suspect? No. She couldn't. She'd assume Kate was as confused about the situation as they were.

Kate got to her feet. If she became paranoid about her team, she would be in real trouble.

The one person she had doubts over – who she knew had been loyal to Dickson – was DC Jamie Webster. However, Jamie was on leave, recovering from injuries sustained during his brave efforts two days earlier in capturing the bolt gun killer, and she didn't expect him back any time soon.

'Yes. We need to know what the official line is going to be on this story.' Kate left the office as quickly as possible. Although she could play it cool with Morgan and Emma, DCI William Chase would be another kettle of fish. He knew her too well. He was also aware there was no love lost between her and Dickson. Nevertheless, this conversation couldn't be avoided.

For a second, she wondered how things would have turned out this morning if she'd rung William instead of Bradley. She'd have probably blurted out everything, including the fact she was behind the publication of the damning article. Any respect from fellow officers would have been tossed out of the window once that nugget of information got loose. Promotion might no longer have been an option either, along with any chance of nailing the other bastards who were part of the syndicate. Maybe her decision to ring Bradley had been the best call after all.

The station was eerily hushed: no loud voices, doors banging, or the usual noises that accompanied life there. It was as though everyone was holding their collective breath.

DI Harriet Khatri emerged from a meeting room and, spying Kate, stopped in her tracks. After Chris's murder, Kate almost injured an innocent passenger on a train, who she had mistaken for a terrorist. Dickson had insisted then on her stepping down, citing her mental health. Harriet Khatri had taken over Kate's old team. On her return, Kate had not been reinstated. It took a while to work out that Dickson was deliberately attempting to sabotage her career in order to stop her looking any further into Chris's death.

Harriet's glacial eyes met Kate's. Neither spoke until Kate had drawn level.

'You've heard?' Harriet's husky voice was at odds with her slight frame and sharp features, which were made more pronounced by the fact Harriet wore her hair scraped back tightly.

Kate returned a nod. 'You believe it?'

Harriet held her gaze before replying. 'My question wouldn't be about the validity of the article. Rather . . . which bastard blabbed all this utter crap to the press?'

'The paper states there's evidence to support the allegations.'

'Then my second question would be: who handed it to them?'

Kate was momentarily floored. Was Harriet accusing her of being the leak? Did she suspect or, worse still, have proof that the information had come from Kate? She maintained eye contact, kept a poker face and shook off her concern. There was no way that Harriet could know. She was being her usual contentious self. Kate refused to be intimidated. Dickson was bound to have found support among those he had favoured. Harriet was one of those.

'Do you have any ideas who might be responsible?' Kate asked.

Harriet didn't blink. 'I'm sure we'll be able to find out. One thing is sure: the super won't take this lying down.'

Kate didn't need any more enemies. Harriet might be her old team's DI – she might have even actively disliked Kate for whatever reason – but there was no need for Kate to exhibit any animosity towards her. Instead, she adopted a more concerned look. 'You're right. It'll be some troublemaker. Superintendent Dickson will deny it, then sue the newspaper. Have you seen him today?'

'No. Nor would I expect to. Would you come in if your name was being libelled by the media?'

'No, I guess not. I expect he's lawyering up.'

'Kate! My office.' William was at the end of the corridor.

'On my way,' shouted Kate.

By the time she walked into his office, William had already taken up a position standing in front of the window. His forehead was a network of creases. 'I take it you know about the article? I can't . . . I can't believe it.'

'Nobody believes it, William.' She took her usual chair, her head held high. He'd spot any tells she might unconsciously display. The key was to not overact. 'I know I've not always seen eye to eye with Superintendent Dickson; however, what they're saying about him is ridiculous, isn't it?'

'Yes. Yes, it is.'

'Are you okay? I know you and he were quite close,' she said.

William gave a small nod. He looked like somebody had punched him in the gut. She got to her feet, broke their usual work protocol and walked around the other side of the table to hug him. William meant the world to her. He was family and she couldn't count the number of times he'd held her when she was hurting.

During working hours, they kept their relationship professional, but Kate had grown up with William in her life, first as her father's friend – an uncle figure – then later as her mentor and personal friend. She had a fleeting vision of him leading her gently from the train where she had discovered Chris's body, when she was numb and alone. He'd supported her and she would forever be grateful he was in her life. It saddened her that her actions were hurting him.

She kept the embrace short, but it was enough for William to give her a friendly smile. She pulled away but held on to his hands for a moment.

'Are you sure you're okay?'

'Yes. I am now. Thanks. Sit down. We need to talk this through.'

She let go of him and headed back to her chair. William remained standing.

'I've known John a great number of years. This sounds wrong . . . It's too much. He and Elaine have had their ups and downs but to do what the paper is suggesting—' He shook his head. 'Listen, you interviewed him about the Maddox Club at the time of the investigation. Did you have any doubts about him then?' His voice was pure concern. That threw her. If William only knew what she had done! It would break him.

'None.' She held his gaze.

'Liar!' whispered Dickson's voice. She held her nerve. Dickson was trying to throw her off track. Fuck him!

William gave a sharp nod. 'Good.'

'Have you spoken to him?' she asked.

'No. He's not at home or picking up his calls. On the one hand, that's understandable. On the other, what is concerning is that he hasn't spoken to the chief constable or anyone else higher up the chain of command. I'd have expected him to have kept somebody in the loop.'

'Have you tried his wife?'

He cleared his throat. 'Elaine rang me a short while ago. He sent her a text message last night at 8.23 p.m. She didn't see it until this morning. It was just one word. *Sorry.*' He paused to make his point. 'Elaine rang him to ask what he meant, but his phone was off. It was only after she spotted the newspaper article that she called me.'

'Sorry for what? Could he have known about the article and be apologising in advance for the fallout?'

'You know as well as I do that sort of message is associated with people who are considering suicide. Up until Elaine called me, I thought – hoped – he might be lying low. Since that conversation, I've changed my mind. I'm concerned for his well-being, Kate.'

She hated seeing William looking so tormented. She should have worded the message differently. She intended it to be ambiguous and to suggest that Dickson knew he was about to be exposed, not that he was about to take his own life.

'I told you that you weren't thinking clearly. Tsk.'

Damn Dickson, he'd been right. She had tripped up. She should have sent something more obvious. Now she had to ensure those investigating his disappearance didn't become fixated on searching for a body. 'Okay, well, we can't discount the possibility that he's taken his own life, but both Harriet and I think he's with his lawyers. That seems far more likely, especially in light of that article.'

'Possibly. I hope so, Kate. Between you and me, I'm worried. Really worried. That article, the text . . . It sounds ominous to me.'

'The superintendent would fight those allegations, not surrender to them, regardless of whether they're true or not. You know him better than most of us. He isn't the sort of person to crawl away and give up, or take his own life, because of this.'

William nodded again. 'Maybe. Maybe you're right.'

Before he could mention suicide again, she said, 'I'm sure he's okay. He'll be working out a way to counterattack. If the lawyers are on the ball, the article will get pulled immediately.'

'And that brings me back to the reason for calling you in. The newspaper won't hand us whatever evidence they have against him. If it's as damning as they suggest, it might have serious repercussions – not just for John, but for all of us.'

'Why? We aren't involved in anything underhand.' Her pulse beat a loud tempo in her eardrums. She hoped her voice didn't sound as high-pitched to him as it did to her.

He sucked air between his teeth, then said, 'But if, and I mean if, they have valid proof he's guilty of corruption, the reputation of the whole force will come under the microscope. After all, how could we have let one of our own operate outside the law? Confidence in us will wane and our handling of the investigation into the Maddox Club in particular will be scrutinised. I don't want you dragged into any mess. Not after what you've been through to get back on your feet.' He shook his head before saying, 'I don't want that to be the case. Your dad would want me to keep you well out of that.'

The mention of her father touched her. 'We didn't do anything wrong. We followed procedure. I took Superintendent Dickson at his word when he confessed that he'd been with a sex-worker the night of the murder. I had no reason to press him for further details.'

'Some might argue you should have asked him about the girl in question's age.'

'At the time, I was investigating several murders, not underage prostitution.'

He rubbed his forehead as if to erase the deep worry lines. 'If it comes to it, we'll point that out. I'll back you every step of the way. I won't let any crap get hurled in your direction.'

'Are you suggesting there's a possibility there's some truth in the article?'

'No! I'm watching your back on the off-chance things turn nasty. You're up for promotion. I don't want anything to taint that.' He sat down at last, elbows planted firmly on the table. 'That aside, and friend to friend, I'm truly concerned about John. For some time now he's been putting in long shifts – become a workaholic. On top of which he's been dealing with his marriage break-up. He's all about reputation. You know how much he values public opinion. He might have reacted badly to this article. We might have to face that inevitability first, and then deal with the fallout from these damning articles.'

'See how he's watching you?' Dickson's voice came out of the blue, making her heart hammer. *'He's looking for tells. William is an expert in body language.'*

'Listen, William. I don't want to get over-worried at this stage. The article was only published this morning. He could bowl in any time today.'

'You might be right. Even so, if we've heard nothing from him by this afternoon, I want your team to start a manhunt. Call it a bad feeling, a hunch or whatever, but I believe something awful has happened to him and I don't want you to delay an investigation.'

'Me?' A sudden itch on her scalp caused her fingers to twitch.

'You slipped up there,' whispered Dickson. *'Ha! He spotted it.'*

She willed her muscles to relax, ignored the infuriating itch and kept her gaze steady. Years of being on the right side of the interrogation room had made Kate aware body language was important. To touch her face, cover her neck, her mouth, or look away could expose her guilt. Instead, she focussed on her breathing, techniques taught to her in the wake of Chris's murder. Outward appearance was everything. Dickson had been a master at maintaining a poker face, even to the very end. She could play the same game – after all, she'd been masking her emotions for months.

Assuming a missing persons team would have been instructed to locate his whereabouts, she'd not allowed for this eventuality: investigating his disappearance herself. Her brain popped and fizzed, assimilating the situation. This turn of events could work in her favour, provided she trod extremely carefully.

'Yes. I'm keeping it in-house. If nobody's spoken to John by lunchtime, I'll be assigning it to your team.'

'Okay. Try not to worry too much, William.'

'I know. It causes wrinkles! Bit late for me to be concerned about that now,' he said with a small smile.

'Oh, by the way,' she said. 'I wanted to apologise again for missing the celebrations last night. I really wasn't feeling too well. Post-investigation fatigue did for me.' William had invited her and her team for drinks at the White Rose pub to celebrate catching the bolt gun killer. She'd missed it in order to rendezvous with Dickson.

He waved away her apology. 'Everyone was done in. You weren't the only one to cry off. Obviously, Jamie couldn't make it, what with being in hospital and all, and Morgan and Emma had something they needed to do. You'd all better attend my official send-off, though.'

'You know there's no way I'd miss that.'

As she took her leave, there was only one thing that she could be certain of. Within the next few hours, she and her team would be called upon. She needed the intervening time to prepare herself and superglue the mask she'd require over the forthcoming weeks into place.

CHAPTER THREE

DAY ONE – AFTERNOON

At two o'clock William beckoned Kate into the corridor.

'Still no word?' she asked.

'I've spoken to Chief Constable Atwell. We're now of the same opinion. That he might have . . . well, taken his own life.'

For the last hour, she'd been preparing her response: concerned yet practical. 'I'm not going to focus solely on that possibility, William. He could simply be keeping his head down. I mean, if there's any truth at all in what this article says, he isn't going to want to come forward. Not yet.'

'Going into hiding only makes him look guilty. The chief constable agrees with me. Moreover . . .' He paused with a heavy sigh. '. . . should this article turn out to be true, John will have to face an inquiry. We must be seen to be actively searching for him to ensure he is answerable. It's our duty.'

Kate left enough of a gap, during which she folded her arms and dropped her gaze as if weighing up his words before mimicking his sigh. 'Okay. I'll prep the team. For the record, I still believe he'll turn up.'

'*Oh, please! This bullshit isn't going to wash.*' Dickson's sinister whisper peppered icy bullets through her veins. She hadn't spoken aloud, had she? She caught William's serious frown and feared she had. He cocked his head and studied her momentarily.

'*He can see through you.*'

She tried not to flinch. William gave another small sigh, making her heart accelerate. Dickson was right. Her performance wasn't fooling the person she was closest to.

'I wish I had your confidence,' he said. 'Find him, Kate. Prove me wrong.'

Relief washed over her. He didn't suspect her. Dickson had once again been toying with her, just like when he'd been alive.

'William, one other thing. Why are you putting my team on it? Why not Harriet's? After all, she has far more manpower than me.'

He locked eyes with her. 'Her unit is currently assigned to Operation Moonbeam.'

A recent tip-off had resulted in the discovery of several illegals, working at a local biscuit factory in Stoke. It had subsequently transpired they were being manipulated by people traffickers who had disappeared during the raid.

'There's been some fresh developments in that investigation, so I don't want to pull them off it at this stage. I know your team has not finished tying up the ends on the bolt gun murder case, and indeed you all deserve time off, but I want you to handle it. Also, I need somebody who'll be level-headed, non-judgemental and who I know has the tenacity to locate him. Wherever he is.'

'I'll do my best.'

'Let me know if you need anything at all.'

He plodded back up the corridor, head lowered. This had hit him harder than she could have imagined. She squared her shoulders and prepared to face Emma and Morgan. It was game on.

Emma looked up from her computer. 'I love this job but filing reports does my head in.'

'Then you'll be pleased to know we've been assigned another case.'

Morgan's head snapped up. 'Already?'

'We're to find the super.'

'What?'

'DCI Chase is worried something has happened to him.'

'What? Like . . . ?' Morgan drew an imaginary blade across his throat.

'He would bloody well think that about me, wouldn't he? Oh, if he knew the truth . . .'

She silenced the voice. 'I guess so. Anyway, we need to track him down and quickly, so, Morgan, start with his mobile phone provider. Emma, his car. Ask the techies to hunt through local surveillance camera footage. We need to find out who he spoke to last, what time he left here yesterday, so check the CCTV cameras overlooking the car park.'

'Wouldn't it be better to pass this over to MisPers?' asked Emma.

Kate shrugged. 'DCI Chase thinks we're the best people for the job. So, let's get on with it.'

She sat behind her laptop, heart thumping. Directing her team whilst in full knowledge of what had transpired was dangerous, yet how many times had Dickson fooled those around him? He had helped to cover up the murder of a young male prostitute, lied when questioned, and kept the scent off him. He'd led an undercover operation into underage prostitution purely to find Rosa, the girl he'd been with the night of the boy's death. Then, once he'd tracked her down, he'd murdered her, or had her killed, all the while maintaining his position as superintendent and going about usual business. If he could do it, then so could she.

Dickson had no social media accounts, which meant they would have to interview relatives, friends and colleagues to ascertain if he had made any contact with them. It felt strange going through the motions, fully aware it was pointless. She set about getting relevant details, pleased with her performance so far. This was how she'd get away with it.

'CCTV shows him leaving the car park at 5.58 p.m.' Emma brought up a capture, Dickson's stern face staring out of the Mercedes' windscreen.

'Okay. See if you can track where he headed.' Kate returned to her computer, ensuring neither of her officers would suspect she wasn't fully invested in this manhunt the way they believed her to be.

A tap on the door made her look up.

'I hear you're hunting for the superintendent,' Harriet said as she entered the room.

'Word spreads quickly,' Kate replied.

Harriet disregarded the comment and continued, 'It was DCI Chase who informed me. I thought he should know that I was with Superintendent Dickson yesterday afternoon, when he took a phone call. He seemed perturbed by it. I didn't think much of it at the time; however, considering what has happened, I thought it prudent to tell DCI Chase. He suggested I let you know.'

Kate was the one who had made that call. Her mouth went dry for a moment, as she searched Harriet's face for any clue that the woman had an inkling of who had rung Dickson. This could be the moment she got caught out. 'Did you overhear any of the conversation?'

'Only that Superintendent Dickson told whoever was on the line he would be with them within the hour. Then he dismissed me.'

Kate checked again. There was nothing to indicate Harriet was aware Kate had rung.

'What time was this call?'

'Five thirty. He wound up the meeting immediately afterwards with apologies that he had to be somewhere else.'

'He didn't mention where?'

Harriet remained stony-faced. 'If he had, I'd have told you.'

Kate forced a smile. 'Of course. It's habit to ask even the most obvious of questions to make sure I haven't missed anything. You know how it is.'

Harriet didn't reply.

'Right. Thank you. This information could be useful.'

'The call might have been from that scumbag journalist, Dan Corrance. I'd check him out if I were you.' Her eyes sparked.

'Will do.' Kate fought the urge to snap that she didn't need telling how to do her job.

'If you need any help, let me know. I'm sure I can release an officer or two to assist.' Harriet turned on her heels and left.

Morgan waited a few moments before muttering, 'The Ice Queen looks cheesed off.'

'She always looks like that,' said Emma. 'Probably doesn't like the fact she isn't in charge of this one.'

Kate held her tongue. As one of Dickson's supporters – even if she was unaware of the depth of the man's corruption – Harriet would want Dickson back and his name cleared as soon as possible. She wasn't going to be thrilled when she found out he'd gone for good.

'Want me to talk to the journalist?' asked Morgan.

'No, I'll do it,' Kate replied as she got to her feet. This was one job she was not going to pass over to anyone else. Although she had faith in Dan, with Dickson missing, he would be under greater pressure than usual to give up his source, especially if the likes of Harriet decided to confront him. 'Stick to tracking Dickson's phone and car for the time being. We really need his call log. Kick somebody's arse, Morgan.'

'With pleasure.'

Emma threw Morgan a wry grin. Kate picked up on it. And the wink he gave her back.

'*They know,*' Dickson's voice hissed.

Her heart accelerated, flustering her as she patted pockets in search of her car keys. Retrieving them from under a pile of paperwork, she casually glanced at the pair again. Morgan was now on the phone while Emma had returned her attention to the computer screen. The imaginary voice was wrong. These two were simply good friends who often shared looks and glances. Kate was too jumpy.

'*Have it your way.*'

She squeezed the keys until the flesh of her palm stung, distracting her from the inner voice. She strode from the office, grateful to be out of the claustrophobic space. If she'd spent any longer in there, she might have crumbled and confessed to her colleagues what had really happened.

Tyler Viking, chief editor at the *Gazette*, greeted Kate with a gentle hug. Chris had thought highly of Tyler, who had never been afraid to put his neck on the line and publish some of Chris's punchier articles. He and Chris had been good friends. Tyler had, on occasion, even dropped around to their house for a drink or dinner.

Kate had only seen Tyler twice since Chris's death, but that was because she had hidden herself away and made excuses for not meeting up with anyone who might remind her of what she'd lost.

'I understand what you're saying, Kate. We knew this story would cause ructions, and might even have serious ramifications, so Dan did the sensible thing. He took off. He's gone into hiding until we've finished running the story and the dust has settled.'

'I understand. Did he tell you who his source was?'

'No. He plays his cards close to his chest. Said it was best if I didn't know.'

'Look,' Kate said. 'I know it isn't my business to tell you how to run your newspaper, but it might be better if you didn't run any more of the feature until we've spoken to Superintendent Dickson.'

Tyler picked up a propelling pencil and rolled it between his fingers and thumbs, all the while considering Kate through half-lidded eyes. 'Here's the thing, Kate . . . We're sitting on a goldmine of information. The fact your superintendent has gone missing only fans the flames of speculation. And you know what they say about smoke and fire.'

She leant towards him, lowered her voice and captured his gaze. 'My concern isn't for the superintendent's reputation, more the backlash Dan will face. You know he and Chris worked together on an article about child pornography and prostitution – a piece, as I recall, that was pulled before it hit the press. The research into that article cost Chris his life.' She left the rest unsaid. Tyler would understand what she was inferring.

Slowly, he turned the pencil two full rotations before speaking. 'Dan already voiced similar concerns. He knew this was hot, which is why, between you and me, he's left the country. Don't ask me where he is, because I genuinely have no idea. We decided it would be best if nobody here knew his whereabouts. He's switched off his phone, and he's emailing his articles as and when they're written from various internet cafés, so he can't be tracked. I understand your concern, but don't ask me to pull the articles because I won't. I've spoken to the newspaper owners and our lawyers. We're confident that we can legally publish this story. We possess damning evidence that proves Superintendent Dickson is not a fine, upstanding officer. It's our duty to expose him. After all, if he was innocent he wouldn't have vanished.'

She knew the damning evidence in question was the video Stanka had shot at the Maddox Club the night a male sex-worker was murdered. The footage proved Dickson not only knew about the incident, but had been complicit in the cover-up.

'And just so we are clear, I'm not giving up that evidence unless I'm forced to. It's safely locked away.'

'I wouldn't dream of it. I'm here because I do have to ask you some questions as part of our inquiry into the disappearance of Superintendent Dickson.'

'Fire away.'

'Do you happen to know where Dan was yesterday evening, around five thirty?'

'Here in my office, revealing what he had discovered. Then we discussed the viability of getting it into print for today.'

'How long did he stay?'

'In the office, until almost nine. I spoke to the newspaper owners, lawyers and then held an emergency meeting with him and our senior team members. After the meeting finished, we set the wheels in motion, and Dan began writing the first article at his desk.'

'Were you all here until that time?'

'All five of us? Yes. We had to drop another story in order to feature this on the front page, which required diplomacy. Worth it, though. That other story was hot enough, but this one was a scorcher.'

'And everyone who knew about this article was in the offices until nine?'

'How much longer are you going to ask these pointless questions?' Dickson's voice was ice cold. She fought the urge to press her hands over her ears and block it out, and focussed on Tyler, leaning closer to catch his words rather than the whispering in her head.

'Yes. Some of us stayed later, until almost midnight.'

'Could you give me the names of those people who were working here during those hours?'

'Blah . . . blah . . . blah. You don't even sound as if you're invested in this. A genuine officer would be all over this man, demanding information. This bastard has that video exposing me and that is down to you.'

Her hands trembled slightly as she tried to listen to Tyler and focus on writing the names he was reeling off. She missed one. Inside her head, Dickson ranted on.

'I bet he suspects that you gave Dan the video. Maybe he'd like to print that in tomorrow's edition. Or better still, a story about a crazy DI who killed her superior!'

'Erm, I'm sorry, Tyler. My pen's given out.' She made a show of shaking it. 'I've got a spare one.' She hunted through her bag, allowing time to compose herself and reasoned that if she allowed it to, Dickson's voice would destabilise her. She was in control of it, not vice versa. Calmer now, she retrieved a black pen.

'Let's try again,' she said, giving Tyler a small smile.

'It's no good pretending. He sees through this charade,' whispered Dickson.

Tyler reeled off the names. Kate nodded as if all this was important.

'Thank you, Tyler.'

'Why do you need to know where we were during those hours? It's as if we might be suspects. Has something . . . happened to the superintendent?'

'Told you!' The voice was triumphant.

Kate feigned a smile. 'Oh, Tyler. You're a typical reporter. Rooting for information. I'm just being thorough. Besides, you know I can't discuss an ongoing investigation.'

'A newspaper editor has to try.' His eyes crinkled warmly.

'If Dan gets in contact or comes back, will you tell him I was asking after him?' She got to her feet.

Tyler joined her and hugged her again. 'Chris was an ace reporter, Kate. I know you've had to come here in an official capacity, but you're always welcome here. I'll pass your message on to Dan. Don't worry, he is perfectly safe. I wouldn't let anything happen to him. As for the story, Superintendent Dickson is very welcome to sue us for libel. We're ready for him.'

'There could be some knock-on effects that you haven't allowed for.'

He lifted a heavy, dark eyebrow. 'What might they be?'

'For one, I was lead officer on the investigation into the death at the Maddox Club. I knew the superintendent had spent the night with a sex-worker. I didn't quiz him over her age.'

'Oh! It wasn't my intention to involve you in any way. Really.'

'I'm sure it wasn't. Don't worry about me. I'll handle any repercussions, but those articles are going to stir up bad feeling among some of the officers at HQ. There are many there who feel no matter what he is accused of, he cared passionately about the community he served and protected.'

'And you? How do you feel, Kate?'

'I remain, as always, unbiased. My job is to find him. It will be up to someone better placed than me to decide whether or not he deserves punishment.'

He gave her a half-smile, fuelling her concern that he had seen through her performance. 'Always the diplomat. Like Chris. Ah, you were a dream team. I'm so sorry you've had to go through . . . Well, you know.' He cleared his throat. 'Like I said, drop by any time.'

She took her leave, heart sore at the mention of Chris. On the way to the lobby, her phone rang.

'Kate, I've some info on the super's phone,' said Morgan.

36

She felt a weight lifted from her shoulders. This was going to plan after all. It had been imperative they locate the mobile, which would in turn lead them to his car, rather than to the reservoir where he'd met his death . . .

◆ ◆ ◆

Now that Bradley is here, a sense of calm finally washes over Kate. Bradley's movements are unhurried, even when he sees what's happened. He's faced death before. Probably numerous times. The sight of Dickson in a heap does not faze him.

'You killed the fucker, then?'

'Not in cold blood. He pulled a gun. We struggled. It went off . . . and I was the only person to walk away unhurt. I recorded the whole thing, but the device broke during the fight. Even if anything could be extracted from it, I'm not sure it picked up enough of what was said. I don't know if I should take the chance and call this in.' She reveals the plastic pieces in her palm.

He takes them from her and shakes his head. 'Absolutely not. It's too risky.'

'You think so?'

'I hate to say it, but yes. Even if you can convince someone to believe you, his supporters will drum up some evidence pointing at you and make sure you go down for his death. And then once you are behind bars, something worse might happen. He and his group of supporters are ruthless and fucking bold. Look what happened to Stanka's friend, Rosa, and to Cooper. Both murdered. And we know who was behind their deaths: Dickson and his contacts.'

She is relieved he has said exactly what she has thought: that to confess will lead her into danger.

Bradley continues. 'You and I both know Cooper didn't take his own life. Dickson had him silenced. Even dead the bastard will have eyes and ears everywhere. I really don't think you should take the gamble. And I wouldn't fancy your chances with a self-defence plea in the courts.' A sneer of contempt fixes his lips in place as he ambles across and kicks at Dickson's lifeless body. 'I should have topped him myself ages ago, as soon as I found out he was behind my best friend's murder. I owed Cooper that much. Look, I know we haven't always seen eye to eye, but you can trust me with this. I'll dispose of him.'

'No. I can't ask you to do that.'

'Then why did you ring me?'

She shrugs. 'For advice. Help. To give me good reason not to call this in.'

'And I'm offering all of that with no strings attached. This snake was involved in the Maddox Club murder. He was the only one present the night of the murder who wasn't killed by that avenging nutjob who took the others out. Dickson had inside information he didn't share with you. He looked after number one and hid in a safe house with no thought for anyone else. My son-in-law was murdered! And you know who I blame? His so-called friends who begged him to keep quiet over the years. And of those, I blame Superintendent John Dickson the most.' He spits the name.

'Dickson should have come clean from the outset. The boy's death should have been investigated, not covered up. If he'd done the right thing, my daughter would still have a husband, my grandchildren would still have a father and Cooper would still be alive. Dickson could have prevented all that shit from happening. The man was evil. Look at the lengths he's taken to protect himself since then – all those who have died or been hunted down because of him covering his tracks. Let me do this for them. For my family. For Cooper and his daughter, Sierra, and for that poor, terrified girl, Stanka. Let me help you.'

She holds his fierce gaze. Bradley is straight-talking. She's drawn to his strength and conviction. Besides, what other options are open to her? 'Okay.' Her mind lurches as she tries to think of the next move.

They must exercise the greatest caution. A plan takes shape. Bradley waits until she nods and says, 'There are some forensic outfits in the boot of my car, which is parked in a lane about two miles up the road. The key to it is resting on the off-side back tyre. I didn't have a pocket in my outfit,' she adds.

He glances across at her bike, then casts an eye over her semi-naked body. 'You need a coat too. I'll fetch you mine.' He begins to walk back to the Land Rover.

'No, it's okay. You don't want my DNA on it. In fact, you need as little evidence as possible connecting us, so get rid of the burner phone that I rang you on. I have a plan. Best if I don't divulge too much about it. The less you know, the better. Would you fetch the suits? There's a hooded zip-up top in the boot too. Bring it and my car keys. I'll wait here.'

Bradley stares again at Dickson. 'What about the gun?'

'Can you dispose of it?'

'Shouldn't be a problem.'

'I don't want it finding its way back into circulation.'

'It won't. Stay here.'

He strides to his car and is gone again in an instant, leaving her shivering in the cold night air. A mournful call of a barn owl fills the silent skies. There are no vehicles. Luck is staying on her side. She crouches down beside the reservoir wall, which affords a little protection against the breeze. Although her plan seems foolproof, it won't hurt to run through it again before Bradley returns.

'Bradley's a civilian,' scoffs Dickson's voice loudly. 'Military-trained or otherwise, he'll still screw up. He's an old man. Dear, oh, dear. You need to up the ante if you think you're going to pull off this ridiculous plan of yours.'

'I thought I told you to shut the fuck up?'

'Ah, but I won't. You're stuck with me. Better get used to it.'

◆ ◆ ◆

'Kate? Are you still there?' Morgan's voice broke Kate's reverie.

'Sorry, the signal cut out my end,' she said. 'I'm outside the *Gazette*'s offices now. Tell me again what you just said.'

'I've got the super's call log in front of me. The call DI Khatri overheard him taking appears to have come from a pay-as-you-go number. I shot it over to the tech team, but they say it's unlikely they can give us much on it. These pay-as-you-go SIM cards are often only used once then destroyed.'

'Well, it wasn't Dan Corrance or anyone else on the publishing team. It appears they didn't decide to publish the article until after the call was made to the super. All the *Gazette*'s senior staff were in a meeting around the time of the call and didn't leave the office until much later. They couldn't have arranged to meet him within the hour.'

'Maybe he met somebody completely unconnected with the newspaper.'

'That's possible too.'

'There are no other records of this number in his call log. There was, however, another call made from his phone, this time at 6.55 p.m., to another pay-as-you-go number. It only lasted ten seconds. According to the mobile provider it was made in the Abbots Bromley area.'

'I wonder who he rang,' said Kate, playing along.

'Emma and I can't work it out. It's odd that it's another pay-as-you-go number. Neither number appears in his call log before yesterday evening. I've tried ringing them and both phones are dead, which raises a large red flag for me.'

'That's definitely suspicious.'

'Then there's nothing else until he sent his wife the text message at 8.23 p.m. Triangulation of the phone at that time puts its location somewhere in the Needwood area.'

40

'Can we narrow these locations down any further?'

'I'm afraid not.'

'Where are we with tracking his movements?' she asked.

'We found footage of his vehicle heading along the A51 from Stafford towards Rugeley but lost it after Wolseley Bridge. He probably took the road over Blithfield Reservoir, through Abbots Bromley and towards Needwood. There are so many country lanes in that area, we'll never locate his car using CCTV. Remember the trouble we had during the Alex Corby investigation?' said Morgan.

Kate was fully aware of the fact there was no surveillance equipment along that route. It was one of the reasons she had chosen it.

◆ ◆ ◆

'You sure there's no CCTV around here?' asks Bradley.

'Positive.' She shimmies into one of the white forensic suits, dragging the hood over her head and tucking her hair carefully under it. She tugs on the shoe covers. Bradley copies her movements, stretching then drawing the tight rubber gloves over his large hands.

'I handled the gun during the struggle. I need to wipe it and then put his prints back on it. And his mobile too,' she says.

'I keep a couple of towels in my car in case I need to dry off the dogs. They're clean. I thought you wanted me to dispose of the weapon?'

'Change of plan. I'll take it with me.'

He gives her a worried look. 'You're not panicking, are you? I've seen trained soldiers make poor decisions because of panic. You should stick to your plan.'

'I hear you. It's better if the gun is found. It'll add credence to the story that I'll create surrounding his disappearance. I need to clean it and then put his prints back on it.'

He grunts a response and extracts a medium-sized towel from his car-door pocket, thrusting it and the gun in her direction. She wraps the material loosely around the handle, and, pointing it away from them, uses the remaining cloth to wipe the barrel with circular motions, before repeating the process on the handle and rubbing the trigger until she is satisfied that she has erased all prints from earlier when she wrestled the weapon from Dickson's hands. She hesitates by the body, unable to draw her regard from his glassy eyes.

'I'll do it. Is he right- or left-handed?' Bradley asks.

'Right.'

Bradley prises the gun from her tightened grip, easing it into Dickson's hand, pressing the dead man's fingers against the trigger and handle. When he's done, he returns the firearm to Kate. She places it in the Mercedes' glove box before wiping down both the box and the passenger door in case she left behind any prints when she was searching for Dickson's phone to call for help.

She then cleans the mobile she used to ring Bradley and, keeping her gaze from Dickson's face, places the phone in his hand as if he were handling it, before pressing his finger against the screen to unlock it. If she can keep the device awake, she won't need his print again. She changes the lockout time to one hour before placing it on the passenger seat of his car.

'I wiped the glove box. I need his prints again,' she says.

'Help me lift him. We don't want to leave drag marks.'

Together they lug Dickson's body to his car, where Kate supports his weight while Bradley presses the man's left hand against the glove box, as if he's leant across from the driver's seat to open it.

'That should do it,' he says, small steam clouds rising as he speaks.

Once more, they carry the body, this time hauling it over the Land Rover's tailgate and on to a rubber boot tray. They lay him on his back. His eyes are still open, staring up at Kate. Blood that has seeped from the gunshot wound has flowered across his chest, dark and sticky like red fruit jam. Kate is sure his lips mouth, 'You'll get caught.'

Blindsided for a moment, her heart hammers loudly in her ears.

'You'll need to deep clean the car,' she says to Bradley.

Bradley stretches to press a button on the inside of the tailgate. The boot lid automatically descends, shutting with a quiet click. 'I'll sort it. I'll get rid of the car boot liner after I dispose of the body. Don't worry, I know exactly what I'm doing.'

'I . . . I don't know what else to say, other than thank you.'

'The fucker deserved to die, so don't take it to heart. You're a good police officer, DI Young. The force needs people like you.' He turns to check the area is clear, unaware of the anguish he has caused with just a few words.

How can she call herself one of the good guys after this? Dickson was evil but what she is doing is equally wrong. There is still time to change her mind. Return the body, ring the police. Give herself up. She's a good officer. This is morally wrong. She's better than this.

Chris's voice is suddenly clear in her head, making her gasp. She hadn't expected to hear it again now that Dickson had appeared. 'Kate, this is no longer about Dickson. You heard what he said about there being others who are worse than him. Are you prepared to let them get away with the same sort of things that he did? There are those people who turn a blind eye to corruption and those who fight against it. I was a warrior. I fought it and it cost me my life. Regardless of the risks, I was prepared to expose those I believed were immoral. Dan Corrance is treading the same path because, like me, he isn't afraid to reveal the rot that exists in some of our institutions. You're one of us. You were the person who exposed Dickson. Why do you think I left you the list of people I felt were corrupt? Because I knew you, like me, would want them held accountable. I thought you would carry on what I had started. Did I die in vain?'

'No,' she whispers. Bradley, a few paces away, doesn't appear to hear her.

'Were my efforts pointless?'

She shakes her head.

'Are you with me, Kate? Will you continue to fight on my behalf?'

A lump fills her throat. She will always be on Chris's side, no matter what. She will continue his fight. 'Yes.'

A rush of cold air causes her to shiver uncontrollably. She rubs her arms. She wants to be the good officer, but sometimes it isn't that simple, and rules have to be changed. She will honour Chris's memory and bring those individuals rotting the system to justice. Chris is right. She must choose sides, and she chooses his. The relief at hearing his voice is immense, so overpowering that she wants to collapse against the car and weep, but Bradley is back, his calm gaze upon her again.

'It's best if we tidy up this mess and say no more about it. If there's no body, there's no crime, right?' he says.

'Not strictly speaking. However, if they have no reason to suspect he's dead, then that would be ideal. Listen, it's probably best if I don't contact you for a while.'

'Okay.'

'You will still look after Stanka, won't you? There might be others coming after her.'

'You reckon?'

She nods. 'I'd like to see her but—'

'I get it. Best nobody makes any connections between you and me. Listen, Stanka will be safe. I'll send you an emergency number in case you need to get in touch with me. If her bloody pimp, Farai, turns up, I'll deal with him, and if anybody else comes snooping they'll have me and the dogs to deal with. Gwen and I will look after her, and if and when she is called on to testify against Dickson, then we'll go with her.'

'Gwen's okay about all of this?'

'She is. I told her enough to explain why Stanka is in our house, but not too much. She knows Stanka was at the Maddox Club the night of the boy's murder and that she and her friend, Rosa, went on the run from Dickson immediately afterwards. She also knows Rosa's death was down to Dickson and that Stanka is afraid that he or one of his men will kill her. Gwen doesn't ask too many questions. She's good like that. Probably down to a lifetime of living with a secretive bastard like me.' He smiles. 'Maybe Stanka will open up to her in time and tell her everything. Either way, Gwen misses our daughter and the grandkids, so she's happy to have somebody to mother again.'

Kate's happy the girl is in such good hands. 'Okay, well, I'll be in touch when I think it's safe to do so. And . . . I suppose you should leave now.'

Bradley nods. 'You can count on me. I shan't say a word to a soul about this. Not a soul.'

'I hope you don't find yourself questioned.'

'If I do, I shall deny any knowledge. Take care, Kate.'

'And you.'

She waits until his car taillights have vanished and she can no longer hear the rumble of his car engine before lifting her bike into the Mercedes' boot. She scrambles into the driver's side and starts up the car. Much hinges on how she sets this up and people's suppositions. She draws away from the reservoir, on to the road. This time she wants to see other vehicles and for them to spot this car. She speeds down the lane, through Abbots Bromley, turning off after she's traversed the village, heading towards the destination she hopes will give those hunting for Dickson a clue to his disappearance. There are no surveillance cameras along this route but a Mercedes driving faster than the legal limit, with its headlights on full beam, will surely attract some attention. She hunkers down in the seat and hopes the glare from the lights will prevent any witnesses from seeing who is behind the wheel.

◆ ◆ ◆

45

'Kate, are you still there?' said Morgan.

'I lost you again for a minute,' she replied. Damn! She needed to focus on the present, not what happened at the reservoir. 'Listen, Morgan. My phone keeps cutting out. I'll be back at the station soon. We'll figure out where the super met up with this anonymous person, and where he was when he sent that second text message. We should talk to Elaine Dickson too. Could you arrange for her to come in and speak to us, or at the very least arrange a video-call?'

'On it.'

She strode from the *Gazette* offices, past the food van where she had met Dan Corrance to pass over the information that he had now spun into front-page news. Like the evening before, the van was shut, outside tables away, a sign pinned to its drawn shutters. A favourite haunt for all those who worked at the newspaper, including Chris, it was unusual for it not to remain open until six o'clock weekdays. She drew level to read the sign. The van hadn't shut early as she'd assumed the evening before. The young man who ran it had met with a minor accident but would be back the following week. As she made for her car, she marvelled how one person's bad luck could be another's good fortune. His absence had ensured she had not been seen meeting Dan. Maybe her luck would hold out.

'Don't bank on it.' Dickson's words sent a shiver through her body. She had to get rid of his voice in her head before it had a seriously damaging effect on her.

CHAPTER FOUR

DAY ONE – EARLY EVENING

Kate didn't return directly to the office. She stopped off at the building adjacent to the police station, which housed the technical department. She tapped the code into the keypad, and entered the first room – reminiscent of her school science laboratory – where two technical assistants were seated in front of benches, studying a line of computer screens, filled with numbers and codes that were completely incomprehensible to Kate. A family-sized packet of tortilla chips lay open between them. The head of technology wasn't in her glass-fronted office.

'Hi, Rachid, Krishna,' she said, addressing the assistants, who looked up from their screens. 'Is Felicity about?'

'She's around somewhere. Try Tech 1,' came the reply.

Tech 1 was one of two rooms used for studying surveillance footage. Kate tapped on the door.

'Enter!'

Felicity was leaning back in a chair, her eyes on the screens. She craned her neck to see who had come in, beckoned Kate over and spoke to the woman who was sitting next to her. 'Can you stop it there?'

The assistant paused the frame. On the wall-screens, two individuals were now frozen as they entered the foyer of what was to Kate an instantly recognisable place.

Stoke-on-Trent railway station was not only a stunning grade-2 listed building, but a place that held horrific memories for her.

It was on platform one that she had encountered the gruesome sight of passengers massacred in a first-class carriage on a train from London – among them, her husband, Chris. The station was where everything had ended yet also begun. It was where she felt she had lost Chris and, for a while, her mind.

She had returned to the railway station only once since that dreadful day, to examine a CCTV tape of a meeting between a Heather Gault, a civilian investigation officer, and a girl named Rosa – the underage sex-worker who'd slept with Dickson at the Maddox Club the night of the boy's murder.

It was on that same footage that Kate had spied DC Jamie Webster shadowing both the girl and Heather. That had been the moment Kate finally understood the depth of Dickson's corruption. Jamie had been planted in her team to keep an eye on her, and report back to Dickson. It didn't matter why Jamie believed he was doing it, but that Dickson had gone to such lengths only confirmed his involvement in the conspiracy.

Kate was becoming immersed in her memories again. Felicity boomed a hello, bringing her back into Tech 1. She tore her eyes from the frozen figures on the screen.

'I understand congratulations are in order. You caught the bolt gun killer,' said Felicity, scraping her orange-framed spectacles over steely grey hair and leaving them perched on the top of her head.

'We couldn't have done it without you and your team.'

'I know. We're utterly brilliant, aren't we?' Felicity beamed. 'So, have you popped around to invite us all out for a celebratory drink?'

'Sadly, no. I need a word with you.'

Felicity picked up on the subtext and asked her assistant to leave them for a moment. Once the door had closed, she folded her arms and said, 'Go ahead. Shoot.'

Kate almost winced at that. If only Felicity knew the impact just hearing that word had on her after the events of the night before. 'As you know, my team's been tasked with finding the superintendent.'

'He'll be in hiding, waiting for a crack team of lawyers to hit back at the newspapers.' Felicity cocked her head. 'What do you reckon?'

'Same as you. Upstairs, however, are concerned about him and the potential consequences of this, so either way, we have to locate him.'

'Emma spoke to me earlier about routes and surveillance cameras. Simon's next door, examining any potential footage we can find. It's tricky as those backroads have little to no CCTV.'

'I wondered if there was any way we could track down his car remotely, using an app or GPS, or something similar.' She'd thought hard about this. Because if Dickson's GPS could be tracked, that would also alert them to the fact that his Mercedes had been parked at the reservoir for almost two hours, which was something she needed to account for.

'Sorry, not possible. Funnily enough, there was a tracking device fitted to his car several months ago. But he disabled it. Or maybe it simply stopped working. He also didn't activate the *Mercedes me* app, which might have allowed us to locate his vehicle. Do you think there's any truth in that article?'

'Tell her you're the source. Or are you afraid of what she'd deduce from that juicy gem? She might wonder what else you were capable of.'

Kate clenched her fists, causing her nails to sink into her palms and distract her from the voice that only served to remind her of her guilt.

'At this stage, I neither know nor care. I simply want to find him. I'll leave the rest up to those who wish to question him.'

'For what it's worth, I'd suggest that disabling a tracking device does rather seem a tad suspicious,' said Felicity.

Kate resisted a smile. Dickson's action would fuel the suspicion surrounding his disappearance.

'I'll make sure Simon gets hold of you the second he finds anything. Short of lending you a couple of sniffer dogs to hunt the superintendent down, I'm at a loss as to how we can help.'

'Have you been granted access to his personal computer or any other devices he might own?'

'Not yet. What about his mobile?'

'It's switched off.'

'Well, when we find it, I'll have it prioritised for processing.'

There was something else on Kate's mind. Although she'd written off the recording device, part of her wanted to . . . no, *had* to know if whatever it had recorded could be saved.

'You're stepping into dangerous territory with that,' whispered Dickson. *'She'll definitely be curious. And if by some miracle she can salvage the recording, where will that leave you?'*

'Felicity, I have a friend, an undercover officer from another station, who was using a tiny recording device. It got broken. They can't get it repaired and I wondered if you or your team would be able to.'

'Oh, bravo! You've signed your own death warrant.' She imagined Dickson applauding as he spoke.

'How badly damaged is it?' Felicity asked.

Ignoring the voice in her head, Kate pulled out a plastic bag containing the fragments. Felicity held it up to examine it and shook her head. 'This is a lost cause. Its size alone would make it darn near impossible to repair and even if by some miracle we managed it, I'd bet six months' wages we'd be unable to download anything from it. I hope whatever was on it wasn't too important.'

'I'm sure my friend will find another way to catch their villain,' said Kate, taking the bag from Felicity. 'Cheers, anyway. I'd better get back. It looks like it's going to be a long night.'

'Ring if you need anything. One of us will be here.'

It was some consolation to know the device was irreparable. It helped justify her actions. Had she chosen to call in Dickson's death, she wouldn't have had any evidence to corroborate her story.

'Come on, Kate. There is no justification for what you've done,' said Dickson.

She raced for the door before the voice got to her. She had to keep telling herself she'd done the right thing, even if she didn't wholly believe it.

◆ ◆ ◆

In the office, Emma was working at her desk, while Morgan was on a video-call with Dickson's wife. There was a peach glow to Elaine Dickson's round cheeks and a hint of matching lipstick on her wide lips. Her chestnut hair fell in soft waves, framing her small face, contoured perfectly to create a more youthful appearance. Small diamond studs in her lobes flashed subtly as she shook her head.

'The last time I spoke to John was three weeks ago, at his insistence. John had . . . has taken our break-up badly. That night, he'd obviously been drinking and was very low. He pleaded with me to give our relationship another chance. I refused. I have . . . reasons for not returning to my old life.'

Kate remained by the door, watching this exchange.

'See what you've done,' said Dickson. 'My poor wife has no idea of what has happened to me. You sent that text knowing she would believe I was going to take my own life. Look at what you are putting her through!'

A flash of guilt warmed her cheeks. Hatred for Dickson had overshadowed her humanity.

'We might have been going through a tough patch, but she loved me for a very long time. You didn't think through the consequences of your actions. You didn't consider those people who actually cared about me.'

Kate hung her head, ashamed of the suffering she'd caused.

She hadn't deliberately taken him from his loved ones, but she had denied them the right to know what had happened. How she had changed! She was becoming the sort of person she hated: acting cruelly and without thought to others. And for what?

The urge to confess everything at that point ballooned. Just when she thought she could stand it no more and was about to give herself up, she heard Chris's calm voice, not Dickson's. His voice was more distant than usual – faint, as if she was hearing him through a hotel wall. Nevertheless, it was him.

'You're doing this for the greater good, Kate. There are always casualties in a war, and you are waging a war on all the corrupt individuals who pollute this institution.'

Relief flooded her, relaxing her bunched shoulders and tightened fists. Chris was still inside her head. He hadn't been usurped. He was with her. They would fight this syndicate together. She turned her attention back to the interview.

Elaine continued speaking directly to Morgan, unaware of either Emma's or Kate's presence. 'To be frank, I was surprised he was as upset as he was about the situation. John's always put his job first. I assumed he'd get over our separation and subsequent divorce with ease and simply bury himself in work as he always did. And I thought he was coping . . . not brilliantly, but coping all the same.

Until I received that message. I've not been sleeping well recently, so last night I took a sleeping pill and turned off the phone. I didn't see his text until this morning. I rang him straight away. I didn't understand what he was supposed to be sorry about, but he has sent some odd messages over the last few weeks, saying how the marriage breakdown was his fault, apologising for neglecting me. I thought this text was along those lines. It was only after I read the article in the *Gazette* this morning that it struck me that John might have been apologising for it. I rang DCI William Chase . . . and you know the rest.'

Kate noticed a wooden dresser behind Elaine, on which sat a line of decorative plates with intricately painted daffodils that stood to attention. Kate could also make out a photograph of Dickson's wife standing next to a handsome man, his arm draped across her shoulder. If he was the new man in her life, it went some way to explaining why she hadn't wanted to rekindle her relationship with her husband.

Elaine lifted a glass to her lips and sipped, leaving a salmon-on-pink smudge against its rim.

'I understand it was a one-word message,' Morgan said.

'That's correct. William took a different view about it. Asked me if John had ever discussed suicide. I told him I couldn't envisage John taking such extreme measures. But then again, I wouldn't have said he was capable of doing any of the dreadful things the press is accusing him of.'

'And you say he's sent you other messages recently?'

'Yes. They're more intimate. I'd rather not share them with you.'

'That won't be necessary, although we might have to ask you for them, to help establish his state of mind.'

'I'd say they were sent after he'd been drinking heavily, if that helps. Separation and divorce take their toll, DS Meredith.'

'Yes, I understand,' said Morgan. Kate was sure Morgan would be giving Elaine an empathetic smile. He had the ability to charm information from interviewees or scare them into giving it away. Today he was kind, and it was paying off. Elaine was opening up to a DS she'd never met before this call.

'I didn't know.'

'About what, Mrs Dickson?' asked Morgan.

'Please, call me Elaine. I didn't know about any of the things the article mentioned. I suspected there were other women in his life. I had no idea they might be underage. John's never displayed any obvious interest in younger women. But . . . as I said, we had drifted apart.'

'Our main concern is for John's welfare. Do you have any idea where he might have headed? A place you and he might call special? A hideaway? Friends or relatives he might have turned to?' Morgan said.

'I could write down a list of anyone I can think of. Should I email it to you?'

'If you wouldn't mind.'

Elaine nodded, her neatly arched eyebrows pulling together. 'I can't think of anybody obvious. His connections are mostly people he works with. He doesn't have any hobbies and many of his friends from years ago have fallen by the wayside. You have tried Alex Corby's family, haven't you? John was appalled by what happened to Alex. They were friends for many years.'

Alex Corby had been the reason Kate had been brought back from sick leave. Dickson had requested that she head up the investigation into his friend's death. Now, she understood the real reason he'd insisted she'd been lead officer. Knowing she was still traumatised by Chris's death, he'd hoped she would slip up, or suffer a lapse in her judgement. Because, if it was pursued intensely, the investigation would have uncovered evidence relating to the murder of an underage male sex-worker. A murder to which Dickson had been party.

'We'll talk to them. Can you think of anybody else?'

'My first thought was William, but he has no idea any more than I do of where John might be.'

'If anything comes to mind, or the superintendent contacts you, would you let me know immediately, please?'

'Certainly. And likewise, let me know when you find him.'

'Thank you for your time, Elaine.'

Morgan ended the video-call and spun his chair to face Kate. 'Alex Corby's family? Alex's house overlooks Blithfield Reservoir, which puts it in the vicinity of Abbots Bromley.'

'I hardly think Alex's wife will be harbouring the super at their house . . . but you never know, so yes, try her,' she replied.

'What about her father, Bradley Chapman?' said Emma. 'He used to be in the SAS. He'd be pretty handy as a bodyguard. As I recall, he still practises Krav Maga. He lives near Abbots Bromley. Shouldn't we try him too?'

Ice prickled up her spine at the mention of Bradley's name, but Kate didn't flounder. Emma wasn't wrong. Bradley *was* guarding somebody. Just not Dickson. It was Stanka who was hiding at his house.

Kate fought the mild panic threatening to wash over her. They'd already discussed the possibility Bradley would receive a visit from the police. He would know how to conduct himself. 'Yes,' she said, keeping her tone steady. 'Why don't you ring him, Emma, and then speak to his daughter?'

'Erm, as I recall, he wasn't very helpful during our investigation into his son-in-law's death. Maybe I should speak to him face to face. If he's hiding the superintendent, he isn't going to willingly confess over the phone.'

Kate couldn't fault Emma's argument, even if she would have preferred her to have rung. 'True. Okay. Head over to his house and see if you can gauge his reaction.'

'Right-ho.'

'Morgan, let's crack on with what we know. We believe the super went somewhere near or in Abbots Bromley for a meeting.'

'There's about two thousand people living in that village, let alone those in the countryside. The words *needle* and *haystack* spring to mind,' he replied. 'Although, if I was meeting anybody, it would be most likely at a pub. Abbots Bromley has three of those and a restaurant.'

'We should make a start there. However, we really need to know where he went afterwards. He could be staying with somebody in the Needwood area.'

'There's a hotel on St George's Park,' Morgan replied. The 330-acre park was the English Football Association's national football centre, boasting fourteen outdoor pitches, state-of-the-art performance facilities and an outdoor leadership centre. The hotel was situated next to a full-sized indoor pitch. 'There's also that estate there, the one with the mews houses and a big hall. What's it called?'

'Rangemore Hall,' said Emma, shrugging on her jacket.

'That's the place. One of those gated communities. He'd be safe from prying eyes if he's hiding there.'

'Worth a try. Pull up a map of the Needwood area, would you? See if there's anywhere else where he might be,' said Kate. She wanted Morgan to identify the location where she'd left Dickson's car. It had to come from him rather than her.

Her pulse hammered in her ears as she kept her head lowered over her own screen, resisting the urge to glance in Morgan's direction. He would have enlarged the map by now and be searching for farms, barns, any place where he suspected Dickson was lying low. He grunted quietly, made a note.

'There aren't many other properties in this area. I suppose he could simply have been meeting somebody here, then gone elsewhere. He could be in Land's End or John O'Groats for all we know.'

Kate muttered, 'I hope not. That would make our job a hell of a lot harder.'

'He's got the skills and wherewithal to hunker down somewhere remote for as long as it takes for this to blow over without being found.'

Kate didn't reply, pretending instead to be occupied, all the while waiting for Morgan to have the Eureka moment.

'He isn't going to take the bait,' said Dickson. *'Maybe Emma would have been a better bet. She's quick off the mark. What will you do if he doesn't make the connection?'*

Kate willed Morgan to point out the destination. She had to ensure her reaction was natural. Dickson's voice – along with the pulsing in her ears – was driving her crazy.

'You're walking deeper into danger. You're banking on your team following your clues to the letter, but what if they turn up something that points to my death? What if they start to notice their DI is not reacting as she should?'

Unable to calm her heartbeat, she rose to go to the washroom.

'Kate.'

The wariness in his voice immobilised her. She prepared to respond.

'There's a small airfield nearby. You don't suppose he could have met somebody there and literally taken off, do you?'

At last! 'Anything's possible. Find out whatever you can about the airfield and talk to somebody at that hotel.' She headed into the corridor, where she lifted her head to the ceiling and exhaled noisily. It was still going to plan. A flash of movement made her jump. For a second, she was sure it was Dickson who was striding

57

down the corridor towards her. The figure marched with authority, head high, the same gait as her nemesis.

'Hello, Kate. Surprised to see me?'

Impossible! It couldn't be Dickson. She blinked to dispel the image.

'You okay, Kate?'

His face came into focus. It was Rich, one of the liaison officers, who bore only a slight resemblance to Dickson. Her nerves had got the better of her.

He regarded her cautiously. 'You look like you've seen a ghost.'

'I'm fine, Rich. Just suffering a sugar dip. I need coffee and chocolate.'

'Don't rely on the drinks machine, then. It's only distributing lukewarm milk or green tea.'

'Tea will have to do. Cheers.'

She scurried off.

'All this subterfuge is harder than you imagined, isn't it?' said Dickson, gleefully. 'You're going to have to take your A-game to Tatenhill airfield because that's where the real test will begin.'

'If you could pull it off, so can I,' she replied, although the churning of her stomach suggested otherwise. She had to. There was no other choice. She'd managed to stay calm last night. She could continue to do so today . . .

There are no dog walkers in Abbots Bromley. In fact, there isn't anyone on the streets. The village is sleepy, with curtains drawn at the windows of pretty cottages and pavements empty. She passes the grocery store, shut for the night, and turns down a lane too narrow and twisty to drive at breakneck speed. It is one thing to attract attention, but another to cause injury or worse. The insides of the nitrile gloves are uncomfortably *damp. Nobody has spied the car. It's imperative somebody does. The road descends, winding past the church, causing her to slow, but on spying two people leaving the pub at the bottom of the hill, she increases her speed and hares past them. She knows even before she checks in the rear-view mirror that they've seen her. One of them is shaking a fist at the car. They might even have seen its number-plate. She checks the time: 8.09 p.m. She is only four minutes away from her destination.*

Tatenhill airfield is in complete darkness. Her headlights pick out the outlines of several light aircraft under covers and parked on the grass in front of a hangar. As expected, there are no lights on the runway, and no sign of life. The place is shut during the hours of darkness. She only knows of its whereabouts thanks to a visit some time ago with Chris, who had come here for a trial flying lesson. She thinks again about the logic of what she is trying to do – convince people Dickson has been picked up from here, yet it would be foolhardy for any pilot, no matter how accomplished, to attempt to land and take off from the airstrip in the pitch dark.

She sits in the car, going through potential scenarios, finally deciding that whilst a landing would be impossible without lighting, a take-off might be viable.

The gates are locked, making it impossible to manoeuvre Dickson's car into the parking area. However, she's already anticipated that situation and will park up close to a group of outbuildings she spotted just before the entrance.

She screws her eyes to better check the exterior of the hangar. There are two surveillance cameras, both aimed at the hangar doors. There is nothing overlooking the car park or the gated entrance. She looks up and down the road, ready to switch off her headlights at the first sign of a vehicle. Again, luck sits on her shoulders. The road is empty, so she reverses back to a lay-by at the bottom of the airfield, next to the buildings. Sometimes it is better to hide things in plain sight. During the day, the road is busy, with employees making for the nearby industrial parks or heading into Burton upon Trent. The Mercedes won't attract a great deal of attention. Plane spotters often park along this stretch.

With the vehicle in situ, she's almost ready. It's now 8.23 p.m. Dickson's phone is still unlocked. She thumbs the contact list, finds Elaine's name and sends a one-word message to her, then resets the auto-lock to its original setting and waits for the mobile to switch off before sliding it next to Dickson's wedding ring in the glove box. She makes for the rear of the car. Vehicles rumble by in the distance. None approach. She opens the boot lid, pulls out her bicycle, then, taking the wrapped gun from the glove box, places it inside the spare wheel. It will add fuel to the theory Dickson has not taken his own life, merely disappeared. At least, that's the idea.

She leaves the car unlocked, removes her forensic clothing, balling it against her chest and zipping it into position under her hooded top, before climbing on to her bike to begin the forty-plus minute journey towards the reservoir and her own car.

'Stupid to leave the car unlocked,' *says Dickson.* 'Anybody could steal it and find the gun. What if they use it to kill somebody? You'll end up with even more blood on your hands.'

'I want people to think you were so panicked you fled without giving much thought to anything. Leaving it unlocked is a risk I'm prepared to take. It's rural Staffordshire, not the centre of London or Birmingham, though, so I reckon it's fairly safe here.'

'Ah, but you can't know for sure. Shame on you. You're supposed to protect the public not—'

She lowers her head and pedals furiously to shut out the constant chatter.

◆ ◆ ◆

Morgan interrupted her thoughts with an update.

'The hotel receptionist confirmed there were five new check-ins last night,' he said. 'None under the name of Dickson. I could head across and check out their CCTV to ensure he wasn't using a false name. Unless you have a different idea.'

'Oh, yes. Well done, Morgan. That would waste some more time. How long can you keep up this act, Kate? Unless they find my car soon, you'll crack and say something you shouldn't, or let that mask of yours slip. Everything depends on your idea panning out exactly the way you planned it. From where I'm sitting, that isn't happening, so how long, Kate? How long can you keep it up? Your heart is thumping so loudly, I'm surprised he can't hear it.'

Morgan unwrapped the chocolate bar Kate had brought upstairs for him. He snapped off a square and popped it into his mouth.

Kate clutched a takeaway cup of tea, periodically blowing on it, going through the motions of normality even though her head was full of Dickson's questions and comments. She had to get out of here before it exploded. She put down the cup.

'Sounds good to me. Did you ring the airfield?'

'I got the answerphone.'

'Oh, dear! Things don't always go the way we hope.' Dickson's sarcasm was infuriating. This was a setback she didn't need. She'd hoped to stop at both places and then the car would be found. She couldn't force that issue. All the same, she couldn't let this purgatory drag out any longer.

'How about we both go? Then, if we have no luck at St George's Park, we'll drive to Rangemore Hall and see if we can spot his car. I know it's feeble, but it's the best I can come up with.'

'We have to start somewhere.' Morgan crammed another piece of chocolate into his mouth and leapt to his feet.

Kate slapped the lid on to her cup and followed him out. The next phase of her plan was about to begin.

◆ ◆ ◆

Emma drove across the reservoir, black water shimmering in the moonlight. She'd never really liked the place, even though it was beautiful. The horror of what she'd uncovered at the Corby residence had tainted it. To her mind, death and beauty were forever entwined here.

Ignoring the turning that led to that house, she decided to visit Bradley Chapman before returning here to speak to his daughter, Fiona.

It had been over a year since the Alex Corby investigation, yet the events were still clearly imprinted on Emma's mind. It had been a horrendous case. All the same, Kate had risen to the challenge, even though she had clearly not been over the death of her husband.

Emma had always held Kate in the highest regard. The effort that had been required to take on such a challenge during a highly stressful period in her life only served to solidify this. Her DI was one of the best. In turn, that made Emma want to be the best officer she could possibly be. She had an added impetus to prove her own worth on this case, even track down the superintendent herself – a six-foot-plus reason: Morgan Meredith. Although they'd been friends for an age, recently her feelings for him had taken a turn. The blinkers were off and their relationship had entered a more romantic phase. In fact, she was falling for him. Too quickly for her liking, perhaps. But something about them being in a couple made her happy and she liked that feeling.

She recalled visiting the Chapmans' home with Morgan, who'd been surprised by her ability to quieten the large guard dogs prowling by the gate. She pretended she'd known how to control them when, in reality, she'd been bluffing. Even back then, she'd sought his approval and liked him far more than she'd been willing to admit.

She followed a narrow lane to a gated entrance. The same two German shepherds bounded in her direction. As she clambered out of the car, they bared their teeth and began barking for all they were worth. This time, calm words didn't appease them. She reached for the intercom button and replied to a disembodied voice asking her to identify herself.

'It's DS Emma Donaldson. I'd appreciate a few words with Mr Chapman, please.'

'What about?'

'I'd rather discuss that inside, if you don't mind.'

A click indicated that the person had hung up. Within seconds the dogs' ears pricked up and they bounded towards the house. Emma returned to her car and waited for the gate to open automatically. It seemed she was still welcome here after all.

Bradley Chapman stood outside the front door, head high, hands behind his back and legs slightly apart. He nodded at her as she approached. 'DS Donaldson. How are you?'

The gruff voice matched the lined, worn face.

'Good, thank you. I'm sorry to disturb you but Elaine Dickson suggested I speak to you.'

His brow furrowed deeply. 'Elaine Dickson,' he repeated, in a way that suggested he didn't know the woman.

'Superintendent Dickson's wife.'

'Oh! John Dickson. Elaine. Yes. I know who you mean, although I barely knew him. He was Alex's friend.'

'Elaine thought you might be able to help. Superintendent Dickson is missing.'

Bradley folded his arms across his broad chest. 'Missing? Or gone into hiding following that rather damning article in the *Gazette* this morning?'

'That's what we're trying to establish. Nobody has heard from him, and his wife is concerned.'

'And, reading between the lines, you think he might be skulking about in our house?'

Emma gave a light laugh. 'Maybe not skulking as such, more looking for some privacy while he sorts out how best to handle the situation.'

'Sorry to disappoint you but I haven't seen or heard from your superintendent since Alex's funeral.'

'Oh, right. Erm, I wonder if your daughter might have heard from him.'

Bradley was one of those people with a natural resting angry face. The cloud that flitted across his features made him look even more cross than he normally did. 'I doubt it. The house has been for sale for over ten months and Fiona is currently living in France. She couldn't stay at the old place, not after what happened to Alex there.'

'Yes, I appreciate it would be difficult.'

'More impossible than difficult. So, sorry I can't be of any more assistance, but John Dickson has certainly not contacted us.'

'Thank you for your time, anyway.'

He spun on his heel and disappeared back into the house. The door closed tight behind him. As Emma got into her car, a movement caught her eye and she looked at the upstairs window in time to see a young woman watching her. They locked eyes for a moment before the girl disappeared. Emma hesitated for a second before deciding, whoever she was, she had nothing to do with the task in hand.

◆ ◆ ◆

Kate received Emma's call as they were about to head off to Abbots Bromley. She had drawn a blank with Bradley, but on learning the Corbys' house was empty, had decided to check it out on the off-chance Dickson had chosen to lie low there.

'We're headed in your direction. It would help if you could drop by the pubs and restaurant in the village to see if anyone spotted the superintendent meeting a third party around 6.30 p.m.,' said Kate.

'Sure. I'll do that. What about you? Will you meet me there?'

'No, we're heading to St George's Park. Ring us if you find out anything.'

Kate stared at the queue of traffic waiting for the lights to turn green. Morgan tapped the steering wheel impatiently. 'I'm not sure going into hiding is the right way to handle things,' he said eventually. 'I'd want to prove my innocence.'

In that instant, she had an unexpected desire to unburden herself to him. Morgan wasn't just one of her team. She'd known him a long time. He was her friend and, as such, he would understand why she'd had to feign Dickson's disappearance.

'No,' cautioned Chris, his voice still sounding distant, but insistent enough to break through.

Regardless of his words, her stomach twisted and the yearning to speak grew. Keeping this hush-hush from people she trusted and cared about was agony. 'That's assuming he is innocent,' Kate replied, edging her way to a conversation that could lead to her divulging the truth.

'Kate. No.' This time, Chris's voice was louder. Reason returned. For all she wanted to spill her soul, she couldn't. Not to Emma, not to Morgan. This had to remain her secret. Hers alone.

Morgan drummed a beat again before speaking. 'Yeah, running for the hills and keeping everyone in the dark sure makes him look guilty. Should we try to speak to his solicitors in case they've advised him to disappear?'

She hesitated before speaking. She trusted Morgan completely, but her revelation could be too much for him to comprehend. She couldn't tell him. 'DCI Chase would probably have already checked with them. I'll ask him when we get back.'

'I know we should all stand shoulder to shoulder and support our fellow officers,' said Morgan, 'but I'm beginning to have . . . doubts about the super.'

'Don't let them confound the issue. Our brief is simply to locate him. Let's keep it at that.'

'When we investigate a murder, we try to think like the killer, anticipate their moves. We should do the same in this scenario. If the super is guilty of any of what is being said in the newspapers, he'll react in one way. If he isn't, he'll act differently. We need to put ourselves in his shoes. If he's biding his time to prepare an attack on the media, he'll be keeping a low profile, presumably somewhere nearby. If he's on the run because he knows he's in deep trouble, he could have gone further afield, even abroad by now.'

'You're right. Given the leads only take us as far as Needwood, that's where we'll start. First the hotel.'

'And afterwards, how about the airfield?'

She nodded. Morgan was following the trail of breadcrumbs as she intended. All she had to do now was wait for him to spot the car and let the rest unfold.

CHAPTER FIVE

DAY ONE – EVENING

Emma trained her eyes on the narrow lane that led to what had been Alex Corby's home. Her headlights spilled over uneven hedgerows that seemed to have swollen to three times their size since her last visit. Their branches clawed at her car as she passed. Trees appeared to dance in the stiff breeze, warning her to stay away.

Emma wasn't of a nervous disposition but, nevertheless, chilled fingers tickled the nape of her neck. Her mind conjured up an image of a neglected castle at the end of the road, and a hero cutting through swathes of undergrowth to reach an imprisoned prince or princess. But life, she reminded herself, was no fairy tale.

This was rural Staffordshire, and town-loving Emma needed to get a grip on her overactive imagination. Around her the fields were populated by animals, not ghosts or monsters. The demon who had murdered Alex Corby, and others after him, was now safely behind bars.

The lane twisted to the right, headlights tracing the line of hawthorn bushes to eventually fall across the large metal gates to the house. She got out, the cold night air nipping at her face as she shone her Maglite on the padlock holding the gates together. It was broken. She swung the heavy gate wide enough to pass through.

Her footsteps crunched over the gravel driveway. There were no lights inside the house, or any vehicle parked outside. She peered through a window into an empty room, drew a deep breath and began to walk around the back of the property. The light swept over flagstones and stone ornaments – a dancing woman, a stone bird bath, a crouching lion – taking Emma closer to the French doors that led into the dining room. It was in this room they'd found Alex's body, facing the windows as if staring out at his garden and the reservoir beyond. A macabre shriek froze her to the spot, heart thumping. When it screeched again, she half-laughed at her reaction. It was only an owl.

She dimmed the light, crept towards the double windows and, steeling herself, looked through the glass. Relief flooded her as she realised it, too, was empty.

What had she expected? The superintendent, tied to a chair, his tongue lolling and eyes staring glassily at her?

Her shoulders relaxed, and she shone the torch with more confidence around the grounds, through other windows, until she was certain there was nobody hiding in the property. She picked her way through wet grass and was heading back to her car when she spotted a weak light emitting from under the garage doors. She tiptoed across, established there were no door handles and that the garage appeared to be locked from within. Maybe someone had simply forgotten to extinguish the light – an estate agent showing round a potential buyer, for example. She turned to leave, stopping when she heard a quiet cough. She spun round and banged her fist hard against the door.

'This is the police. Open the door!'

She was met with silence. Emma's mind raced. Could her boss be hiding here?

'I won't ask again. Open up!' she yelled.

There was some shuffling from within. Emma waited. When nobody appeared, she hammered hard with both fists. 'Okay. This is your last chance before I break open the door.'

'One minute,' came the reply, followed by the scraping of a bolt being tugged loose. There was further rasping as another was released. The right-hand door eased outwards, causing her to jump to one side, and a figure emerged.

'I wasn't doing any harm.'

It was difficult to put an age on the bearded man. His hair was long and streaked with grey, but his eyes were clear and bright. He was about the same height as Emma, his frame shrouded in a thick padded jacket, wide jeans and oversized woollen socks. She spied a grubby sleeping bag laid out in one corner of the room. Muddy work boots stood beside it along with a bag of crisps and two cans of lager.

'What's your name?' she asked.

'Digger.'

'Digger, how long have you been living here?'

'A couple of days. I stumbled across it the night before last.'

'This isn't the sort of place you stumble across. I suggest you broke the padlock and forced your way into the garage.'

'No, honestly. The padlock was already broken. This door was open. I wouldn't have come in otherwise. Really. I'm not doing anything wrong.'

'Breaking and entering,' she said.

'No. The garage door was open. I wandered in,' he insisted.

'Is Digger your surname?'

'I'm just Digger.'

'Do you have a home address?'

'I'm looking for a new place.' He shuffled from one foot to the other.

'Are you local?'

He nodded. 'I've lived around here for ten years.'

'And where were you staying before you came here?'

He hesitated before saying, 'A farm near Uttoxeter.'

'Which farm?'

He hung his head. 'I can't remember the name.'

'Really? Come on, Digger. You expect me to believe that? You've lived in the area for a decade. You must know every farm around here. Was the farmer aware that you were there at the time?'

'No. People don't mind if I only spend a night or two in one of their outbuildings. I always clean up after myself. Never cause damage.' He looked so downcast Emma couldn't help but feel sorry for him.

'Listen, you can't stay here. It's private property. I'll run you into the nearest town and find you a bed at a hostel,' she said.

'No hostels,' he muttered, moving back into the garage.

'It's okay. I can drive you to Lichfield, where we'll fix up some temporary accommodation for you. A bed. Food.'

He began thrusting his provisions into a carrier bag. 'Thanks, but I can look after myself.' He bundled up the sleeping bag and shoved it into a large, shabby backpack.

'It's dark and you have nowhere to go. I'll drive you. Come on.'

There was a long pause until he finally grunted, 'Okay.' He hoisted the bulging backpack on to his shoulders and picked up the carrier bag.

Emma's communications unit burst into life. Kate wanted an update. Emma turned away from the man as she spoke.

'There's a vagrant at the Corby residence. I'm going to take him to Lichfield to find somewhere for him to sleep tonight, then I'll return . . . Hey! Wait up!'

Digger had raced across the garden and was almost out of sight. Emma started after him.

'He's done a runner,' she said into the Airwave.

'Leave him. Head to Abbots Bromley instead.'

Emma shone her torch into the blackness, picking up nothing but vegetation before returning to the garage to extinguish the light. She pushed the door shut. She'd ring Bradley and let him know it was unlocked and the padlock on the gates was broken before anyone else decided to take up residence.

Kate and Morgan were close to Needwood and the airfield.

'Who on earth would doss down at the Corbys' house? It's in the middle of nowhere,' said Morgan.

'Beats me. However, that person isn't our priority and I doubt he has anything to do with the superintendent's disappearance,' Kate replied.

'Knowing Emma, she's probably already belting after him and will drag his sorry arse back to her car.' His eyes twinkled as he spoke. 'Still weird, though. Of all the places to break into, he chose that house. I suppose it's coincidence.'

Kate didn't comment. There was something disagreeably strange about the intruder being found on the premises. All the same, she didn't believe it was connected in any way to Dickson, unless . . .

Her mind somersaulted.

Unless the person was searching for Stanka.

Her mind shuffled through the possibilities: Stanka had been spotted getting into Bradley's car, which in turn had been traced to him. Could this be one of several people staking out Bradley's and his daughter's homes, hoping to find Stanka at one of them?

'My people will always be one step ahead of you, Kate.'

By digging her fingernails into her thighs, she found the focus to mute Dickson's voice. She was overreacting to the situation.

Nobody could know that she and Bradley had driven to Blackpool to meet and rescue Stanka. They would have spotted it if anyone had been following his vehicle. They'd been ultra-cautious. There was no way that the syndicate members could have traced Stanka to Bradley's house. Not in such a short space of time. Could they?

She was glad when Morgan spoke again.

'Do you support a football team, Kate?'

'Er, no. Sorry. Not something I'm into. Chris wasn't either. He was more a rugby man.'

'Me too. I enjoy watching the odd football match, but you can't beat a game of rugby. I wondered if there'd be any top footballers training at St George's Park this evening.'

'I wouldn't know any of the England squad if I fell over them,' she replied. They were closing in on the airfield. She turned her head to study the fields opposite. Dickson's car would soon come into view on the right, parked directly in front of a barred gate leading to the airport café, and she shouldn't be the one to spot it first. She counted to eight before sensing the car slowing.

'Kate, there's a Mercedes estate car parked ahead, by the gates. No! That's Dickson's car registration, isn't it?'

Even though she had known this moment would arrive, her heart began a rapid *rat-a-tat-tat*. The time had come to play her most convincing role yet. What had seemed easy when in the planning now seemed impossible. What if she unconsciously gave away something? Morgan knew her well. The slightest change in her behaviour and he would suspect something was up.

'It's not easy being deceitful. It takes years of practice to become as accomplished as me and my colleagues. You're out of our league.'

Morgan pulled the Jeep over beside the Mercedes and bounded out, followed swiftly by Kate, who couldn't bear Dickson's asides. Of course she wasn't good at covering her tracks or keeping secrets from her friends; it wasn't who she was! At the same time, she recognised the fact she'd become that person. Reminding herself this was, as Chris had said, *for the greater good*, she began her performance. If she treated this investigation as if it was anyone other than Dickson, she'd be able to carry it off.

'Don't touch anything,' she warned.

Morgan crouched to look through the driver's window. 'There's nobody inside and the keys are in the ignition.'

'Got any gloves?'

'Yes.' He opened the Jeep's rear passenger door and delved into a cardboard box on the seat, pulling out a pair of nitrile gloves for each of them. They circled the Mercedes before Morgan tried the driver's door handle. It opened. Locating the boot release button, he pressed it and the lid lifted effortlessly. He made for the back of the car, sighing with relief as he looked inside. 'For one horrible moment, I expected to find his body in here.'

'I can't see any signs of a struggle,' said Kate.

'So, what the fuck has happened? What made him drive here, leave his car unlocked, with the keys in the ignition, and then disappear? Oh, shit! What if he . . . he's taken his own life? That message to his wife and all—'

'Then why not do it inside the car?' said Kate, countering Morgan's plausible argument. She had to get him off the subject of suicide and thinking more along the lines that Dickson had done a runner. 'If somebody intends taking their own life, they usually do it somewhere familiar. At home, at work, in their car, or in their garage. They don't drive to an airfield, miles away from their home.'

Morgan seemed to digest her words as he rubbed his large hand over his forehead.

'Okay. That's true. But to leave his car like this? What if somebody forced him to drive here?' he said.

'You mean you think somebody kidnapped him?'

Morgan shrugged. 'I was thinking more along the lines that somebody brought him here to execute him. That sort of shit happens.'

Kate struggled to maintain the conversation while trying to quell the mounting anxiety that was making her palms sweat. She was about to 'discover' Dickson's phone and it was imperative she acted exactly as Morgan would expect. She popped the glove box, peered inside and pulled out the mobile, holding it up for Morgan to see. 'Here's one mystery solved. Now we know why he hasn't been answering his calls.'

'Is it his?'

'Don't know for certain. It requires a biometric password. It looks like his.'

'Is there anything else in there?'

Kate patted inside the box, ducked down to squint into the space before withdrawing the wedding ring. She adopted a hushed tone. 'Yes. This.'

Morgan's eyebrows drew together tightly. 'Fuck! Isn't that the sort of thing somebody does when they plan on taking their own life? They leave behind objects they no longer want or need. Kate, this really looks like suicide.'

With his eyes on her, Kate sighed heavily as part of her act. 'Okay, I really hope we're wrong about this, but I guess we must face up to the possibility. We'll get a forensic team here pronto to check over the car and search the area.'

She rang the head of Forensics, Ervin Saunders, to explain the situation, all the while struggling for normality. Glancing at Morgan while she spoke, she tried to read his face, worried he might have seen through her act. The solemn expression he wore was probably down to the thought Dickson had topped himself rather than anything else. She had to continue to treat this as a genuine disappearance, then she would perform realistically.

Once the brief call to Ervin ended, she addressed Morgan again.

'We should look around, see if . . . he's anywhere close. I'll get hold of Emma.'

'I'll start there,' said Morgan, pointing at a group of low-roofed buildings, ex-RAF billets.

She spoke to Emma on the Airwave, keeping one eye on Morgan as he climbed effortlessly over the gate. His flashlight bounced along the walls of a larger building which housed the café and offices, then across the cracked tarmac towards the furthest billet. Having instructed Emma to join them, she pulled out her own torch and pursued Morgan.

Dickson's voice whispered, *'The net is tightening, Kate. Once Forensics examine my car, they'll discover your DNA. It'll be there somewhere. And I was wearing my wedding ring when I was shot. Don't you think there might be a teeny-weeny amount of blood on it somewhere, or on the driver's seat, or even in the glove box? You know how thorough the forensic team are. You might have to rethink this ridiculous charade.'*

Surely, Dickson was wrong. If a drop of blood were to be found, it would be too microscopic to cause alarm. Forensics would deduce it had come from some small nick or cut on his person.

She peeled away from Morgan to head in the opposite direction, her heart jumping in her chest. Things could so easily unravel. She suddenly needed reassurance. 'Chris?' she said, softly. When silence ensued, she whispered again, the need for her husband's voice intensifying.

'While you continue to be deceptive, you're only going to hear me,' said Dickson. *'Chris has gone.'*

She shook her head angrily. That wasn't the case. She'd spoken to Chris's voice earlier. He was on her side. They were a team. 'Chris?'

The urge to hear her husband's voice, assuring her that she was in control grew, and yet she was aware of nothing other than a dim chuckle that sounded exactly like Dickson's.

◆ ◆ ◆

The pub at the far end of Abbots Bromley was empty apart from two men by the bar who didn't give Emma a second glance when she walked in. The bartender, a woman in her forties, threw her a smile. 'Sorry, no food tonight. Drinks only. It's the chef's night off.'

'I only came in to ask a few questions.' Emma lifted the ID card on the lanyard around her neck. 'I'm DS Donaldson. I'm investigating a disappearance that might have taken place in the local area.'

'Oh, right.'

'Were you working here last night?'

'Every night. I'm the manager.'

Emma brought up a photograph of Dickson on her phone and showed it to the woman. 'You didn't happen to see that man in here, did you? It would have been around six thirty.'

She stared at the picture. 'He's the policeman who was in the news today. The sex scandal story.'

'Did you see this man yesterday evening?'

'No. He didn't come in here. It was dead until about eight.' She turned her head. 'Wasn't it, Garth?'

The man closest to Emma looked up. His face was broad and ruddy, broken veins across his cheeks and nose. 'Nobody but me and Bert.'

The second man joined the conversation. 'No one came in. Not while we were here anyway.'

'Thank you both for your time.' She paused. The pair, dressed in grubby overalls and wellington boots, looked like they might be farm labourers. 'I don't suppose either of you have heard of a man called Digger?'

Garth burst out laughing. 'Drifter Digger? Of course. We all know Digger around these parts. What's he been up to?'

'I happened across him. He was sleeping somewhere he shouldn't have been. I was going to drive him to a hostel, but he scarpered . . . pretty quickly too.'

He grinned again. 'You'd never have managed to drag Digger to any hostel – or town, for that matter. He's a born countryman and a loner. He roams the farms around here, doing a spot of manual work if there's anything going, in exchange for food and shelter. He prefers sleeping in a barn to a house. Sometimes, he beds down in a place even when he isn't working there. Nobody minds as long as he doesn't do it too often or overstay his welcome. He won't have strayed far. I heard the Tollers over towards Colton are expecting him to turn up and help them out in the next day or two.'

She thanked them again before taking her leave.

In her car, she rang Bradley to let him know that the gate to his daughter's house was insecure and the garage doors unlocked. He was as surly as usual, assuring her he knew about the padlock and intended replacing it, then, as an afterthought, thanked her for alerting him about the garage.

'Bloody estate agent will be to blame. I keep telling them to lock up properly after they show somebody around.'

She was going to tell him about Digger, then changed her mind. The man hadn't left behind any rubbish or damaged the place. If Bradley locked the doors, Digger wouldn't return. No sooner had she rung off than Kate's voice came over the comms.

'We've found the super's car. Can you get here? It's parked on the side of the road next to Tatenhill airfield.'

Emma started up the engine. She had a bad feeling about this. Something serious had happened to the superintendent.

CHAPTER SIX

DAY ONE – LATE EVENING

Flashlight beams arced left and right as officers combed the fields behind the old RAF billets. Kate greeted Ervin as he got out of his Volkswagen Beetle convertible. He and Kate had known each other for years, and when Chris had been alive, they'd often attended Ervin's outrageous parties or met him for after-work drinks. Since Chris's death, Kate had refused the invitations that had come her way and now only saw Ervin for the occasional night out. With her free time given to searching for evidence to bring down Dickson, those evenings had become rare over the last year.

Ervin remained unhurried, pausing to pick a fleck of dirt from the lining of his black velvet jacket, the same deep crimson as the large red roses patterned all over his crisp white shirt. He shrugged it into position, did up the buttons and smoothed the black tie into place, then brushed invisible creases from his dark grey trousers and turned to face her with, 'Please don't comment about the tie. I've come from a wake.'

'I'm so sorry. I didn't mean to drag you away.'

He held up an elegant hand to stop the apology. 'It had gone on far too long. I was glad of an excuse to finally escape Aunt Nora's quizzing. She always makes me feel like I'm ten years old and she knows I've been stealing from the cookie jar.' He gave Kate a wink. 'Right, what have we got here?'

'Superintendent's unlocked car with the key in the ignition, a mobile phone and a wedding band in the glove box.'

'I suppose we can't be one hundred per cent certain the phone and ring actually belong to him until we examine them, can we? Are all the items tagged and bagged?' he said.

'Yes, and already on their way to the lab.'

'Good. I gave my officers a lecture about how we had to be super-efficient on this investigation. I'm sure HQ will be watching our every move . . . so I include your team in that statement. What's your take on the newspaper's accusations?'

Ervin, like her, had harboured suspicions about Dickson. She was sorely tempted to tell some of the truth, even hint at what had befallen Dickson. Anything to relieve the mounting pressure that had her heart beating too quickly and was air-drying her mouth so often she had to keep swallowing.

Unable to get Chris's voice to speak to her, Ervin was one of the few other people she felt close enough to who she knew would listen.

All the same, she didn't dare say a thing. Once she started talking, it would snowball and before she knew it, she'd have confessed her crimes and, as close friends as they were, she knew Ervin would still be shocked to the core.

She couldn't even discuss the accusations being made about Dickson in the press, not while she was feeling so vulnerable. And even if she wanted to, she couldn't do it here, where they might be overheard. Instead, she shrugged a response, which seemed good enough for Ervin.

He stepped towards the back of the car, where one of his team was searching inside the boot. 'Anything, Ammad?'

'It's clean, boss. Just about to check below deck, so to speak.' The man lifted the cover to reveal the wheel well containing a spare tyre, a tool wrap and a first aid box.

'What's that?' asked Ervin, pointing immediately at the towel shoved into the middle of the rubber tyre.

The man lifted and unfolded the material. Kate feigned surprise with a gasp. Ervin released a low whistle. 'A Baikal handgun. A Baikal IZH-79, to be exact. Oh, Superintendent Dickson, you have been a naughty boy!' He clicked his tongue in disapproval. 'It's a sure bet that's an illegal weapon. Of course, it might have been planted, so maybe I shouldn't cast aspersions before facts. Check it for prints before you bag it, Ammad. Then test all the area with luminol.'

'Yes, boss.'

Ervin ran long fingers through his styled grey quiff – a modern hairstyle that took ten years off his age.

'Boss!' It was another officer, working on the driver's seat. Kate wandered to the gate to calm her heartrate. Had the officer found something she'd been careless enough to leave behind? She spotted Emma walking alongside Morgan, matching his pace, step for step. She focussed on her breathing: in through the nose, out through the mouth.

Ervin joined her at the gate. 'There's a small amount of blood on the glove box. It might be something, or it might be nothing. We've taken a swab.'

Kate swallowed down panic; calmed herself with logic. It had to be Dickson's blood, not her own. 'Okay. That's not much to go on. Is there anything to suggest he might have been attacked or was forced into driving the car?'

'It's not looking that way. No blood in the boot. No evidence of a struggle.'

She pretended to give this some thought. 'Unless somebody held him at gunpoint, forced him to drive here and then . . .'

'Then what? Kate, there's no body.'

'We haven't yet searched the entire area.'

'I'll grant you that. But for what it's worth, I don't believe he's here. I also think it's highly unlikely he was hijacked, brought here under duress, or even murdered.' He lowered his voice. 'I suspect he drove here of his own free will, deliberately sent an ambiguous text to his ex-wife, left his personal effects in an unlocked vehicle and disappeared. The question is why?'

'To take his own life?' she offered.

'Over the years, as a forensic officer, you develop an instinct about certain cases and people. I can't see Superintendent Dickson taking his own life. Can you?'

Kate tried not to react. Of course, Ervin wasn't going to just accept the idea of Dickson committing suicide. She should have been better prepared. The thought of her friend uncovering her lies was somehow worse than the prospect of losing her job or position in the force.

She shook her head. 'Not really. Why do you think he chose this spot?'

Ervin flashed a smile that enhanced the creases around his bright eyes. 'Come on, Kate. You're anything but slow-witted. Don't pretend you haven't questioned why he would drive to a private airfield that is closed overnight. If somebody wished to escape from the public eye, or from an inquiry into his behaviour, what better way than by a light aircraft? He wouldn't have to worry about surveillance cameras tracking his car or his movements. Small planes can even get away without filing flight plans and can land on private airstrips. Do you have any idea how many places he could reach without raising any questions?'

'Quite a few, I'd imagine.'

'There are roughly seven hundred and fifty airfields in the UK, if you include the numerous licensed strips in fields, and before you ask why I am cognisant of such facts, let's just say I am an aircraft-spotting enthusiast who often checks out airfields. By the way, please keep that nugget of knowledge to yourself. I have no desire to be labelled an anorak.'

Kate chewed her bottom lip.

'Hmm, that face suggests either you don't agree with my hypothesis, or you are merely baffled as to why a genius such as myself would be interested in what some may consider a dull hobby,' said Ervin.

'Dull? No. I get the whole plane-spotter thing. I'm also leaning towards your theory, but if we uncover his body—'

Ervin shook his head. 'I think we both know that's unlikely. We'd have found him by now. He wouldn't be too far from his vehicle. If he'd truly intended ending his life here, he'd have used the gun we found. It looks to me as if Superintendent Dickson wanted to vanish and, as far as I can tell, he's succeeded.'

'It's a sound theory.'

He took a small bow, then said, 'Heads up! Emma is coming!' He flashed Emma a wide smile as she came closer. 'Hello, Emma, dear. I must say you're looking rather radiant. The fresh air has put colour into your cheeks, or might that be working in such close proximity to the rather gorgeous DS Meredith?'

Emma punched Ervin lightly on his upper arm. 'Don't tease me or I might have to put you in a headlock.'

Ervin's eyebrows raised in unison. 'If that's going to be the outcome of my ribbing, I'm tempted to torment you further. However, duty calls, and I must rally my troops. I'll speak to you later, Kate.'

'He's far too cheerful for this time of the day,' said Emma, shaking her head. 'I don't know how he manages to be so energetic.

Kate, I'm going to hit the other pubs in Abbots Bromley before they close.'

'Okay. It's not looking promising here. We passed another pub on the way, in Newborough.'

'Oh, I saw it too. I made a mental note to call in there when I headed back.'

Kate hadn't intended directing Emma towards the pub, but since speaking to Ervin, she felt a need to push things along, encourage the idea that Dickson was alive and in hiding into everyone's heads. With luck, Emma might come across the same people who had seen Dickson's car speeding through the village, which would add fuel to that speculation. She heard rather than saw Emma's car drive away, her attention drawn to another vehicle that came to a halt in the space Emma had just vacated. William Chase emerged, his face grim. She made a beeline towards him.

'No sign of him, William. We've been searching for an hour.'

William pushed his hands deep into the pockets of a well-worn overcoat. 'I've been doing some digging of my own. After you rang to say you'd found his car, I asked about. It appears John Dickson held a private pilot's licence for ten years before it lapsed in 2018. By the way, I'm not suggesting anything, merely providing details I think you should know.'

'Then the super might have known or still know fellow pilots.'

William nodded. Kate wanted to punch the air. Dickson was making this easy for her. Speculation would soon be rife.

'No matter how good the pilot, landing an aircraft in pitch darkness on an unlit runway would be crazy and dangerous,' she said.

'I agree. However, taking off might be possible.'

'I'll check the details of everyone who flies out of Tatenhill, and those who own aircraft here,' she replied.

The torch beams continued to bounce their light show against the night sky. William watched the flickering for a while before speaking again. 'What do you think has happened to him, Kate?'

She surreptitiously wiped more sweat from her palms, grateful that William couldn't see her face clearly. The lying wasn't getting easier, especially when she was speaking to someone she cared for deeply. William was more than her boss and friend. In some ways, he'd replaced her father, which meant that lying to him caused physical pain: a tightness in her chest. 'I can't call it yet. We need to examine the facts, let the tech team establish that the phone is his, then wait for them and Forensics to carry out their checks. Meanwhile, we should keep asking questions. It's too easy to jump to conclusions.' As she spoke, she had a lightbulb moment.

Although she hadn't spent a great deal of time looking through it, there'd been nothing on Dickson's phone that raised red flags regarding his extra-curricular activities. He was far too clever to use his work phone for such matters. But that suggested he might have used a burner for those. There hadn't been a second phone either on his person or in his car, yet there had to be one. She mentally kicked herself for not thinking of it sooner.

Her mind raced back to her earlier conversation with Harriet. Dickson had curtailed their meeting, yet hadn't left the station to meet with Kate for a further half an hour. What had he been doing during that time? He certainly hadn't rung anyone from the phone they found. Kate had checked the call log, revealing her call from Chris's phone to have been the last received and the call to Bradley the last made. Could Dickson have left a burner somewhere at work?

Dickson's voice started up. *'I might have owned a burner. I might have got rid of it. Did I? Didn't I? This is going to have you spinning like a top. See, you have no idea what you are up against. Maybe somebody else in the syndicate already has it. For safe keeping. Maybe they have dumped it. We could be one step ahead again, eh, Kate?'*

She suppressed a groan, choosing instead to ask William, 'Can I have permission to search the superintendent's office?'

He replied with a subdued, 'Yes. Go ahead. I want a word with Ervin, so would you excuse me? I'll catch up with you later.'

Kate spotted Morgan heading her way and called him over so she could recount what William had told her. 'There are a couple of houses close by. I'd like to establish if the occupants heard any aircraft noise last night,' she said. It was another time-wasting exercise that had to be carried out. Any deviation from standard procedure would only invite suspicion, especially from the Dickson supporters.

She climbed into the Jeep. In the distance, the searchers kept up their steady hunt. All this manpower being wasted on a man who couldn't be found was down to her. Another criminal act that would have her banged up if it ever came to light. She was getting deeper and deeper into the mire. She buckled up and turned her mind to Dickson's burner phone. Although only a hunch with little evidence to support it, she was sure it existed. If so, she had to be the person to find it. It might allow her to track down his contacts, allies or other officers who were corrupt.

'Good luck with that,' whispered Dickson. *'Don't you think they'll also be looking for it?'*

CHAPTER SEVEN

DAY ONE – NIGHT

Kate stood to one side, allowing Morgan to converse with the man at the front door who was now engaged in a full rant about the noise from the airfield, caused by low-flying aircraft that flew over his property.

'I'm afraid I'm unable to do anything about the noise pollution; however, if you continue to write to your local counsellor, that is probably the best way of handling the situation,' said Morgan, interrupting the tirade. 'I'm here to ask if you heard any aircraft last night, after hours.'

The man shook his head. 'I was watching television. I didn't hear anything.'

'But if there'd been a flight, you'd have probably heard it?' Morgan continued.

'Only if they'd flown overhead. It depends which direction they take off and land. There are two strips, see? It also depends on wind direction.'

'Then you heard nothing after the airfield shut for the night?'

The man shook his head. 'Can't you take down my complaint while you're here?'

'I'm afraid it's a district council matter, not one for the police. Thank you for your time.' Morgan stepped away, Kate by his side.

The man slammed the door shut after them.

'You wonder why he moved to a house near an airfield if he hates airplanes,' muttered Morgan.

'He probably just enjoys complaining. Nobody else around here seems to mind,' Kate replied. 'Still, we've established that an aircraft could take off or land without any of the nearby residents hearing it. Now we need to find out who owns a plane and if anyone moved or flew one yesterday evening . . . all of which will have to wait until the morning. After you drop me off back at the station, you can head home.'

Morgan leapt into the driver's seat with a grin. 'I was hoping you'd say that.'

The comms unit burst into life before they'd gone too far. Emma had struck out in Newborough and Abbots Bromley. Kate wasn't too disappointed. There was still time to track down the people who'd been outside the pub in Newborough when she had raced by in Dickson's car.

However, her thoughts were now on the burner phone. She chose not to share her suspicions with Morgan, who might either poo-poo them or volunteer to help her search Dickson's office. This was an avenue she wished to explore alone.

'Why?' murmured Dickson. *'In order to single-handedly hunt down everyone in my contact list? Or to prove beyond any doubt that I was as corrupt as you believe? You're obsessed. You've tipped past the point of reason.'*

She shut out the whispering monologue.

Morgan had been doing some musing of his own.

'You were right. If the super had intended taking his own life, he could have stayed at home or gone somewhere remote. Maybe somewhere that held a special meaning for him. On reflection, I don't think that was why he went to Tatenhill.'

'Neither do I. Since we recovered the handgun, I toyed with the idea he was forced to come here, then . . . I don't know what. As for heading elsewhere by plane . . . Well, I still have my reservations.'

'It's the most viable theory we have.'

She gave a non-committal grunt.

'Unless all of this has been staged,' said Morgan.

Kate's heart stopped for a moment. Morgan was too close to the truth for comfort.

'By whom?'

'The superintendent,' said Morgan, restarting Kate's heart. 'It's part of his plan to drop off the radar until he can explain himself or launch an attack on the journo who wrote that piece. Or both.'

'Yes, I could see that being the case. We'll discuss it further at the briefing tomorrow.'

'Yeah. I can understand he'd want to throw the media off the scent. What better way than to set up a trail that suggests he has left the area or country? Like a wily fox being hunted by hounds.'

Kate nodded, unable to continue the conversation. Duping Emma and Morgan was horrendous. It would have been far less complicated and easier on her nerves if her team hadn't been assigned this investigation. As it was, she was walking on eggshells, keeping truths from those she cared about, people who were her family. Both were brilliant officers, neither of them to be underestimated. They were capable of uncovering what really happened and if she didn't stay fully alert, this situation could get stickier at any moment. She was relieved when her phone rang, stopping further conjecture on Morgan's part. She was less pleased when she learned who was calling and why.

DC Jamie Webster's voice was concern personified. 'I heard our team is looking into the superintendent's disappearance,' he said. 'I'm coming off sick leave. I don't have any major injuries, just a load of bruising and a couple of broken ribs.'

'Shouldn't you wait another few days—'

'Nah. The doctors have prescribed pain relief and say I'm fine for light duties. I really want to be involved. I don't want to sit about here feeling sorry for myself when you've got something this big going on. I'm okay. The painkillers are doing their job. Really.'

'Well . . . only if you're up to it. We could certainly do with your help. I'll bring you up to speed at the briefing. See you at eight o'clock.' The words didn't sound forced even though they stuck in her gullet. The last thing she wanted was one of Dickson's followers involved in the search for him.

'I'll be there, guv.'

'Mr Duracell is coming back to us, then?' said Morgan, after she dropped the phone back in her lap. 'You have to admire him. Gets the stuffing knocked out of him, is patched up in hospital and two days later comes back for more punishment.'

'He was insistent. I've no idea how much pain he really is in but we'll make sure he doesn't overdo it.'

'I've never met anyone as enthusiastic as him: first into the office every day, first to volunteer, and he bounces about tirelessly. I can hardly keep pace with him some days. Still, he's okay, I suppose. Just a little over-effusive. Maybe being kicked half to death will have calmed him down a little.'

Kate noted the respectful tone in his voice. It had taken Morgan time to warm to Jamie, but Jamie's bringing down the bolt gun killer had earned him a great deal of kudos from his fellow officers. It had even helped change Kate's attitude towards him – slightly. While she couldn't deny he had been a team player during the investigation into the bolt gun murders, a question mark remained over him.

Kate had been convinced from the start that Jamie was a mole planted by Dickson, a theory that grew legs when she discovered Jamie had worked undercover for the superintendent on an investigation into underage prostitutes, one of whom Dickson had slept with.

Kate was still unsure whether Jamie had known exactly who he'd been searching for at the time, or whether he, like Heather Gault, had been duped into believing Operation Agouti was a legitimate investigation.

She did, however, know for certain Jamie had lied about his whereabouts the day he had followed Heather and the young sex-worker, Rosa, to Stoke-on-Trent railway station. Moreover, he'd never confessed to Kate about being there. Consequently, to her way of thinking, he was untrustworthy. Then, when teamed together on a lookout for the bolt gun killer, he had divulged information not only suggesting he was disillusioned with Dickson but that his loyalty lay firmly with Kate.

Now, though, she found herself once again doubting Jamie's sincerity, and questioning the reason for his return. Maybe he really had become a team player or maybe he'd been instructed by Dickson's cohorts to keep an eye on Kate and ensure she was following up on everything as she should.

'Or he's coming back because somebody on my side suspects you,' hissed Dickson. 'You forgot to ask him one pertinent question – who informed him that you were in charge of hunting for me?'

'Everything okay?' asked Morgan.

'Fine. I was thinking I wish we had more evidence to go on.'

'We'll get it.'

She fell silent again, wondering who'd spoken to Jamie. Dickson had warned her there were other dishonest officers like him. One of them could be controlling her DC's movements. Or maybe Jamie knew more than he was letting on.

It was almost ten o'clock by the time Morgan dropped Kate back at the station. She took the stairs two at a time, slowing only when she reached Dickson's floor. She didn't want to run into anyone, and listened carefully for sounds that would alert her to the presence of other officers on the floor. At this late hour it was unlikely there'd be many people still working. The corridor was brightly lit, and from the office next to Dickson's there came the white noise of a vacuum cleaner. Kate hesitated for a second, eyes drawn to the brass nameplate bearing Dickson's name, before slipping through the door and switching on the light.

Dickson's office was contemporary in design. He'd opted for a black, ergonomic chair placed behind a huge walnut desk balanced on a black metal arc, slap bang in the middle of the office. Black shelving stood out against the cream walls, each section artistically filled with books and box files arranged in various positions to create a more pleasing look, alongside artificial succulents in grey holders. From his seat, he looked at a large whiteboard filled with information about ongoing operations written in small, neat writing, nothing like Kate's lopsided scrawl. She felt the layout and choice of furnishings were more suited to modern business premises rather than the old station, stealing from the building its soul and identity. The historic charm she associated with it had been blatantly ignored in the redecoration of this room.

Aside from the bookshelves, there was nothing in the office other than a password-protected computer, which she ignored, and a metal filing tray containing documents that awaited signatures on top of the drawerless desk. She began searching the shelves, lifting books, mostly military history, one by one, and flicking through them to ensure they contained no secret compartments, at the same time acknowledging it was a cliché to hide anything in such an obvious place.

'You're wasting your time, Kate. There's nothing here.'

'Here's as good a place as any. You'd need to keep it somewhere accessible. If it's not in this office, it must be nearby.'

Her retort silenced Dickson's voice, leaving her to hunt in peace.

The books were in good condition, with little to no sign of use. Kate wondered if he'd ever read any of them or if they were there for show. She returned Stephen E Ambrose's *Band of Brothers* to its position, next to a photograph of Dickson with his friends on a skiing trip. It had been this photograph that had provided a clue into the torture and death of Alex Corby and others in the picture. She was surprised to see Dickson had kept it, especially as he had been party to events that had resulted in those murders. She lifted it from the shelf, studied the men, thirty years younger, smiles on their faces. It was then it struck her the picture didn't quite fit into its frame. She turned it over, unclipped the back and blinked. A small, flat key was taped between the back of the photo and the cardboard holding it in position.

'Gotcha!'

She teased the object from the sticky tape, then repositioned the photo, placing the frame exactly where she'd found it. Turning it over in her palm, she wondered what sort of lock it would fit. It was too small for one of the locker keys at the station. She began looking in the drawers at the bottom of the shelving unit, hunting for a box small enough to take the key.

A rap on the door caused her to jump.

'Sir?'

It was Harriet Khatri. Kate scrambled to her feet, debating whether to remain silent and pretend nobody was in the office before deciding Harriet wasn't somebody who'd buy that. She slid the key into her pocket then opened the door. Harriet's face fell.

'Oh, I saw a light under the door and thought Superintendent Dickson had returned.'

'No, I'm afraid he hasn't. DCI Chase asked me to check the office in case he'd left any clues as to where he was headed.'

'I see.' Harriet's features reset into their usual, emotionless expression. She fiddled with her earlobe and the stud she wore there. 'Have you any idea yet what's happened?'

'We've got some theories we're working on.' Kate wasn't giving anything away to this ruthlessly ambitious officer. If there was any way she could replace Kate on this investigation, she'd try it. It was no secret she was hoping to make DCI. Kate was certain that Dickson would have warned her Kate was also up for the same promotion. Kate wasn't as competitive as Harriet; nevertheless, she wasn't going to allow the woman anywhere near this case. She'd already taken over Kate's old unit. She wasn't muscling in on any more of Kate's turf.

'I'd better leave you to it, then.' Her glacial eyes were trained on Kate's face.

It was late. Harriet's team hadn't been in their office earlier when she'd passed it. The suspicion that Harriet might have come searching for Dickson's phone ballooned. 'I couldn't find anything, so I guess I'm done here,' Kate replied. She caught sight of the cleaner leaving the room next door.

'You can come in here now,' she said to the man. Then, turning to Harriet, she pointed at the briefcase and asked, 'You on your way home?'

'Yes. I better get a move on. You?'

'Got to prepare some briefing notes for first thing before I leave.'

Kate accompanied Harriet down the corridor, peeling off into her own office, where she waited, door slightly ajar, for the sound of the heavy front door to slam shut. With no window to peer out of, she allowed two minutes to drift by before going back outside and checking the car park. Harriet's black Volvo had gone. Now she could puzzle over the key in peace.

She tried the men's changing room, where she examined the lockers. The key was far too small to open any of them, including Dickson's.

'Cold, Kate. You're stone cold. I guessed this would be the first place you'd look,' said Dickson. She could almost see him, arms folded, watching her as he leant against other lockers.

Dickson was devious. Where on earth would he hide a small box? Where would be the last place Kate would search? She ran through a list of possibilities. Dickson only had thirty minutes to hide whatever it was. It wasn't in his office. It wasn't in the changing rooms. She tried the toilet cubicles, lifting the lids on the cisterns.

'Freezing cold, Kate.' His laughter echoed in her head. She hated his tormenting voice that had usurped Chris's. At the same time, she understood why she was hearing him. It was guilt.

'More than guilt. You're losing your mind. Why? You've gone against everything you believed in. Look at you, Daddy's precious girl, who believed in justice and morality. You're a criminal, Kate. You're no better than me!'

'Don't you dare mention my father!' she shouted, then stopped, clamping a hand over her mouth. What if somebody were to hear her yelling? Crap! She was really losing it big time. This was Dickson's fault. All his damn fault. How dare he bring up her father, who he'd treated badly. He'd not been a good friend to either him or William. Her mind slowed. *William.* Why hadn't she thought of that sooner? The last place she would look would be William's office. If William had been out, Dickson could have sneaked in, hidden the box and then left for his rendezvous.

'You're getting warmer,' he called after her as she raced back upstairs.

94

William's office was as familiar and welcoming as home. She ran hands over his chair, feeling the worn leather against her fingertips. She couldn't imagine how her life might have turned out had it not been for him.

She didn't spend time looking at the various knickknacks and objects that were part of William's life here; she hunted immediately for places he wouldn't use on a regular basis, somewhere Dickson would have slipped a locked box. She tried desk drawers and cupboards, hunted behind books, all in vain. The floorboards creaked under patches of carpet as she trod carefully, hunting among box files and behind radiators.

'Cold, cold, cold,' said Dickson.

She was about to give up when she noticed a slight gap between the free-standing shelves and the wall. She knelt beside it, slid her fingers into the space and brushed against something. There was little room to work her fingers and it took some effort before she'd teased it out. She tugged gently, then squatted on her haunches, a slim black box in her hands.

'Not cold. Hot. Boiling hot,' she said as she waved the box above her head. She got to her feet, a sudden desire to escape the office and the station overcoming her. She would open it at home, before deciding what to do with its contents.

Her own phone vibrated in her pocket. She grabbed it. An unknown number flashed on the screen.

She held it to her ear and heard Bradley Chapman's voice.

'We have a new problem. The package has gone walkabout.'

'How?'

'Meet me. I'll explain.'

'Where?'

'Lay-by on Newton Hurst Lane.'

'Half an hour.'

The phone went dead. The package was the young sex-worker, Stanka, who'd been pivotal in exposing Dickson. It made no sense for her to leave so she must have been snatched. Who would have managed to pass Bradley's security and steal her away? Was it the damn vagrant Emma had rooted out at Bradley's daughter's house?

She stormed out of William's office. Anxiety knotted itself in the pit of her stomach. Things were beginning to unravel. Moreover, she was going to have to pass the exact place where Dickson had died, yet again. This wasn't how it should play out.

'I warned you there were others. You can't trust anyone, Kate. Don't be too sure I planted that phone either. I might have given it to William for safe keeping.'

She covered her ears to silence the voice, to no avail. Dickson continued to taunt her as she gathered her belongings. If she didn't get her shit together soon, she'd crack completely.

CHAPTER EIGHT

DAY ONE – LATE NIGHT

Kate's nerves were like firecrackers, fizzing and popping throughout her body as she descended once again towards the reservoir, where she caught sight of the solitary swan that lived there, asleep with its head under its wing.

She concentrated on the woods beyond the water, all the while willing herself not to stop and check the area where she and Dickson had struggled. If only she could be sure there was little evidence left of the fight, or that she hadn't left behind bicycle tracks or anything else that might give away her presence on that night.

She reminded herself there was no reason for anybody to suspect Dickson had died at this spot, repeating over and over, 'It's fine. Nobody knows.'

She turned at the junction and travelled the short distance to the next turning, where she found Bradley's Land Rover at the designated meeting spot. He hopped out of his car and made for hers, climbing into the passenger seat.

'She took off,' he said without preamble. 'At least, I assume that's what happened.'

'Go on.'

'She received a phone call about six o'clock, just as we were about to eat. She went into another room to talk but she was clearly agitated and raised her voice a couple of times. She wasn't speaking English. When she came back, she was subdued. I asked if everything was okay, to which she replied there was nothing I could help with. It was a family issue. We ate, although she only picked at her food, then she went upstairs. Said she had a headache and was going to lie down. Neither of us heard her leave. She took everything she brought with her and crept out.'

'What about the dogs?'

'They were inside at the time, being fed. She picked her moment to do a runner.'

'Whoever rang sent her scurrying.'

'Somebody who spoke Bulgarian. That's where she told me she's from – Bulgaria.'

'I don't know what to do about her. The investigation into Dickson's disappearance is . . . taking up all my mental energy.'

'The way I look at it is, no matter what's going on in her life, she's safe from Dickson, which was the reason you asked me to protect her. I'd have liked to have told her that, but I could hardly tell her she had nothing to worry about because the big bad wolf was no more, could I?'

Kate shook her head. 'How did she seem before the call?'

'Quiet. Nervous. Understandable given the sort of life she's been leading up to now. One minute she's on the streets, running scared for her life; the next, squirrelled away in a farmhouse in the middle of nowhere. She's got your number. If she wants to ring you, she will.'

'I guess so. I wish I knew what spooked her, though. And I'm uncomfortable about her taking off like that without a word. Plus, she knows about us. Dickson had officers searching for Rosa and Stanka. If one of them finds her—'

'Kate, one thing I've learned in life is how to hold my nerve. Don't worry about situations until they become real. Then deal with them. Dickson has gone. *Corpus delicti.* There is no body. There is no evidence to suggest he is dead. Remember that and all will be fine and dandy.'

'There was blood left behind at the reservoir . . .' she began.

'I've dealt with it.'

'It should be cleaned up by professionals. There could be biohazards, blood-borne pathogens. They're a danger to people who use that route. I didn't think it through properly last night.' Unable to control it, she heard the mounting panic in her voice. Bradley grabbed her upper arm, squeezed gently.

'Kate, calm down. It's fine. I returned after my visit to the pig farm. There wasn't as much blood as you imagined. I threw disinfectant over it and then covered the area up with a couple of large buckets of earth. It's blended in with the gravel and earth already there. I've checked. There's nothing to see.' He released her.

She drew a deep breath. 'I'm sorry. I'm allowing my imagination to run riot. Thank you for having my back.'

'I told you I would.'

'Nobody is that loyal,' whispered Dickson. *'Can you truly trust him?'*

She gave a tired smile.

'Rest up. Don't fret over Stanka. She's capable and extremely distrustful of the police. I doubt she'll say a word to anyone. Unless she reappears or something crops up, I shan't contact you again.' He rested his hand on her car door handle. 'Look after yourself, Kate. You've got this.'

She watched the Land Rover's taillights fade into the distance. Bradley's reassurance was insufficient to quiet her concerns.

Unable to summon Chris's voice, there was only one other person she could trust enough to turn to: her sister, Tilly. Galvanized by the thought of talking to someone who might at least be able to understand, she started up the engine to make the journey home.

As she drove, she wondered how best to break the news to her stepsister that she had committed a crime. Had, in fact, committed several.

◆ ◆ ◆

Kate tossed her bag on to the floor by the staircase, then marched straight into the room that had been Chris's office. More recently, it had become the room she used for her personal investigation into Dickson.

She threw herself into Chris's chair, mentally calculating it would be coming up to eleven o'clock in the morning in Sydney. Tilly would be at work at the woman's refuge. The urge to talk to her sister was strong, and she didn't know how much longer she could wait without changing her mind.

All the way home, she'd thought of how best to broach the subject, deciding in the end to be brutally honest. It wasn't so much that she wanted Tilly's advice, more her understanding, compassion and comfort. Tilly would comprehend the predicament she was in.

She lifted her phone, fingers hovering over the FaceTime icon before putting it back down. She couldn't do it. To confess, even to Tilly, would be crazy. Only Bradley knew what had transpired. Given he was seriously implicated in covering up the death, he would never spill the beans. Even if Tilly understood and vowed to keep it hush-hush, she might repeat the conversation to her husband, Jordan, who in turn could blurt it to a good friend and so on until, suddenly, Kate found herself in the deepest possible shit.

She balled her fist and thumped the desk so hard that pain shot up her forearm. There was nobody she could talk to. No one she could completely trust with such a dreadful secret.

'Chris,' she said, knowing full well he would not reply. The silence was heartbreaking. It almost made her wish Dickson's voice would jump in, just so she'd have somebody to talk to. 'I'm lost. Completely lost.'

Her ringtone sounded loudly, making her jump. The FaceTime icon lit up with a photograph of Tilly. Surprised at such an odd coincidence, Kate accepted the call and soon Tilly's actual face was beaming at her.

'Hi,' said Kate.

'Hi, yourself. I have a lull at work . . . and thought I'd check in to see how you were. I had one of those weird feelings that something was wrong.'

'I'm . . . fine.'

Tilly peered closer at the screen and pulled a face, accompanying it with a mock, 'Eww! You look like shit, sis. You been on the razz?'

Kate half-laughed. 'Drinking alcohol alone? Not me.'

'I expected you to be celebrating after catching that crazed killer.'

'The euphoria was short-lived. I've since been tasked with hunting for our superintendent, who has disappeared. I've only just got home.'

'Cripes! It's all go in sleepy Staffordshire, isn't it? Has he been kidnapped?'

Kate realised that here was her opportunity to unburden herself. She could also ask her stepsister what to do about the box she'd found and still had to unlock.

The fact Tilly had rung at that very moment, when Kate was at such a low point, was spooky, proving there was a connection between them – a sisterly intuition. 'It's . . . complicated. A damning article about him appeared in the newspaper this morning.'

Tilly leant in closer to the screen, her grey eyes shining. She lowered her voice. 'Shit! Is this the same guy you spoke to me about the other day?'

Kate hadn't forgotten the conversation she'd recently had with her stepsister about an officer she suspected of corruption. No names had been mentioned at the time, but Tilly's mind was razor-sharp. She nodded.

'The one who you think was involved in Chris's murder?'

'Yes.'

'Who you think killed a female officer?'

'Yes.'

'Then it's a bloody good thing I warned you to back off from him. Especially as some journalist was on his tail. He must have been on to him too. Did they mention either of those things in the article?'

'No, it was about him sleeping with an underage sex-worker.'

'The one you were looking for! How did this journo get on to that?'

Kate struggled to reply. If she confessed that she'd given Dan the ammunition for the article, then Tilly would know Kate hadn't heeded her advice. Luckily, Tilly wasn't waiting for an answer and continued, eyes sparkling, as she conjured up a picture of how she imagined the scenario to have played out.

'I bet your crooked guy's done a runner. If he's up to his neck in crap, he has no other option.' She revealed perfectly white teeth. 'You're hunting him down, then? Bit like you were before, only officially this time. My sister, the ace detective.'

'We're not sure at this stage what's happened,' said Kate. 'We're following several lines of inquiries.'

'Pfft! You sound like some police automaton when you say stuff like *several lines of inquiries*. It's police rhetoric, isn't it? Or bullshit. Are you stumped or have you found somebody willing to snitch on him? Come on, this is me. Dish the dirt. I won't tell anyone.'

'I can't discuss an ongoing investigation with you, Tilly.'

'Give over! You wanted to discuss stuff last time we chatted. As I recall, you ran a load of things past me and asked for my advice. Come on, I'm your sister.'

'Okay. It looks like he might have taken off in a plane from a small airfield. He left behind his mobile and wedding ring in his car, which was unlocked and parked by an airfield.' Kate stuck to the facts. She simply couldn't bring herself to tell Tilly, yet something in her manner must have given her away. Tilly's eyelids narrowed, reminding Kate of a cat weighing up its prey before pouncing.

'You did give up investigating this corrupt officer, didn't you? You didn't, by any chance, decide to carry on, and then leak information yourself? After all, Chris was a journalist. I'm sure you know some of his colleagues at the *Gazette*. If you wanted to expose someone . . .'

Caught out, Kate was too slow to deny that Tilly was on to something. Her sister barked, 'Ha! I can tell when you're not being completely honest with me. You carried on regardless! You and your ex-SAS chums found the pimp and sex-worker you were hunting for, and then you handed the story to the journalist.'

Kate gave a half-hearted shrug. There was no way she could deny it, not with Tilly able to recall every detail of their recent conversation.

'I don't suppose you expected the so-and-so to scarper, though. You were no doubt hoping he'd be investigated and face up to allegations in court.'

'That's a lot of assumptions,' said Kate testily.

Tilly raised an eyebrow. 'And your reaction confirms I'm right. I can read you, Kate. Much like you can read me. See, I should have joined the force alongside you. I have good instincts. We'd have made a formidable team, eh?'

'We probably would,' Kate replied, still debating whether she wanted to be dragged into a deeper conversation, one in which she confessed everything. Tilly, on the other hand, was now intrigued and putting forward more theories.

'I imagine he read the story in the newspaper, realised he was in over his head, then upped and left. Or . . . maybe somebody gave him a heads-up about the article beforehand, which gave him time to plan an escape. He'd have needed time to arrange a flight from an airfield. *Or* maybe it's a set-up to throw you off the scent.'

As Tilly scrabbled closer to the truth, the urge to divulge everything grew stronger, threatening to burst from Kate's lips.

'Did you tell him about the article, Kate?'

'Why would I do that?'

'To make him squirm. To make him realise you were on to him.'

'Telling him would give him the advantage, time to prepare a response or go into hiding, wouldn't it?'

'Hmm. I suppose so.' Tilly pressed her thumb against her lower lip, squashing it flat.

Kate hadn't denied it, merely responded with a question, a technique often used in interviews by those who were guilty. Tilly was in full sleuth mode now, her face contorting as she puzzled over what might have occurred.

'What if . . .' she said. 'What if somebody he worked with has silenced him?'

Tilly was too close for comfort. This was the pivotal moment during which Kate could tell her all. 'Tilly . . .'

'Yes?'

'I . . . I . . .' It was no good. Kate couldn't burden her sister with this. 'I think you're a wonderful sister. All the same, you should leave the detective work to us.'

'Hey, hang on a sec. It is possible, isn't it? If he was mixed up with bad sorts, somebody might have wanted to make sure he kept his mouth shut for good. After all, if he started talking, he could help you put away a lot of other crooks or other police officers who were involved in his dealings.'

'I'll give you that. Yes. It's possible. However, we're not really investigating what he got up to, more where he might be.' Kate clenched her fists. After all of this, she'd bottled it. Stupid! She'd had the chance and now . . .

'Surely the two are connected?' said Tilly.

'Like I said, it's complicated. I've no doubt it will all get sorted in due course. In the meantime, we have to track him down and let the bigwigs deal with him.'

Tilly straightened up. 'Yes, sure. I admit I can get a little carried away. Your life is way more colourful than mine, plus you did ask for my advice before.'

'And I took it. I backed off.'

Tilly laughed. 'Yeah, right. You might not be looking into his dealings any more, but you've successfully brought them to the attention of people who can. Still, I'm happy. At least you're no longer in danger. I was worried he'd come after you if he found out what you were up to. When you find him, do you think he'll ever admit to killing that officer or having something to do with Chris's death?'

'I really can't say.'

'You understand you might never find out, don't you?'

Such was the look of compassion on Tilly's face, Kate longed to hug her, then tell her she knew the truth, that Dickson had confessed before he'd died. If only the recording hadn't been destroyed.

There was the sound of somebody calling Tilly's name in the background. She turned away briefly, allowing Kate to glimpse a poster, advertising a self-help group for women on the wall behind her. When Tilly looked back, her face had lost some of its brightness. 'Sorry, Kate. I'm needed. Talk again soon. Ring me whenever, won't you?'

'I will.'

'Love you!'

'Love you too.'

The screen went blank. Kate curled her hand around the phone as if some residue of Tilly's confidence and belief in her could be transmitted through the plastic. She'd blown her opportunity to come clean. She was truly on her own.

CHAPTER NINE

DAY TWO – WEDNESDAY MORNING

Emma left Morgan's place early to give herself time to have a shower and change for work. She didn't want everyone to know just yet that they'd become an item. She'd almost told Ervin when they were at the airfield, after he'd commented on her happy disposition, saying it was down to Morgan's presence. The fact was it had been. She didn't think Kate suspected anything, but they shouldn't hide it from her. However, it was very early days, and Emma didn't want to jinx it.

A few days ago, she and Morgan had been best buddies. Then, on Sunday, the tenth anniversary of her mother's death, she'd finally accepted he meant a whole lot more to her. They'd been in the friend zone for so long she'd been blinkered to the deeper feelings she had for him.

It had been Morgan who'd been the first to break cover, show he really cared about her on more than one level and, without warning, she'd fallen for him. The expression 'head over heels' applied to her. It was, however, a complication she could do without.

She wasn't the sort to settle down, have a family. She shuddered at the thought. Her own family was a right mess. Her father had died when she was a kid, her mother had gone to pieces and the children, all six boys and Emma, had fended for themselves as they groped their way to adulthood.

The arrival of a new man in the house – her stepfather – had complicated matters further. Emma had packed her bags and left to stay with her grandmother. It had taken a long time before she'd returned home, and only then for visits. The last one, she'd walked into the worst scene possible.

◆ ◆ ◆

'Mum?' Emma's key sticks in the lock and she has to tug it out.

The house seems to hold its breath as she drops her bag on the hall carpet and heads for the living room. 'Todd? Bayley?'

Neither of her brothers reply. She'd expected them to be sat in front of the television, gaming controllers in their hands, gunfire rat-a-tatting as they shot zombies and high-fived each other when heads exploded on the screen.

It's been six weeks since she last visited and stormed off again after another blazing row with her mother. Her nan has managed to drum into her that Emma only has one mother, and they need to make amends. It's down to Emma to take the first step. Emma places the bunch of white roses on the kitchen table. She was told they were the right flower to buy to say sorry, although she doesn't want to apologise, just smooth things over. She misses her mother.

A thump coming from the bedroom above her makes her jump. She makes for the stairs, leans on the banister and calls again.

'Mum, it's me!'

There's no reply. She strains her ears and picks up the sound of sobs. Slowly, with heart thudding, she treads the stairs, one at a time, holding on to the banister.

'Mum?' This time she is wary. Something is wrong. Muffled sobs reach her ears and without hesitation she lurches for the door handle.

She can't process the scene: the naked figure on his knees, head lowered, rocking as he whimpers; another naked body lying on the bed, a plastic bag over her head, but she recognises her mother's bracelet, a gift from all her children for her last birthday.

Her stepfather lifts his crumpled face. Snot leaks from his nostrils, over his lips. 'It was an accident.'

Emma can't speak for the rock in her throat. It is too late to make amends.

That day had messed with Emma's head for a long time. She'd been dreading the anniversary and yet it passed better than she expected because Morgan had checked in with her, made sure she was okay, and when she'd visited her mother's grave, he accompanied her and waited while she'd laid white roses on it.

As she fumbled for the key to her flat, hoping the elderly neighbour didn't spot her and start asking questions, a text came through.

Had a great time last night.

Hope I haven't made you late for work!

XX

She smiled to herself. She and Morgan should have hooked up sooner. Much sooner.

The black box Kate had found in William's office lay on the kitchen table. The size of a watch box, she was certain it didn't contain a timepiece. She'd put off opening it because once she did, she would have another decision to make – to hand it over or investigate the contents herself.

The key she assumed fitted the box shone in the early morning sunlight that streamed through her east-facing window. She was deeply involved as it was. Hiding evidence was only one more thing to be added to the list of offences she had committed in the last forty-eight hours. Some police officer she was turning out to be.

She tipped the remains of lukewarm coffee down the sink before returning to the table, where she pulled on nitrile gloves. She eased the key into the slot and heard the quiet click as it unlocked. She wrestled the lid open and lifted out a small phone.

A Nokia 3310, just over eleven centimetres in length. She turned it on and cursed. It was password protected.

'Bastard!'

'What did you expect?' said Dickson. *'I'm not an idiot.'*

'What's the damn code?' she shouted.

'Like I'd tell you. You'll have to hand it over to a tech team and who's to say somebody won't wipe any incriminating information from it? I've a lot of friends, Kate. Far more than you.'

'Fuck. You!' she said, replacing the phone in the box. She slid it into her bag. There was no way she was giving up easily. The phone might contain details of other officers who were as dishonest as Dickson, and Kate wanted to know who they were.

Kate drew up outside the station to find journalists blocking the entrance. She didn't fancy running the gauntlet of noisy questions, therefore she was happy to see Morgan pull up beside her Audi.

'Even more fuckwits hanging about than yesterday,' he muttered. 'If any more turn up, we'll need a battering ram to get through. Here, I'll go first.'

Morgan marched determinedly towards the crowd, arm out in front of him to clear a path. 'No comment!' he yelled as he cut a swath, Kate close by his side.

'DI Young, have you heard from Superintendent Dickson?'

'Has he been in touch?'

'Is there any truth in today's article?'

She faltered for a moment. Regardless of her concerns, Tyler had gone ahead and printed another article.

'Who's the witness willing to testify against the superintendent?'

Dan had mentioned Stanka! Surely he wouldn't have mentioned her by name in the article. If he had, it would help explain why the girl had bolted. She ignored the barrage of questions. Morgan shoved the door hard, holding it open for her to dive through. She only relaxed once it had clattered shut behind them.

Morgan strode over to reception and leant on the counter to address the officer behind it. 'Get somebody to shift that bunch. They're making a bloody nuisance of themselves. DI Young would have been mobbed if I hadn't been there to help her through. They need moving on before anyone else turns up to work.'

'I'll sort it,' came the reply. Morgan thumped the desk with the flat of his hands by way of a thank you.

'Have you got a copy of today's *Gazette*?' Kate asked the officer.

'It's in the back office, ma'am. The super made front-page news again. I'll fetch it for you.'

'They need to stop releasing these articles. We can't be expected to do our job if we're going to be pursued by the media wherever we go,' grumbled Morgan.

'I'll talk to DCI Chase,' said Kate. 'We ought to be able to get a blanket injunction or find some way of stopping them from printing daily.'

Emma burst through the door, a figure by her side.

'Bloody hell! Can't somebody move those fucking journalists? They nearly trampled us to death,' she said.

'It's being sorted, Sarge,' said the officer, making for a door behind the desk.

'Good thing too. So, look who I found outside,' said Emma.

Although Jamie sported a large vivid purple and blue bruise on his cheek and was pale faced, he seemed bright enough. He delivered a salute. 'Morning, guv. Morning, big guy!'

'Hey, mate. How are you?' asked Morgan.

'A few scrapes and bruises, the odd broken rib, nothing major. The doctors suspected I was concussed, then decided I'd always been this stupid.' He laughed, then stopped with a grimace.

Morgan patted him gently on the back. 'Good to see you.'

'Thanks for coming in, Jamie,' said Kate. 'Make sure you don't overdo it. Desk work only and go home the moment you're in too much discomfort.'

'As long as I don't have to chase after any gun-wielding criminals for a few days, I should be fine,' he replied.

The desk officer reappeared, a copy of the *Gazette* in his hands. 'Here you are, ma'am.'

'Thank you. I'll return it later.'

'No, don't bother, ma'am. We've read it.'

She took it from him, unable to gauge his true reaction to the story. By now, several officers would be beginning to question the validity of the articles. She followed the others upstairs.

While Morgan and Emma brought Jamie up to speed with the investigation, Kate scanned the article to see if Stanka had been named. However, Dan had been circumspect and only referred to her as 'a witness'. Once again, the article focussed on the events that had taken place in the Maddox Club and the Gold Service offered to members. Farai, who'd provided the club with the prostitutes for that particular service, wasn't named, merely referred to as Mr Y, who, in the wake of the boy's death, claimed he was ordered to no longer supply the club with sex-workers and was warned by Superintendent Dickson himself to keep silent about his dealings with the club. Next to photographs of the interior of the Maddox Club was a statement from the club owner, Raymond Maddox, denying all knowledge of any Gold Service. The article ended with promises that an incriminating video would follow shortly.

Folding the paper back up, she laid out the briefing notes on her desk. There wasn't a great deal to discuss. With no body or evidence that the superintendent had been involved in any altercation, they were only left with the possibility he had caught a plane from Tatenhill.

'Morgan . . . you came with up something interesting last night. Would you share your thoughts, please?' she said.

'Yeah, sure. It struck me this all seems a little . . . bizarre. I know we have to look into the possibility he took off from the airfield . . . But surely, if he really had flown out from there, wouldn't he have left his car somewhere less obvious, and certainly not left it unlocked like he did? It got me thinking. This seems a bit staged. Like somebody wants us to suspect he took off from Tatenhill and that person could be the superintendent himself.'

Emma, who was sitting on her desk with her ankles folded, shrugged. 'Why go to all that effort?'

'No, I get where the big man is coming from,' said Jamie. 'The super could be creating a bigger mystery – his disappearance – and using it as a smokescreen to detract from the other stories they keep printing. Which is genius, really, when you think about it.'

Morgan snorted. 'Sounds a bit James Bond to me.'

'No, it makes some sense,' Emma said. 'The big question then is . . . has he flown off into the sunset, or set it up to appear that way?'

'We still have to follow up on every lead we have,' said Kate, pleased that they were now all thinking along these lines. 'Let's crack on. I don't need to remind you that he's been missing for over thirty-six hours.'

The team set to work, leaving Kate to ponder the issue of the burner phone. Lost in thought, she didn't notice Jamie until he was by her side.

'This might seem a bit bonkers, guv, but somebody might have had it in for the super.'

His statement caught her off guard. Why had he jumped to this conclusion in such a short period? Had the thought been planted? She continued to play it cool, pretend she found no credibility in the newspaper article and was on her boss's side. 'The only people who seem to have it in for him are journalists, and judging by today's article, they're still trying to bring him down.'

'I was thinking more along the lines of criminals.'

'If that were the case, we'd all be in trouble. Every villain we arrested could be wanting revenge.'

'Not convicted criminals.' He dropped his voice. 'Can I have a word with you outside?'

'Sure.'

He followed her along the corridor to a vacant briefing room.

'Okay, what do you want to tell me?' she asked.

'It's a bit . . . awkward.'

'I'm listening.'

'Do you remember our discussion in the car the other night, about me working a covert operation with Heather Gault?'

'Of course I do.'

'I'm not sure how much I should mention, but given the superintendent appears to be in deep trouble, you ought to know what I know.'

'Go on.'

'I can't discuss the operation, but I can tell you someone working on it was not . . . a good cop. They were trouble. Heather found some evidence against this person and went to the superintendent about it. I didn't hear any more on the matter. I wonder if that officer might have had it in for Superintendent Dickson. Even want him out of the picture before he could expose them.'

This was a different version to the one Jamie had recounted on Sunday night, while high on pain meds in the back of the ambulance. Then, in his very relaxed state, he'd revealed Heather had thought the person *in charge of the investigation* was using it for their own purposes, as a front, to find one prostitute in particular – Rosa. Heather had challenged Dickson over it before being taken off Operation Agouti. Jamie clearly didn't recall telling Kate any of this. She pretended it hadn't happened.

'I'm taking what you're telling me seriously, but it's too speculative. Unless you give me actual names, I can't follow it up. Who else was on the operation with you?'

'That's the trouble, guv. The super didn't want us to know each other's identities.'

'Why not?'

'We were working undercover, talking to druggies, prostitutes, dealers and pimps. We couldn't have our covers blown. We were partnered up, though. I was paired with Heather. I haven't a clue who else was on that gig. The super only contacted us by phone. After Heather left, I worked alone for a while, then I got word the operation was being wound up.'

'Why? Was it successful?'

'I don't know. All I know is I did my bit. Like I said the other day, I'm merely a soldier. I do as I'm asked. Anyway, yesterday, before I rang you, I was thinking about the operation and the fact the super only communicated by phone. So I retrieved my phone records dating back to that time.'

The hairs on the back of Kate's neck began to rise.

'I went through all my calls to identify the ones the superintendent made to me. I asked Morgan about the superintendent's call log earlier and, before the briefing, I cross-referenced them with mine. The phone numbers don't match.'

'What do you mean?'

He lifted his hands in apology. 'The superintendent didn't ring me from his work mobile or a landline. The calls came from a different number altogether. Which got me thinking that he probably has a second phone, and if he's taken it with him, it might give us an idea as to his whereabouts.'

A buzzing like an angry bee started to sound in her ears. Jamie was either doing great detective work or had been primed about the phone and was trying to corner her. Either way, he knew there was a burner, which meant hanging on to it would be even riskier than she first thought. She forced a smile.

'Good work. Pass the number of that phone to the tech team. Let's see if they can locate it.'

'Erm, I wasn't sure if I should mention the operation in front of the others. I was instructed to keep quiet about it.'

'I understand. Just for the record, I prefer transparency. Thank you for telling me.'

He nodded earnestly. 'I'll pass the info over to the techies, then I'll tell Morgan and Emma. Well, I'll give them an abridged version.'

Kate gave another smile. 'Good.'

He made for the door and, hanging on to it, turned back to say, 'There's no I in team, is there? Although I'm not really into all that blue-sky-thinking bollocks.'

◆ ◆ ◆

Kate thrust her hand into her pocket and gripped Dickson's burner. She'd chosen to keep it on her person rather than leave it at home. In recent months her house had been broken into by someone she believed to have been searching for evidence linking Dickson to corruption.

That evidence had existed, secreted on USB sticks hidden in a bird feeder, and was at present in Dan Corrance's hands.

Damn Jamie! Now what was she going to do about this phone? She couldn't say she'd happened upon it or return it to its hiding place. The fact it was switched off might prevent the technical team from locating it, yet they might have other ways she knew nothing about of finding it and if she was caught with it . . . ! She had to act quickly. Without any further thought, she raced downstairs. She was going to have to put her trust in somebody. And that somebody was Felicity Jolly.

She walked into the lab, empty of technicians, the only sound an ominous whirring. She spotted Dickson's work phone, hooked up to a computer, then a muffled shout caused her to look up. Felicity was beckoning from behind her desk in the glass-fronted office.

'Hi. Sorry to disturb you again. Erm, are you alone?' asked Kate.

'Only for a short while. Rachid and Krishna are trying to recover data from a waterlogged iPad. And when I say waterlogged, I mean some buffoon tried to flush it down a toilet. A rather full toilet if you get my drift. Did you want them?'

'As it happens, I actually wanted to speak to you in private.'

'What about?'

'The superintendent.'

Felicity perched her glasses on top of her head. 'I'm all ears.'

'Then I'll get straight to the point.'

'That's the best way. I hate shilly-shallying.'

'You already know I had my doubts about him, especially after he asked you to delete information from Heather Gault's computer.'

Felicity nodded. 'I shared those doubts.'

'Following that, I did some digging, which only served to further my suspicions. I have reason to believe what the press is saying about him is true.'

'Okay. Where are you going with this?'

Kate pulled out the burner phone. 'I think this belongs to him. Nobody else knows I have it. I ought to declare it, allow it to pass through the correct channels to reach you, yet here's my problem: I suspect the superintendent involved other officers in some of his *dealings*. There are some people who still have his back who could be incriminated, thanks to this device. I can't take a chance it will be intercepted and information on it deleted before it comes to light. This is a big ask, but would you hack into it and relay the information directly to me?'

Felicity's expression didn't change. Kate said no more. She was asking a lot of the woman. Not only could this jeopardise her work position, but also her safety. Kate had no way of knowing how much support Dickson had or to what lengths his soldiers would go to protect him and themselves. Seconds that felt like minutes passed before Felicity cleared her throat.

'How do I know you're being truthful? That phone might hold information implicating you.'

Dickson, in her head, barked a laugh.

Kate felt her jaw slacken. Felicity was doubting her! She tapped the phone now on the desk. 'DC Jamie Webster knows of this phone's existence. It was used during Operation Agouti to contact team members. Heather had doubts about a member of that team, somebody who'd been tampering with evidence, yet the only person she knew to be on it, other than my officer, was the superintendent himself. When she confronted him, she was taken off the operation. That was the reason he asked you to delete all her computer files appertaining to Agouti. That might even have been the reason she was killed. The man convicted of her murder has always claimed she was alive when he last saw her. Now, I don't know how fanciful that sounds to you, but I believe it to be true. Since the Maddox Club death, I suspect the superintendent has been trying to cover his tracks. That's something he couldn't do alone. This phone could contain vital evidence to prove I'm right. If it does, it should be protected until it can be used in court.'

Kate took a breath. 'It's up to you, Felicity. If you refuse, then I'll hand this immediately to DCI Chase and let it make its way to you via the proper channels.'

There was another long pause, during which Felicity studied Kate before saying, 'Right answer. If you were willing to hand it over, then you couldn't be concerned about its contents.'

'You were testing me?'

'Uh-huh. I do that a lot. I like to make sure I know what is really going on in people's heads. For what it's worth, I didn't doubt you for one moment. I recall your reaction when we had all that kerfuffle over Heather's computer. You were outraged the superintendent had bypassed you and requested I dealt only with him. I admit, it sounded shady, even to me, a humble techie.' She reached for the phone. 'You sure it's his?'

'Yes.'

Felicity lowered her spectacles to examine the phone. 'An old Nokia. We still see a surprising number of these. Very popular among the criminal fraternity.'

'There's another problem. Jamie gave this phone's number to your team to trace.'

Felicity's eyebrows danced up and down. 'Ah, and if they do, they might find it here in my lab. That is slightly challenging. Still, forewarned is forearmed as they say, so if I ensure that request is passed to me, that ought to resolve it.'

'You could get into trouble should you be found out.'

'It's highly unlikely they'd pin anything on me.'

'You sure?'

'Positive.'

'Can you crack the password?'

'Do pandas eat bamboo?'

Kate gave a half-smile. 'That's a new one on me.'

'Bev's been doing the graphics on a children's video game. She had me testing it out with her last night until the wee hours. Panda gets superpowers whenever it finds bamboo sticks. The images are burned into my retinas so every time I shut my eyes, I see that damn panda in a coral costume, swinging through trees.'

Kate couldn't imagine Felicity playing computer games with her partner, Bev. Ordinarily, everything tech-related went out of the window after she left work, allowing Felicity to relax with a book, music and, invariably, a large glass of wine.

'This shouldn't present any problems. I'll need to use the lab equipment, though, which means I'll have to work on it out of hours. Bev's at some meeting tonight, so I'll hang back and see what I can do.'

'Thank you.'

'Save your thanks. Let's wait to see what we find on it first. He might have wiped it clean.'

Kate thought she heard Dickson's quiet laugh.

'My door is always open for you, Kate. Now, bugger off before anyone appears and starts asking what I'm doing.'

Kate took her leave. It was only as she walked back towards the station entrance that she realised the journalists had been disbanded.

'Very clever, taking it to Felicity and getting her on board. You overlooked one thing, though,' said Dickson. *'There's nothing to prove the phone belongs to me. It could be William's.'*

'He wouldn't have hidden the key to the box in your office. And you forgot another thing,' she replied as she crossed the car park, wind tugging at her jacket. 'Jamie has a record of your phone number. The two will match up.'

Dickson's voice fell silent. She pushed open the heavy door to the station. The visit to Felicity had buoyed her. It was good to have somebody else on her side. She felt a lot less lonely.

CHAPTER TEN

DAY TWO – AFTERNOON

By lunchtime, they were no further forward. Kate was becoming tired of fronting an investigation that would never be solved. Moreover, she was weary with all the duplicity. She was only too pleased to leave her industrious officers to continue their fruitless task while she visited Ervin, who had rung her.

It was a short drive to the laboratory on the university campus, but long enough to give her some perspective. She was going to have to see this investigation through to the bitter end before she could look to rounding up Dickson's wretched cohorts. She would make sure Chris's efforts to expose the rot in the force hadn't been in vain. Maybe if she succeeded, Dickson would release him, and she'd hear her husband's voice again.

'What the fuck! You think I've somehow kidnapped your husband's voice? Overpowered it, maybe . . . but kidnapped? Ha! You are really losing your marbles. You can forget about hearing him again. You're not only going to be stuck on this case for months and months with me in your ear the whole time, but the lack of progress will scupper your chances of promotion. Harriet, meanwhile, will become DCI and you, DI Young, will be stuck in a rut for evermore.'

She hated hearing his sanctimonious tone, echoing her fears. For all that she knew, the voice was manifesting itself because of the enormous guilt she was feeling. Dickson was her conscience, there to remind her of her wrongdoings and constant failings. And . . . she was powerless to snuff it out. If anything, it had intensified over the last few hours.

She pressed her lips tightly together to stop herself answering back. This talking to herself, this mimicking of Dickson's voice, was crazy.

Speaking to Chris had seemed more logical and cathartic: a natural part of the healing process. She'd missed him so badly it had left a gaping wound in her heart. Now his voice was being suppressed by Dickson, she missed him more than ever. Yet, try as she might, she couldn't hear him. While Dickson remained the dominant voice in her head, Chris's voice was effectively imprisoned. She needed to work out how to reverse that.

She parked close to the windowless building and slammed her door shut, pretending Dickson was locked inside the car, then trotted up the steps to the forensic laboratory. The security guard greeted her, checking her ID before buzzing her into the restricted area. There was nobody in the corridor and her heels clattered along the polished floor until she reached the main door, where she pressed the intercom button to gain entry.

Ervin, wearing a white lab coat over what looked like a frilled dress shirt and kilt, answered the door, gesturing grandly as he spoke. 'Come in. Come in. Excuse the chaos. We're somewhat inundated with work at present.'

Kate glanced around the clinically clean lab, where two assistants were working through an enormous pile of soiled clothes. Another was using optical instruments, data flashing on a screen beside them. Two more stood behind a glass screen, heads lowered over an array of gadgets and displays.

'Let's go to my office,' said Ervin, leading the way. She followed, eyes drawn to the woollen green socks that reached his knees and the flash of red material below their patterned turnovers.

Ervin dropped lightly on to his chair. The lab coat opened further, exposing the frill of his white shirt that clung to his chest. The kilt was a green and red tartan, complete with a red sporran.

'Very smart,' she said, admiring the outfit. 'Did you make it?' Ervin was no stranger to a sewing machine and would often alter garments or create them from scratch depending on his mood. Clothes were his passion and Kate was sure, had he not become a forensic scientist, he could easily have been a designer.

'I upcycled it. I was aiming for James Bond's Highland dress in *On Her Majesty's Secret Service*. I'm still working on the jacket. It requires a few more buttons. Judging by your expression, you haven't seen the film.'

'Er, no.'

'You should watch it. George Lazenby plays Bond. Only the once, though. Sean Connery resumed his role as Bond afterwards. Anyway, that and obvious good dress sense aside, I wanted to see you in person rather than talk over the phone.'

'You said it was about the handgun we found in the superintendent's car.'

'Yes. What do you already know about it?' he asked.

'Erm, that it's a Baikal IZH-79, which is a commonly seized firearm, made in Russia, usually procured legally in Eastern Europe. The weapons enter the criminal market, get reactivated and transported to a transit hub, such as Holland, then smuggled into the UK, by private boats crossing the Channel, or concealed in vehicles coming through the ports, then get sold on, usually to gangs and drug dealers here.'

He tipped an imaginary hat, then said, 'What you might not know is that it's been converted from a blank-firing weapon into an active one.'

'It is active, then?'

'Not only active, but it has also been fired.'

'Can you be more specific?'

'Kate, we have worked faster than the speed of sound to gather as much information as possible for you regarding Superintendent Dickson's disappearance. Miracles take a little longer than a few hours. More to the point, as talented as I am, I am not a firearms or ballistics expert, nor does my laboratory have all the necessary goodies – by which I mean equipment – to examine the weapon in detail. This isn't the movies, where I can slide a pencil through the trigger guard, hold it to my nose and say, "Oh, yes, this has been recently fired." It could have been discharged yesterday, or years ago. We simply can't tell. Without a crime scene, gunpowder residue, bullet, cartridges or further evidence to link to this weapon, I can only tell you the firing pin has struck, which indicates the gun has been discharged at some point.

'I've sent it to the National Ballistics Intelligence Service, which manages databases for all recovered firearms. They'll be able to tell us if it has been used in any crime. Once we know that, we might be able to work out what it was doing in the superintendent's car. He could well have seized it, prior to his disappearance.'

'Then left it in an unlocked car?'

'Public safety was probably low on his agenda at the time. Who knows the workings of a highly stressed individual's mind? He might have forgotten it was there, or assumed you'd quickly track down his car and find it.' Ervin crossed his legs, the red material catching Kate's eye again.

'Ervin . . . what is that?' She pointed at the material, almost afraid to ask.

'A hose flash,' he replied, raising the sock cuff to expose the material attached to a piece of elastic. 'Dual purpose – looks good and keeps the socks in place.' He replaced the sock cuff once more. 'So . . . back to the gun. Whilst I can't tell you when it was fired, I can tell you the serial number has been filed off, it has undoubtedly come from Eastern Europe and . . . we found a fingerprint. Getting prints from a weapon is extremely difficult, which makes our discovery even more surprising. You'd think we could get them from the trigger, but that's not usually the case. If we find any at all, they're more likely to be from the gun magazine or unspent shell casing.

'Did you know, the chances of finding a latent print on a gun can be as low as five per cent? Usually because of their design with rough edges and ridges and so on. Most of the time, guns are wiped down after use, so we were fortunate to find one on, of all places, the trigger.'

Kate held her breath. When would he get to the point?

'We matched it to the superintendent's prints.'

'Are you suggesting he fired the gun?'

'No. The opposite, in fact. Firstly, he's a police superintendent, not a half-witted druggie. If he had used the weapon to kill or maim somebody, he surely would have wiped it clean and disposed of it. Secondly . . . a print on the trigger? Really! It's far more likely he was trying it out for size.'

'Ervin, what are you saying?'

'The gun is a red herring.'

'All of this to tell me the gun has no significance?'

'I thought the same until it struck me that it has been deliberately left behind.'

Kate braced herself. Shit! Ervin was on to her.

'If I'm right, the superintendent is trying to create some sort of smoke screen. To confuse those who are hunting for him. He's added a few confusing details into the mix to keep you running around, while giving himself ample time to make good his getaway.'

He leant across the table, his face suddenly serious. 'I think he's dicking us all about.'

Kate emulated his expression, even though inside she was rejoicing that Ervin had come up with this credible explanation, one she could share with William and the others.

'Do you mind if I pass this all on to DCI Chase?' she asked.

'Be my guest. Although maybe change the phrasing of that last sentence.'

'Thanks.'

'Don't be misled by my peevishness. If there's anything further you want me to investigate, then I shall. My irritation is directed at the man who is causing all this inconvenience. Some of us have investigations requiring our urgent attention and can ill afford to waste time.'

'I understand how you feel.'

'I'm sure you do. The sooner we put it to bed, the better. If I were you, I'd suggest it gets passed across to Missing Persons.'

'I do as I'm instructed, Ervin.'

'No, Kate. You're far too shrewd to simply obey orders. More to the point, you know who you're dealing with.'

With that, he stood up. 'If you don't mind, I'd better return to my fold and help assist. Keep me informed.'

'I shall. For the record, you look very dashing. George Lazenby, eat your heart out!'

◆ ◆ ◆

'This is becoming ridiculous,' she said, as soon as she'd sat down in William's office. 'Unsurprisingly, nobody at the airfield will admit to flying the superintendent or lending him an aircraft. The blood found in his car belongs to him, yet is such a small amount it's likely to have been produced by a minor injury, ruling out the possibility he was involved in an altercation and taken to Tatenhill against his will.

'There are no fingerprints other than his on the steering wheel, glove box or driver door handle. Other prints have yet to be identified. They could be anybody's – Elaine's, even yours if you hitched a ride with him. It's all bizarre and the strangest thing in all of this is the handgun we found in the wheel well. I've just got back from the lab.' She added a sigh for effect, then recounted what Ervin had told her.

William drew his thumb across his chin as he thought. 'You're suggesting Superintendent Dickson took possession of an illegal weapon, handled it, then deliberately left it behind to confound us.'

'Ervin says the gun hasn't necessarily been recently discharged. And unless NABIS tell us otherwise, we don't know if it has been used in any firearm incident. I have no idea why it was in Superintendent Dickson's possession, and fail to see what bearing it has on his disappearance, although it is suspicious that it was in his possession and begs the questions why he had it and what he intended doing with it.

'Gun aside, we've spent all day chasing up flying schools, pilots and owners of aircraft: all of which has got us nowhere, while Ervin has wasted time on this firearm. We're going around in circles. I'm wondering if there's really a chance the superintendent has staged this.'

William folded his hands and looked Kate in the eye. 'The chief constable has asked me to hold off my retirement until we resolve this. It's imperative we succeed in locating John Dickson. His disappearance is rapidly becoming an embarrassment for the force. No matter what you and I think, we must keep working the evidence until we track him down. If you're right, then I can't allow him to outwit us. I won't let that happen.'

'You know this would be best handled by Missing Persons,' she said.

'No. The chief constable has requested that for the time being we keep it in-house, purely because there is a chance John Dickson has gone into hiding. There's already a large enough spotlight being shone on him by the press, and it's felt this might be better managed by us rather than those who don't know him as well as we do. Until that decision is reversed, you'll remain on the case. You talked about dead ends but what about the phone call he made around the time of this supposed meeting? Have you traced it yet?'

She sighed. 'Only to a pay-as-you-go phone.'

'Kate, are you okay with this? I know it's a lot to handle and you do seem off your game—'

He can see right through your pretence,' said Dickson. *'He knows you rang Bradley from my phone.'*

She shook her head. 'I'm absolutely fine, William. It's just that it's difficult when you are being given the run-around, that's all. And this is the superintendent we're hunting for, not some stranger.'

'Are you certain you're up to continuing with this investigation?'

'Yes.'

'Then I'm sure there's a way to track the owner of that phone. You've managed it before.'

Dickson whispered, *'He's playing cat and mouse with you.'*

She fought to keep focus on William.

William continued, 'What about this second phone he supposedly had?'

She didn't falter. 'We've yet to find it.'

'I'll issue a warrant for you to search his house. We need to be seen to be actively hunting for clues as to his whereabouts. If there is another phone, it might be there. We can't throw in the towel.'

'What about gaining access to his house?'

'Elaine says one of the neighbours, Mrs Gillespie, has a spare set of keys. She's invariably at home. Try her first.'

'Have you spoken to the newspaper about these articles they keep publishing?'

'The chief constable is dealing with the matter. Our media office will be issuing a statement later. Kate, I understand this is frustrating for you. I feel the same way. We have to put our best foot forward.'

She nodded.

'Locate this second phone and find out who he rang that evening. Then report back to me. I'm not letting go of this. And neither are you.'

'Meow! Are you going to squeak, Kate?' said Dickson.

She curled her fists and wished she could pummel the voice into oblivion. She was being pushed into a corner and she didn't like it one little bit.

Back in her own office she was met with a similar sense of frustration. Morgan was reclining in his chair, staring at the ceiling.

'What's up?' she asked.

'Hit another brick wall,' he replied, without looking at her.

She sympathised. 'It is frustrating. Why don't you take a break? We could do with a coffee run. Try the café down the road. See if they have any of their demon doughnuts left. My shout.'

Morgan straightened up with a grimace. 'Sure. I need to stretch my legs.'

'I'll come with you,' said Emma, then added in a louder voice, 'Only to make sure he doesn't snaffle any before he gets back.' She leapt to her feet, leaving her computer switched on and connected to the police database.

It was unusual for Emma to firstly interrupt her work and secondly not turn off her computer when she left the room. Kate observed the pair, taking in the subtle wink Morgan gave Emma and then how she seemed to deliberately brush against his arm as he held the door open for her. Was their relationship blossoming into something else? There definitely seemed to be more than a friendship vibe between them. She hoped that was the case. She was ridiculously fond of them both.

As soon as they'd gone, Jamie spoke again. 'Guv, I've been thinking about the call made to the super that interrupted his meeting with DI Khatri.'

'The call you made,' said Dickson.

Kate had executed caution when ringing Dickson, replacing the existing prepaid SIM card in Chris's mobile with a different one, which she'd purchased online. Afterwards, she'd destroyed it.

'Because whoever rang him was probably the last person to see him. We really need info on that call.'

His persistence was exasperating. To ward him off before he got in too deep and made her feel very nervous, she said, 'I agree. Why don't you get on to the techies and see if you can push that along?'

Although she wanted to be one of those who searched Dickson's home, in case there were any clues as to the members of his inner circle, it would be wiser to delegate the task to Emma and Morgan, again deflecting attention from herself. She jotted down the neighbour's name and address. 'Jamie?'

'Guv.'

'Could you also get a phone number for this person? She's one of the superintendent's neighbours. DCI Chase wants us to search his house for that phone.'

'Sure, I'll do it as soon as I've spoken to Rachid again.' She dropped the details on his desk before meandering back to her own, wondering what she should do next. This pretence was becoming tedious. Her mobile vibrated soundlessly in her pocket.

When she thought no one was looking, she checked the message. It was from Stanka.

Need help

Victoria Park Stafford

Please come

Kate glanced at Jamie, who was on the phone with his back to her. He hadn't spotted her reading the text. She made for the door before he finished his call. Outside, she waited in her car until she caught sight of Morgan and Emma returning from the café. They were holding hands.

As they turned into the car park they let go and moved apart a couple of inches; now just two colleagues returning from a coffee run. Kate couldn't help but smile. They were like teenagers trying to hide a relationship from their parents.

Winding down the Audi's window, Kate called them over. 'DCI Chase is organising a warrant to search the superintendent's house. When you've had your coffee and doughnuts, would you head over there? Jamie should have details of a key holder.'

'What are we looking for?' asked Emma.

'A second phone, as well as anything to help us locate him. I'll join you later. I have something to check on.'

She left them to it. If she was quick enough, she'd be able to meet Stanka and then reach Dickson's place while Morgan and Emma were still there.

Victoria Park linked Stafford station to the town centre. A little under five acres, the Green Flag award-winning park stood on the banks of the River Sow. Kate followed the pathway past the cast iron Alderman Mottram shelter, built in the early 1900s, towards the white arched bridge that crossed the small river. She had no idea where Stanka might be waiting, although it seemed sensible to head towards the round structure that was Albert's Café.

She strolled on to the bridge, where she paused to scan the immediate area for the girl. When she couldn't spot Stanka, she continued on her way, intending to first try the coffee house before heading towards the thatched cottage shelter and aviaries. She'd only walked fifty metres when she spied the slight figure, sitting on a bench, reading a magazine. She drew level and sat down. Stanka continued reading, as if she didn't know Kate. Kate played along with the pretence, leaning back against the seat.

'Why did you run away from the safe house?' she asked quietly.

'A friend called to say my sister is in trouble.'

'Is that why you messaged me?'

The magazine pages fluttered and turned, revealing women in stylish outfits, strutting on catwalks. 'Yes. Maja was supposed to be coming to Stafford. I waited at the stop-off point to grab her, but she was not on the minibus. No girls were on it, only the men who bring . . . brought . . . them. They are the same men who bring me. I think she is a prisoner, like me.' The girl's dismay caused her to fumble for words, her accent thicker than Kate had heard before.

'Tell me what happened to you, Stanka.'

The girl had the look of somebody accustomed to being hunted. 'In my country, I had no job. One day, I was with my friend, Bisera. We meet . . . meeted . . . met men who tell us we are beautiful and can get a good job in UK where we will become models and send lots of money home to our families to help them. Bisera says we must do it and be famous together. The men say we must leave in one week, because they have friends driving to England who will take us. We must not tell parents or anyone, or they might stop us. The men will get us passports and we do not need to pay them for passports or travel. They say when we make money as models, then we will pay them. We wait for one week. I didn't tell anybody, only my little sister, Maja. She was so excited for me and wanted to come with me, but I tell her she is too young. I promise when I make money, I will pay for her to fly to England too.'

She pressed her lips together as she struggled to find the words she needed, then continued, stumbling through her story. 'We meet . . . met . . . the men who drive us in van to the border, then we catch a minibus. One man, his name is Ognian, said we must tell border officials he is our cousin. There is another girl on minibus – Rosa. We are all going to England to be models. We wear best clothes, make-up and are happy. But when we get here, Ognian take our passports from us. We cannot have them back until we pay money for travel. Then he takes us to a room in block of flats and locks us in.'

She laid the magazine down in her lap, her voice weakening as she spoke. 'We become scared. Ognian is not nice. He brings his friends. We are *given* to friends . . . for sex. If we do not do as he says, he beats us. Bisera . . . Bisera, she fights back. She spits . . . scratches. Ognian ties her up. He hits her. Burns her face with cigarettes and tells her she will never be a model now she is ugly. Rosa and me, we look after Bisera. She cries . . . cried . . . all the time, then Ognian gets really angry and takes her away. She does not come back, and I think she is dead.

'We stay in room. Never go out, only to other room for sex.' Her brow wrinkles at the memory. 'No money. Ognian keep passports. Tell us we cannot go home. We cannot escape. I speak only little English. Rosa, she speaks better and teaches me. Then Ognian, he says Rosa and me are leaving. Tall, skinny man comes to get us. He is called Farai. You know him, I think.'

'Yes, I know him.'

'He was nicer than Ognian, but he tells us we must work. We must have sex with men. Men who like young girls. He gives us a little money and food. We live in flat with other girls who he pays. No more bad men. No more Ognian. No job as model. Only prostitute.'

Bitterness coated Stanka's words. Kate's heart was heavy. The girl had been duped and brought here with the sole intention of turning her to prostitution. Naïve and young, she'd fallen prey to people traffickers who'd stolen her youth. She doubted Farai was a great deal kinder than the men who had brought Stanka, yet he had in latter months tried to protect her from Dickson, moving from town to town and giving her a phone and Kate's number. Maybe there was a heart hidden somewhere in his scrawny chest, after all.

'And Maja?'

'Maja is only thirteen. She is a child.' She shook her head, tears pooling in her eyes. In Kate's opinion, the girl didn't look much older than thirteen or fourteen herself.

'Stanka, who was this friend who rang you and told you this?'

'She also works for Farai. She saw him talking to Ognian. He told Farai my sister was on her way and he wanted Farai to buy her.'

Kate wondered why Stanka wouldn't divulge the name of her friend. The girl was incredibly guarded. She didn't press her on the matter. It was more important that Stanka felt she could open up to Kate.

'Was she sure it was your sister they were discussing?'

'Yes. Ognian said Farai must like me very much to keep me after the trouble at the Maddox Club and that Maja was like me, even prettier than me. Farai said no. That he doesn't want any more

135

girls at moment. Kate, my sister will be taken to a room. Men will rape her. Then she will be sold. I . . . I don't know what to do. Please help me.'

The right thing to do would be to hand this information over to William. He would pass it across to another team, maybe even Harriet's, who were already involved in a people-trafficking investigation.

The issue with that was twofold. First: Stanka was Kate's problem. She couldn't afford for anyone else to get involved and uncover details about Kate's involvement with the girl. Kate had broken many rules and regulations while hunting for Stanka, including involving a civilian to help bring the girl back from Blackpool and keep her hidden at his house. Discovering this information would certainly lead to Bradley, which was something she really couldn't afford to happen. Second: Stanka was probably still in danger from other corrupt officers wishing to protect themselves.

The only way to handle this would be to plead with William, explain that this was connected to the Maddox Club investigation and as such ought to be kept in-house, with her team.

'Risky,' hissed Dickson. 'You had opportunities to tell William about Stanka before now. William might wonder what else you've been keeping secret from him.'

Her stomach flipped at the words. She hadn't considered this before.

Shit!

William would forgive many mistakes and mess-ups but not being kept in the dark. Stanka's earnest look brought her back to her senses. She had to help this girl regardless of the consequences. 'I can't promise anything yet, but I'm going to talk to my boss.'

The girl's grip tightened on the magazine, her eyes widening. 'No, please, no boss. I cannot go to the police. The superintendent,

136

he was bad. There are others like him. They already have killed Rosa. Next, they will kill me.'

'My boss was my father's best friend. I trust him.'

'Your father's friend?'

'Yes. My father was a police officer too. He and my boss were very close.'

'He is still alive, your father?'

Kate shook her head.

'My father is also dead,' said Stanka.

'I'm sorry to hear that.'

Stanka nodded. 'Dead when I was five. It was hard for us.'

'I can imagine. My mother died when I was young.'

'Also hard.'

It had been difficult for Kate after her mother's death. However, her father had still loved and guided her. To that end, she'd fared much better than Stanka. And she knew that part of the reason she had to help Stanka was to somehow make up for the opportunities the girl never had. 'Trust me. I shall keep you safe. Let me take you back to Bradley.'

'No. I have very good hiding place in Stafford.'

'You would be safer with Bradley.'

'Better I hide here. It is too quiet at that house. I like towns, not country. I will run away if you make me go back.'

The set of her jaw and the fierce determination in Stanka's eyes swayed the argument. Kate couldn't risk her bolting again. At least she knew, if she acquiesced, Stanka would keep in touch. She wanted so much to reach out and hold the girl's hand, connect physically with her and let her know that she was fully on her side, yet she did not, for fear the girl might misconstrue the gesture.

'I'll ring you later to let you know what is going to happen,' she said.

'You will find Maja?'

'We will do our utmost,' she replied. 'Where are you staying?'

'Best I do not say where. Phone me when you have news. We meet again, yes?'

Kate nodded. 'Yes, I'll call you. Take care. It's important you stay safe. Maja will need you.'

'You must find her before these men . . . You know. Before they . . . hurt her.'

Kate swallowed bile that rose in her gullet. These men would treat the teenager as a plaything, ensuring her will was broken, and then sell her on. It was imperative that Maja was found before that happened. Kate knew she had to follow this through to the end.

Keeping her eyes fixed on the road ahead, heart thumping, she rang William on the hands-free as she drove towards Dickson's house to meet up with Morgan and Emma.

She'd only visited the place once before, during the investigation into Alex Corby's death, when it looked like Dickson had been going to be the killer's next victim.

Kate had little recollection of the house itself. What she remembered was more Dickson's attitude when she questioned him about his time at the Maddox Club. The bastard had lied to her face without giving away any sign of so doing, and she hadn't noticed a damn thing.

'William,' she said, when he picked up the line. 'Something has cropped up that demands our urgent attention.' Before he could interrupt and say nothing was more important than finding Dickson, she added, 'It's highly relevant to our current investigation and I don't want it going to another team.'

'Okay, I'm listening.'

The only way she would swing this was to bend the truth. 'The girl who slept with the superintendent at the Maddox Club has contacted me. She's deeply concerned about her thirteen-year-old sister, who's been transported into our patch by the same people traffickers who brought her here.' She recounted an abridged version of Stanka's story, giving William sufficient information to persuade him to take on the case, yet not so much that it might risk Stanka's life. The silence that ensued threw her into a panic. She was unsure if she'd said enough to persuade him. She needed to follow this up herself, so, adopting what she hoped was a confident tone, she said, 'If we can find her sister, this girl will be more willing to cooperate with any team investigating these claims about the superintendent.'

'Your brief is purely to find Superintendent Dickson.'

'William, the girl is wrapped up in all of this. We don't know why he has gone to ground or if indeed something has happened to him. What we do know is she might help us unravel the truth.'

'I'm not keen on adding further complications to this if they prove unrelated. This should be passed across to Harriet's unit. They're best placed to look into this girl's concerns.'

'Because they're dealing with a gang of people traffickers? It doesn't necessarily follow this youngster is in the hands of the same gang.'

'You have enough to do hunting for the superintendent.'

'This could help lead us to him!'

'Unless he's abducted the girl in question, I can't see how.'

The hesitation in his voice suggested he was wavering. She had to ensure he would topple.

'You were the one who pointed out that the accusations against the superintendent could have repercussions for my team. This girl was at the Maddox Club the night of the murder, which was our investigation. She's *our* responsibility, not DI Khatri's. Give me the opportunity to track her sister, William. The girl is willing to talk to me, and no one else.'

'Does this girl have a name?'

'Yes, but for the moment, it's best if I keep it to myself. She's risked such a lot to come forward. She's petrified, William. I don't want to say any more than is necessary, to anyone, including you. Sorry. I will once I can.'

'You're sure she's telling the truth about having sex with Superintendent Dickson?'

Kate mentally crossed her fingers at the blatant lie. 'As sure as I can be.'

'I suppose I'll have to trust you on this, Kate.'

There was a pause, during which she pulled up at traffic lights. A man walking a dog crossed in front of her. She tapped her fingers impatiently against the steering wheel. *Come on, William. Don't make this harder for me.*

'One condition. I'm going to get actively involved in hunting down the superintendent. You can't manage without assistance. How do you intend to go about this?'

'The girl has a friend who has a contact – they know where the sister is. I'll start with the friend.' She avoided mentioning Farai, who probably knew where Maja was being kept. As much as she trusted William, she couldn't give away anything that might get back to one of Dickson's cronies. Given recent history, anyone with information could end up dead.

CHAPTER ELEVEN

DAY TWO – LATE AFTEROON

DCI William Chase put down the telephone and sat back in his chair, his fingers lightly tracing the cracks in the leather arms. His conversation with Kate had left him in a quandary. He should have argued that she and her team should be putting all their energy, time and resources into locating John Dickson, not hunting for a girl who'd been trafficked. The trouble was, Kate was his Achilles heel. It might have been the urgency in her voice, or the fact he knew her well enough to understand she wanted this badly, or that he trusted her instinct, that had persuaded him to agree to her demand. It was, though, he concluded, madness to have told her she could hunt for the girl, especially when they should have a full unit rather than a handful of people assigned to something like this.

The leather was cool beneath his fingertips. Comforting. John's disappearance should be Kate's priority and he hoped she wouldn't lose sight of that fact. The sole crumb of comfort was that he believed in Kate. If she thought this nameless girl held information that would clear or condemn John, then she was right to pursue it. Whether the girl also knew something that might lead to the man's whereabouts remained to be determined. He rested his head against the chair and shut his eyes. He was tired of all of this. He should be looking forward to retirement now, not be thrown into this mess.

He no longer had the appetite for policework. He'd already been counting down the days and looking forward to getting out.

He'd been banking on Kate to find John quickly. There was nobody more suitable to handle the task. He, better than anyone, knew just how capable she was. She was his protégée and he was incredibly proud of her. He cared about her. Too much. Which was another reason he'd let her follow her instinct regarding the nameless girl's sister. However, the fact Kate had kept the girl's identity from him was a worry. Withholding information hinted at mistrust.

His finger tapped a staccato rhythm on the firm armrest, his eyes still closed. Surely, he hadn't slipped up in any way and allowed Kate a glimpse behind his front. She was sharp-witted. Had she finally seen through him?

Damn! He really needed her to continue viewing him as a loyal friend and confidant, because there would come a point soon when he would have to confess to what he'd been up to, and he would need her on side. Their relationship had been forged over many years, partly because he owed it to her father and his best friend, Mitch, and partly because he saw in her a drive and determination, a sharp mind and loyalty to the force that was unquestionable. He needed her on side. Never mind that he hadn't been entirely honest with her.

It had been his decision and his alone to request she and her team handle John's disappearance. Others in the building had already begun questioning why such a small unit was dealing with such an important investigation. Harriet Khatri, for one, had already voiced doubts. None of them, however, were aware of the details regarding the Maddox Club investigation. John had lied to the team about his involvement, something which would only serve to motivate Kate even further. Others may want to find him, but Kate would be more determined than most. She'd allowed John to pull the wool over her eyes and one thing he knew about her was she would want to rectify that error. Finding John would help her, and her team, to save face.

John had voiced doubts about Kate more times than William cared to remember. He'd been wrong. Kate was as tenacious as she was dedicated to the service. William might not be happy about her being side-tracked at the moment, yet he had confidence this circuitous route would lead to a good result. Hopefully one in which John was found – alive – and the aftermath dealt with.

He looked at the name he had written on his notepad. Kate might not have been able to find out who owned the pay-as-you-go phone that John had rung, but he knew people she didn't. William had called in all manner of favours to get this information and now he needed to act upon it.

Tracing the owner should have been impossible. However, his friend – a military cyber expert – had succeeded in pinpointing the location of the mobile device at the time it received the call, to a property not too far from the village of Abbots Bromley. A house that belonged to somebody they'd held in custody during the Alex Corby investigation – Bradley Chapman.

William rose from his comfortable seat. Given that Bradley had not only been uncooperative during that case, but had complained about Kate and her officers, and coupling this with the fact Kate's team was stretched hunting for a missing girl as well as John, William decided to pursue this lead himself.

He collected his overcoat from the peg behind the door. There was no need to discuss the matter with Kate. This was something he would handle alone.

As soon as she'd finished her phone call with William, Kate rang Stanka to explain that she would take on the hunt for her sister. They arranged to meet again in an hour, which would give Kate time to see what the team had uncovered at Dickson's house. Having already found his mobile, she could easily skip this visit, yet she wanted to see if there was anything else that might point to his corruption. Thanks to the broken recording device, Dickson's confession would never be heard.

But the desire for everyone to find out exactly what an evil bastard he had been still burned inside her, along with a hope that there would be something else in his house to prove he was complicit in the murders of Chris, Rosa and Cooper.

The front door was ajar when she pulled on to the drive and parked up beside Morgan's Jeep. She entered calling, 'It's me!'

'In the kitchen,' Emma called back.

The house felt different to the last time Kate had been here. It had once felt homely, if not a little old-fashioned, but now it felt oddly cold. The ornaments that had been displayed in a glass cabinet had disappeared, the hooks on the walls had been emptied of pictures, and there were indentations left in the carpet where a console table had stood.

A pair of men's boots, thick mud on the soles, lay cast by the door and a coat was thrown over the banister.

Kate peered into the lounge, where cushions lay squashed on a settee, a blanket had been left on the carpet, and an empty whisky glass stood on a coffee table. She was momentarily startled by her own reflection staring back at her from a mirror opposite. For a split second she imagined Dickson to be in the room.

'You shouldn't be here. This is my private space, bitch! You have no right to pry.'

The venom in his icy whisper sent her scurrying to the kitchen, where she wrinkled her nose at the stale smell that hit her. Takeaway boxes piled high had forced the top of a pedal bin wide open. Unwashed crockery and glasses filled the sink. Plates, dirtied with dried tomato sauce, conjured a vision of the stain that had billowed on Dickson's chest. She squeezed her eyes shut momentarily to eject the image from her mind. Emma looked up from letters and paperwork that were littering the kitchen top in time to catch her reaction.

'Not pleasant, is it? You know, this reminds me of my brothers' student flat. Two of them shared a place in Manchester with another couple of lads. Nobody emptied the bins or even washed up. It was horrible. They seemed to think I should clean up their mess when I visited. I only went the once. Arrogant sods.'

Kate cast about. It was difficult to imagine Dickson living like this. At work, he had portrayed a man for whom appearance was everything: well groomed, suits clean, trousers pressed and shoes polished. His office was ordered, neat and logical. Yet here, without his wife, he had existed in chaos.

'Any sign of a mobile?' she asked.

'Nothing so far, although we found a computer. It's bagged up for the tech team.' Emma replaced the paperwork, then rooted through a wide drawer under the marble kitchen top. Kate left her to it and climbed the stairs.

In the time Elaine had been gone, it seemed Dickson had done no housework. Carpet fluff had gathered in tiny mounds where his feet or furniture had scuffed up the pile. She peered into the first room to spy an unmade bed, its duvet thrown carelessly in a heap. A glass of water had been left on the bedside cabinet along with a John Grisham novel, a bookmark sticking out from its pages. The digital clock was flat on its back, numbers flashing. The twin cabinet at the far side of the bed was empty.

Kate walked into the room, noting the hastily drawn curtains that hadn't been fastened into their matching blue floral tiebacks.

A wing-backed chair with wooden arms stood in one corner. Over it lay crumpled clothes. She pulled on a brass ring to open the nearest wardrobe, tugging hard to free it of its frame. It had been cleared. Nothing belonging to Elaine remained. Kate made out more indentations on this carpet: four outlining where a chair or small table had once stood and six more, indicating another, larger piece of furniture, no doubt now set up in Elaine's new abode.

An object caught her eye. The corner of a picture frame. Bending to retrieve it from under the bed, she studied the photograph of a couple in evening dress. Elaine Dickson in a cream and black dress, with her thick, dark hair heaped elegantly on her head, pinned in place with diamanté clips, John Dickson in full police regalia. There were no smiles, no sense of intimacy, yet they made a striking couple.

'Get out. Get . . . out . . . of . . . my house!'

She shook herself free from the grips of her imagination. Dickson was dead. Nevertheless, she left the bedroom, crossed the landing to a second bedroom, where Morgan was on his knees, searching through cardboard shoeboxes at the bottom of a wardrobe. From what she could gather, they contained various memorabilia: old coins, faded photographs dating way before the digital age, and folded newspaper articles.

'It feels wrong to be going through his personal items when we don't even know what's happened to him. If he returns, I'm going to find it so hard to look him in the eye having turned his place over,' said Morgan.

'I know what you mean,' she replied. 'Try not to think so much about whose house it is and focus on finding anything that might lead us to him. Treat it like any ordinary investigation.'

'It isn't, though, is it? This is the superintendent we're investigating.'

146

'We're only looking into his disappearance, Morgan, not what he may or may not have done.'

'I suppose so.' He flicked through some more photographs of a group of schoolchildren. 'It's creepy, though. I keep expecting him to turn up any minute and yell at us.'

She noticed an open door into a bathroom. 'You been in there yet?'

'No.'

She walked into a family bathroom. A claw-footed bath stood in the centre of the room, a wooden tray used for soaps and face-cloths stretching across its width. An original painting of a seaside village with white, hillside houses reaching an azure blue sea hung on a wall, the artist a foreign name that looked Spanish to Kate. A dark oak unit containing his-and-her sinks was devoid of soaps, toothbrushes or any hygiene products. She stooped to open the cupboard below it, where packets of toilet rolls were stored along with cleaning products. She reached in, moved the objects around, dislodging a make-up bag bearing a chequered pattern that had been squeezed in behind some plastic spray bottles. She pulled it out and examined the contents: a small bottle of oily liquid. The bottle bore no label, but nevertheless Kate's heart began to jack-hammer. She twisted off the top, then sniffed. There was no smell.

Gamma-hydroxybutyrate, known as GHB. The same colour and had no odour. Commonly known as a date-rape drug, although it was also used by some addicts. It was also the very drug that had killed Rosa.

She licked her dry lips. Could this be the very evidence Heather Gault had taken to Dickson? If Kate took it to Ervin, he could test it, as he had tested the liquid Heather had secretly passed to him. He might even recognise the bottle.

Morgan hadn't followed her into the bathroom. She could hear him grunting as he sifted through the contents of another box. She had to make a rapid decision: put the bottle in an evidence bag and have it tested, or take it to Ervin herself? Again, if this fell into the wrong hands, it could go missing. She'd already crossed a line by keeping quiet about his mobile device. She shoved the bottle back in the bag, and returned it to its position behind the toilet rolls before shutting the door. She knew where it was. She needed more time to consider her options. She checked the cistern, noisily replacing it so Morgan would hear.

'No phone here,' she called.

She made for another room on the landing, still thinking about the bottle and its contents. Dickson was already dead; what did it matter if they amassed further evidence against him suggesting he was corrupt? The newspaper had sufficient material to annihilate his reputation. She had already won, hadn't she?

William sat outside the gates to Bradley Chapman's house. He reached for the Nokia in his coat pocket and checked it again. There were no messages or missed calls. How many other syndicate members had repeatedly performed the same act this morning, each of them checking for messages from John Dickson? He dialled the number under the name Alpha, only for it to ring out. This was the fifth time today. Wherever John was, he was keeping well out of contact. He returned the device to his inner pocket and got out of the car. The Alsatians that had been barking at his vehicle ever since he pulled up hurled themselves at the bars of the gate, outraged at his ambivalent attitude. He was a cat person rather than a dog person and, like his pets, he moved towards the intercom without a care for their noise.

'Yes?'

'Is that Mr Bradley Chapman?'

'Yes.'

'I'm DCI William Chase, sir. I would appreciate a few minutes of your time.'

'I'll call in the dogs and open the gate. Come up.'

William smiled at the dogs. 'Off you trot, you noisy pair.'

He returned to his car and watched the dogs as they eagerly pounded towards the house. It wasn't like John to stay incommunicado. Although William had already searched John's office before Kate, he had not upturned John's second phone. Therefore, he could only assume, if the team didn't find the device in his house, that John had it on his person or had ditched it. Even supposing he'd done the latter, John would have found some other way to contact his lieutenants.

The gates opened and William nosed his vehicle through. Why on earth would John have telephoned this man? Hopefully, within the next few minutes, he'd find out.

Kate assisted with the search for another hour before telling Emma and Morgan that she'd see them back at the station. The bottle of what she believed to be GHB bothered her.

'You should have taken it when you had the chance.' She pictured the sneer that accompanied Dickson's voice in her head. *'Of course, you can't be sure it was GHB. You want to associate me with Rosa's death so badly that you are making assumptions. The bottle could have been my wife's – some simple beauty product with no odour.'*

'Don't bullshit me. It's GHB. Forensics will recover and analyse it. Then questions will be raised as to why it was there.'

'If you say so. It makes no odds to me. There isn't an evidence trail linking it to Rosa's death or to Heather Gault, for that matter. Of course, you could insist you follow it up, but it would only take up an

enormous amount of your valuable time, and maybe only serve to show everyone you have a personal vendetta against me.'

'All your crimes will come to light in due course.'

He laughed. *'Wishful thinking on your part. You know that isn't going to happen.'*

'Oh, go screw yourself!' Without thinking, she turned to give him another piece of her mind and, seeing the empty passenger seat, was brought to her senses.

She gripped the steering wheel more tightly, forced all thoughts of Dickson from her mind.

She was now minutes away from seeing Stanka again. With William's backing, she could invest her energies into locating her sister. She hoped the girl could give her enough information for this to happen quickly. She understood Stanka's anxiety for her sister's well-being – after all, she had seen the devastating after-effects of rape with her own sister, Tilly, who'd been raped when she was a teenager. Maja's situation was even worse, and Kate felt more than duty-bound to prevent that from happening. She swung her car into a parking space and leapt out. There was no time to lose.

This time, she met the teenager in a popular coffee house at the far end of town. Sitting at one of only four tables in a second room to the rear of the café, they were alone. Not only did the window in the room overlook the main road, affording Kate a good view of anybody passing by, but from her position, she was able to see anyone entering or leaving the café.

It was almost six o'clock, and there was little passing trade. Stanka clung to her cup of tea, eyes on every car that drove past the window until Kate told her to stop it.

'Nobody is watching us. I checked before I joined you.'

'You never know where these people are,' was the response.

'They're not here. Stanka, I can't talk to you if you're not focussed. You want me to find Maja, don't you?'

'Of course.'

'Then tell me everything you know about the men who took you and now have Maja.'

The girl reluctantly tore her gaze from the window.

'You mentioned the name Ognian before.'

'Yes, he is the boss. There are three men: Ognian, Grozdan and Doncho.'

'Do you know their surnames?'

'No.'

'Can you describe them?'

'Ognian is a big man. He has long black hair to here.' She indicated her shoulders. 'Always like this . . .' She made a motion of tying her hair back in a band.

'A ponytail?' Kate said.

The girl nodded. 'He has many tattoos on hands and neck.'

'Any on his face?'

'No. On his neck and throat. And his body too.' She grimaced and sipped the tea as if to get rid of the sudden bad taste in her mouth. Kate could only imagine what horrors the teenager had experienced, but for the moment she had to remain detached, gather all the information she could without allowing emotions to cloud her judgement.

'Grozdan is smaller. Thin. He has no hair but has a funny nose. It is from fighting.'

'A broken nose?'

Again, Stanka nodded. 'Doncho is also big. Not as big as Ognian, but with large arms and neck from weights.'

'Like he works out with weights? In a gym?' Kate asked, mimicking lifting weights.

'Yes. He has a thick gold chain around his neck.'

'Any tattoos or markings?'

'No.'

'Do you have any idea where the men live?'

'They had an apartment in the same block where we lived but they didn't sleep there.'

'Where was this, Stanka?'

'I don't know the name of the street. There were many apartments all the same.'

'When you looked out of the window what did you see?'

'Road. More apartments.'

'No shops?'

'No.'

'No people?'

'Sometimes people. When we went outside, I saw big chimneys.'

'Chimneys?'

'Like towers but not so big.'

Was she talking about cooling towers? Kate wished she had an interpreter so Stanka could describe her experience in her own language. Stanka meanwhile was struggling to explain herself. 'Brick chimney. Like bottle. Brick bottle.'

Kate suddenly grasped what she meant. The teenager was trying to describe bottle kilns. Kate used the search engine on her mobile, and eventually held up a picture. 'Like these?'

Stanka nodded enthusiastically.

There were approximately fifty bottle ovens in Stoke-on-Trent, so she continued to scroll through pictures, showing each one to Stanka until she said, 'Yes. Those are the chimneys I see.'

The circular kilns – once ovens for the pottery industry – had since been preserved and were landmarks that stood on the canal bank amidst a housing development. The block where Stanka and her friends were held captive couldn't be too far from them. Although, even if Kate could find it, what would be the use if it was no longer owned, rented or even used by these men? It was likely that they'd moved to other premises to avoid arousing suspicion. Stanka lowered her head, her fingertips white from gripping the cup.

'You're doing really well, Stanka. This is very helpful.'

The girl lifted her face. 'But I think Maja is not there.'

'We don't know that for sure. I can look. You went to Stafford to a stop-off point. Where was that?'

'It is a hotel on the road. They take us girls to be photographed in nice clothes . . . and also . . . without clothes. Ognian told us the pictures are for agencies . . . to help us be models. Then he takes our passports, phones, possessions, everything. After one night at the hotel, we move to the apartment.'

Kate made a note. There were at least a couple of hotels she was aware of. No doubt Stanka would be able to point out which one.

'You said they brought you here in a minibus. Did they drive any other vehicles? Vans? Cars?'

'Ognian has a big Mercedes.'

Again, Kate scrolled through her phone, hunting for Mercedes websites that displayed the newest models, only to be met with head shaking every time she showed Stanka an image.

Finally, she tried a classic car website, where the girl pointed out an older silver-grey S-Class. 'Just like this one.'

'Do you remember any of the letters or numbers on the registration plate?' She was met with a helpless shrug. 'Okay. What else can you tell me?' The blank look floored her for a moment. 'Did they ever mention another place? Hotel name? Another town?'

Stanka frowned in concentration. 'I can't remember any other places. Only dairy. They were laughing one time about milking the cows in a dairy.'

A farm seemed an unlikely place to keep young women. A converted barn would be a better bet. She would investigate places named The Dairy. The minimal information she had gleaned would have to suffice for now. She'd first make a start with the hotels, then work her way around to the apartments. She checked the time – twenty to seven – then gave the girl a gentle smile. 'I need you to come with me. To help me find these places, not to come inside. Would you do that?'

Stanka's cup clattered against the saucer. 'Yes. We should go now.'

It was a start.

◆ ◆ ◆

Bradley Chapman leant against the kitchen top, legs apart, arms folded with bulging biceps on display. He shook his head.

'I wish I could help you, but I'm completely in the dark. I certainly don't recognise that phone number, and this is the only phone I own.' He indicated the iPhone on the table. 'I haven't spoken to Superintendent Dickson since the investigation into my son-in-law's murder.'

William, sat on a stool, was fully aware of Bradley's tactics. The man was like one of his dogs: marking his territory by ensuring William felt slightly intimidated both by the man's size and his aggressive stance. He had remained standing while insisting William took a stool that barely accommodated his backside.

But William was too long in the tooth to be unnerved. Besides, he was good at playing games too.

'Well, it's a mystery. The phone call was definitely made to this address.'

'I expect *this address* includes the area in front of the house and the lane leading to it. Anyone could have pulled up here and received a call.'

'That would be rather odd, though, wouldn't it? Especially as the house isn't visible from the main road. I can't imagine

154

why anybody would turn off, unless they intended visiting you.' William maintained a friendly, slightly bamboozled tone, as if he didn't suspect Bradley of lying to his face. 'Did anybody visit you that evening?'

'What time was this call again?'

'Five to seven.'

Bradley appeared to be thinking even though his face remained impassive. 'No, sorry. I was the only person here. My last driving lesson finished at six. I came straight home. Gwen was out with a friend, so I ate supper alone.'

'What about the dogs? They'd have alerted you to a vehicle's presence, wouldn't they?'

A muscle in Bradley's jaw twitched. 'The dogs were inside, so even if somebody pulled up by the gate, they wouldn't have reacted. They'd bark if somebody rang the doorbell, though.'

William doubted the truth of the statement. The dogs had not only charged at the gate when they saw his car, he'd heard them barking while he had been sat in the kitchen.

'I'm stumped,' said Bradley. 'I can only suggest your information is inaccurate. To my knowledge, it's impossible to accurately pinpoint an exact location in these matters. There's plenty of surrounding woodland. Any call received out there might easily be mistaken for one made to this house.'

There was no further point in pushing the man. He was lying, which meant he was hiding something. William stood up. 'Yes. I shall have to consider that possibility. Sorry to have troubled you, Mr Chapman.'

Bradley unfolded his arms and walked him to the front door, holding it open without a word. William returned to his car. The man may have thought he'd got away by offering minimal information, but William saw through him. His silence or reluctance to assist only made him more culpable. William knew John Dickson and was certain he wouldn't have phoned this man for help. He must have rung Bradley about something that had come to light during the meeting. Once William established who it was John had met, he would have an idea as to why he'd rung Bradley.

Bradley was wrong if he believed William had bought his act. William was well versed in looking for what wasn't spoken rather than what was, and an expert in body language. The tell had been the muscle twitch in his jaw, so minor, it might have gone unnoticed. Bradley was full of bluster, like a lionfish blowing itself up to huge proportions to frighten off its attackers. William would bring him back down to size.

CHAPTER TWELVE

DAY TWO – EVENING

Emma slammed the cupboard door shut. 'I give up. No phone, nothing whatsoever to indicate any foul play, only a feeling of awkwardness about sifting through somebody's personal belongings, especially when that person is somebody you work with – or rather, for.'

'That's exactly how I feel. Like some sort of voyeur. The state of this place. Looks like the poor man is having a mental breakdown.'

'Eating badly, drinking too much, neglecting housework. You know, Morgan, he could have tipped over the edge, and on finding out about the newspaper article, lost it completely. I mean, look at Kate and how she was after Chris's murder.'

'She was on medication, though, wasn't she? I couldn't find anything to indicate the super was taking any pills or substances. Nothing to suggest he was on anything – apart from the alcohol, that is. Who's to say he knew about the newspaper article? He might just have flipped,' said Morgan.

Emma pulled the front door to and locked it. 'True. I blame the pressures of the job. It's got to be a right juggling act, staying on top of everything while managing time for family life. How many of our colleagues from our old unit are still in a steady relationship or marriage?'

'Jamie for one.'

'That's only one. Besides, he wasn't part of our old unit.'

Morgan began naming officers as they made their way over the gravelled driveway. 'There's Flynn.'

'No. He and his wife split up last year. She went off with their son's teacher.'

'Oh, yes. Shit. I forgot. Erm, Hugh?'

'Hugh is about a hundred years old and has been married three times.'

'He's still married to Yasmina.'

'Yeah, only for the last six months. Give it time. Seriously, it's hard work being in a relationship yet giving your all to the job.'

Morgan stopped in his tracks. 'Is this your way of warning me off, Emma?'

She faced him, a smile on her face. 'No, you goofball. I'm making an observation about other people's relationships. I'm happy we've taken ours one step further.'

'Then, given how long it's taken me to make a move on you, I doubt we need to worry about splitting up for at least another two decades.' He stepped towards her, put a hand on her cheek, allowing it to rest there. 'We'll be fine. We're different to the others. First and foremost, we're good friends.'

She covered his hand with hers. 'Yeah. I think we'll be okay. Besides, if I were you, I wouldn't even think about pissing me off. I might be smaller than you, but I could kick your arse any day.'

He laughed.

'No, seriously, Morgan. Becoming intimate is a big step for us. I don't want our friendship to suffer simply because we jumped into bed together. I'd rather we took a step back and remained as good friends than go through something that rips us apart and ruins everything we've known.'

'That's never going to happen. I only make right decisions. Besides, I'm a keeper. Now, before I do something very unprofessional and kiss my colleague in front of the superintendent's house, we'd better get going.'

'What do you think has happened to the super, Morgan?' she asked as they jumped into his car.

'Between you and me?'

'Of course.'

'Something bad.'

'Even though we didn't find his body at Tatenhill.'

'Uh-huh.'

'Why do you think that?'

'Because the car by the airfield, the text to his wife, the phone and wedding ring left behind and the gun are all too damn convenient.'

Emma chewed on her lower lip as they drove along the darkening roads. She trusted Morgan's instincts, and her own were also telling her something was weird about this whole business. Kate hadn't stayed long at the house, racing off on some undisclosed mission. She'd been increasingly aloof again, which worried Emma. If this case was getting to her, she might turn to the pills, as she had after Chris's death, or maybe, in this instance, she knew something about the superintendent that she wasn't willing to share. Just what they were investigating was becoming a blur. It could transpire to be something far bigger than an officer gone AWOL.

Thanks to Stanka, Kate had now located the hotel where the girls had first been held during their ordeal. Even though the reception team had been as helpful as possible, the descriptions of Ognian, Grozdan and Doncho rang no bells for any of them. Certainly, none of the men had been spotted in the last day or two. Leaving her business card and instructions to ring her if any such men or young women were spotted, she joined Stanka again. This time they drove towards Stoke to locate the apartment block near the kilns. Regardless of the teenager's limited language skills that made conversation stilted, Kate marvelled at how well she communicated, especially as she'd had no English lessons prior to arriving here. Kate turned the conversation to Rosa, mindful of what she assumed to be GHB in Dickson's bathroom.

'Do you know how Rosa died?'

'Somebody killed her.'

'Do you know how?'

'They say Rosa took an overdose, but this is a lie. Her brother died two years ago, because he took heroin. She hated drugs. She never even smoked a cigarette. Somebody put those drugs in her or made her take them. I don't know how. I only know Rosa would never kill herself and never take drugs.'

'You, Rosa and Farai . . . you were all running from Dickson, weren't you?'

She pulled out a packet of cigarettes with shaking hands. 'Is it okay?'

'Wind down the window,' said Kate. 'To let out the smoke.'

She never ordinarily allowed any smoking in her car or home. This, however, was different. Stanka needed to quell her nerves. Once she'd lit up and blown smoke into the cold night air, Kate tried again.

'Tell me about you, Rosa and Farai.'

'We knew we were in danger after the night at the men's club. Farai too. If he didn't stay quiet, the bad policeman, Dickson, was going to send Farai to prison and in prison he would be killed. Farai was scared, for him . . . himself . . . and for Rosa and me. It was not safe in Stoke, so we travelled to Manchester. Dickson sent officers to Manchester. One was the woman, Heather, who warned Rosa that Dickson was going to hurt her. We moved to other towns, then to Blackpool. Always moving. Three months here, three months there. We stay in many places, rooms, hotels, in parks, we keep moving.'

'Did Farai make you work all that time?'

Stanka dragged on the cigarette for what seemed like a minute. 'All the time,' she replied quietly. 'He gave me a phone.'

'Have you got his number?'

'It does not work any more.'

'When did you last speak to him?'

'The day I rang you. He told me to call you.'

'Did he say where he was going?'

'No. He is hiding again. When the newspaper tells the truth about Dickson, Farai can work again, and have many girls. No more hiding.'

'Maybe not as altruistic as I imagined,' Kate muttered.

'Please? I do not understand.'

'Not important,' she said. 'He wanted to save you.'

'Yes. Farai said while I had Rosa's video I am in danger. He is in danger. All the girls are in danger. He said I must give it to you. Then Dickson will go to prison, and everyone will be safe.'

'And one of Farai's other girls rang to tell you about Maja?'

'Yes. Nevena. She was a friend to me and Rosa when we were in Stoke.'

Her name at last. Stanka was beginning to trust Kate.

'If we could speak to Farai, he might be able to tell us where the men are keeping Maja,' said Kate.

'I don't know where he is.'

'Could you ring Nevena and ask her if she knows where he is, or if she could help us to find him?'

Stanka sucked on the cigarette, then held it so the smoke could escape through the open window. Kate cranked up the heating to compensate for the cold air filling the car's interior.

'Farai is good at hiding.'

'We need to talk to him,' said Kate. 'If he knows you have handed me the video, he'll believe he is safe.'

The girl nipped the end of the cigarette between her fingers, then cast it away. The glass whirred back into place. 'Maybe.'

'You have to try. It's the only way to find Maja. Please ring Nevena, and others who know him, while I drive.'

Kate drove towards the bottle kilns while Stanka spoke at high speed in an unintelligible language on her phone. Kate gathered by the frequent use of '*da*' the teenager was agreeing with whoever she was speaking to, although that was the limit of her comprehension. No sooner had Stanka finished one call than she began another, words machine-gunning into the mobile. Farai was their biggest hope. If he had indeed spoken to Ognian, he might know where Maja was being held. If they could get him to agree to take the girl, they could rescue her.

The plan sounded simple yet was fraught with difficulties, the greatest of these being Farai. He would not take kindly to Kate's interference. He wasn't some Father Christmas figure. He was a man whose trade involved children who should never be working the streets. The girl next to her ought to be at home with her family and friends, maybe without a job but at least with her innocence preserved and her dignity intact. Men like Ognian and others like Farai and Dickson had robbed her and others of that, and gone on to exploit these youngsters further. It made her sick to her stomach.

'You're forgetting Harriet and Operation Moonbeam. This gang of traffickers is already under investigation. Tread on toes at your peril. You don't want to make an enemy of Harriet.'

Stanka looked at her, the frown deepening. 'That is a strange voice. What did you say?'

'I was just talking to myself,' replied Kate.

The girl continued to view her suspiciously. 'Why did you speak like that, like a man?'

Kate coughed. 'I have a dry throat.'

The silence that ensued was awkward until it broke with Stanka pointing ahead towards the tops of two bottle kilns. 'There! There is chimney.'

Relieved at the distraction, Kate cleared her throat again for effect. *Shit!* She was going to have to be much more careful. Voices in the head were one thing; speaking aloud in front of others was another. She could tell Dickson was gloating.

'You're cracking up,' he whispered.

She checked to make sure she hadn't spoken aloud again.

Fortunately, Stanka, back on her phone to another friend, hadn't noticed.

William reclined in his favourite chair beside the open fireplace. His cats, Wayan and Made – Balinese names given to the eldest and second-born children – were wound together in the opposite chair, creating one furry cushion. The animals were strikingly beautiful, with sapphire-blue eyes, silky white fur and plume tails. Expensive to purchase, William hadn't hesitated when he'd discovered a breeder with a litter for sale. Intelligent, friendly and playful, they were ideal company for a lonely widower who spent too much time at work.

His other love – his bees – were housed in hives in the back garden. He'd become an apiarist to help his mental health; an alternative way to cope with the stress and depression that invaded his life after his wife died. He'd read up on 'beekeeping therapy', discovered veteran soldiers suffering from PTSD had gone into beekeeping programmes with success, and decided he would try it. The results had been positive. Each time he pulled out a deckchair from the shed, sat down and watched the bees flying in and out of the hives, he felt calmer. Over the years, he'd become passionate about his hobby. Bees were a dying species and without them nature would suffer.

While William didn't have strong political views, he believed humans should do their bit to care for other creatures sharing the planet. But sometimes he wondered if that would ever be possible. During his time on the force, he'd seen horrible things he would never forget. He'd witnessed how depraved humans could be, uncaring and cruel. If his wife had lived, he would have retired many moons ago, taken up a different job, maybe even moved abroad. She had always loved the idea of visiting Italy.

He glanced over at the photograph on the mantelpiece. A pixie-faced woman with sparkling brown eyes and a bright smile. Sometimes he couldn't believe she was gone. Tanya Chase had died of complications during childbirth, which had also cost the life of their child. Losing her had transformed him. She had kept him anchored, helped him be a nicer, kinder person. After she died, he'd untethered himself from the values she'd upheld and for a long while resented the world and everyone in it. He'd immersed himself in dealing with scumbags and criminals, wife-beaters and any other lowlife he deemed unfit to exist on his patch. Maybe that was another reason he'd chosen to keep bees. They were social animals. Intent on working together for the common good rather than ripping into each other emotionally and physically.

Nowadays, he was a milder version of himself. One who would soon be freed from shackles that had bound him for decades. He was not proud of his actions over the years.

Tanya would be ashamed of some of the decisions he'd made, yet she'd left him to flounder, and flounder he had.

He sipped from a glass of orange juice and screwed up his face. On a normal day, he would be on the gin and tonic by now. He looked forward to unwinding with a drink, his cats and some music. Today, however, he was back in the saddle, requiring his wits. Bradley Chapman was hiding something. What could it be?

He lifted the laptop from the table and plugged in the USB stick he'd received that evening. His hacker friend was still helping him out and had sent over images from a well-disguised surveillance camera on a property along the main road to Bradley's house. The black and white images flickered into life.

His friend had only provided the relevant sections, each with a time stamp in the corner. William played the first segment of footage.

There was nothing to see other than the waving branches of a large tree to the side of the driveway until a vehicle came into view. William paused the video, selected the time stamp that showed 7.01 p.m., then pressed 'Play'.

A Land Rover passed by at speed, the camera capturing a side view of the vehicle. Rewinding the footage to when the vehicle first appeared, William watched it again, freezing each frame until he could make out the figure driving it. Enlarging the capture, he peered hard at the driver. It was difficult to make out who it was, but it certainly looked like Bradley Chapman.

The second video was time-stamped 8.04 p.m. This time the car was returning in the direction from which it had come. At that point, William would have assumed Bradley was returning home for the evening except there were two more videos: one at 9.12 p.m. when the Land Rover reappeared and at 10.09 p.m. when it headed back in the direction of Bradley's house. Where had the man been going? William studied the map of the area. Unless he was travelling to and from Lichfield, the only other direction he could take would be towards Rugeley, taking him over Blithfield Reservoir. As William recalled, Bradley's daughter lived close to the expanse of water, yet Emma had said the house was empty and up for sale. If the man had been toing and froing from the place, why hadn't he mentioned it? His version of events didn't tally with what William now saw on his screen.

The cats stirred, unravelling themselves so two distinct faces appeared, pink tongues on display as they yawned in unison.

'Go back to sleep, boys,' William said. 'I have to nip out for a while.' He got to his feet. Emma might have scoped out the house to make sure John Dickson wasn't hiding there, but he, on the other hand, wanted to search for clues that would lead to an explanation as to why Bradley had been beetling backwards and forwards that evening.

Kate and Stanka were making progress with their own investigation. Having pulled up in front of the two brick bottle kilns, they were able to work out where Stanka and her friends had been held hostage.

Kate left the girl in the car with instructions to keep the doors locked, and to ring should anything untoward occur, even though Kate was confident the identical red-brick buildings would be empty by now.

She navigated her way to the block Stanka had identified, looking up at the large floor-to-ceiling windows protected by bars so they could be opened in warm weather without any risk of an accident occurring. The apartment where Stanka had been held captive was right at the top of the block. The blinds in front of the windows were closed, so she couldn't tell if anybody was inside. A large satellite dish hung from the railings of the apartment directly below it, and the sound of canned laughter floated on the breeze in her direction, confirming someone was at home.

She headed for the main entrance, where she tried pressing a buzzer for what she assumed was the top-floor flat. When there was no response she stabbed at the one underneath, hoping it belonged to the person with the satellite dish, and struck lucky: the front door unlocked with a loud click.

Upstairs, she found a slender man in his late forties – wearing mismatched socks, joggers and an oversized T-shirt with shoulders that hung low on his skinny upper arms – standing in an open doorway.

'You're not from Pizza Palace.'

'No.'

'Then what the hell are you doing here?'

'I was trying to get hold of somebody in the apartment above yours. I rang your bell to see if you knew anything about them. You buzzed me straight in.'

'Shit! I thought you were the delivery person.' He peered at her through round-framed glasses, a prominent Adam's apple bobbing as he swallowed. 'What do you want?'

'Your help, if you don't mind. I'm a police officer.' She showed her ID.

The man swallowed again. 'Er, what about? I haven't done anything wrong.'

'If you have, I'm not here to quiz you about it.' Her attempt at levity fell flat. The man looked like he wanted somebody to wave a wand and spirit him elsewhere.

'It's about the occupants of the apartment upstairs.'

'I don't know anything.'

The answer came too quickly.

Kate changed tack as well as tone of voice.

'What's your name, sir?'

'Why?'

She pulled out her notebook. 'Because I'd like to know the name of the person who is being obstructive.'

'I'm not being . . . ob . . . ob . . . obstructive,' he spluttered. 'I don't know anything.'

She studied him with narrowed eyes. 'You mean to say you never noticed the three men who lived here, or the girls who were brought in and out of the place?'

His shoulders sagged; his chin dropped. 'Maybe.'

'Good. "Maybe" is a start.'

'Listen, detective, I don't have anything to do with any of the residents. Not them upstairs or anyone else in this block.'

'Can you tell me what little you know, Mr . . . ?'

'Fisher.'

'Anything you can tell me would be of a huge help, Mr Fisher.'

'I really don't see much of them. I . . . well, I generally stay out of their way. They're not exactly what you'd call friendly.'

'I understand that to be the case. I imagine noise gets transmitted quite easily in these buildings. You must have heard what was going on above you.'

'Erm . . . to be honest, there's usually not any noise. Only when their girlfriends or relatives or whoever the heck they are turn up. Then sometimes there's yelling and crying.'

'Did that not concern you?'

'Why should it? If people fall out and have a shouting match at each other, it's none of my business. It's not like there was any screaming or gunfire. I figured they were . . . you know . . . doing drugs and shit. Like I said, it's none of my business. I only want a quiet life.' He scratched wildly at his thinning hair. 'Live and let live.'

'I understand. Did you ever hear them shouting?'

'Now and again. I didn't understand what they were saying, though.'

'When were they last here?'

'Over a month ago.'

'What about the girls?'

'I never really saw them. They stayed inside the whole time they visited. I knew when they were here, though.'

'Have there been any female visitors recently?'

He shook his head. 'None. Last lot were here about the same time as the guys. It's been dead quiet since then.'

'Did you ever see any of the girls?'

'Once or twice. I saw them getting into a car.'

'Would that have been a silver Mercedes?'

'Yeah.'

'Do you happen to know its registration?'

'No idea. I don't curtain-twitch.'

It was clear Mr Fisher was scared rigid of the trio and probably his own shadow. 'Do you know if anyone has a key to the place?'

'The manager should have a master key.'

'Where can I find him?'

'First block on your right as you come on to the street. Bloke called Gary Shardlow.'

'Thank you, Mr Fisher. If you happen to hear anything upstairs or see any of these men again, would you give me a ring, please?'

He took her business card and peered at the name. 'DI Kate Young. That rings a bell,' he said.

'Thank you, sir.' She left before he could continue the conversation. Her name had been plastered over the newspapers following the train massacre. As not only the first detective on the scene, but also the wife of one of the victims, she had made headlines. It was little wonder he recognised her name.

Stanka was sitting so low in her seat she was almost hidden from view. Kate waved at her before striding to the block where the manager resided and soon found herself inside his ground-floor apartment. His wife, who introduced herself as Bernadette, bustled about, tidying up after their evening meal. Kate apologised for disturbing them, only to be told it wasn't an inconvenience and was part of the job description.

'Got to be on hand to help out at all times,' said Gary, pulling on a large fleece jacket. 'It's amazing how many of them lock themselves out regularly or need me to let in a workman.'

'What do you know about the occupants of this particular apartment?' she asked.

She couldn't miss the look that passed between husband and wife.

'Let's say we've had our suspicions about them for a while.'

'What suspicions?'

'Drugs. Hookers. Parties. It was obvious something was going on. They'd always turn up with a harem of young, attractive women.'

'Don't you have rules about such things?'

'We do, which is why they've gone.'

'When?'

'Last month. It was hard to get rid of them. The chap they were renting from wasn't an easy man to contact, or very helpful.'

'They didn't own the apartment?'

'It would have been a lot easier if they had. No, it's owned by someone who lives in South Africa. He let it out to them, that and another apartment in one of the other blocks. There was some legal issue preventing him from kicking them out. He'd agreed to a six-month let so he couldn't evict them until that date.'

'I need his name and contact details, please.'

'Sure, I'll sort those for you after I've shown you the place. I should tell you it's been cleaned since they left so there's nothing to see.'

That was a blow. She'd hoped to come across something to indicate where they might have gone. 'Then I'd also like the name of the cleaning company who saw to it.'

'Not a problem. I can give you that too.' He picked up a torch from the sideboard. 'In case the electricity is off,' he explained.

He opened the door. 'After you, DI Young.'

Back at the apartment block, Kate found herself in the middle of a decent-sized room for a couple rather than a family, with a long settee at one end and a kitchen/dinette at the other. The furniture was basic but functional, a four-seater settee, wooden table and shelving and a mounted television screen at one end, a table in the middle of the room with six high-backed chairs and a kitchen with the usual appliances and a microwave. The place smelt of bleach.

'When did the cleaners come in?'

'A couple of days ago. It was a mess. Needed what they called a deep clean. You should have seen the bathroom. Hair dye stains on the mat, nail varnish on the sides of the bath . . .' He rolled his eyes.

Kate ambled into the bedroom next door, where green and cream check curtains on brass rods had been pulled to. A lamp-shade in the same moss green hung from the ceiling, its dim light falling over two single beds that had been pushed together to make room for a spare mattress laid on the cream carpet. There were faint marks on the pine wardrobe, as if somebody had stuck on pictures with Sellotape. She could imagine the girls adorning the door with photographs from magazines to brighten the gloomy atmosphere. There was barely enough room to walk about, let alone for three girls.

Kate opened the wardrobe door, noting there was space for one person's clothes. 'Is this the only bedroom?'

He nodded. 'Bathroom's next door.'

She was about to shut the door and follow him when she caught sight of something scratched with a sharp implement into the back of the wardrobe: 'Bisera, Rosa, Stanka'. And below their names, another ten. The girls held had left behind a reminder of their existence.

She photographed the list before joining Gary and completing the tour, keen to get out of the flat and re-join Stanka.

Her next priority was Farai. He was probably the only person who could lead them to the girls' whereabouts.

Thanking Gary, she rushed to the car, only to discover Stanka had disappeared.

'Stanka!' she called, turning a full circle, heart pounding. There was no sign of the girl.

She walked a few paces in both directions, hoping to spy the girl, but nobody was about. Why had she gone without letting Kate know?

She rang the girl's number, and with the phone pressed to her ear walked aimlessly up the road in the hope of seeing her. The phone went to voicemail.

'Somebody got to her,' said Dickson.

'No, they can't have.'

'Then maybe she got another call with information about her sister and has gone racing off to find her.'

'But she would ring me if she had.'

'Not if she was told not to. Not if it is a trap!'

Could that be the case? Stanka was walking into a trap? She shouted the girl's name loudly. When there was no reply, she jumped into the car.

She had to find Farai.

CHAPTER THIRTEEN

DAY TWO – NIGHT

Kate rang Stanka's number for the second time, only to be transferred to voicemail again. Had somebody forced her from the car? Or had she left of her own volition? She hoped it was the latter, although why she'd leave without contacting Kate was a mystery.

It was fast approaching eight thirty and Kate was now on the hunt for Farai. He would know where to find the traffickers. If she found them, she might find Stanka and Maja. She'd last tracked the pimp down in Manchester. She could try the café where he used to hang out again, although that was a wild shot. Since then, he'd moved a few times.

'You really shouldn't trust the word of a streetwalker. Have you considered that Stanka invented the entire trafficking story, just so she could mess with you? Most of those sorts of girls hate the police. She's probably giggling about it with her mates already.'

'That's ridiculous.' She had seen the sincerity in the girl's eyes. There had been no faking that sort of anguish.

'You're right, of course. Somebody, one of my cohorts even, got to her. Hmm. I wonder where they've taken her or even if she's alive.'

Now that Dickson had voiced it, she couldn't get that idea out of her mind. The desire to find Farai became even greater. He'd been protecting the girl from Dickson all this time, so there was a slim chance that Stanka had heard from him and run to him. After all, he had been her protector for a long while. With Dickson now in the spotlight, thanks to the newspaper article, Farai might have returned to his original stomping ground in Stoke.

Then came a lightbulb moment. Stanka had told her that Nevena *saw* Farai and Ognian talking. At the time, Kate had thought the choice of word was down to Stanka's limited English, but if she actually meant 'saw' rather than 'heard', and was still working in Stoke, it suggested Farai could also be in the area, meeting Ognian face to face. Should that be the case, she stood a better chance of finding him, especially as she knew his usual haunts. She floored the accelerator pedal and the Audi raced along the dual carriageway. There was no time to waste.

William pulled up outside the Corby residence. The padlock on the gate hadn't yet been fixed, allowing him the opportunity to access the grounds. The curtained skies imprisoned the light from celestial bodies, ensuring the isolated property and its land were swathed in inky blackness. The car headlights shone on the magnificent house, standing in the shadows of ancient trees, before they extinguished automatically, leaving him in complete darkness.

He switched on his torch, the light scattering over a bed of late-summer flowers, their petals graphite, charcoal, jet and midnight black. The only sound came from the breeze that seemed to call from the 'reservoir, a soft whisper that rustled dry leaves, and tinkled windchimes somewhere in the garden.

He traced a path from the front door to the rear. Here the lawns swept downwards, affording a superb view of the reservoir. Because of the darkness, however, William could see nothing out there in the distance. He walked to the middle of the grass, where he faced the house. The windows were Vantablack hollows in the building.

He trudged over the damp grass, torch beam bouncing in front of him, unsure of where to search or what he was looking for. The house was clearly unoccupied. Why would Bradley come here, unless it was to meet the superintendent? Branches of an oak tree creaked ominously. The sound didn't bother William. He wasn't somebody who spooked easily. In the distance stood a small building, an outhouse or shed. Not knowing where else to look, he headed for it, huffing in frustration when he discovered it to be locked. His gut told him something was off about Bradley. If he hadn't come here the night John disappeared, then where might he have gone? The wet penetrated his footwear, making his socks damp. He was making no headway. Maybe his instincts were becoming more unreliable with age.

He sighed heavily. He'd been so sure there'd be some clue here. He trailed the torch beam over the ground, picking out the thick blades that required cutting. Then it struck him. The grass had been flattened where somebody had walked on it recently. He strobed the Maglite over the area, following the light to a circular area; a darker patch of grass. Bending down to examine it more closely, he realised it wasn't grass he was looking at, rather the remains of a recent bonfire. He tucked the torch under his armpit and, retrieving a pair of latex gloves from his pocket, dragged them over his wide hands. He picked through the ashes for clues, finally landing on a tiny scrap of material. Sitting on his haunches, he could only come to one conclusion. Bradley had driven here to destroy something.

The big question was what?

Leaving the warmth of her car, Kate crossed the road to speak to the woman outside the boarded-up pub. The area was a notorious hot spot for prostitutes, so it hadn't taken Kate long to find one she knew worked for Farai. Spotting Kate, the woman turned on her heel and began walking away.

'Hold up, Moira. I need to speak to you.'

Moira kept walking. 'I don't speak to coppers.'

'I'm trying to help one of your friends. One of the girls on the street. She's in danger,' Kate shouted.

Moira turned. Her heavy-lidded eyes gave the impression of being sleepy, yet Kate knew she was as sharp as a knife. As Kate approached, she struck up a defiant position, arms folded, sulky lips downturned. 'Hurry up. I've got work to do.'

'I need to speak to Farai.'

'You've been needing to speak to him for months. I heard you were charging about the country looking for him.'

'This is urgent. Stanka is in trouble.'

'Stanka? I don't know any Stanka.'

'Don't piss me about. Of course you do. She's a teenager, Moira, and now her sister – who's even younger – has been trafficked. She's only thirteen.'

'Not my problem.'

'You've got a kid, haven't you? Do you want her to end up on the streets at thirteen?'

Moira shook her hair back from her face. 'She won't.'

'This girl didn't ask for this life any more than Stanka did.'

'She came here to work, didn't she? She found it. Not my fault if she doesn't like it.'

'You don't understand. Stanka was duped. She was raped, Moira. Raped repeatedly until she lost all self-respect and was too terrified to try to run. Then she was sold to Farai.'

Moira shuffled from foot to foot. 'I didn't know that.'

'You remember her friend, Rosa?'

Moira shrugged.

'The same thing happened to her and now she's dead.'

Moira dropped her head. 'I didn't know them well.'

'Just give me an idea of where I can find Farai. That's all I'm asking. Unless you know anything at all about a man called Ognian.'

'I've never heard of him.'

'Then tell me where to find Farai. Please. Before another child gets raped and ruined.'

'I haven't seen him in months.'

'Do you still work for him?'

'Uh-huh.'

'Then how does he get paid?'

She looked around before answering. 'He collects the money from Big Harry. Harry should know where he is.'

'Where can I find Harry?'

'Tony's Pool and Snooker Hall. He's there every evening.'

'What does he look like?'

'You won't miss him,' she replied with a dry laugh. 'Can you piss off now? I have to make a living.'

'Sure. And thanks.'

Without any further discourse, Moira ambled back towards the closed pub, head lowered.

Kate tried Stanka's phone once more, leaving yet another message begging the girl to ring her. The pool hall was a five-minute drive away and one of the more run-down offerings in the town. Kate left her car parked in a nearby street and made her way on foot along dank, broken pavements and past buildings with lichen attached to brickwork. Wrappers, lifted by the breeze, scurried alongside her as if racing her to the end of the street, dancing and falling, only to be lifted again and continue their journey. Her heels tapped loudly, emulating her heartbeat.

The snooker hall, attached to a car wash, was set back from the road. The original white render was now a crumbling, dingy mess, the car park was weed-infested and the once-smart lettering had degraded so only half of the business's name remained. She shoved the entrance door with her shoulder, climbed the stairs and found herself in a large room, set up with seven tables, a mixture of pool and snooker. The green baize on each had faded over the years, the wooden edges damaged through knocks and stains from glasses balanced there. There was little conversation; the only sounds seemed to be the *kerplunk* of snooker balls as they struck each other.

Two tables were occupied by men who ignored her arrival as they concentrated on their game. The onlookers outweighed the players by a ratio of two to one, some with pint glasses in their hands, others with bottles. She wandered across to the bar, where the bartender was drying a glass with a grubby tea towel. 'You want to play?' he asked.

'No, I want to speak to Big Harry.'

A languorous voice mumbled, 'I smell pork.' His comment prompted chuckles among his companions.

'I find that reference offensive, sir,' she said loudly, striding towards him.

'Ain't no reference to anything. You shouldn't jump to conclusions, lady.'

'No, not pork. Bacon,' said a tall man with piercings in his eyebrow and lip, and several in his nose.

'Did you know, according to our public order act, it is a criminal offence to use threatening, abusive or insulting words or behaviour in a public place with the intention of causing harassment, alarm or distress? I find your language offensive and suggest you desist in making derogatory remarks or I might have to deal with you officially.'

One of the men snorted loudly. She spun in his direction. 'Have you got a problem with me?' she asked, fury seeping from her pores. She didn't need this shit from these idiots.

Something in her look quietened them. She eyeballed the nearest man, holding a cue. 'Do you know Big Harry?'

He nodded.

'Do you know where he is?'

'He's right behind you,' said a deep voice. She turned again. The man standing by the bar rested his spade-like hands on his large waist. His shiny red skin seemed stretched over his round cheeks and his neck hung in folds, like small tyres. 'What do you want with me?'

'I was told you know where Farai is.'

'You were told wrong.'

'It's not official business.'

'Sorry, can't help.'

'Well, that's a shame, because now I'll have to call in my colleagues from Vice who won't be as polite as me. I'm sure they'll find plenty of reasons to take you and your friends here in for questioning.' She'd hit her target. The men who'd been rude suddenly looked uncomfortable. 'And if they don't turn up anything this time, they'll keep this place in mind and do spot raids until they do.' It wasn't her strongest argument; however, these chumps seemed to be buying it. The man with the cue gestured with his chin.

'Harry, what does it matter if you tell her?'

'Shut the fuck up, Weasel.'

'No, Weasel's right. I don't have any beef with Farai. I'm not going to arrest him. I need his help.'

The man hoisted his joggers. 'I don't think Farai is up for Boy Scout of the Year.'

'It's about one of his girls. He's been protecting her for a while. I'm sure you already know he's been hiding out with a couple of them over the last few months.'

Harry rested his elbows on the bar and studied her through small dark eyes. 'What do you want to ask him?'

'I'll only speak to him. He knows he can trust me.'

'I'll tell him you're looking. If he wants to speak to you, then that's up to him.'

'Okay, but make sure you tell him that the person he's been hiding from can't hurt him any more. And give him this number. It's vital he contacts me immediately.' She handed him a business card. 'It's crucial,' she urged.

She didn't wait for an answer.

This is all too little too late. Stanka's dead,' said Dickson. *'One of my team got to her. One down, eh? Who will be next?'*

She snapped off the voice in her head and made for the door. She wasn't going to give up. The trouble was she half-believed what he was saying. Stanka could already be dead.

William rubbed his chin, Columbo style, and tried his slightly confused, bumbling act out on Ervin. 'I wasn't sure if you could help me, what with it being burned.'

Ervin continued to peer at the material through the high-powered microscope, poking at the fibres with a pair of tweezers. He made non-committal noises, which William took to mean he had found something. Eventually Ervin looked up.

'I'd like to run it through the spectroscope to determine the chemical composition of fibres.'

'Not something you can do quickly, then?'

'I was rather hoping to have clocked off by now, but even if I stay on, I'd need to run a few other tests to be sure, which means I won't be able to give you any definitive answers for at least twenty-four hours. We have some sophisticated equipment which should help identify the fibre, type of clothing and even colour. We might also be able to pick up something indicating who it belongs to, if we are extremely lucky and there is a drop of DNA on it.'

'New technologies, new ways. I'm a little behind the times. All of this, what you do, has always seemed magical to me. Like David Copperfield.'

'Ah, magicians are masters of exploiting nuances of human perception, attention and awareness, whereas I am a scientist, or a criminalist, if you prefer. I rely solely on analysis and scientific techniques to examine evidence. I am a pedigree bloodhound rather than a clown-like but lovable Labrador.'

'I get your analogy, although I'm more of a cat person myself.'

Ervin continued placing fibres into individual tubes. 'I read that in humans the cerebral cortex – the region of the brain that controls thinking and rational decision-making – contains 21 to 26 billion neurons. Cats possess 300 million neurons compared to dogs, who have 160 million neurons. The cerebral cortex not only governs higher functions of rational thought, but also problem solving. In summary, I imagine cats would make better detectives than dogs.'

'I'm sure my boys will be delighted when I share that nugget with them.'

'You're welcome.' Ervin looked up from his task. 'It doesn't take a great brain – cat or otherwise – to establish that you never get your hands dirty these days. I'm curious as to why you've brought this to me yourself and why you asked me to meet you here, out of hours. Does this scrap of material have anything to do with the disappearance of our superintendent?'

'To be honest, I don't know.'

'I take it you wish me to be discreet about it.'

'I'd like you to keep it entirely to yourself, Ervin. I want you and only you to work on it and I would like you to share any information with no one other than me. Nobody else.'

Ervin lifted an eyebrow. 'Discreet is my middle name.'

'Funny, I thought it was Clyde.'

'Which, as it happens, means "the keeper of the keys". Your secret is safe with me, DCI Chase.'

William gave him a small salute, much like Columbo might, causing Ervin to smile. His performance had worked. Ervin was unlikely to tell anyone about the material he'd just examined, which was good because if William's suspicions were correct, John was dead. And the fewer people who knew that William was following that line of inquiry the better. Because the only way to catch his killer was by stealth.

Kate was running out of energy and patience. She'd tried every streetwalker she knew, each one claiming to have no clue as to Farai's whereabouts. It was looking like her best chance remained with Big Harry – a thought that depressed her.

She drove slowly down Nile Street, an area that police had clamped down on in recent years, fining kerb-crawlers and driving many of the sex-workers elsewhere. As was usually the case, once the heat was off, they returned, so she wasn't surprised to see several touting for business. A couple made for her car, shrinking into the shadows once they saw her face.

'*They know you're a police officer,*' said Dickson. She caught sight of her own lips in the rear-view mirror, mouthing his words. For crying out loud! She had to stop this fucking voices-in-the-head shit. It had gone from internal voices to her talking to herself when she was alone, to even talking to herself when other people were present.

Dickson piped up with, *'Maybe Stanka ran off because she thought you were crazy when you were talking in a funny voice.'*

She checked in the mirror again. This time her lips hadn't moved. Good. All the same, Dickson was wrong about Stanka and he was wrong about the prostitutes. They'd slunk away from her because she had the look of somebody on a mission.

She'd given up leaving messages on Stanka's phone and was now sure something had happened to the girl. Getting a trace put on her phone would have to wait until daylight, which worried her further. Anything could happen overnight.

A woman in her twenties, leaning against a wall, watched idly as Kate's vehicle slowed to a halt before ambling over. Kate dropped the window a few centimetres. The woman put her hands on the car roof, allowing her crop top to rise higher, exposing flesh and breasts.

'What's on offer?' Kate asked.

'Depends on what you want,' the young woman replied.

'Information.'

'Then you got the wrong person.' She began to turn to walk away.

'I'll pay.'

The woman stopped in her tracks. 'How much?'

'Depends on what you know.'

'Try me.'

'Farai. I need to locate him urgently.'

'I don't know no Farai.'

'How about a girl called Nevena? She's friends with Stanka. You remember Stanka, don't you? She and another kid called Rosa worked this street a few times.'

The woman stared at her. Close up she was older than Kate had first imagined, angry spots on her pale skin, hair greasy and stretch marks on her stomach.

'You police?'

'I am, but I'm not here to caution them or give them a hard time. I'm offering help.'

'Help? Pfft! We all need help from time to time. One of the girls on this street got her face punched in last week by a dissatisfied customer. Asshole couldn't get it up and blamed her. We don't get any protection. We don't get help, so why are you so concerned about these girls? Listen, never mind. I don't care. I have work to do.'

Kate held out a twenty-pound note. 'Nevena? Have you seen her?'

The woman snatched the note before stepping away from the car. 'She was here earlier, but she took a phone call then raced off. Haven't seen her since.'

'When?'

'A couple of hours ago, I guess.'

'Do you know who the call was from?'

'Are you joking? How the hell am I supposed to know that? We don't chitter chat! Besides, I didn't understand what she was saying. It was all gibberish.'

'Did she shout, seem upset?'

'Dunno. She scarpered straight away.' She shrugged.

'Do you know where she lives?'

She rolled her eyes. 'No. Now fuck off or you'll frighten away the customers.'

The woman strolled back to the wall, took up her earlier position and pointedly looked away from Kate's car. Kate moved off, nursing the thought that Stanka might be with Nevena. The timing was right for it to have been Stanka who rang. Maybe Nevena arranged to meet Stanka and hide her. Of the two options, this was one she clung to. The idea that Stanka had been snatched was

184

one she couldn't handle at present. Yet, if the girl was with Nevena, why hadn't she rung? A dull headache was beginning to take hold. Kate needed time out.

'Go on. Take a break. Take as long as you like. It doesn't matter if you take all the time in the world. It's too late for Stanka.'

Afraid of what she might see, she didn't dare look in the mirror.

CHAPTER FOURTEEN

DAY THREE – THURSDAY MORNING

Kate rolled up to the station to discover Jamie had arrived at the same time as her and was struggling to get out of his car. He clutched the side of the door to heave himself forwards before hobbling up the steps to the entrance.

'I'll get that,' said Kate, racing for the heavy door, which required a heave to open it.

'Cheers, guv. Least we're not swamped by journos today.'

'I don't think they'll give up easily. They probably got moved on before we arrived.'

'You seen today's *Gazette*?' he asked.

'Picked up a copy on my way in. They're still at it.'

'This reflects badly on all of us, not just the super. I bet every *Gazette* reader is wondering not only if what they're saying about him is true, but if any other officers get up to the same sort of tricks. If the public lose trust in people like the superintendent, they'll lose it in us as well. The papers shouldn't be allowed to print this shit.'

Kate wished Jamie would walk a little quicker so she could get to her desk and ignore his rant. As it was, every few steps, he'd slow or stop to speak again.

'It's a bummer about his second phone. Morgan told me they couldn't find it at his house.'

'That's right.'

'I still reckon his disappearance is a smoke screen. The super is trying to sort out this shitstorm, hoping the story about his disappearance will make the headlines rather than the crap they're saying about him. He might have the phone with him.'

Kate took his defence of Dickson to mean Jamie still had loyalty towards the man. Maybe Jamie really was ignorant of how corrupt his superior was.

As he continued to talk, she wondered if Felicity had managed to unlock the mobile overnight as she'd planned. There'd been no word from her, leading Kate to suspect she had either not yet found time to check it out or had failed to get it operational.

'So, where do we go from here, guv?' Jamie had finally made it to the meeting room.

'We have a new angle to explore. I'll explain at the briefing.'

'Good, because at present, we're pissing in the wind.'

She opened the door to the room, larger than their office, and made a show of checking her notes so he wouldn't talk further about Dickson. Within moments, Emma appeared, fresh-faced and energetic.

'Morning!'

'Wow! You're extra cheerful,' said Jamie.

'Slept well,' she said smoothly. 'I guess you've read today's paper.'

Kate looked up and spied Morgan lurking in the corridor. Why hadn't he come in with Emma? It only took a moment to work out why not. It confirmed the little looks she'd noticed pass between them, the fact Emma had rushed to accompany him to the coffee shop the day before. The handholding. They were trying to hide the fact that they were now more than friends from their colleagues.

'Yeah,' said Jamie. 'They're really trying to create a drama, aren't they? They keep going on about this video. I wonder what's on it that is so incriminating.'

'My guess is they're running it past their experts and lawyers to ensure it's the real deal,' said Emma. 'Otherwise, they'd have already put it out there. The articles so far are all about the same thing: titbits of information, suggestions of what more is to come. It's a lengthy build-up. They're after selling more newspapers. They might not have much at all.'

Jamie grunted. 'What's been printed so far is damning enough. Suggestions of corruption at this level is bad news for all of us. We'll all be under the microscope before long.'

'We don't have anything to worry about. Even if they do, we're squeaky clean.'

'Ah, I don't think so,' said Morgan, who appeared at last. 'What about the mysterious disappearance of my packet of Hobnobs last month?'

Emma punched him playfully on the arm. Kate hid a smile. They'd soon be outed at this rate. 'I only hid it from you for a day or two. It was for your own good.'

Kate cleared her throat and caught their attention. It was time to get down to business. 'Okay, everyone. Before we begin, I should let you know we're waiting for DCI Chase. He will be helping investigate Superintendent Dickson's disappearance. There was a development yesterday that means we must keep this in-house. Ah, here he is. I'll let him explain.'

William entered, shutting the door behind him. He stood in front of it to address the room.

'As you are fully aware, this is rapidly escalating into an awkward situation. Unless we find the superintendent and he can deny the serious allegations being hurled at him, we can't launch a counterattack. What is more concerning is that there might be some truth in what is being written about him.

'The girl who alleges she had relations with Superintendent Dickson at the Maddox Club has come forward and is willing to talk to us, but only if we can find her sister, who we believe to be currently in the hands of the same people traffickers who trafficked her.

'Before you say anything, I appreciate we are a very small unit. I understand the task in hand is onerous and you may think I ought to involve another team. After serious consideration, I've decided not to. The young woman will be an important witness should Superintendent Dickson be brought to trial. We need her to be cooperative. Furthermore, she might even be able to give us a clue as to the superintendent's whereabouts. To that end, we must try to find her sister.'

Kate's phone vibrated in her pocket. She didn't recognise the number, but she breathed a sigh of relief when she read:

Am OK.

Will contact you soon.

S

Stanka was safe! Kate tuned back into what William was saying.

'What is being printed about Superintendent Dickson is not our concern, finding him is. For that reason, I shall be assisting in the investigation. I'll be concentrating on trying to locate Superintendent Dickson, freeing most of the rest of you to search for the people traffickers. Given the grave nature of the allegations being made about the superintendent, I suggest nothing regarding this investigation is to be repeated outside. Do I make myself clear?'

There were nods and Jamie said, 'Yes, sir.'

'Then I'll pass back to Kate.' William pulled out a chair and sat down.

Kate spread her hands out on the desk and explained what she knew so far about the people who had taken Stanka. She left out no details, other than the girl's name.

'For the time being, because she insists on anonymity, I'll refer to her only as Girl X. However, I have a description of her thirteen-year-old sister, who is called Maja. I'd like Emma and Morgan to speak to all the residents in the blocks of flats where Girl X, along with other trafficked girls, was held. See if any of them spotted a car like this one. We need a registration for it. It might have been spotted there about a month ago. I believe it belongs to a man called Ognian. He appears to be the ringleader.' A photo of the old model S-Class Mercedes appeared on the screen behind her.

'He works with two other individuals.' She gave names and descriptions of Doncho and Grozdan, explaining that Gary Shardlow was the manager who could let them into empty properties, then put up another photograph on the screen.

'These names were found scrawled on the back of a wardrobe at the flat where the girls stayed before being moved on. I have no idea where these girls might be. Since Girl X doesn't know their whereabouts, I suspect they are no longer on our patch.' She waited for a reaction. Jamie would recognise at least one of the names – Rosa – if not both Rosa and Stanka. As part of Operation Agouti, he had been tasked with hunting for them. He did not, however, comment.

'On the basis that Girl X was pimped, shouldn't we at least speak to streetwalkers to see if they know the whereabouts of any of these girls?' asked Morgan.

'I spoke to a few of them last night. Nothing doing. Maybe you'll have more success. You could try this evening when they are active. In the meantime, let's concentrate on these three men, see if we can find the Merc and take it from there,' said Kate.

Jamie, who'd kept his head lowered for most of the brief, spoke up. 'DI Khatri's team are investigating a people-trafficking ring. Could we piggy-back their investigation – two heads . . . or two teams in this case?'

William cleared his throat. 'Can I answer that, Kate?'

She nodded.

'I considered merging the teams, or at least having two-way communication as an option, before discounting it. In light of what has been discovered so far, I suspect we are dealing with two different gangs of traffickers. There's been nothing to link those being investigated by DI Khatri's team to prostitution.'

Kate glanced at Jamie. She wanted him to step up, say something about being involved in hunting for a sex-worker called Rosa, whose name was written on the back of a wardrobe, yet he remained silent. She was about to call him out when Emma spoke.

'Can we speak to Girl X at all?'

'Not until we find her sister.'

'Then what happens if we don't find her?' Emma asked.

'We'll cross that bridge when we reach it. For now, I have her assurance she will talk to us.'

'Is she in a safe house?' Jamie asked.

Kate maintained her sang-froid. 'I'd rather not divulge her whereabouts at present. You understand how important it is that as few people as possible know where she is.'

She saw a cloud flit across Emma's face. By keeping information from her team, she was running a risk of losing all the trust that had built up over the years.

Jamie gave a small cough. 'Erm, there's something I should say. As you know, I was involved in working undercover for the super.

The operation was to find underage sex-workers. One of the girls we were hunting for is on that list – Rosa.'

At last! thought Kate. Maybe he could be trusted after all.

'Did you speak to Rosa?' she asked.

Jamie shook his head. 'I located her, but she gave me the slip. I passed on the details to the super. I don't know if he or any others in that unit managed to track her down. Guv, is she Girl X?'

There was too much at stake to tell her team the truth. To her knowledge, only she, Stanka and Farai knew that Rosa was dead, killed by Dickson or somebody working with him. Kate had decided not to bring it to anyone else's attention until she could gather proof to support her suspicions. If word got out to any of the syndicate about Stanka, the girl would be in incredible danger. And for all her desire to trust Jamie, she couldn't be certain he wouldn't leak the information to one of the syndicate members. She needed to keep in mind that her mission was to uncover every one of them and bring them to justice. That's what all of this was really about. Yes, they had to save poor Maja and whoever else was with her, but after that, Kate was determined to redirect her energies into uncovering those people who pretended to safeguard citizens yet were twisted and corrupt themselves. There was no option but to perpetuate the lie. 'I can only tell you that she claims to have slept with the superintendent.'

'What about transparency and teamwork?' said Jamie. 'You told me that was how we worked in this team.'

'Hey, that'll do,' said Morgan. 'If Kate wants to keep the girl's identity a secret, that's fine. Trust comes into this as well.'

She was grateful for his interjection. 'Thank you, Morgan. Once we find Maja, you'll learn her sister's identity and can interview her. If what she claims is true, she'll be pivotal in bringing the superintendent to justice and, like it or not, we must protect her from harm. Jamie, are you okay with that?'

He shrugged. 'I suppose so. I don't see how she can help find the superintendent, though. It's probably bullshit simply to get us to rescue her sister. We should drag her in here and ask her what she knows right now, not pussyfoot about.'

'Yeah, cos she'll really open up if we do that, won't she?' said Morgan. 'Use your head, Jamie. If we get her what she wants, she'll help us. Sometimes it works that way. Besides, the sister is only thirteen! How would you feel if one of your kids was duped, trafficked, raped and then set to work on the streets in some foreign country? You'd lose it bigtime. The best thing we can do is get out there and track down these three blokes.'

Jamie gave a huff of irritation. 'What about the super? How are we going to keep up the hunt for him?'

Kate directed her answer at him. 'You'll work closely with DCI Chase. We've already done a lot of the legwork. We're in agreement that Superintendent Dickson is lying low for the time being. Even you felt everything was an engineered smokescreen so he could assess the situation and deal with it before returning. All the same, I'd like you to continue checking with his friends and family and follow up on those pay-as-you-go numbers. You got anything on them yet?'

'No, I'm still waiting on Rachid.'

Given her wavering uncertainty about Jamie's loyalty, Kate had decided it would be best to keep him under William's watchful eye and away from any information about Stanka or Maja. William would need help and Kate wanted her best two officers to assist her. 'Emma was checking out pubs in and near Abbots Bromley to ascertain where he might have met the person who rang him. Maybe continue with that. What was the name of the pub in Newborough, Emma?'

'The Red Lion. It was on my to-do list for today. The bar person I spoke to wasn't the same one who was on duty the night the superintendent went missing. They were due back this lunchtime.'

'Are we sorted on how to play this, then?' Kate looked around the room. 'DCI Chase, are you happy with that?'

'Absolutely.'

'Okay, thanks, everyone. I know this isn't our conventional way of handling things, but this isn't a conventional case. Have you anything else to add, DCI Chase?'

'Only to ask that everyone be circumspect and under no circumstances whatsoever are any of you to talk to the media.'

Kate packed up her notes and iPad. The others moved off. Jamie, the last to leave, hung by the door.

'Guv, if Girl X has information about that night at the Maddox Club, suggesting the super was involved in that murder that took place there, he would be in seriously deep water.'

'I'm aware of that, Jamie. That's why it's imperative we keep this all to ourselves. We need to exercise damage limitation. You weren't part of that investigation, but you are part of this team now. That case was our responsibility and if we overlooked something as important as this, we will also be held accountable. So now you understand why I'm playing my cards close to my chest. Not to exclude any of you but to protect you.'

'Yeah, okay. I get that.'

'So, let's find the superintendent. We need to hear his version of events.'

She waited until he had left the room before letting out a sigh and dropping on to the chair. She wasn't sure what she was saying or doing any more. All she wanted was to find Maja, make certain Stanka was out of harm's way and then wait for the dust to settle.

If the *Gazette* exposed Dickson for covering up the boy's death, she and William would ensure that none of her team would be held accountable. After all, Dickson had deceived them all, and they'd had no reason to disbelieve the word of their superior, who had assigned them the investigation. If she was guilty of exaggerating the situation to Jamie, it was only to keep him on side and to ensure he trusted her.

There was something about the younger detective she couldn't put her finger on: a feeling that he was playing along. No matter how hard she tried to shake it off, she still believed he was tied to Dickson and the syndicate, and because of that, she was going to continue to watch him carefully.

Her phone flashed up a message. Felicity wanted to see her. Scooping the desk debris into her bag, Kate hastened to the technology unit.

Felicity beckoned Kate into her glass-fronted office. She took the offered seat, her back to the large glass windows overlooking the laboratory, where three white-coated individuals were bent over desks, working on various electronic gadgets.

Placing her elbows on the desk and leaning forward conspiratorially, Felicity lowered her voice. 'The phone is unlocked but you aren't going to be happy. I only succeeded in retrieving twelve contact numbers in total. They'd been deleted but not completely obliterated, which leads me to suspect everything other than that list was professionally erased at some point in the past, probably using a specialised program. Ten numbers have been assigned Greek letters, beta to lambda, rather than names. I assume alpha would be the phone owner's code name.'

'No text messages?'

She shook her head. 'I matched one of the two unnamed numbers to DC Jamie Webster's phone, and the other with Heather Gault's. As for the remaining ten, I can only tell you they belong to unregistered pay-as-you-go phones.'

'They're all burner phones?'

'It would appear so.'

'Is there any chance of obtaining a call log, so we can establish when calls were made?'

Felicity pulled a face. 'Possibly. You'd have to request it from the provider and . . . well, you don't want to alert too many people to the fact you have this phone, do you?'

Kate chewed on her bottom lip. Dickson had been extremely cautious. Interestingly, only Heather and Jamie had not used burners. Could they have been mere soldiers, used for Operation Agouti but who fulfilled no other role? Whereas those with untraceable phones were all part of the syndicate? Maybe those members with code names also had soldiers in their contact list. Kate paused to consider the scale of corruption that might exist.

'Kate?'

Felicity was staring at her.

'I was just trying to get my head around this.' Another thought struck her. 'Felicity, could somebody work out that the mobile is here? I mean, you had to turn it on, didn't you, to get the information?'

'Don't fret. We techies have software to unlock phones without a password or PIN or access broken phones to recover data, photos, contacts, etc., without having to switch on the device. If I had turned it on briefly to recover the contacts then turned it straight off again, that might have resulted in a signal to the nearest mast. Even then, that information would only be available to the phone service provider at that time and would only cause a problem if someone else rang the number while it was switched on. Don't worry. I erred on the side of caution. Best in these situations, don't you think?'

Kate felt her lips stretch into a smile that matched her friend's.

'I'm not sure what to do with this information,' Kate said. 'Could you place a watch on these pay-as-you-go numbers?'

'For what it's worth, I think they'll remain switched off until the superintendent reappears. I doubt the owners of those numbers will want to be associated with him at present.'

Kate sighed. Felicity had made a good point. Some of them might even have ditched their phones altogether.

'I'll keep an eye on them, all the same,' said Felicity.

'I'd appreciate that.'

'You can do me a favour, in return.'

'Sure, anything.'

'Come to dinner at our place. We haven't seen you socially since forever.'

Kate smiled again. 'I'd like that.'

'Great. It's a date. You'll be doing me a huge favour. I need somebody else to play that damn panda game with Bev! Okay, what do you want to do with the phone?'

'I ought to take it.'

Felicity picked up a bunch of keys from the desk, unlocked the top drawer and removed the black box, which she slid towards Kate.

Kate pocketed the phone then got to her feet. 'Thanks again. I'd better get back to the troops now. We've a stack of work to get through.'

'Always here if you need me,' said Felicity. 'And I'll get back to you on that dinner date.'

Kate slipped out of the building into the dull day. A pair of crows were squabbling over the contents of a discarded burger box tossed into the car park, intimidating each other with hops and angry squawks. The phone seemed to radiate heat in her pocket, almost convincing her it was glowing, so everyone could see she had it. She marched to her car parked at the far side, dispersing the crows in her path, and opened the boot.

She looked up at the brick building where she had worked for the last few years, eyes drawn to blinds that remained shut at Dickson's office window, half-expecting them to twitch, before slipping the box into a small compartment housing an oil can. She'd work out what to do with it later. For now, she had more important matters to deal with.

As she shut the boot lid, she looked up again at Dickson's window. She clamped her lips together to prevent herself from speaking aloud in his voice, leaving the words screaming in her head.

'I can see you!'

CHAPTER FIFTEEN

DAY THREE – AFTERNOON

Emma and Morgan trudged towards the block of flats where Gary Shardlow, the manager, lived. They'd spent all morning knocking on doors, only to be met with guarded looks or mumbled assistance from residents who had little to offer. It seemed nobody was willing to discuss the trio of men or their entourage of young girls who had lived here temporarily.

'That's how these bloody criminals get away with it,' grumbled Morgan. 'People want a quiet life. They don't want to stand up to thugs or shady individuals, so they stay schtum.'

'Could be that they're simply scared or didn't see anything. If the girls didn't live here permanently, and only came and went during the hours of darkness, many of these people wouldn't have clapped eyes on them.'

'Why are you so reasonable about things like this? I want to shake everyone by their throats until they spit out everything they know, while you look at the situation from their point of view and reason that they know nothing. And you're probably right. It's damn frustrating!'

'Them not talking or me being right?' she said, holding back the smile.

'Them, of course. You're almost always right. I've got used to you almost always being right.'

'Almost?'

'Don't push it,' he growled, with a twinkle in his eyes. He rapped on Gary's door sharply. When the man appeared, he held up his ID card. 'Officers DS Meredith and DS Donaldson, sir. You are the manager of these apartments, Mr Gary Shardlow?'

Gary's voice was a mere tremor. 'Yes.'

'Could you spare a few moments, sir? It's with regards to the empty flats we understand were rented to three foreign men.'

'Er, yes. Come in. I spoke to another officer last night. I told her everything I know.'

'That would have been DI Young.'

'That's right. I told her that we'd had our suspicions about the men, what with the girls appearing whenever they did.'

He led the way through a narrow hall to the kitchen, where he sat on a chair already pulled out from under a round table, shut an open magazine on top and clamped his arms across his body. He didn't invite either of them to join him, leaving both standing.

'We're keen to find these men. Is there any information you could give us to help do that?' asked Morgan.

'No, sorry. I only deal with the owners, and the owner of those two flats sublet them without my knowledge.'

'Yes, we contacted him earlier and he said he'd rented the places to a Mr Brown.'

'Right. Okay. I can't add to that,' he said with a light shrug. 'I never spoke to the men.'

'You never challenged them about what was going on in the flats? I'd have thought it was your responsibility to ensure residents behaved appropriately.'

'My role is more as caretaker. I make sure the buildings, grounds and apartments are in good order. I handle complaints and problems, and since nobody complained about the occupants of either flat, I didn't have grounds for challenging them.'

'But you were suspicious of activities going on?'

'Sure, I was. Look, three blokes turn up and bring a bevy of girls, of course it looks suspicious, but if they want to party, then as long as they don't disturb others, I don't need to interfere.'

Emma spoke for the first time. 'Did it not strike you, Mr Shardlow, that the girls were very young?'

'Were they? I can't say I thought so. It's difficult to pin ages on women, especially when they're dressed up and wearing make-up. Hand on heart, I thought the guys used the places to party with hookers. I suspected they were taking drugs and shagging and so on, which was why I told the owner. He told them to get out and now the guys don't come here. That's all I know.'

Emma wasn't completely satisfied with his response. While she accepted not everyone on site would have noticed the comings and goings of the men and the girls, she was sure the manager would have been more astute. It was, after all, his job. 'How often did the men appear?' she asked.

Gary tucked his hands firmly under his armpits. 'Erm, maybe every three months or so.'

Emma looked up from her notebook. 'Could you be a little more specific?'

'Not really. I don't stare out of my window all day, waiting to see who's about. They were only here for two to three weeks at a time. It varied.'

Morgan took over. 'When was the last time you saw them?'

'August. I remember because we went away for a break to Wales and when we returned, they were here. They brought six young women with them that time. Yeah. That will have been the beginning of August. They moved out two weeks later.'

'Did you have any contact with the girls?' Emma studied the man as he replied. His thumbs rubbed nervously against the fabric of his fleece, and he wouldn't meet her eyes.

'No. I only saw them from a distance.'

'What about your wife? Did she speak to any of them?'

'No way.'

'Why not?'

'She thought . . . we thought . . . they were prostitutes. She wouldn't have anything to do with people like that.'

'Could we speak to your wife?'

'Sorry, Bernadette won't be back until late this evening. You'd be wasting your time talking to her anyway. She prefers not to mix with anybody living here.'

Emma stared at him. 'Why not?'

'She doesn't like living in Stoke-on-Trent. We're only on this complex because of my job. She'd rather we moved to Wales, where she's from. I'm looking for similar positions there, but it's tricky to find something suitable that offers accommodation.'

Morgan, who'd been relatively quiet, moved towards the sink. 'You've got a good view of the road from here,' he said. 'I don't suppose many cars would pass by without you knowing about it.'

'I don't tend to stand at the sink. Only as long as it takes to rinse a cup.'

Morgan turned around, pointed at a pile of car magazines stacked near the sink. 'You like cars?'

Gary nodded. 'Yeah. I'm mostly into sports models. Can't afford one, though. Dream cars. All of them.'

Morgan pointed to the glossy magazine in front of Gary on the table, a vibrant orange Lamborghini on the cover. 'That one's way above my pay grade.' He moved towards the pile of magazines, lifted the first one. 'I see you like classic cars too.'

'Sort of.' The man gave a nervous look in Emma's direction, and she instantly knew what Morgan was up to.

'Do you own the Mark 1 VW Golf GTI parked outside?'

'Er, yes.'

'Lovely motor. Best hot hatch produced,' said Morgan.

Gary unclamped his hands. 'It was that car that started the small car revolution.'

'My dad thought the Renault 5 did that.'

'Nah, the Golf GTI is the second most recognised model after Porsche 911. It's iconic.'

'You know your stuff,' said Morgan, replacing the magazine on to the stack. 'Those guys who rented the flat, they drove an old classic car, didn't they?'

'An S-Class.'

'What model was it?'

'I'm not sure.'

'A car buff like you! I bet you saw it drive past and checked it out. You'd know the model and year it was manufactured. Come on, Gary, don't mess about. I know you know.'

'Mercs aren't my bag.'

'If I went through that pile of magazines, I bet I'd find plenty of articles about all makes and models. You'll have read about Porsche, BMWs and Mercedes. In fact, I see you have a copy of *Mercedes Enthusiast* magazine among your collection. And if I examined your computer browsing history, I'd find you watch a load of car videos, wouldn't I? Why don't we stop with the crap? What model was it?'

Gary shifted on his seat. 'I can't be totally sure. I think it was a second-generation model, a 126.'

'And what year would that make it?'

'Anything from between 1979 to 1991.'

'But we could narrow that down if you gave us its registration.'

'I don't know it.'

'Oh, come on. You must have taken note of it. It would have driven right past this window, and you'd have gone to check it out.'

'No. I don't know the car's registration. I have an interest in Mercs, from the classic car point of view, but I didn't pay attention to the car reg, honest!'

Morgan gave a brief smile. 'Oh, well, we'll have to leave it at that, won't we?'

The man nodded. 'If there's anything else I can help you with . . .'

'We'll be sure to ask you. You are aware that I can charge you with perverting the cause of justice if you refuse to assist me with my inquiries?'

'Er, yes. But I'm not refusing.'

'Or if you deny knowing a detail that could help us in tracking down these men.'

'I don't know anything else.'

Morgan gave him a gimlet eye. 'Then thank you for your cooperation. If anything springs to mind or your wife happens to know the car registration for that Mercedes, call me.'

He placed his business card on top of the magazines and both he and Emma left.

Outside, Emma turned to him. 'How did you guess he was into cars?'

'Take a look at the VW Golf parked over there. It's in pristine condition. The paintwork is immaculate, the chrome is buffed. I bet there isn't a spot of dirt on it. Whoever keeps it in that condition is a car enthusiast and most car lovers are usually into all sorts of motors. The magazines were another giveaway. I mean, what man keeps a pile of car mags in the kitchen?'

'Only somebody who reads them there.'

'Exactly, and from where he was sitting, he could see vehicles arriving or leaving the complex. He must also spend loads of time outside working on his car, cleaning it, polishing it and so on.'

She nodded. 'In the parking area, where he'd see who else was about.'

'Uh-huh. I think Mr Shardlow observes all the comings and goings here. He knows exactly who drives what and for some reason is keeping his trap shut.'

Emma agreed. 'His body language suggested the same. He was dead nervous.'

'I suppose the suspects could even have threatened him or his missus.'

'Then how do we get him to talk?' she asked.

'I need to think about that. At least we've narrowed the car down to a specific make and model. Maybe the tech team can find out who owns it.'

'Could be worth a shot.'

'Come on, I need a coffee. You can treat me to one and a nice sticky cake for being a genius.'

While William was waiting for news regarding the burned material found at the Corbys' house, he continued ringing John Dickson's contacts.

The defamatory articles in the *Gazette* were annoying. Not only because they were gaining gravitas every day John was missing, but readers online had begun commenting, many believing there was no smoke without fire. Their anger was no longer about the unseemly conduct of one high-ranking police officer, but had spilled over to include all police officers. Public distrust in the force was now becoming apparent, with every fresh article inciting further rage from the public. HQ would have to make a greater effort to quell the unrest.

Rumour was bad enough; these articles were on another level, with their damning claims and supposed evidence to back them up.

William was old school. Over the decades, he and his fellow officers had fought hard to keep crime off the streets and the people of Staffordshire safe. It hadn't been easy and sometimes they'd failed to get it right, but they'd worked hard – bloody hard. To lose face in such a way was sickening. He wished he'd got out before this shit-storm. Now, he was not only obliged to stay on for longer than he intended or wanted, but he'd been tasked with finding somebody who would be impossible to unearth.

John had contacts that the chief constable knew nothing about. He could melt away, disappear forever if he so desired. It would only take one phone call. What kept William from throwing in the towel was that the only person John had rung on the night he vanished did not appear to be one of his trusted associates. In fact, he had barely known the man.

William could always smell trouble. And Bradley Chapman was trouble.

William suspected that Bradley had been racing back and forth to his daughter's house, while the ashes there told their own story. Whether this was related to John Dickson's disappearance was yet to be established, but William's mind was conjuring numerous possibilities, all of which seemed plausible.

At the same time, he supposed John might have been involved in some underhand business with the man and it was even Bradley who had rung the office to demand a meeting. After all, John had been friends with Bradley's son-in-law, Alex Corby. A question mark now hung over the events that had transpired at the Maddox Club, when both John and Alex had stayed overnight, and the boy in the next room had died. Of the five men present that night, four were now dead. Bradley, whose best friend Cooper had buried the boy's body, might be linked in some way.

A knock at the door interrupted his thought process.

'Come in,' he called.

Jamie entered the office, his eyes shining, and stood to attention in front of the desk. William was struck by the man's enthusiasm. Jamie had shown loyalty and discretion in the recent past, and John had been considering recruiting him into the syndicate.

'Sir,' said Jamie. 'I've just been on the phone to the pub in Newborough. The bartender doesn't remember seeing the superintendent but a couple of his customers, who are there now, said a car passed through the village at high speed that night. I thought I should nip over and speak to them.'

'I'll come with you,' said William. He got to his feet. Taking a break from the office might help him think more clearly.

Kate cursed. She'd rung the number that Stanka had messaged her from earlier, only to find it switched off. What was Stanka playing at?

She'd sent Emma and Morgan to the apartment blocks near the kilns, while she'd headed downtown to talk to those people who lived on the streets. Once more, she was on the hunt for Farai. This time as part of her investigation into finding Maja.

She began her search at an encampment not far from the main shopping area, where tents and makeshift shelters were pitched on scrubland. Among the detritus were sleeping bags, gas canisters and even a filthy frying pan.

Kate stepped over the abandoned food packets and empty plastic bottles, towards a mound covered by several tatty blankets. Squatting beside it, she shook the person underneath awake. She tried not to recoil at the foul breath that spat, 'Fuck off!'

She shook the person again. 'I'm looking for a man called Farai.' She described him.

The blankets moved and, like a creature shedding skin, fell away to reveal a grubby-faced woman with matted brown hair. 'What's it worth?'

Kate held out a twenty-pound note. 'Yours if you can direct me to somebody who knows where Farai is.'

The woman licked dry lips. Her eyes darted to the money and across the scrubland. 'Him. Turk. He knew something.' The man she was pointing at was sifting through a brown paper bag. Kate pushed the money into the woman's hands and made for Turk. He caught sight of her at the last minute, jumped to his feet and began running.

'Turk! I only want to ask some questions.' She pounded across the scrubland, diving over large rubbish bags that were scattered like black boulders. Turk was fast on his feet. He'd almost reached the street. She raced on, shouting for him to stop. Turk darted across the road. Behind him, traffic impeded her crossing. By the time she had made it to the other side, Turk had disappeared. She stomped back to the scrubland only to discover the woman had also gone. Kicking out at the pile of discarded blankets, she swore again.

'Give in, Kate. Admit it. You aren't up to this. Jack it all in. Go to Australia and spend time with your family. That would be best for everyone.'

A man looked up from a can of cider and laughed. 'That's the first sign of madness, you know. Talking to yourself,' he slurred.

'What the fuck do you know about anything?' she snapped.

He bared his yellow teeth. 'Fuck you, copper!'

She stormed away, annoyed with herself for acting out of character. The man wasn't at fault. She was. She was becoming somebody she didn't recognise.

CHAPTER SIXTEEN

DAY THREE – LATE AFTERNOON

William immediately liked the feel of the Red Lion. It was his sort of pub; a reminder of the good old days when he and his colleagues would gather, joking, enjoying each other's company.

He stood beside the roaring fire and studied the painting of red-coated riders on white horses, hounds at their feet, while Jamie questioned two men. His mind drifted to evenings spent in establishments like this with Kate's father, Mitch, way back when they were both young sergeants. The years had flown past. What would Mitch have made of his daughter? William guessed he would have been proud of how she had turned out. She had integrity and determination, a rare combination, but one that made her an obstacle for the likes of John Dickson. She'd identified him for what he was, and since then had been on his tail.

John's disappearance would be confounding for Kate. She must be frustrated that he wasn't around to face the accusations. William had a fair idea it was her who had leaked the information to the *Gazette*. He just wasn't sure what to do about it. Not while John was missing. He had checked his own burner again before leaving the station. There was still no news from John Dickson. Had he gone to ground like a fox chased by hounds, or had he been mauled to death?

'Sir, these gentlemen have been helpful. They claim they saw a silver Mercedes estate driving at speed through the village in the direction of the main road at around ten past eight,' said Jamie. 'No reg, though.'

William crossed the short distance to join the two witnesses, both on bar stools. They looked at home here. *Regulars*.

'The car didn't slow down,' he said.

'No. In fact, it sped up, didn't it, Charlie?'

The second man nodded. 'That's right. It took off up the hill at a rate of knots.'

'Did you see if there were any passengers?' William asked.

'I'm pretty certain the driver was alone.'

'You didn't catch sight of the driver's face, by any chance?'

'I'm afraid not. It shot past so quickly, I couldn't see the person at all.'

'And you're certain of the time?'

'Absolutely. I'd promised to be home by half past eight,' said the first man. 'I checked my watch as we left the pub, just before the stupid sod came haring down the road.'

William thanked the men. He cast about the pub one last time. He liked the look of the stylish leather chair next to a single table. He might come back when he retired, spend a quiet hour with a pint in front of the fire and reminisce about times gone by.

'I thought we might stop off at the Corby residence on the way back to the station,' he said to Jamie.

'Any reason for that, sir?'

'A whim. Alex Corby was one of the superintendent's close friends. Maybe he stopped off there for some reason, could even have met somebody there.'

'I'm on board with that theory, sir.'

No matter that he'd already visited the place, William still believed there was some connection between it and whatever had happened to John.

Maybe daylight would throw up more clues. And four eyes were better than two.

◆ ◆ ◆

Kate sat at the rear of the coffee shop, eyes on the front door. She'd been told that a man matching Farai's description had been seen here on a couple of occasions. The oat milk latte was lukewarm and unappealing. Nevertheless, she remained in situ, aware of wasting precious time, hoping beyond hope that he would appear. If he didn't, she was out of ideas. She hadn't been able to locate the pimp the last few months, so why should now be any different?

She was desperately weary of everything. It was obvious, even to her, that it had taken its toll. She really should let go. After all, Dickson was dead. Her crusade to bring him down ought to be over, yet still she was embroiled in what felt like a Groundhog Day.

The door to the shop opened and Kate's muscles tensed. Harriet Khatri strolled to the counter and ordered takeaway coffees. Catching sight of Kate, she wandered across.

'Tell me you're closer to finding the superintendent,' she said quietly.

'We're following up a number of leads,' Kate replied.

Harriet's face remained impassive. 'That's the usual crap we feed the media. I take it to mean you have jack shit.'

Kate felt her lips tighten. She refused to be intimidated by her colleague. 'We're pursuing several lines of inquiry. When we have something concrete, we'll be sure to pass it on. That's all I'm prepared to say on the matter. You surely understand how sensitive this investigation has become.'

Harriet didn't blink. 'You need to track him down and fast. Every lie the paper prints is another he has to deny. The longer this goes on, the worse it will become for him.'

'I'm fully aware of the situation, Harriet. I want to find him as much as you do.'

'Probably not for the same reasons, though.'

'What's that supposed to mean?'

'I don't think I need to explain myself.'

'No, carry on.'

Harriet gave a tight smile in response.

Kate lowered her voice even further. 'If you have a problem with me leading the investigation, take it up with DCI Chase or the chief constable, because I'd like nothing better than to let somebody else take the reins on this. I have the whole of the top brass waiting for me to magically produce the elusive superintendent. When I do, he'll have to account for his actions, possibly even face charges. Then where will that leave me? I'll be the one accused of having pursued some sort of witch hunt, determined to catch him. I can't win, Harriet, so if you want to step up and take over, be my bloody guest!'

'Ha!' Harriet's voice was hollow. She began to turn away. Kate pulled at her arm, forcing her fellow detective to face her again.

'Let me make myself perfectly clear. I don't give a fuck if those articles are telling lies or truths, my sole aim is to do my job as best as I can and track him down. What transpires after that is out of my hands. I'll do my job because I was asked to, not because of any personal feelings.'

Harriet's lips twitched. 'Then why are you skulking in here?'

It took every ounce of effort not to snap at the woman. 'Following a lead . . . Not that it's any of your business.'

She stared hard into Harriet's eyes, fists clenched, ready to do battle. Then, without warning, her anger evaporated. It would be a welcome relief if Harriet or somebody were to see through her act.

She would be free of this horrendous subterfuge and deceit. She could be herself again.

The barista called out Harriet's order. She raised her hand in acknowledgement. 'I'd better get those drinks back before they go cold. And, just for the record, I don't believe you are trying hard enough. If I were you, I'd be concerned something bad has happened to him. You need to pull your finger out, Kate, or I *shall* take it up with the chief constable.'

Her words fired Kate up again. *Bitch!*

Harriet collected the cardboard carrier before leaving without so much as a glance in Kate's direction. Kate uncurled her fists. *Damn the woman!* She had succeeded in unnerving her.

The chair legs scraped against the flooring as Kate jumped to her feet. She reached the door and paused. Further down the road, Harriet was climbing into the back of a surveillance van.

Kate stepped away from the door and moved to a table where she could observe the van without being seen. After ten minutes passed and the vehicle was still stationary, she wondered if Harriet was watching the café. Operation Moonbeam was a people-trafficking investigation. They'd already picked up some illegals from a biscuit factory. What if they suspected there were more working here? She shut her eyes, tested her memory and recalled seeing the van parked in the same spot when she'd come into the café. In which case, Harriet would have seen her arrive. Her spurious coffee run was purely to find out what Kate was up to and if she was trampling over her operation.

'In a contest between you and Harriet as to who can reach the traffickers first, I know which horse I would back,' hissed Dickson.

'Then it's a bloody good thing you can't place a bet,' she muttered under her breath.

◆ ◆ ◆

Emma and Morgan had returned to the office to find it empty.

'What do you suggest we do now?' said Emma.

Grabbing her by the arm, Morgan pulled her towards him. 'Do you really need me to answer that?'

She pushed him away. 'Not here, you oaf. We can't be seen . . . you know . . . here. The bloody walls have ears.'

'Let them talk. I don't give a toss.'

'Well, I do.'

His face turned serious. 'You are okay about us seeing each other, aren't you?'

'One hundred per cent. It just feels wrong to carry on at work. I'm so used to you being a colleague, that while I'm happy – more than happy – to be with you outside, I can't break from habit. You know how seriously I take my job.'

He nodded. And with a solemn face said, 'I understand. No necking in the office or corridor, and definitely no humping against the filing cabinets, especially when Kate is briefing us.'

She spluttered, and laughed.

He sat down at his desk with a sigh. 'First the super, now a teenager and some traffickers. Missing Persons should be handling this. We're a special crimes unit.'

'It doesn't get more special than hunting for your own superintendent, who might, incidentally, be dead.'

'I really hope we aren't going to get stuck with this case for much longer. We've gone straight from capturing the bolt gun killer to this without a break. We're due some leave, and I was hoping we could spend it together.'

'Then Kate would only have Jamie.'

'Who has proved his worth. It's not like we have to deal with a murder every day, or week for that matter . . . or month. Besides, if something big turned up, they could draft somebody in to help.'

'Given DCI Chase is currently assisting us, I reckon they're horrendously short-staffed.'

'Are you looking for excuses?'

His face was earnest, eyebrows slightly raised. She had the urge to hug him.

'Not in the least. I can't think of anything nicer, but if we both go at the same time—'

'Oh, come on, Emma. Think about it. See how this investigation pans out, then we'll bugger off for a week or two somewhere sunny and warm. You. Me. Cocktails on the beach: margaritas, frozen strawberry daiquiris, even piña coladas. What do you say?'

'I say I had you down as a pint-and-pie man.'

He cocked his head. 'I'm offended. Listen, why don't I take you out to a bar tonight and show you what a gentleman I really can be?'

'It's a school night.'

'And we're not at school.'

'But we're working an investigation. Two investigations. How about at the weekend? If we're not up to our necks in work.'

'You're on.'

'And as for your idea about getting away together, well, I'm warming to it.'

Morgan rubbed his hands together. 'Great. Now that's been decided, let's get back to the task in hand.'

'Looking for the proverbial needle.'

'Not like you to be defeatist, Emma. Let's go with what we know. We have a make and model of car and an idea of when it was last in the bottle kilns area. There must be some footage somewhere. Let's run with that for the time being.'

215

The rear garden at the Corbys' house looked far more friendly during the daylight when William could see across it to the reservoir. It wasn't the best weather, yet the woodlands were beginning to display their autumn colours, the water was reflecting clouds that scudded across the pale blue sky and a formation of geese flew a circuit that returned them to the water, where they honked noisily before taking off again.

William casually made for the outhouse – a wooden structure which he knew to be locked. For the sake of appearances, he tried the door again, knowing Jamie was only a few paces behind him. From there, he wandered across to the ashes where he'd found the material and crouched down. There was nothing else to be seen. Jamie caught up with him.

'Have you found anything, sir?'

William had considered telling Jamie about his earlier find, then decided against it. For all his enthusiasm, Jamie wasn't part of the syndicate and until William was certain of John's fate, he didn't want to share his thoughts. He got to his feet. 'Nothing. What about you?'

'Well, the place is definitely not lived in. Every window and door are tightly shut, and I'd imagine the alarm system has been set. Nobody could break in. I doubt the superintendent would rendezvous at the house, although he might have agreed to meet somebody outside. After all, the gate locks are broken.'

'I wondered if that might be the case.'

'Then he would only have arranged to meet somebody who's familiar with this place, knew it was empty and the gates were unlocked.'

'I've spoken to the owner's father, Bradley Chapman, who denies ringing Superintendent Dickson.'

'Is there anybody else who knew both the super and the Corbys?'

'His wife, Gwen. She was out that evening. Yes, we should check out her alibi, Jamie. Other than that, I'm stumped. Unless . . . unless it was somebody connected to the Maddox Club murder.' A name popped into his head. 'Cooper Monroe's daughter – Sierra.'

'Did she know the people who lived here?'

'Her father worked for Alex Corby.'

'But how would that be relevant? Why would she ring the super?'

Maybe Sierra knew something about the night the boy had died and had rung John to discuss it, or even blackmail him. Her father had taken his own life in prison, but there was every chance he had passed on some information beforehand, for Sierra to use when she needed to. William grunted. This was a supposition worth pursuing.

'We'll speak to Sierra,' he said. As he crossed the garden, things seemed to fall into place: Bradley was Cooper's best friend, and he and Sierra had challenged the coroner's report on the death of her father. Neither were happy with the verdict of suicide. It was possible Sierra had arranged to meet John here.

However, none of this explained why John Dickson had then got in his car and tear-arsed to the airfield. It didn't make sense yet, but it would. William would get to the bottom of it, and nobody would stand in his way.

CHAPTER SEVENTEEN

DAY THREE – EVENING

Kate was on her way back to the station when she received a call from Big Harry.

'Farai will meet you at the Golden Moon at eight o'clock tonight. He says to come alone.'

The phone went dead immediately, leaving Kate relieved she no longer had to search for the elusive pimp. It was a breakthrough she badly needed. She tried Stanka again, only to find the phone still switched off. Stanka had gone to ground. Cursing, she typed out a message, urging the girl to contact her immediately. With luck, Stanka would sporadically check her phone and read it.

With an hour to go before she could meet Farai, she decided to head home, grab some food and arrange another Skype call time with Tilly. Talking to herself in Dickson's voice, imagining he was watching her or in her house, was a complete mindfuck. She needed to talk to somebody unconnected to all the shit going on here, who would in turn anchor her. With Chris's voice gone, Kate recognised she was becoming unhinged. Tilly was the only person who could help her crawl out of this dark place.

Because Sydney was ten hours ahead, Kate didn't expect Tilly to pick up her message immediately, even though her stepsister was a very early riser and, like Kate, ran regularly each morning, usually before the day got too warm. It was springtime in Australia, a time of renewal and hope, whereas in the UK, the days were becoming shorter and the temperature cooler.

Settled in front of the computer, a mug of tea by her side, she read online national newspapers, not that she was interested in what was going on in the world, rather she needed to keep Dickson's voice out of her head.

She jumped when the Skype ringtone sounded, and Tilly appeared. 'Hi, Kate. Surprise! We're up with the larks and look who I have with me today,' she said immediately.

A small face joined hers. 'Hi, Auntie Kate!'

Kate's heart swelled. Even though she'd only met her nephew once, she adored him. A familiar ache, a reminder of how empty her own life was, began in her chest. She ignored it.

Talking to five-year-old Daniel was the tonic she needed, his happy smile lifting her flagging spirits. Words tumbled excitedly as he told her about a school trip to the Taronga Zoo planned for that day, reeling off the animals he was most excited about seeing, including the five baby lion cubs that had been born in August.

His enthusiasm made her smile. For the first time that day, she felt relaxed.

'Now you've told her your news, off you go, sweetie,' said Tilly. 'You can watch telly in your bedroom for a while. Let Mummy talk to Auntie Kate.'

'Okay. Oh, and Auntie Kate, Daddy's going to make omelettes and strawberry smoothies for brekkie, before I go.'

'Wow! Sounds delicious.'

'Love you,' he shouted, then bounced from the seat. The screen was adjusted, and Tilly came into view.

'Daniel was desperate to speak to you,' she explained. 'He's been ridiculously excited about this trip for days. He got up three times during the night to ask if it was time to go yet. By 4 a.m. I gave in and got up with him. He'll be pooped tonight when he gets back. Anyway, when I saw your message, I thought I'd call you so you could speak to us both. Daniel is still your number one fan. He keeps asking when you are coming to visit us. And as for that dinosaur you bought him – well, nobody but nobody is allowed to touch it. You'd think it was made of gold.'

As Tilly spoke cheerily, Kate couldn't account for the sadness that suddenly flowered in her chest.

'It's so . . . nice . . . to . . .' Tears stung her eyes. The truth hit her. She missed them. More than that, she wanted what Tilly had: a normal family life. One where she and Chris made omelettes and smoothies for their child's breakfast. She swallowed hard in vain. The internal sorrow continued to balloon.

'Hey, are you okay?'

'My hormones are playing up,' said Kate, waving away Tilly's concerns.

'Don't give me that. You're upset.'

Kate couldn't halt the tears. Once the first few escaped, others followed and soon she couldn't control them or the sobs that accompanied them.

'Hey! Come on now. Stop that, or you'll set me off.'

Kate snivelled, wiped her face with the back of her hands. 'I'll be . . . okay . . . in . . . a sec. Sorry.'

'You have nothing to be sorry about. Kate, you're overdoing it. You've gone from one major investigation straight into another. You've had no *you* time.'

'I . . . miss you.'

'Well, get your arse over here, girl!' Despite the bright smile that accompanied her words, Tilly looked concerned, lines forming on her forehead.

'I shall. I . . . promise. As soon . . . as this investigation . . . is over.' Kate inhaled and sniffed again to regain further control. She'd spoken the words before; however, this time she meant them. Once she'd found Maja, she was going to walk away from the Dickson investigation, tell William to hand it over, and catch a plane. Staying with her sister and her family would fix her. She had to do something before the madness set in even deeper.

'You'd love it here,' said Tilly. 'And we'd love having you to stay. Now, tell me, what's bothering you?'

'I was feeling lonely. Seeing Daniel made me realise how lucky I am to have family. I miss Chris. So badly. Time isn't a healer, Tilly. Not for me, anyway. I need to get away altogether, from this house, work, everything Chris and I shared. Just for a short while until I can feel better.'

'Oh, honey. You never gave yourself a chance to get over his death, did you? You've been pursuing that corrupt cop, determined to find out if he'd had anything to do with his murder, driving yourself mad. You need to step away. Look at you! You need looking after.' Her voice was gentle, making Kate feel sad again. 'You could really do with this cop showing up and getting slammed in jail or at least finding his body. Then you could get closure. That's what you need.'

'She's right. Still, there's no chance you'll tell her what happened. Especially as you bottled it last time.'

Kate flinched at the voice in her head. The last thing she needed was to be listening to Dickson when she was talking to Tilly. This was *her* time. How dare he invade it.

'Then you'll have to add her to the list of people you care about so much that you're hiding a dark secret from them all!'

She flinched again, causing Tilly to ask if she was okay.

'Yes, there's an annoying fly buzzing about in the room,' she replied smoothly.

'Are you still looking for him?' asked Tilly.

221

'Half of the team is. The other half is searching for a trafficked teenager.'

'They spread you thin over there, don't they? If you're running two investigations, it's little wonder you're struggling. I know making DCI is important to you, but don't put yourself through the wringer over it.'

'The cases are related to one another. I find the girl, then I might be able to find the officer.'

Tilly rested her eyes on Kate. 'Kate, is there something you're not saying about this investigation, because you seem to be . . . different. You have a worried look when you talk about this officer. A haunted look.'

Kate swallowed again. Even though they'd been separated for years, the connection they had always shared as youngsters was still there. She could read Tilly, and Tilly could read her.

This was Kate's opportunity to come clean. To unburden herself.

'You won't say anything. You disposed of my body and covered up my death! She'll be horrified. You will lose your sister forever. She won't want to know you if you confess to her what you've done.'

She shut down the voice. It was now or never. Tilly loved her. She *would* understand. Emotion coursed throughout her body, forcing her lips apart and releasing the words she fought hard to retain. 'Is Daniel in earshot?'

'No. Nobody is. The door is shut. Why?'

'Tilly, nobody will ever find him. He's dead.' There. It was out in the open. Just speaking the words was a blessed relief. But now she had to face the consequences. She held her breath as she waited for Tilly to respond.

Tilly blinked several times before speaking. 'Did you . . . Did you?'

She nodded quickly. 'Yes. It was self-defence. He tried to shoot me. We wrestled for the gun. It went off. I didn't kill him in cold blood.' Her guts writhed uncomfortably. She couldn't read Tilly suddenly, as though that valued connection between them had vanished.

'*I warned you,*' said Dickson. '*You called it wrong. You've just gone down in her estimation. She'll probably even turn you in.*'

Tilly's eyes were like saucers. 'Jeez, Kate.'

'I know. All I can do is wait for the heat to go off, for them to decide he's gone into hiding and let it drop.'

'Will they, though?'

Kate shrugged.

Tilly edged closer to the screen and lowered her voice. 'Kate, are you out of your mind? What the hell are you thinking of? You should give yourself up. You were only trying to protect yourself. Tell them.'

Kate swallowed hard before saying, 'I got rid of the body.'

'Fuck!' Tilly lifted her head to the ceiling. 'Why?! Why didn't you call the police and explain? Do it now. Tell them where to find the body.'

'I can't. No one will be able to find it. It's . . . gone. Tilly, I had no other choice. I'd lured him to a meeting to get him to confess he'd had something to do with Chris's murder. I riled him. Now I'm in way over my head and the only way to get through it is to keep playing along with this charade. There are other officers tied in with him and his plans, who will come after me if they suspect for one second that I've had anything to do with his death. I can't take that risk. They mean business. They'll kill me.'

Tilly shook her head. 'I can't believe this. It's madness.'

'I wish that weren't the case, but it is. I'm in such a mess. I have to bluff my way through, pray the case gets dropped due to lack of evidence.'

'You're being foolishly optimistic if you think that'll happen any time soon.'

'But it will. In time.'

Tilly sighed for the longest while before saying, 'Did he confess to having something to do with Chris's murder?'

'Yes. I recorded everything, but the device got broken during the scuffle, leaving me with nothing to support what had taken place.'

She detailed the events of the evening and explained how they would seem suspicious to anyone interviewing her.

After she'd finished, Tilly remained silent. Kate tried to read her stony expression.

As I predicted. You've blown it,' said Dickson.

Her stomach continued to squirm and twist. She'd banked on Tilly supporting her, especially as Kate had guarded her sister's own secrets in the past.

At last, Tilly spoke. 'Are you sure they can't find the cadaver?'

'Positive.'

'And you've covered your back.'

'Yes.'

'Then as I see it, you have two choices: give yourself up immediately, or keep your cool and play this out. But, honey, if you choose the second option, you'll be taking a massive gamble. It could backfire spectacularly on you. There's no way they'll give up searching for this man. For heaven's sake, he's a police officer! They're never going to let go of this until they know exactly what's happened to him. They might even bring in more officers to investigate. And then there's the fact that modern forensic methods might just cough up something you thought you'd got away with.'

'She's speaking sense. At some point when your team has finished shilly-shallying about, they'll bring in a whole new team and you'll have no control over what they find.'

Kate shook her head. She refused to listen to him. She clung to the belief that she would get through this so she could help Stanka, and others like her. Somebody had to stop the rot that currently was permeating the force. Somebody had to stand up to the syndicate. She couldn't do that if she was behind bars. 'I hear you, but I won't give myself up. I can handle this. I just need time.'

Tilly cocked her head. 'Sis, I love you but is that really the right way to go about things?'

'I've gone too far. I've left myself with little choice other than to see this through.'

Tilly gave a heavy sigh. 'Okay. Do what you have to. Then when the time is right, you should think about distancing yourself from Staffordshire. Maybe you should think about giving up the force altogether. Start a new life here.'

Her words found their mark, lifting Kate's mood in an instant.

'You'd be happy for me to do that?'

'You know I would. You've had my back in the past, Kate. I'll have yours, no matter what you decide to do.'

'Thank—' The lump that rose in her throat cut off her speech. Tilly had just given her the strength she had so desperately needed to battle on.

'Hey, you can always count on me.'

Kate jumped at the sound of a small voice. 'Mummy, I can't find my animal book.'

Tilly turned her head. 'Can't Daddy help?'

'He's still asleep.'

'Have you looked in your bedroom?'

'I've looked *everywhere*. It's not there. Mummy, I *need* it.' The voice reminded Kate of the way Tilly had sulked when they'd been younger, a lengthy whine that spurred on the recipient to deal with whatever was troubling the child.

'I'll come and look in a minute.'

'But I need it *now!*'

Tilly gave Kate an apologetic look. Kate helped her make her decision.

'You go. I'm fine. I'll deal with this, Tilly. Then we'll discuss me coming over.'

'I can call you back.'

'It's fine. I have to go out. Really. I'll call you again. Soon.'

'I won't say a word. Not even to Jordan.'

'I know I can trust you. Thank you.'

'Love you, sis.'

'Love you more.'

Long after the screen had gone blank, Kate continued to stare into space. The initial euphoria of having unburdened herself passed suddenly, drowned by doubts over her actions. Telling Tilly had been downright stupid. She'd allowed her emotions to rule. Now she felt vulnerable. A hazy vision of Dickson sitting opposite her kept her glued to her chair.

'If you want to stay safe, you should never confide in anybody. Not even family. Nobody can be trusted. Once sense kicks in and Tilly realises her son admires somebody who is a criminal, she'll be unable to keep it to herself. You can't go to Australia. You can't run. By this time tomorrow, Jordan will know. He'll tell his best mate and then . . .'

Kate's mouth was bone dry. The words caused her heart to thud against her ribcage like a prisoner banging against a door for release. She'd never be able to start afresh, not with a secret that big out of the bag. What had she been thinking? She'd had everything under control. Pouring her heart out to her stepsister had been a huge mistake.

◆ ◆ ◆

William had dropped Jamie off at the station with instructions to obtain Sierra's address, then set off alone to interview Gwen Chapman. He had considered taking Jamie with him, but if the woman knew something about John, William wanted to be the first to hear it. Jamie was somebody who would jump through fire, no questions asked, which was the reason William had asked Kate to divide the team, ensuring he and Jamie worked together. Morgan and Emma were far sharper and keener. They'd question his methods, whereas Jamie simply went along for the ride.

Knowing Bradley would be obstructive, William wasn't going to the Chapmans' house, but rather a health club in Uttoxeter that Gwen used on a regular basis – a fact that had been uncovered when they'd been investigating Alex Corby's death. A quick call to the club had confirmed Gwen was scheduled an hour-long facial at 5 p.m., which meant he could be there when she came out from her appointment.

He hummed in tune with the 'Flower Duet' from the opera *Lakmé*. He knew nothing about the opera and the French lyrics eluded him; nevertheless, he liked the duet. Classical music was his go-to when he needed to cogitate.

The music came to an end as he pulled into the car park. He turned off the radio and waited for Gwen to emerge, casually getting out of his car as she walked to hers. He called out to her and made his way towards her.

'Mrs Chapman, what a surprise.'

Her perfectly arched eyebrows raised. Gwen was a fine-looking woman, older than her husband by several years, yet still giving the impression of somebody in their forties.

'Do I know you?'

William held out his hand. 'DCI Chase. We met at the station, last year.'

'Ah, yes. I remember you.'

'Funny running into you like this. I was at your house only the other day.'

Her face took on a guarded look.

'Oh, nothing serious. I was hoping your husband had been in contact with Superintendent Dickson, what with him being a close friend of your son-in-law's.'

'We never saw anything of him. He was Alex's friend, not ours.' The response was similar to Bradley's and William couldn't help but wonder if it had been rehearsed. Gwen brushed at some invisible dust on the sleeve of a velvet jacket. 'Well, it was nice seeing you again, DCI Chase. Erm, are you a member here?'

'No, I was checking out the place. I'm due to retire very soon, so I thought I'd see what amenities they offered. I need to keep fit and I'm not very self-motivated. I ought to enrol in some gentle classes to get me started. Would you recommend it?'

'Yes, there are lots of different classes and quite a few men, also retired, who attend. Now, if you'll excuse me.' She made to leave.

'Actually, I'm glad I bumped into you. Your husband told me you were out Monday night.'

She stiffened at his words. 'What business is it of yours?'

'I'm investigating John's disappearance. It sounds odd, but he might have met somebody at your daughter's old place by the reservoir. It would help me to know it wasn't you.'

'Met at Fiona's?'

'It's only a theory, but the timings fit, and John knows the house.'

She shook her head vehemently. 'It wasn't me. I haven't been there since Fiona moved out.'

'Then could you tell me who you went out with? Just so I'm clear on the matter.'

'Am I under suspicion for something?'

'Far from it, Mrs Chapman. You'd be helping me hugely if you told me your whereabouts. I already know Mr Chapman was at home.'

'I was with Francesca Gibbs. We went to Stafford for the evening. You can check with her.'

'If you could give me her contact details, that would be most helpful.' He gave a smile he knew would disarm her, pulled out a notebook and jotted down the details.

'Thank you, Mrs Chapman. I wish you a pleasant evening.'

She caught his gaze. 'I hope you didn't come here to deliberately ambush me, DCI Chase.'

He held up both hands in surrender. 'Not at all. I'm here purely to check out the health club. Maybe see you here in a few weeks after I've taken my retirement.'

She gave a sharp nod and headed towards her car. William left for the club, aware she was watching him and spent ten minutes talking to the gym instructor manning the desk before coming away with leaflets that he tossed into his car.

He was sure Gwen was telling the truth about her evening out, but all the same, she was nervous about something. The Chapmans were definitely keeping secrets.

Kate had washed her face and given herself a stern talking to. Now she'd confessed to Tilly, there was no turning back. She had to hope her stepsister would be true to her word and say nothing about their conversation. In the meantime, she had a meeting with Farai, who she was determined would tell her whatever he knew.

The streets were mostly empty as she drove through town, a fact she put down to the heavy rain that had begun an hour earlier and was flooding her windscreen. Her wiper blades squealed complaints with every movement. The rubbers needed replacing, a job she'd sort out when she had time. She turned on the radio to drown out their noise. Water whooshed under the chassis as the car splashed through the black puddles that had rapidly pooled. One Direction's 'The Story of My Life' came on, causing Kate to snort angrily. Her story was rapidly becoming a series of disastrous chapters. She felt the spectre of Dickson watching her from the back seat and, even covered by warm sleeves, gooseflesh pimpled along her arms. She reminded herself self-reproach was creating these hallucinations, messing with her head. She had to assuage it, or she would continue to plummet.

'Chris, help me,' she whispered. The only reply came from the torrential rain that beat an angry rhythm on the Audi's roof, drowning out the chorus of the song. She was horribly alone.

Then it struck her that there was somebody else she could ask for assistance – Farai. He'd spent months protecting himself, Rosa and Stanka from Dickson, which proved he had some humanity.

'Don't be naïve. He was only hiding them because he knew if I got to them, I'd get to him too.'

This time, Dickson's voice didn't startle her. She was aware he would offer a counter-argument to every one of her considerations. In a way, he was like Chris, only Chris had offered solutions, whereas Dickson brought up her failings. It came as no surprise. After all, it was how she'd perceived him in life – her nemesis. What scared her was how easily she had come to accept his voice.

'It's because you've changed, Kate. In killing me, you've traversed to the dark side. You know, you'll never hear Chris again. He won't associate with somebody who has gone rotten.'

She clamped her lips shut. She turned up the radio, now playing Sia's 'Unstoppable'. Two streets from the Golden Moon, Stanka rang her.

'Thank goodness you called. Are you okay?' she said.

'Yes. We found Farai.'

'I'm on my way to meet him.'

'No, you don't understand. We went to meet him. He is dead.'

'When?'

'Ten minutes ago. We left him there. We ran.'

'Where, Stanka?'

'Behind the Golden Moon.'

'I'm almost there. Where are you?'

'I must talk to you, Kate.'

'Okay. Tell me where you are, and I'll come and meet you.'

'I'm not safe.'

'I can keep you safe.'

'No. You can't. Meet me in two hours. I'll be where I found you last time.'

'Okay. I'm at the Golden Moon now. I'll have to call this in.'

'He is in the alleyway, by the bins.'

Stanka hung up.

Sia returned, now singing the chorus, and Kate noticed the rain had eased during the brief conversation. She pulled up opposite the pub, a dingy affair with poor outside lighting and curtains drawn at the windows. Exiting the Audi, she crossed the road, oblivious to the steady drizzle that soaked her hair. She felt for the Maglite in her pocket and aimed its beam towards the entrance to the dark alleyway beside the pub. Sia's song continued to play in her mind as she swung her torch from side to side, wondering if this might be a set-up into which she'd walked blindly.

'Anyone here?' she called. 'It's the police. Show yourselves.'

There was no reply. She took a few more paces and swung the torch again. There was no sound. She set off again. This time the beam reached a collection of large recycling bins. She trained the light on each in turn, then along the ground, over a pile of black refuse bags. She edged forwards again, closer to the bins, torchlight falling on a discarded cardboard box, a broken chair, more bin bags and landing on a trainer, then another. The shoes were at odd angles to each other and attached to a pair of legs. She rushed forwards and stood in front of the body on the ground, recognising immediately the skinny frame, the dark hair, the sunken – almost skeletal – cheeks. A dark stain had mushroomed across his chest.

Transfixed by the sight, she watched as his face morphed into Dickson's. *'You won't get away with it.'*

She yelped in terror, dug her nails deep into her palms. 'You're not Dickson,' she murmured. 'You're not him.'

The lips seemed to move again. *'Go on, Kate. You've done it before. Dispose of the body.'*

She squeezed her eyes tightly shut. Instinct urged her to bolt before somebody suspected she was the perpetrator of this crime. 'It's Farai,' she told herself. 'Farai.' She opened her eyes. Dickson had disappeared. In his place was the pimp she'd spent months searching for. She should walk away from this. Ensure the murder was assigned to another team, but Big Harry knew she was meeting Farai and that would come back to bite her if she scarpered. Like it or not, this was part of her investigation and her responsibility. She turned her face from the sight to phone for assistance. The last thing she needed was another episode where she imagined the body to be Dickson's. She had to hold it together or she would fail.

CHAPTER EIGHTEEN

DAY THREE – LATE EVENING

Kate had rung her team and asked them to meet her. Although she was the first officer on the scene, she couldn't afford to remain there, given she had to travel to Stafford to meet Stanka. However, she wasn't going to play this one by anything other than the book, so she secured the scene while she waited for the others to arrive.

It gave her time to decide what to do about the young sex-worker. The girl might have witnessed the killing, or she might have been responsible for it. Either way, this was something Kate wanted to keep under wraps for the time being. Until she'd had the chance to speak to Stanka about this, she didn't want the team to discover the teenager had made contact with Farai, or even been in the vicinity of the Golden Moon.

She'd secured and then, using her phone, videoed the scene. She'd not spotted a murder weapon, but it was obvious Farai had been shot. Her money was on the traffickers silencing him before he could talk to either Stanka or Kate. The linchpin in this was Big Harry, who knew Farai was going to be at the Golden Moon that evening. Now it was a question of who else he had told.

Morgan's Jeep pulled up, and both he and Emma leapt out. Kate couldn't help but notice that both were dressed in tracksuits and Emma's hair had been pulled back hastily into a short ponytail.

It added fuel to her speculation that they'd progressed from friends into a more serious relationship.

'Who've we got?' Emma asked, as she stood beside the cordon to pull on shoe covers.

'Pimp by the name of Farai. He supplied the Maddox Club with underage prostitutes. He's been on the run, hiding out ever since the night of the boy's murder.'

'Looks like somebody caught up with him at last,' said Morgan.

'Could be the traffickers we're after. Farai bought some of his girls from them.'

Morgan ducked under the tape and spoke again. 'Why shoot him, though?'

'Maybe . . . they found out he'd arranged to meet me,' said Kate.

Morgan's jaw dropped. 'What the fuck! Meet you?'

'I know I should have kept you in the loop. But it was complicated. Farai was unwilling to speak to the police and took some convincing. In the end, I had to go through a contact who passed on a message. Farai had agreed to meet me, then . . . this!'

The rain had stopped and a small crowd was gathering outside the pub. As they stepped closer, Kate waved them back.

'Away from the cordon, please!' She turned back to Emma and Morgan. 'Morgan, can you deal with the onlookers and take statements from them? Find out if anyone saw anything at all.'

He looked for a moment as if he might challenge her, but a gentle nudge from Emma brought him around. With a quiet 'Sure,' he made for the people.

She spoke again to Emma. 'I hate to cut and run, but I really can't hang about any longer. Could you take over?'

'Where are you going?'

'Trust me, Emma, I'll tell you when the time is right.'

'Kate, you can't keep going solo. We're a team.'

'I'm aware of that. But this investigation is different to anything else we've dealt with. It has to be handled differently.'

Emma faced up to her. 'It doesn't seem to be working so far. There's a potential lead lying dead over there, murdered before we got a chance to interview him.'

'And I need to speak to another before the same thing happens.'

'Who?'

'I can't discuss that.'

Emma's lips tightened.

'Emma, I'll explain everything as soon as I can. I promise. You do trust me, don't you? Listen, I don't like this any more than you. I hate keeping things from you all. But there are times when some things aren't ready to be revealed. Isn't that so?' She looked at Emma then pointedly at Morgan.

Emma flushed. 'We were going to tell you. It's only been a few days—'

'And I don't mind. It's your business. For what it's worth, I'm happy for you both.'

There was a pause during which Emma glanced across at Morgan. 'You should tell him yourself that you're going.'

'He's busy. Besides, I don't want to get into an argument with him. I haven't got the time. Would you tell him that I had to follow up an urgent lead and I shall lay everything out on the table as soon as I can? A life is at stake here. I wouldn't do this to you otherwise.'

Emma nodded at last. 'Okay, I'll handle it.'

Blue flashing lights appeared at the end of the street.

'Looks like the support teams have arrived. Over to you,' said Kate. 'I'll talk to you later.'

She marched back to her car, stopping only to instruct a couple of uniformed officers. As she pulled away, she was aware of Emma observing her. She hoped she hadn't broken any trust between them. Part of her would have liked to have told Emma everything, or even simply that she was meeting Girl X. Another part counselled her to hold her tongue. She'd kept every aspect of her investigation into Dickson from her team, including Stanka, who was tied up in it all. Until she knew what it was Stanka had to tell her, she had no choice other than to continue to keep her officers in the dark.

It would take her half an hour to reach Stafford, which left her time to stop off at the pool hall and find Big Harry. With the chorus of Sia's song still playing in her head, she accelerated. Big Harry owed her some answers.

◆ ◆ ◆

The cat purred contentedly on William's lap as he scratched its ear. Sierra placed a mug of tea in front of him.

'You seem to have made a friend. Crystal's not normally keen on humans. Other than me, of course.'

'I guess she knows I like her. I've got two of my own. The secret is to not make a big fuss, and let them check you out. Slow blinks always work too. They soon work out what sort of person you are.'

'Crystal has decided you're okay, so that's good enough for me.'

He gave her a fatherly smile. Sierra had been through a lot over the last year. She'd been held hostage, almost losing her life to a crazy she-devil, discovered her father wasn't the upstanding citizen she'd believed him to be, watched him be sentenced to prison, then lost him forever. Following his death, she'd moved out of their family home, set up a new place on her own as well as handling his funeral arrangements and sorting out his estate. All of which had taken its toll. There was no youthful spark in her pale blue eyes. She had grown into adulthood before her time.

'I was really sorry to hear about Cooper,' said William.

'He didn't take his own life, no matter what the autopsies said. He was murdered.'

William sipped his tea. He had heard that under Bradley's stewardship, Sierra had challenged the original autopsy, and fought for a second, independent procedure to be performed. That pathologist hadn't found anything to contradict the first report, so her accusations were thrown out. However, it seemed she still refused to accept her father would take his own life.

'I understand the pathologists couldn't find any proof to suggest he was murdered.'

Sierra shrugged. 'Either whoever killed him was really clever or there was a cover-up.'

'You were very close to your father, weren't you?'

'Yes. Mum walking out as she did brought us closer.'

William nodded and gave her a small smile. 'It's always hard when you lose those closest to you. You rage against the world for a long time. I felt that way about my wife, Tanya, after she died.'

'Oh, I'm sorry.'

'Thank you. It was a long time ago. I'm simply saying I understand your anger, your frustration. It's only natural to feel the way you do. I blamed a whole bunch of people for Tanya's death before coming to the realisation it was fate.'

She shook her head. 'Maybe that's how you coped with your wife's death, but I knew my dad and there is no way he would have taken his own life.'

Although he hadn't come here to discuss Cooper's death with Sierra, he was curious. The young woman was adamant that her father hadn't taken his own life, and it didn't appear to be grief talking.

'Do you want to run your thoughts on the matter past me? I'm a good listener.'

'No, it's okay. I don't suppose you could do anything about it.'

The cat shifted on his lap, the purring like a small motor running. It was soothing.

Sierra changed the subject. 'You wanted to ask me about Superintendent Dickson.'

'That's right. It may seem odd, but I'm following up on everybody who knows him or had contact with him the last year.'

'I only saw him at Dad's trial.'

'You haven't seen him since?'

'No. I've had no reason to see him.' She looked blankly at him. William sensed confusion rather than anxiety. 'I know he's gone missing, and the papers are saying all sorts of things about him, about that night at the gentlemen's club. Is it true?'

'Honestly, we don't know, and until we locate him, we're unlikely to get to the bottom of it.'

'Why would you think I'd been in contact with him?'

'I'm simply crossing the Ts and dotting the Is.'

'Anyway, what would I talk to him about?'

'Your father?'

'I didn't talk to him about Dad!'

'My mistake, I assumed you might have spoken to him about your concerns over your father's death.' He offered an apologetic smile.

Sierra's forehead wrinkled. 'No. I didn't speak to him. I did speak to DI Kate Young, though. She was very understanding. Even encouraged me to request a second post-mortem. I like her. She's kind.'

'She's one of the best officers we have. I've known her since she was a child. I was best friends with her father.'

'Were you?'

'Uh-huh. We were work colleagues and friends. I was really pleased when Kate followed in his footsteps. Didn't expect to be her boss, though.'

'Then you know she was supposed to meet my dad the day he died. He wouldn't have killed himself if he arranged a meeting with her, would he?'

This was the first he'd heard of any such arrangement. Trying to disguise his surprise at this news, he lowered his head, pretending to pay more attention to the cat and answered, 'The mind is fragile. Maybe his reason for seeing Kate wasn't as important as you suspected.'

'Oh, it was. Didn't she tell you?'

'We don't discuss every aspect of every case. Why did he want to speak to her?'

'He wanted to tell her something he'd kept secret, something to do with a train.'

'Hmm. That doesn't ring any bells with any investigations I can think of,' he replied as casually as possible. 'I'll ask her about it. Now, I'd better get on my way. I have a few more people to talk to. Thank you for the tea.' Although he carefully lifted the cat and placed her in Sierra's hands, his mind was already elsewhere. This was a turn of events.

Why had Kate kept this visit from him? And if she'd kept this a secret, what else was she hiding?

'So where did Kate disappear to this time?' Morgan asked Emma as they waited for the pathologist, Harvey Fuller, to examine Farai's body.

'To follow a lead. Dashed off before I could find out more, but she promised to update us later.'

Morgan lifted the cordon, allowing forensic officers to duck under with thanks. 'I don't think we can do a great deal more here.

Jamie and I have spoken to everyone in the pub. Nobody heard a thing.'

'I suppose the shooter might have used a silencer.'

'If so, it sounds like a professional hit. The guy's a pimp. I wouldn't be surprised if this was over turf wars.'

'I'd agree, except Kate was on her way to interview him when he was killed.'

'Yes, I suppose so. Could be the thugs we're after got wind and topped him before he could speak to her.'

'Speak to who?' said Jamie, who'd appeared as they were talking.

'Whom, not who.' Seeing a confused look on his face, Emma shook her head. 'Never mind.'

'Who are you discussing?' Jamie asked.

'Kate. She was supposed to speak to the deceased, but somebody took a pop at him before she could.'

'Bummer. I wonder what he might have been able to tell her.'

Morgan turned away from the officers now checking out the alleyway. 'Maybe it was something to do with that bunch we've been looking for. He's a pimp, they're trafficking girls. Two plus two and all that.'

'Makes sense. Fucker can't help us now, though, can he? Listen, guys, I've sent uniformed officers to canvas the area. I reckon I'm done here. Any chance I could go home? Sophie threw up this morning and I *am* supposed to be on light duties.'

'Not still morning sickness, is it?' asked Morgan.

'Not at this stage it isn't. Probably some twenty-four-hour sickness bug. She's been exhausted recently, what with the baby kicking all night and Zach playing up all day.'

Emma nodded. 'Sure. Go. I hope Sophie feels better soon.'

'Me too. It's difficult to play nursemaid to a heavily pregnant wife and Daddy to a hyperactive toddler, especially in my present condition. See you in the morning.' He shuffled away, Morgan watching his movements.

'He's a trooper, isn't he? He didn't have to turn out for this.'

'Wow! This is a turnaround. You're always having a go at him. Why the change of heart?'

'Because he isn't the muppet that I took him to be. He's a grafter. If I'd been pummelled half to death in the line of duty, I'd take my due leave and rest up, not come back to help look for the superintendent and turn out for all this shit.'

'You've got a point. He's clearly not finding it easy,' she commented as Jamie lowered himself slowly into his car.

'And I'd expect to be pampered.'

'Oh, you would, would you? Let me assure you here and now, I don't do fuss. You'll have to toughen up, big man, if you want to stay with me.' She punched him playfully on the arm and headed back to Harvey to see what he could tell her.

'Gunshot wound to the heart. Professional hit or somebody got very lucky indeed,' said Harvey. 'He hasn't been dead long. Less than an hour, I'd say. Apart from that, there's little else I can tell you at present. There's no sign of a struggle.'

Emma cast about the alleyway. Maybe Forensics would find a spent cartridge that might give them an indication as to what weapon had killed Farai. In the meantime, they were no further forward than when they had first arrived on the scene.

That was until Morgan shouted for her.

'Just had a call from the techies. They've got a match for that S-Class Mercedes, and we have a registration plate and an address for Ognian Ivanov. Come on.'

◆ ◆ ◆

Tony's Pool and Snooker Hall was jam-packed, leaving Kate squeezing past spectators and players all seemingly irritated by her presence and questions. After twenty minutes, she had to accept Big Harry wasn't there, or if he was, he certainly wasn't going to speak to her.

She stormed outside, clung to the metal railing at the top of the steps and sucked in the damp air, preferable to the body odours she'd been obliged to inhale inside. The bastard might have heard what had happened to Farai and was lying low. This damn underworld! She couldn't find anyone she needed to talk to. Once people decided to vanish, it was almost impossible to unearth them, not without vast resources.

◆ ◆ ◆

William shut his front door and stood in the hallway, absorbing the silence. At first, coming home to an empty house had been a daunting prospect. After he'd lost Tanya and their unborn baby, he'd spent every night after work at the pub, ensuring he was out of his skull before he could face returning to a place that tortured him with memories. Night after night, he'd come in and tumbled on to the bed they'd shared, hugging one of her jumpers that still bore her fragrance and shedding tears. Worse still was entering the nursery they'd painted together. Staring at the cot filled with soft toys had caused him such sorrow he'd considered ending the misery and joining his small family.

With support from his colleagues, he gradually overcame the pain. Work skewed his anger towards criminals, and he'd been the toughest, cruellest, least forgiving cop on the force for a long while, until his friendship with Mitch, Kate's father. He understood what William was going through, and before too long Mitch and Kate had become his replacement family. Mitch was the brother he never had and Kate, well, she was the daughter he'd almost had.

William had never wanted to return to being the person he'd been back then. He'd got involved in something he should have shied away from and become indebted to John Dickson. It was a mistake that had kept him tethered to the man ever since.

He hung up his jacket on the row of empty pegs by the door and placed his boots side by side as Tanya would have expected, before shuffling into his fleece slippers. He'd become used to the solitude and now this refuge – the same cottage purchased for his family when he was a young DC – was where he found solace. He now treasured the memories held within the four walls and valued the privacy. Here, he could hide from all the crap going on. From John Dickson.

He sighed. If Mitch had been alive, he'd have hauled William out of the mess, ensured he had nothing more to do with John. As for Kate, she would do her fruit if she ever got wind of what William had been up to.

The cats, a mass of creamy white fur in their basket, didn't stir. He resisted the urge to stroke them and wake them from their slumber. They wouldn't appreciate his fussing.

A dull ache in his back and pelvis made his movements slower. Old age was coming for him. He was prepared for it. A few years of peace and quiet would suit him. If only he could get to the bottom of John's disappearance. He pulled out the burner phone and tried it again. Still no message. Something heavy was going down. William scratched his bristly chin. If he got caught up in it and the truth got out about his involvement with John, all hell would break loose. If John was still alive, he had to reach him before anyone else did.

◆ ◆ ◆

Rain had begun falling again. A steady patter this time, rather than a deluge.

Kate followed a bus down the main street; on its rear was a large advertisement for an open morning at a local school. For a moment she was transported back to her days in Uttoxeter when both she and Tilly attended the school there. Tilly had always fitted in better than Kate, who'd been quite the loner until Tilly had arrived. For a while, as teenagers, they'd been close, sharing clothes, cosmetics and secrets. To her knowledge, Tilly had never divulged any of Kate's. Moreover, Kate had kept all of Tilly's, even the more recent ones. Could Tilly still be trusted to stay quiet? She hoped so because now she knew something that could ruin Kate.

The bus slowed to a halt and a passenger disembarked. Unable to overtake because of oncoming traffic, Kate eased back in her seat and contemplated her next move. Stanka might have to go into protection. The bus rumbled forwards. Kate glanced to the left in time to spy a familiar figure outside the Royal Oak, in conversation with DI Harriet Khatri. What was Jamie doing there? She craned her neck as she passed them, but couldn't make out what was going on. Shit! She'd been struggling to accept Jamie was loyal to her.

'You can't trust anybody,' said Dickson. *'Khatri is one of my many operatives. They're all on to you, Kate. They know I'm dead, and they'll soon work out who was responsible. You won't be able to keep up this façade. Look at the state of you already.'*

Her hands began to tremble as she chanted, 'Don't listen to the voice. Dickson's dead.' She repeated the words, accepted that emulating his voice was a product of paranoia.

'And that's before you start to worry about Tilly. I expect she's already blurted out everything to her husband. She probably feels she can trust him, but he'll tell a friend who'll tell another and so on. You will soon be up shit creek.'

Tilly wouldn't betray Kate's confidence. They had a special bond.

'You forget she ran off with Jordan, who was your boyfriend at the time. It wasn't that special a bond then, was it?'

'Shut up! That's all water under the bridge.'

'Touched a nerve, have I? Well, you might think you have a relationship with a woman thousands of miles away, but she shares a bed with him. Two words, Kate: pillow talk.'

'That's enough! Stop this!'

'You've a lot on your plate, what with Tilly and Harriet—'

She couldn't take any more. There was only one way to quell her fears. Find out why Jamie had been in conversation with Harriet.

Gripping the steering wheel more tightly, she rang Emma.

'Hi. I'm checking in to see how you're getting on.'

'We've got a lead on Ognian's Mercedes. We're headed to his address now.'

'Great! You with Morgan or Jamie?'

'Morgan. Jamie's gone home. Sophie's not too well and he was feeling a bit ropey himself. How about you? Anything yet?'

The sinking sensation worsened. Jamie had lied to them. She didn't let anything slip. Jamie was her problem.

'I drew a blank. I've got someone else I need to speak to before I call it a day. I'll catch up with you afterwards.'

'Sure thing.'

Her clammy hands stuck to the steering wheel. Blasted Jamie! He was still up to no good. The bus's indicator flashed repeatedly, and the smiling face of a pupil gradually disappeared down a street. The Audi growled away. She forced thoughts of Jamie's treachery from her mind. She would deal with it in the morning.

◆ ◆ ◆

'Kate sounds pissed off,' said Morgan.

'Not surprising given she's hit another dead end.'

Morgan glanced at her. 'You always stick up for her, don't you?'

'Not always.'

'Yeah, you do.'

'Fuck off. I do not.'

'You want to know what I think?'

'Not really.'

'I think she's the big sister you always wanted instead of all those brothers.' He threw her a triumphant look. 'Ha! Your face says I'm on the money.'

Emma was unwilling to admit there was an element of truth in his deduction. 'She's the only role model I have.'

'What about the Ice Queen?'

'Are you for real? Why would anybody want to be like her?'

'I know she's colder than a brass toilet seat on the shady side of an iceberg, but she's no fool and she's going places.'

'So is Kate, without the froideur.'

'*Froideur*,' he repeated with the same heavy French accent Emma had just used. 'You sure you're a copper and not a linguistics professor?'

'Ha! Seriously, I admire Kate. I like the way she operates. If I'm going to cut it as a DI, then I'd feel happier modelling myself on Kate than on that other frosty bitch.'

'I get it, just make sure you don't go all weird like she does from time to time. Ever since Chris was killed, she's acted differently. Especially the last few months.'

Emma couldn't disagree. While she'd accepted Kate had her own coping mechanisms that were helping her deal with losing Chris, she could also see a change in her boss, and not just physically. From time to time there was a troubled look in her eyes, and the low mutterings to herself were unnerving. Emma wasn't even sure Kate knew she was doing it, but Emma had heard her on a few occasions, when she thought everyone was out of earshot. 'To be clear, I look up to Kate. End of. I wish you'd stop banging on about it. It's not the first time you've mentioned it.'

'I just like to tease you. Your cheeks go a really pretty shade of pink, which is rather sexy.'

As she looked away, aware of the heat rising up her neck, she couldn't stop the small smile tugging at her lips.

'We're here,' he said, his tone changing.

The road looked like any other, a pavement running past semi-detached houses, most with bricked driveways rather than front gardens, filled with vehicles haphazardly parked. Emma wondered how they orchestrated their exits each morning. Maybe they had a rota as to who would leave first. It would drive her crazy. At least she had a designated parking space next to the flat where she lived. They got closer, counting off numbers until they reached the address the technical team had given them. There was no sign of the Mercedes, only a white van parked on the road outside the place.

'Crap! Looks like Ognian is out,' said Emma.

'Maybe one of his goons is at home.' Morgan undid his seatbelt and was about to get out when Emma stopped him by placing her hand on his leg.

'No. We don't want to warn them off. We should wait. See if he returns.'

'Fucking hell, Emma. We could be here all night. Or longer. I'll take a quick look. See if anyone is inside. I'll be subtle.'

'Over six feet of subtlety. I don't think so. You'll get spotted. I'll go. You check out the van's VRN. It might be registered to the same address.'

'Okay. I'll keep an eye out for Ognian as well. Don't hang about.'

Emma leapt out and sped across the empty road. Rain fell steadily, a persistent drizzle that left droplets hanging from strands of hair. She made for the front door and listened for any noise, then crept past the front window, where the open curtains revealed downstairs to be unoccupied. She skirted around the side of the building, found the gate to the back garden locked and returned to the car.

'The van belongs to a neighbour,' said Morgan.

'Looks like nobody's at home.'

'How do you want to play this, then? Stay or go?'

Emma shrugged. 'We've no idea if he'll return tonight. Let's try again tomorrow.'

'Okay, boss,' he said.

'Boss. I like that. You're obviously already getting used to the idea of who is in charge in this relationship.'

Morgan maintained a straight face. 'You bet. Besides, I didn't fancy spending a night with you in the car. A bed sounds far more appealing.'

'As long as you don't snore.'

'I wasn't planning on falling asleep.'

'Drive! Just drive. You're becoming too much of a distraction.' She grinned as she spoke. It was fun flirting with Morgan. It released a lot of the pressure the job placed on them. As long as they kept it this light and breezy, it would be great, although that was easier said than done.

The call from dispatch changed the mood. A body had been discovered in the boot of a car only five minutes from their location.

◆ ◆ ◆

All was quiet at Victoria Park. It closed at 8 p.m., so Kate jumped the gates and jogged down paths to the bridge, where she stopped, turning left, then right in the hope of spotting the girl. Seeing nobody, she crossed to the other side and began walking towards Albert's Café, when her phone rang.

'Water wheel,' said Stanka, before hanging up.

Once part of the old town mill that overlooked the mill pool towards the railway station buildings, the large black wheel was set among stones, outside the park gates. Having ensured she wasn't being followed, Kate began running again. As she approached the entrance, she saw the girl, hiding in the shadows. She slowed down, checked behind her in case anyone was nearby. Stanka had slid next to the water wheel out of sight.

'Why did you run off last night?'

'I was scared. You came outside with that man, and I thought he saw me and . . . I ran down the path by the water and hid in the bushes. I lost my phone. I looked and looked but couldn't find it. When I went back to flats, your car was gone. I had to find Nevena and use her phone to text you.'

'Why were you frightened by the man? He's the manager of the blocks of flats.'

'He was one of the men who raped me.'

'What?' Kate could hardly believe her ears. 'Are you sure?'

'Very sure. He came to the flat. He was . . . disgusting pig. Ognian let him. He told me to shut up and let the man do whatever he wanted or Ognian would cut out my tongue.' Her voice was thick with emotion.

The lying piece of shit would pay for this. Kate would make damn sure of that. He'd withheld information, lied to her officers. Not to mention having had non-consensual sex with a minor.

Kate clenched her fists, desperate to hit something, only to kick out at the wall instead. The fucker!

'What are you going to do about it. Kill him? Should be easier second time around, eh?'

249

Dickson's words angered her further.

'Kate, I must tell you about Farai.'

The urgency in her voice helped lift the red mist that had descended. 'Did you see who killed him?'

'No, he was already shot when we found him.'

Kate felt her jaw tighten. She'd hoped Stanka had witnessed the killing, then she would at least have had another lead to pursue. This was hopeless. She needed to round up Gary and pump him for information.

'Farai told me something. Before he . . . died.'

'He spoke to you! What did he say?'

'Tell Kate that a police officer, a woman . . . Harriet? . . . is working with the traffickers.'

Kate almost gagged. Harriet Khatri! Farai had to be wrong. Harriet was dedicated to the force. A vision of Jamie talking to Harriet outside the pub floated before her. Pieces slotted together. Harriet could have been in cahoots with Dickson. Jamie too. Kate ran a hand over her damp hair, flattening it against her scalp. Shit! It made sense.

'Stanka, I must find you a safe house.'

'The police can't be trusted. One of them will find out and I will be killed.'

'I can look after you.'

'No! You must find Ognian and my sister. I will be safe. I will phone you again from a different phone.'

'Are you staying with your friend, Nevena?'

'No more questions. It is best you do not know. I will phone you. Please look for Maja.' The girl shrank further away from Kate, who stepped closer to prevent her from bolting.

'How did you know where to find Farai?'

'Big Harry. I wanted to ask Farai where my sister was but . . . he didn't tell me.'

The thought Farai had chosen to warn Kate rather than help Stanka find her sister saddened Kate. She'd almost lost Tilly to a crazed killer and would have given her own life to save her. She reached for Stanka's hands. 'I'm going to find Maja. Before anything bad happens. Trust me.'

The teenager nodded.

'Ring me from Nevena's phone. Soon. Stay safe.' With that, Kate turned around and began running back towards her car.

Once inside and on the move, her phone rang.

It was Morgan. 'More bad news. Gary Shardlow's body has been found in the back of his car.'

She groaned loudly and thumped the steering wheel repeatedly until she felt weak.

CHAPTER NINETEEN

DAY FOUR – FRIDAY, EARLY MORNING

Kate pressed her fingers against her eyelids, gently massaging them to alleviate the gritty sensation. She was running on almost empty, as were Emma and Morgan, who were slumped by their desks. Discovering that both Gary and Farai were dead had been a huge blow. For Kate, Stanka's revelation that Harriet was somehow involved in people trafficking trumped even that.

Although she believed the girl, part of her doubted Farai's word. After all, he wasn't exactly an upstanding citizen. If Harriet had crossed him somehow in the past, then he might have wanted revenge and fed Kate a falsehood. She cast about in her mind. She was so hellbent on tracking down corruption within the force – a fact Farai knew – that maybe she was simply being manipulated. Harriet was a stickler for being seen to play by the book. Could she really be as rotten as Dickson?

'Your instincts aren't up to scratch. You missed this. It didn't even cross your mind Harriet might be a member of my syndicate. I don't rate your chances of working out who the others are.'

'Kate?' said Morgan.

'Erm, yes. Sorry.'

'I said, do you think we should return first thing to interview Mrs Shardlow?'

Bernadette Shardlow had been distraught to learn of her husband's death. She'd been so inconsolable, she'd been given a sedative and Morgan and Emma had been unable to talk to her.

'Er, yes. Definitely. We need to find out what she knows about those men.'

She'd requested extra officers to maintain surveillance on Ognian's house even though she had a hunch he wouldn't return any time soon. If he was responsible for the murders, he would be keeping well out of the way.

'Then I don't think we can achieve much more for the moment.'

Morgan's weary face said far more than his words. A quick glance at the wall clock reminded her they'd been at work for almost eighteen hours. She couldn't drive them into the ground, no matter how imperative it was that they found Maja.

'Sure. Take off. The pair of you. We'll resume this later.'

'What about you?'

'I'll be right behind you.'

Morgan removed his jacket from the back of his chair and looked at her. 'You need rest too, Kate.'

'I know. I'm not quite ready to leave. Got some more cogitating to do.' She tapped her head. 'I might even help Rachid run through CCTV footage for that Mercedes.'

Emma stopped by Kate's desk. 'Who's to say Ognian was even behind the murders or, if he was, that he was driving his Mercedes?'

'I feel I ought to be doing something productive. There's a vulnerable girl out there who is in danger, and every hour that goes by—'

Emma rested a hand on top of Kate's. 'We're doing what we can. We're not robots. And neither are you. If you don't rest up, you'll make poor decisions, which might lead to her never being found.' She gave a smile before following Morgan out of the office.

Even though Kate knew Emma was right, she couldn't bring herself to depart. That Farai and Gary knew the traffickers and were now both dead was no coincidence. It was also significant that Big Harry had vanished. Maybe he too had fallen victim to the gang. The only lead she had was Harriet Khatri.

'You believe that low life, Farai, do you? He only ever looked out for himself. He didn't flee with Rosa and Stanka to protect them. He fled because he was scared shitless that I'd find them first and they'd lead me to him. He knew what I'd do to him. He hated me even more than you did. I wouldn't trust a word that came out of his mouth. He pimped children! He knew damn well they were underage. His conscience didn't prick him while he was earning good money from sending them to the Maddox Club, did it?'

For once, Dickson's voice sounded earnest and credible. Farai was scum, so why was she even considering the possibility Harriet was corrupt?

'Go on. Check out her work record. See for yourself. Or are you just the teeniest, weeniest bit jealous of her because you know she is the better officer, that she isn't the one having a mental breakdown?'

'That's enough!' she yelled. She jumped to her feet, paced around the small space, pulse thrumming in her ears. Bloody hell! Dickson's voice had touched a nerve. Harriet was far more in control than Kate. She was in a long-term relationship, married to a lawyer, and had a ten-year-old boy who attended a private day school, and whose photograph was proudly displayed on her desk. Of course Kate was jealous. When Harriet left the office at the end of the day, she went home to people who loved her. She had stability and support. In essence, Harriet had everything Kate desired and was now leading her old team. Where once they'd looked up to Kate, they now followed Harriet.

Kate stopped by the filing cabinets and kicked out at them; the tinny clattering that ensued was satisfying. She was about to launch another firm kick when a musical tone announced the arrival of a WhatsApp message. She picked up her phone and saw it was from Tilly.

You awake?

She replied, asking if Tilly wanted to talk.

Can't talk.

At work.

Wanted to say you can trust me.

X

Kate permitted herself a small smile. There was at least one person who had her back. She typed a reply.

Thank you.

That means such a lot to me.

Love you.

Love you too.

Be careful.

Go to bed!

X

It was a relief to know she could trust Tilly. Now in a better frame of mind, she logged on to her computer and began checking Harriet's work records. If she couldn't find anything to raise the slightest suspicion, and if Jamie came up with a reason as to why he was at the pub, she would let it drop. This whole business of corruption was sending her over the edge. It was time to refocus on being a good officer and earning the promotion that beckoned.

◆ ◆ ◆

William poured warm milk into his favourite mug. Just when did he turn into his father, who would also prowl the house in the early hours, unable to sleep? He filled the pan with cold water, and, leaving it to soak, took his mug into the sitting room, where the television was showing an old western. He gave a quiet groan as he flopped on to his chair – another sign of old age – and sipped his drink.

Horses thundered along the ground, raising dust clouds. Men in wide-brimmed hats called to each other and pounding music accompanied what appeared to be a chase through a desert. William wasn't concentrating on the scene, more on what he'd discovered in the last twenty-four hours.

John's disappearance was taking Kate in a whole new direction, one that would inevitably lead to her stepping on Harriet's toes, and William knew from experience Harriet Khatri would not stand for that. He would have to intervene, which would only make Kate more determined. She shared her father's dogmatic belief that if she pursued something for long enough, she would get results. The only problem with that was William didn't want her to stumble on to something else, something connected to the trafficking operation that could blow months and months of planning. If only John hadn't vanished!

The cowboys were now making their way into a one-street town, reins loose, heads held high. William watched as they drew to a halt in a line to face a man on a white horse, a sheriff's badge on his chest. There was a stand-off for the longest minute, with close-ups of each man's determined face, then the man on the white horse pulled a gun and bullets rained down the street, pinging off saloon doors, and drilling into the dust around the horses' hooves.

His phone rang and he muted the television. 'Chase,' he said.

'Oh, DCI Chase. I expected to get the answerphone. I intended leaving you a message.'

'No need, Ervin. I'm wide awake.'

'Pressures of the job causing insomnia?'

'Something like that.'

'I have some information that might add to your concerns.'

'Go ahead.'

'The material you gave me appears to consist of black wool and cashmere fibres. To be completely accurate, they are a blend of ninety per cent virgin wool and ten per cent cashmere, the sort used in overcoats. As you know, I'm somewhat passionate about fashion; I happen to know that ratio is used in some Hugo Boss overcoats.' He paused to clear his throat. William already guessed what he was about to say. He'd seen the coat hanging in the office. 'I appreciate we shouldn't speculate or jump to any conclusions, but Superintendent Dickson owns such a coat. I remember commenting on it when he came to see me. I'd been looking for one just like it.'

'But it isn't exclusive to this brand. I'm sure many overcoats use the same ratio of virgin wool to cashmere,' said William.

'Indeed, that is so. I merely flagged it to you as a possibility.'

'And I appreciate that, although, as you rightly pointed out, we shouldn't speculate. Nor is any of this for public consumption, Ervin.'

'I completely understand. My lips will remain superglued on the subject.'

'Thank you. Thanks too for getting back to me on this so quickly.'

'Not a problem. Let me know if I can be of any further assistance.'

'I shall. And, Ervin, remember, it doesn't necessarily follow that the material belonged to the superintendent's coat.'

'I know that. But you wouldn't have given it to me if you didn't think there was some connection.'

'Let's settle for saying it might be significant.'

'Indeed. I hope you get some sleep, DCI Chase.'

'I'll try.'

As soon as the call was over, William hunted for the USB stick he'd brought home. Plugging it into his computer, he watched the footage of John Dickson leaving HQ the evening he disappeared. He was wearing a long black coat. William finished his drink and picked up the remote control. The one-street town was empty, tumbleweed rolling down the road and bodies by the sidewalks. The saloon doors creaked as the sheriff holstered his pistol, satisfied he had cleaned up his patch. As he turned to mount his horse, one of the villains on the ground reached for his gun and, with his dying breath, shot the man. The sheriff slumped beside his horse, blood pooling under his head. The credits rolled to mournful music.

William sniffed at the irony. He had his own one-street town to patrol and was doing as poor a job keeping it clean and free from crime as the poor schmuck on the screen.

CHAPTER TWENTY

DAY FOUR – MORNING

Kate swung into the car park with a low groan. The journalists had gathered on the pavement opposite the station. They'd been joined by members of the public, who held up placards and chanted, 'Corrupt police are criminals.'

She rolled up the copy of the *Gazette* with its headline 'Superintendent Covered Up Boy's Murder', shouldered her bag and kept her head down, ignoring the shouts from the journalists.

'Who else knew, Kate? Who else knew he covered up a murder?'

'When is he going to come out of hiding?'

'Did you know about this?'

'Come on, Kate, give us something!'

She spun on her heel, ready to tell them not every officer was as crooked as Dickson but checked herself in time. It was thanks to her the *Gazette* was exposing Dickson. She'd fully expected him to be alive, to answer for his crimes.

'This is on you, Kate. You'll have to accept the repercussions.'

She marched to the entrance. Jamie, who had been watching her arrival, moved towards her as soon as she cleared the doors, his lips parted, ready to speak. She didn't give him the chance.

'You. Briefing room. Now!' She stormed ahead, leaving him to struggle up the stairs alone. By the time he reached her, she had calmed down enough to ask questions without flying off the handle. This whole Dickson thing was out of hand, but she couldn't let anyone, especially Jamie, suspect she was angry for any reason other than she didn't like or believe what was being written about Dickson and was frustrated as to where the leak had come from.

'Sit down,' she said.

'Is everything okay, guv? Those journos—'

'I don't want to discuss the journalists, Jamie. I'd like to know where you went last night.'

'Oh, right. I asked Morgan and Emma if I could go home. I'd been on duty for twelve hours and it was taking its toll.'

'So, you went home?'

His brow furrowed. 'Yes. Was that wrong of me? I'm supposed to be taking things easy, guv.'

His pathetic attempt to act innocent was irritating.

'Let's not fuck about, Jamie. Why were you spotted outside the Royal Oak last night?'

His mouth flapped for a moment before breaking into a grin. 'Oh, we were at cross purposes. I thought you were bollocking me for skipping off. Phew!'

'The pub, Jamie. Why were you there?'

'I was on my way home when I spotted Trev – I mean, DS Wray – having a smoke outside the pub, so I stopped to speak to him. About Operation Moonbeam. He and I used to work together in Manchester, and we got on well. I did him a few favours back then, before he made DS. I thought I'd get him to repay the favours, so I asked a few questions about who they were after, to see if they were looking into the same people. It turns out they are. The three we're after are also part of a much larger gang that Operation Moonbeam is trying to bring down.'

She blinked hard. 'You were pumping him for information?'

'Yeah. I used my initiative. I thought you'd be pleased. Especially as he told me DI Khatri's team are going to raid a hotel in Newcastle-under-Lyme this morning. They believe some trafficked women are being held there.'

His face had taken on the expression of a schoolboy keen to impress his teacher. She shook her head in disbelief.

'You were talking to DI Khatri not Trev Wray!'

'Was I? Oh, yes, but that was only for a minute. She'd been in the pub too. I think the team was having some sort of out-of-hours meeting there. She saw me talking to Trev and asked me how I was, after my run-in with the bolt gun shooter.'

'DS Wray wasn't there, Jamie. You were only talking to DI Khatri.'

'Look, whoever told you this has got it all wrong. I stopped to talk to Trev. DI Khatri came out after we'd finished our conversation and DS Wray headed back inside. She had a few words with me and then we both went our separate ways. There's nothing more to it than that.'

Was he messing with her head? Had he already prepared this concocted story to throw her off his scent, or was he being truthful? The questions buzzed in her ears like angry wasps, causing her to shake her head to dispel the noise.

'Have I fucked up, guv? I thought you'd be pleased. I wanted to show you I've got what it takes. You know? To make strides. You said you'd back me, put in a commendation after my heroic tussle. I figured this would be another feather in my cap.' His eyes crinkled.

The buzzing continued. She fought to gain control, forcing calm to flood her veins. It sounded plausible. She couldn't let her imagination run riot. She had to keep Jamie on side. 'I did. I told you I would, and I did. You deserved it. I'm not so sure about your recent lone venture, though. It's not good protocol to muscle in on another investigation. This should have gone through DCI Chase.

At the very least you should have told me about it last night, not waited until now.'

Jamie's face fell. 'Sorry. I thought you were busy following other leads, and I knew it could wait until today. Guv, I only wanted us to make progress. I know it's important we find the sister so Girl X will talk to us. The sooner we do that, the sooner we can find out what's happened to the super. You don't have to do anything with this info. Trev won't blab to DI Khatri. I . . . I haven't stuffed up my chances of promotion, have I?'

'I told you before. We're a team. We don't ride solo. Everything goes through me.'

'I understand. I'm sorry, guv.'

He hung his head, the enthusiasm that had shone in his eyes had evaporated and Kate couldn't help but feel guilty for popping his bubble of euphoria. Moreover, he had given them a lead to Maja's possible whereabouts. The buzzing waned, allowing her to process the information. 'I'll talk to DCI Chase and request we tag along in an observational role. If the girl's sister is among those that DI Khatri's officers bring in, we'll step in and take charge of her. If not, we'll withdraw.'

He lifted his head. The enthusiasm had returned. 'Yes, guv.'

'You can't be part of it, though. You're on light duties. Besides, DCI Chase needs you to work with him.'

'Guv.'

'And don't ever pull a stunt like that again.'

'No, guv.'

'Right. We're done here. I need to let the others know what the plan is.'

He gave a snappy salute.

Kate made for William's office to let him know what she'd just discussed.

William's mood seemed off when she entered. He didn't invite her to sit down or even smile in her direction.

'You okay, William?'

'Not really. I won't beat about the bush. I had an interesting chat to Sierra Monroe yesterday. She told me her father had asked to meet you the morning he killed himself.'

'That's correct.'

'You didn't think to bring this up at any point?'

'I don't know what he wanted to see me about and the prison governor rang to inform me of his death before I got to the prison. It didn't seem relevant to bring it up.'

'Weren't you curious as to why he'd ask to see you, then take his life before doing so?'

She shrugged. 'I was more focussed on our investigation into multiple murders at the time. I assumed he didn't really have anything important to tell me.'

William steepled his fingers together. An act she found unnerving. It was the equivalent of one of his cats twitching its tail.

'Oh, dear, Kate. You're in hot water now. William hates being kept in the dark. He'll lose trust in you, and he won't stop at Cooper. He'll keep digging now until he finds out exactly what transpired at the reservoir. By keeping this from him, you've made matters worse for yourself.' Dickson ended with a laugh.

She had to defuse this situation immediately.

'Okay, so I thought at the time that he might have some information regarding Chris's death. Sierra mentioned he wanted to talk to me about a train. I could only think of the one Chris was shot on. But there had been plenty of opportunities for him to speak to me before he was sent to prison and as for me, well, I wanted to put Chris's death behind me, not rake up the past. However, I was surprised he took his life that day. It seemed somewhat extreme and ill-timed, so I supported Sierra's decision to request a second autopsy only because I know what it's like to live with doubt.'

She held William's steadfast gaze and counted her heartbeats until he grunted, 'I see.'

'The second pathologist also confirmed Cooper had taken his own life. I don't think Sierra has got over it.'

'You've visited her, then?'

'A few times. She's so young, William. She's lost the one person she'd relied on. Her mother turned her back on her. She only had Cooper. I was luckier than her. After Dad died, I had you. I felt sorry for her. I drop by her place now and again, to see how she is. If anyone understands what it is like to be left bereft with nothing but unanswered questions, it's me. Whatever you think of me for following up after an investigation, I haven't crossed any lines.'

'Liar!' whispered Dickson.

William tapped his fingertips together before dropping his hands to the desk and giving her a half-smile. The tension knot in her neck untied itself. He'd bought her story.

'Okay. I understand. I couldn't work out why you'd keep something like that from me.'

'It wasn't a conscious decision. I didn't think it was important enough to share, especially as we were up to our eyeballs hunting for a serial killer at the time.'

'True. Right, now we've cleared the air, what did you want to see me about?'

'There's something I wanted to run past you.' She explained about Harriet's tip-off and wanting to ride along.

'How did you find out about this?'

There was no way she was going to tell him the truth and drop Jamie or DS Wray in it. She had enough on her plate without trouble between her and Harriet over the matter. 'From an external source.'

'Really?'

'Yes. One of my personal sources who knows I'm looking for Maja. They received the information from the same person who gave DI Khatri the tip-off.' She maintained eye contact until William broke off with a sigh.

'I'll sanction it, but I don't want DI Khatri feeling you are undermining her, or that you're interfering in her operation in any way. You can send Emma and Morgan to observe, but only if they stay well back. Only after the traffickers have been arrested and brought back to the station will they be permitted to speak to any girls who are being held captive. I'll let DI Khatri know. It would be discourteous to go ahead with this without informing her so I'm glad you ran it past me first.'

'Thank you. I'll brief the team.'

'Would you ask Jamie to check out this name? She's Gwen Chapman's alibi.' He passed her a slip of paper.

'Francesca Gibbs,' she read out. 'The name rings a bell. We might have spoken to her during the Maddox Club investigation. Do you think Gwen had something to do with Superintendent Dickson's disappearance?'

'At this stage I suspect everybody and anybody.'

'But Gwen?'

'She lied to us during the last investigation.'

'To protect her family.'

'Whatever the excuse, she lied.'

'If you need me to step up and speak to either of them, let me know.'

'I shall. Now I ought to butter up DI Khatri.'

Kate took her leave and exhaled loudly in the corridor. That had been a close shave. She hadn't anticipated William talking to Sierra. He had almost found her out. She'd need to sharpen those wits of hers even more if she was going to remain one step ahead of those people searching for Dickson. A phone call from Felicity surprised her.

'I've been out this morning and when I returned, I discovered another burner phone went live at eight o'clock. It transmitted from somewhere in the town centre, but I can't pinpoint it. Phone belongs to a contact called Iota, who made a thirty-second call to another unregistered number which is no longer operating. I think they've ditched the phone. Sorry, I have to rush off again. I'm late for a meeting. Catch you later.'

Kate pocketed her phone and made for her office. Who on earth could Iota be? And who had Iota rung?

◆ ◆ ◆

Morgan passed the packet of chewy mints to Emma.

'No, thanks.'

He took one himself, then replaced the packet in the centre console storage box. 'This is all wrong. We're piggybacking another operation. We should be doing this ourselves, not waiting for leftovers.'

'You wouldn't like it if another squad took over our investigation.'

'Huh! They can have this one with pleasure. It's a right ball-ache. I've got to the stage where I want to leave *Have you seen this man?* posters on every pole in the city. We've gone from looking for one person to hunting for a teenage girl in the hope another anonymous girl, who also doesn't want to come forward, will provide information that will lead us to our original quarry. And we have two dead bodies. I wonder if DI Khatri will do a swap?'

He glanced across the street to where a silver Ford Mondeo was parked. Harriet's team were now in position and maintaining radio silence. Morgan sighed. 'This is so dull. It's like watching the most boring detective series ever. Are they going in or not?'

'It's only boring because we're observing. It feels unnatural.'

He chewed for a while, then after swallowing said, 'I can think of a hundred other things I'd rather be doing. Most of them involve you.'

'Most?'

'Yeah, a couple involve a steak, fries, some cold beers and a decent box set.'

'Don't you mean Netflix and chill?' she said.

He grinned widely. 'Don't give me ideas. We're on duty.'

There was movement as two plain clothes detectives made for the hotel entrance. 'We're on,' said Morgan. 'Should have brought popcorn.'

Emma watched the men as they hung about on the pavement outside the budget-priced hotel. Another two walked past Morgan's car and veered off into the car park, followed by another pair.

'The animals went in two by two,' Morgan sang.

'Don't take the piss. They're doing their jobs. Wasn't so long ago we were part of that unit.'

'Yeah, makes you feel kind of left out, doesn't it?'

'In a way.'

'Oh, there go another pair. Maybe they should hold hands and form a crocodile to make sure they don't get lost.' He reached for another sweet, chomped it quickly.

Harriet got out of the Ford Mondeo.

'Aha, the Ice Queen emergeth,' he muttered. 'Maybe now we can flush out these bastards and rescue the girls.'

Emma let him ramble. His zany comments amused her. It was a bitter pill to watch her fellow colleagues homing in on an arrest, yet not be part of the unit, especially as she and Morgan had worked with these officers.

Harriet must have given the command because, like a well-re-hearsed troupe, several officers in body armour and carrying weapons spilled out from the back of a plain white van to swoop on the hotel, then disappear quickly from view. Those positioned at exit points stayed in situ, as did Morgan and Emma.

Morgan rolled another sweet around his mouth. 'Fancy a bet?'

'On what?'

'How many girls they come out with.'

'What's the stake?'

'Closest to the actual number wins. The loser cooks dinner for the other person.'

'You're on. Ten,' she said confidently.

'Nah, there'll be fewer. I'll say eight.'

They waited. Nobody exited the building.

'What intel did they have on this place?' Emma asked.

'Toady Trev reckoned they got a tip-off from a bloke called Big Harry, who hangs out at a snooker hall.'

'Great! Trustworthy source, then?'

'Toady seemed to think so. At least, that's what Jamie claims. To be fair, we've no reason to doubt Trev or his source. There's no way the Ice Queen would go ahead with this raid unless she was certain the traffickers and their quarry were here.'

'There's no sign of Ognian's Mercedes. Not here, not in the car park or down the other street.'

'True.'

There was a flurry of activity by the entrance; officers emerged, hands motioned and arms waved.

'Not looking hopeful, is it?' said Emma.

More officers came out of the building to gather in the car park. Harriet soon joined and addressed them, then they gradually returned to their vehicles, most with sullen expressions. As Trevor drew level with the Jeep, Morgan wound down the window.

'What's happened?'

'Nothing. There was nobody there. Somebody tipped them off.' His tone was accusatory.

'Don't point fingers in this direction. We needed them caught as badly as you did.'

'Yeah, well, we're all going to be disappointed, then, aren't we?'

He eyeballed Morgan with something akin to hostility before retreating towards his vehicle.

Morgan turned on the engine and threw his vehicle into gear. 'If these guys can't bring home the bacon, then I suppose it's up to us to do it.' He reversed at speed up the street, executed an impressive turn at the junction, then sped off back to HQ. 'Best break the news to Kate before somebody else does. By the way, you owe me dinner.'

'There were no girls. Neither of us got it right.'

'But I was closest to zero, so I win. I'll let you decide what you cook me.'

With Emma and Morgan at the hotel, it fell to Kate to interview Gary's grieving widow, Bernadette. Kate had intended questioning her at the station until empathy got the better of her. She rolled up outside the flat a little after nine and knocked on the door.

Rich, the liaison officer she'd briefly mistaken for Dickson in the corridor, let her in. He greeted her in a soft Brummy accent, nothing like Dickson's voice. 'I've been here half an hour. And in that time she's hardly spoken a word. I think she's still in shock.'

'Do you think she's up to answering a couple of questions?'

'You can try. Come in.'

Bernadette was in the kitchen, back against the fridge.

'Hello again, Bernadette. I'm very sorry for your loss. Do you remember me?'

She nodded, then spoke. 'He was murdered!' Bernadette didn't look up from the mug, which bore the name Bernie. 'He didn't keel over with a heart attack or anything. He was in the boot of his fucking car!'

Kate spoke as gently as possible. 'I understand this is very painful for you, but I have to ask you a few questions about Gary.'

When she got no reply, she asked, 'Would you like to sit down? You might be more comfortable.'

Bernadette drilled her with a look. 'I'd rather stay here. What do you want to ask me?'

'It's really more about getting a picture of what happened to Gary. Whatever you tell me might help me find the person or persons responsible for this crime.'

'What do you want to know?'

'Can you start with the time you found him?'

'Around seven. He'd been messing with the car. He was always outside polishing it, making sure no bird crap ate into the paintwork, that sort of thing. It was his pride and joy. I suppose in a weird way, he'd have wanted to have . . .' She faltered and swallowed hard. '. . . died in it.'

'I'm sorry to put you through this, but did you notice any comings and goings around the time your husband was outside?'

'I was in the sitting room, watching television. I didn't see or hear a thing. We normally eat after the early evening news. I'd made a slow cooker stew, so there wasn't much for me to prepare. I went into the kitchen at six thirty and looked out of the window to signal it was time for dinner, but there was no sign of him. I assumed he'd seen one of the neighbours and begun chatting to them. Once he got started talking about cars, wild horses wouldn't drag him in for any meal. I waited for him to appear and when he wasn't back by seven, I went looking for him. He wasn't outside any of the flats, and it was only when I went to see if he was doing some work underneath the car that I noticed the boot was ajar. I lifted it to drop it back down and shut it and . . . and . . . he . . . he . . . was lying there.' This time she couldn't control the tears.

Rich put an arm around her and guided her through to the sitting room, encouraging her to sit down, then offering her tissues. It was a while before Kate could talk to her again.

'Bernadette, can you think of anyone who would want to do this to your husband?'

'Erm . . . no . . . no, I can't.'

'Remember I spoke to you both the other day, about the men who rented two flats, who only came for a few days at a time but who brought girls with them. Your husband said he'd notified the actual owner who'd been subletting the flats.'

She dabbed her face with a handful of tissues and spoke nasally. 'I know who you mean.'

'Were you aware that your husband was friendly with these men?'

'Don't be ridiculous! He wasn't friends with them. He was polite only because he didn't want any trouble. Nobody spoke to them. I certainly didn't.'

'He told me you weren't happy with their behaviour.'

'I don't think any of the residents were. We could see they were trouble. Do you . . . Do you think they killed Gary?'

'I'm looking into that possibility, which is why I'll need to ask you further questions.'

'I can't answer them. All of this! Finding Gary like that. It's too much,' she wailed.

'Bernadette, please try. I need your help.'

'I want to be left alone.'

Rich gave Kate a small shake of the head, suggesting she quit pressing the woman. Bernadette covered her face with her hands, muffling her sobs as she rocked backwards and forwards.

In the hallway, Rich said, 'I'll let you know when she's more able to assist.'

'Time isn't on my side. I'm going to wait in my car. I'll come back in fifteen minutes. See if you can calm her down by then.'

Back outside, she crossed to the cordoned area where Gary's car had once stood. It had since been impounded and was waiting for Forensics to check it over. The memory of Gary's body was still fresh in her mind. As soon as she'd got the call from Morgan, she'd come over to see the damage for herself. It had, in her view, been a professional hit: a single bullet straight to the heart. It remained for Ervin to establish if the bullet had come from the same gun as killed Farai.

Kate didn't need the verification. She was certain the same person was responsible for killing both men. Gary had been shot first, then Farai, within an hour of each other. The only common bond between the two men was their connection to the traffickers.

Had Dickson not been dead, she might have suspected him of cleaning up after himself. This time, though, there was no finger-pointing in that direction.

The street was as silent as when she'd visited with Stanka. She looked at the empty spot where she had left her car to check out the apartments. She imagined the horror the girl would have experienced on seeing Gary exiting his front door with Kate, to show her the place where Stanka and her friends had been imprisoned – and then it struck her. There was one other connection: Stanka. Could she have arranged for both men to be killed? This new thought swelled, causing her to doubt herself once again.

'Kate.' Rich was outside. 'She's probably up to a few questions if you want to give it another go.'

She followed him. It might be painful. It might be ugly. Whatever it took, she had to squeeze some information from Bernadette.

◆ ◆ ◆

William was shown into a room Gwen Chapman called a snug. To William, it was anything but. He'd sat in smaller hotel lounges.

Two damask cream silk settees adorned with an array of red and gold cushions were pushed against gold papered walls. William hadn't dared sit on either and had chosen instead a matching wing-backed chair. He kept his feet still, having already ruched the red silk carpet under a glass coffee table so that, instead of it lying flat, ridges like small speed humps had appeared. He tried stamping them down without success and gave up, throwing himself back into the chair, which attempted to swallow him and caused him to emit a small growl of contempt.

The huge gilt-framed mirror over the fireplace reflected a grey-haired man, with a saggy neck and wide hands that covered the chair arms.

He looked away, eyes resting on a gold clock, ornately designed, with a splendid silver and gold pendulum that swung silently. He ran a finger around the collar of his shirt, which threatened to cut into his neck. Another bonus of retirement would be no longer having to wear suits every day. He would donate those that were still in good condition to charity, certainly not bin them or burn them. That last thought brought him back to the reason for him sitting in what appeared to be a set for a glossy home-and-garden magazine.

Bradley entered with his usual authority, head high and limbs loose. William marvelled at how he'd managed to keep in such good shape.

'Sorry to have kept you. I was on a call,' he said. 'How can I help?'

Yet again, he remained on his feet, towering over William.

'We're both busy men, so I'll get straight to the point. You were seen heading to and from your daughter's house on the night Superintendent Dickson disappeared. I'd like to know the reason for the two trips I believe you made.'

'I didn't make any trips to her house.'

'Could you take a moment to reconsider your answer, please?'

Bradley cocked his head, appeared to take his advice, then said, 'I've considered it and I repeat, I didn't go to her house.'

'I don't wish to make this difficult for you, but I am in possession of footage showing you travelling up and down the main road four times that evening.'

'That would only prove I drove up and down the road. Nothing more. Do you have footage showing me at the actual house? No. I didn't think so.'

'You told me you didn't go out that evening.'

'I must have got my dates confused.'

'Where did you go?'

'For a drive. Driving helps me to relax.'

Given Bradley was a driving instructor, William seriously doubted he would want to get into his car and drive after a day of instructing others.

'Maybe the occasional drive does, but you went out on two separate occasions within a short time of each other.'

'I was extra stressed that day.'

'Please don't treat me like a fool. I deserve some respect,' said William.

Bradley sighed. And put his hands up in the air. 'Okay, you got me. I went out to bag myself some partridge. I know it's illegal to shoot them one hour after dusk but, in my defence, I didn't catch anything. Hence the toing and froing. I tried Bagots Wood and the woodlands by the reservoir. I didn't go to my daughter's house at any point.'

The young William would have wanted to launch at the man, knock the arrogance out of him with his fists. The old William knew he had to utilise his most powerful muscle to beat Bradley – his brain.

'Right, that seems to answer my question. Could you tell me when you last went to your daughter's house?'

'Today, as it happens. A short while ago, to replace a broken padlock. DS Donaldson kindly let me know the gates were open when she was checking out the place.'

William decided retreat was the best option for the time being. The material he'd found in the garden was still an ace up his sleeve. It could remain there a while longer.

'Then it appears I have the information I require. Thank you.' He got to his feet.

Bradley accompanied him to the front door. 'Gwen tells me you bumped into her as she was coming out of the leisure club.'

'Yes, I was thinking of joining the club after I retire.'

Bradley looked him up and down. 'Might I suggest somewhere in Stafford? Seems rather a waste to travel all this way when you have such excellent facilities on your doorstep.'

William didn't respond. Bradley had thrown down the gauntlet. His message was clear: stay away from Gwen. He couldn't help but wonder why.

CHAPTER
TWENTY-ONE

DAY FOUR – AFTERNOON

Bernadette's eyes were red-rimmed. She dabbed at the mucus dribbling from her nose.

Every time she was asked a pertinent question, she began crying again. The subterfuge was wearing thin for Kate, who'd ascertained the woman was hiding behind this curtain of grief. She'd asked Rich to make some tea, hoping she could get Bernadette to talk while they were alone.

'I know you're upset, but I'm going to have to come clean with you about something which will be difficult to hear,' said Kate.

'What do you mean?'

'There's no easy way to put this, but your husband took advantage of the services those men provided. That is to say, he had sex with one – maybe more – of the girls who were being held in that flat.'

Bernadette pressed the tissue against her lips.

'And, Bernadette, I think you found out about it,' said Kate.

Tears leaked from the corner of her eyes.

'Come on, Bernadette. This is important. Gary knew what these men were up to, didn't he? He told you. Probably an abridged version, or maybe you even guessed he'd had sex with the girls. Either way, you were so disgusted by it, you insisted he spoke to the owner of the flat and made sure those men couldn't stay here again. Am I right?'

The woman moaned softly to herself.

'I can only imagine how you felt discovering Gary had cheated on you, with such young women.'

The moaning ceased. 'He's always had a thing for youngster women. We started going out together when I was thirteen and he was seventeen. Maybe it was because they made him feel young. He watched a lot of online porn. Girls. Always girls. I didn't know about the flats, not at first.' The sobs began building back up.

Kate crouched beside the woman. 'You're bearing up really well, Bernadette. I know this has been a horrible shock, but all this information will help us find his killer. When did you find out about the girls in the flat?'

'The last time the men came. Up until then, I thought they were party girls, or hookers, for the men. I'd only caught glimpses of them and thought they were all women in their late teens or twenties. Then one day, I saw one of them being dragged to the car. She was crying and it was at that moment I realised she was only a kid. She couldn't have been more than fourteen or fifteen. I told Gary I was going to call the police. He said he'd handle it, and the next minute they were gone.'

'You didn't report it afterwards?'

'Gary told me not to. It would reflect badly on him. He might have been fired. We're on the bones of our arses and Gary's job is the only thing between us and living on the streets.' Her face was puffy and misshapen through crying.

'Did you know about Gary's visits?'

She shook her head. 'No. I swear I didn't know. Not until you visited the other day. He was so worked up after you left, he confessed. He was sure you were going to find out and press charges.'

'Do you happen to know if he was in contact with the men?'

'I'm sure he wasn't. I checked his phone before the police took it. There were no messages or phone calls to strange numbers.'

'You said you saw the men dragging the girl into a car. Did you mean the Mercedes S-Class?'

'Er, no. It wasn't that car. It was a Mercedes, though, a silver estate car.'

'I don't suppose you noticed its registration?'

'I made a note of it on my phone because I was going to call the police about it. Actually, I don't think I deleted it.' She wiped her eyes with a fresh tissue and, hiccoughing tears, scrolled through some apps, before handing it to Kate.

Kate couldn't speak. She knew the registration off by heart. Bernadette had spotted Dickson's car.

'You showed this to your husband?'

The answer was no more than a puff of air. 'Yes.'

Thoughts swirled, none of them anchoring long enough for her to make sense of what she'd discovered. She had to get back to the office and think this through. Dickson, the traffickers, the child prostitutes, Farai and Gary were all connected.

Bernadette rocked back and forth again, arms tightly wrapped around her waist. 'I know Gary wasn't perfect, but I loved him. I loved him!'

'And we'll do whatever we can to bring those people responsible for his death to justice.'

Kate hoped she could hold true to her promise. It might go some small way to making up for all the mistakes she had made.

◆ ◆ ◆

William walked into Kate's office, where Jamie was working.

'The alibi for Gwen Chapman appears to check out,' said Jamie. 'She and Francesca Gibbs went to a restaurant and on to a show, a local production. The restaurant staff remember both women.'

'Then we can be sure Gwen didn't meet up with the superintendent that evening.'

'I'm almost through with the list of friends who know him.'

William nodded thoughtfully.

'Okay, stick at it. I'll be in my office if you need me.'

He meandered back up the corridor. There had to be a way of finding out exactly where Bradley had gone that night. The whole shooting partridge story was garbage and they both knew it. Ordinarily, William would request a warrant to examine the Land Rover's satnav, which would provide a record of the car's movements. However, in this situation and without concrete reason, his hands were tied. Besides, it was unlikely that the car would have satnav. After all, someone with Bradley's experience would make sure there was nothing on board that might track him. William could do nothing other than wait for the man to trip up. The scrap of material was the only potential clue that suggested Bradley might have been in contact with Dickson, and even that was tenuous.

He returned to his chair, looked at the notes he had made on a piece of A4.

Phone call received 6.55 p.m.
Car drove past camera 7.01 p.m.
Car returned 8.04 p.m.
Car drove past camera 9.12 p.m.
Car returned 10.09 p.m.
Bonfire – recent
Material John's coat?

He picked up his phone and called his hacker friend. They might know of a way to extract information from Bradley's vehicle.

◆ ◆ ◆

When Kate got back to her office, she found all three members of her team looking subdued.

'The bust went tits up. Somebody tipped off the traffickers, who cleared out with the girls before we turned up. We came away empty-handed,' said Morgan.

'Oh, shit! They're going to be so spooked they might start off-loading the girls even sooner than we anticipated.'

'Maybe they'll move them somewhere else and stay under the radar. They know a team is on to them. It's going to make movement harder,' said Emma.

'Then we need to act quickly. Try Big Harry. I couldn't find him last night. He wasn't at the snooker hall and nobody there would or could tell me where he was. Find him, and we're still in with a chance of finding them.'

She updated them on everything else, apart from the information about Dickson's car. For now, she wanted to keep that to herself.

Emma spoke up. 'We've been focussing on catching a car on CCTV, but what if the killer travelled on foot?'

Kate's flesh went cold. She'd done something similar when she left her car hidden down a lane and cycled to the reservoir to meet Dickson.

'That's possible. They could have been dropped off or left the car elsewhere. Is there a pedestrian route?' she asked. Stanka had mentioned running off near water. There had to be a route nearby. Why hadn't she thought of this sooner?

'Because you've become fixated on any connection between Harriet and me rather than this investigation. I warned you that you would make mistakes. They'll be noted. You won't get that promotion to DCI.'

She kicked herself at Dickson's words. This really was yet another cock-up on her part.

Jamie brought up a map of the area on his screen. 'There's a canal towpath close to the blocks of flats with an entry point by the bottle kilns.'

'If you'd looked for that last night, instead of racing about like a headless chicken, you might have found Stanka and saved yourself all the pointless running around. Tut, tut, Kate.'

She gripped her pencil tighter, desperate to shake off Dickson's criticisms. What was done was done. 'Morgan and Emma, see if you can squeeze information out of Big Harry. Jamie, find out if there are any surveillance cameras close to the canal. Check out places where somebody could have left a vehicle.'

'I'm supposed to be assisting DCI Chase, guv.'

'I'll square it with him. Everyone clear on what they're doing?'

'Yes.'

'Get cracking, then.'

Leaving them to it, she went in search of William, who was staring at a piece of paper on his desk. He moved it aside and beckoned her to sit down.

'I hear the raid didn't work out,' he said.

'So I gather. I was with Gary's widow. I'm sure the same person or persons who shot him also killed Farai. I've asked Jamie to look into some stuff for me. Is that okay? I know you needed somebody to help you search for the superintendent.'

'It's fine. I can manage without him.'

His downbeat demeanour hit home. He'd been looking forward to retiring; the last thing he wanted was to be up to his neck in an investigation he would never be able to solve. He shouldn't end his career on such a low point. She felt she should offer some conciliatory words. 'It's only been four days, William. Once the press stops plastering defamatory articles about him over the front pages, he will show up.'

'Do you really believe that? Have you seen the crowds outside? This is becoming less about him, and more about what we're doing to hold him to account. The public are beginning to think we're protecting him . . . and that reflects badly on us. The chief constable is going on camera later to assure everyone we are concerned and doing whatever we can to find John so he can deny these allegations. I'm not sure, though, that they can be denied.'

Now was the moment for her to come clean about Dickson's involvement with the trafficked girls. She told him about Dickson's car being at the flats.

He rested his head against his hand. 'Jeez, Kate. What a holy mess! Have you shared this with the team?'

'I thought you should know first. It's highly incriminating. My job is to find him, not judge him.'

He gave her a smile. 'You are so like Mitch. He was level-headed too. I say we keep a lid on this until we find him. You okay with that?'

'Sure.'

'Thank you. We don't need to add fuel to the rumour mill.'

'Will you draft in more officers to hunt for him?'

'The chief constable has already instructed me to do so. Now that people are baying for blood, we must be seen doing everything we can to locate him. We'll be putting out appeals for witnesses, to encourage people who might have seen him four evenings ago to come forward. A team of officers will man the phones and follow up on all leads. I'm sticking with it too. I urgently need whatever information Girl X has.'

'I can't get her to talk until we find her sister.'

'Then find her, Kate. Before this whole thing blows up in all our faces.'

Alone with her thoughts, she questioned William's decision to keep the information about Dickson secret. It was something he ought to share with the higher authorities and yet he'd chosen not to. Whether it was to protect what remained of Dickson's shattered reputation or out of loyalty, it suggested one thing to Kate: that he was one of Dickson's supporters.

◆ ◆ ◆

Kate stopped at the vending machine and was carrying drinks back to the office for her team when DI Harriet Khatri confronted her in the corridor.

'For the record, I'm not happy about your officers' involvement in my operation,' she said.

'As far as I know, they were not involved. As requested, they stayed within the confines of their vehicle, did not interfere in any way and left the scene as soon as it became apparent nobody was being arrested.'

Harriet stepped closer to Kate, who stood her ground. 'If it had been up to me, they wouldn't have been allowed anywhere near my operation.'

'As it happens, it didn't matter how many officers were there. You struck out.'

Harriet's eyes sparked. 'Everything was going well until your lot got involved. Somebody tipped off those traffickers. The girls were moved before we got there! That's not a coincidence. We had them, Kate. They were within our grasp.'

Kate understood that Harriet was frustrated, but not why she would suggest Emma and Morgan were to blame. She was about to bite back when it struck her that this could be some sort of trap. Harriet was trying to rile her, to make Kate lose her cool and say or do something stupid. The reasons why she'd do such a thing spun in her head. Maybe Harriet hoped she could launch a complaint and have Kate taken off the hunt for Maja, claiming she was endangering the success of Operation Moonbeam. If so, the investigation might go to Harriet, who, once she found Maja, would locate Stanka. And, if Harriet was part of the syndicate, it would be like signing a death warrant for Stanka. Kate couldn't allow that.

Regardless of the reasons Harriet was confronting her, Kate was not going to let her hurl accusations about either Emma or Morgan. She took the bait. 'What are you inferring, Harriet? Spit it out.'

'One of your team warned the traffickers.'

It took every ounce of self-control to not push Harriet out of the way. 'Oh, please! Nobody on my team would do that.'

'How can you be so sure? You weren't there at the time.'

Up this close to her, Kate noticed how controlled Harriet seemed to be. If this performance wasn't to discredit Kate and her team and prevent them from finding Maja, then the only other reason Kate could think of was that Harriet was trying to thwart Kate's chances for promotion. Just like Dickson had. She kept her voice level. Harriet would not win this contest.

'Because I trust every single one of them! We had a vested interest in finding one of the girls. There is no way on this earth any of us would jeopardise finding her.'

Harriet's eyebrows lifted. 'Why is she so important?'

Ah! This was the real reason Harriet had confronted Kate. She wanted information about Maja. There was no way Kate would give up that. Moreover, she could box clever too. 'I can't divulge that any more than you can tell me more about these traffickers you are after. Not unless you want to join forces.'

Harriet's expression didn't change. 'You'd be willing to do that, would you? Hand over control to me?'

'Actually, I said *join forces*. Not surrender my team to you.'

'Then it's no deal.'

'As it happens, I wasn't offering.' She took pleasure in seeing Harriet's eye twitch at the comeback. 'Out of curiosity, though, would it be of interest to trade information?'

'I doubt you have anything I would be interested in.'

'A name of somebody who might know where the traffickers are.'

Harriet gave a quiet snort. 'If you had a name, you'd be following it up, not dangling it in front of me. What are you after in exchange?'

'Same as last time. You allow my officers to attend any raid and bring out the girl we are after.'

'Your coffees will be getting cold, Kate.'

'Your loss.' Kate cocked her head. 'Excuse me. You're in my way.'

As she strode along the corridor, she could feel Harriet's eyes burning into her back. She'd piqued the woman's interest. If she could hook her further, she might be able to lay a trap to expose her. Then she would know once and for all if Harriet was to be trusted.

The atmosphere in the office was tense, the air thick with concentration as her team tapped at keyboards and murmured on phones. Jamie was so close to the monitor his nose almost touched it.

Kate distributed the coffees silently, receiving a nod of acknowledgement or a mouthed 'thank you'.

Morgan was speaking in low tones to what Kate took to be a source. They'd all worked the streets long enough to have a collection of go-to informants. Not all of the snitches – a word she disliked – would be obliging, but one or two might know where Big Harry was hanging out.

'Guv? Might have something.'

She made for Jamie's desk, where he pointed at a building on his monitor. 'If you look closely, you'll see there's a surveillance camera on the side of that warehouse. It appears to overlook the canal towpath.'

She peered at the enlarged photograph. It was difficult to spot the grey box but Jamie encircled it for her. 'Do you know who the warehouse belongs to?'

'FD Building Supplies.'

'Get on to them. See if they've any footage for last evening.'

'Have to shoot out for a while,' said Morgan.

Kate didn't ask why. It was clear he was meeting his source. Some of them preferred to meet in person rather than talk on the phone. They were a paranoid bunch, concerned their calls were being recorded.

'Me too,' said Emma.

Kate's informants wouldn't be out and about for another few hours, so she settled for a call to Harvey Fuller to find out if Farai and Gary had been shot with the same weapon. Until she knew for certain, she was working on an assumption, and that could lead them down unnecessary paths.

Harvey was a little terse with her. 'I haven't been able to perform full autopsies yet. The morgue is full, and so far I've only been able to do preliminaries.'

'I appreciate that. I'm not hassling you. I only need to know if you extracted cartridges from both victims.'

He sighed. 'Yes, I did that immediately. I figured you'd need to know if the deaths were connected.'

'And are they?'

'I'm not an arms expert. The bullets looked the same to me, so I sent them to Forensics. Now if you don't mind, I really need to get back to work.'

'Thanks, Har—'

The phone had already gone dead. She was about to ring Ervin when Jamie spoke. 'They've got footage. They're sending it across now. I'll go through it.'

'Great. We really need a breakthrough.'

William tapped on the door and stood in the doorway. 'Breakthrough? I could do with one of those as well.'

'No joy, sir?' said Jamie.

'Nothing but dead ends and unanswered questions. That bonfire at the Corby residence is still bothering me. Somebody had recently been there.'

'Probably the gardener, burning garden refuse,' said Kate.

Jamie spoke without looking up from his screen. 'Or that vagrant Emma found there.'

William stepped further into the room. 'What vagrant was this, Jamie?'

'Erm, a local drifter. He was squatting in the garage, but he ran off when Emma was going to take him to a hostel. She'll be able to tell you more. Maybe he lit the fire to cook something.'

William sighed. 'Maybe so. Is Emma around?'

Kate shook her head. 'She's gone to meet a source.'

'When she gets back, would you ask her to drop by? I'd like to know more about this individual.'

CHAPTER TWENTY-TWO

DAY FOUR – LATE AFTERNOON

Emma shrugged off her jacket and tossed it on to the back of her chair.

'Anything?' asked Kate.

'Not sure. Apparently, Big Harry got spooked by the recent shootings and is lying low. The word is that his cousin, Frank, has a place in the country that Harry has used before when he's needed to get away for a while. I've got to do some more digging to find out where it is.'

'Did DCI Chase speak to you?' said Jamie.

'Yes, he caught me on my way in. He wanted to know about the drifter that ran off the other evening.' She settled in front of her computer and began typing.

Kate tried to shake off the sudden concern that the vagrant might have spotted Bradley's car when he went to fetch the white suits from her Audi. She reminded herself that the man had been living inside the garage; however, if he had been outside, beside a bonfire, could he have seen what happened? Ervin's name flashed up on her phone, sending all concerns scattering.

'Both Gary Shardlow and Farai were killed by nine millimetre cartridges which we believe to be Czech in origin.'

'Can you give me an idea of the weapon used?'

'Sorry but nine millimetre ammunition is one of the most popular used in handguns today. Find us a weapon, however, and the experts would be able to tell you if it was the one that fired them. Could be from the same gun or two separate weapons.'

'Czech cartridges, you say?'

'Yes.'

'Okay. Thank you, Ervin.'

'All in a day's work, although my days are becoming so long, they encroach into my evenings, nights and following mornings.'

Kate replaced the phone on her desk. It wasn't unusual for ammunition to be smuggled in from other countries. Recently, one of the teams had uncovered a load of cartridges from South Africa. Dickson's handgun was also illegal. How he had come by it was anybody's guess but she'd bet it had come via the syndicate. If the members were as corrupt as she suspected, they would have access to seized firearms or those who trafficked them.

William knocked on the farmhouse door. Emma had told him that the drifter, Digger, might be working at a farm in Colton for a family called the Tollers. A phone call had confirmed that Digger was indeed there, so William arranged a visit.

Ed Toller was well into his seventies, with so many broken veins across his cheeks and nose, he looked like he'd been daubed with red paint. William introduced himself.

'He's in the bottom field,' said Ed. 'I didn't tell him you were coming, as you requested. He isn't in any bother, is he? He's a bit odd but he's a good chap. Hard worker. He helps a lot of us farmers out when we need it.'

'No. He's not in any trouble.'

'That's good, cos I wouldn't want you to take him away. There's a fair amount of repair work to do and I'm not as strong as I used to be. I need him for a good week or two. If you follow the path behind the sheds, you'll see him.'

William followed the directions past the cavernous sheds, from which came a strong whiff of what his mother would have called 'country air'. He navigated around steaming cow pats that led to a five-bar gate. Ahead of him, black and white cows roamed in the field, none of them interested in the figure searching for Digger. A loud hammering gave away the man's location and after clambering over the gate with difficulty, William crossed the field and into the next, where Digger was ramming fence posts into position. William could feel the steady vibrations thudding through the uneven ground as he approached. He shouted out the man's name and, after a third attempt, Digger looked up and set down what appeared to be a heavy steel tube with handles.

Digger wiped his nose on a grubby sleeve. 'What do you want?'

William held up his ID card. A shadow crossed Digger's face.

'Just a few questions, that's all. I understand you spent a couple of nights in the garage belonging to a house overlooking Blithfield Reservoir.'

A frown deepened as he spoke. 'I didn't do any harm.'

'I know you didn't. You're not in any trouble. I need your help.'

'Help?'

'While you were there, did you notice any unusual activity?'

The man's head lowered and greasy hair tumbled forwards, hiding his features.

'Digger, you aren't in any trouble,' William repeated. 'Did any-body else come to the house while you were there?'

'Yeah.'

'Okay, this is important. Can you tell me exactly what you saw?'

'I heard a car. I hid in the garage until it left. After it had gone, I went to the garden. Somebody had lit a bonfire and it was almost out.'

'Did you see the car?'

'No. I stayed out of sight.'

William clicked his tongue in frustration. Digger looked at the pile of wooden posts near the rammer. 'I have to get these posts in for Mr Toller.'

William wasn't ready to give up yet. 'Were you in the garage all night?'

Digger stiffened. William knew he was on to something. 'You must have gone outside for a pee or for a walk or to get some fresh air.'

'I . . . I might.'

'Did you?'

'Uh-huh.'

William gave it another go. 'Did you see anything unusual while you were out?'

The man looked away. 'I don't want to get into bother.'

'You're not. I promise. Come on, Digger. I'm asking nicely for your help. I think something bad happened that evening.'

Again, the man looked away, a small jerk of his head reveal-ing his discomfort at this line of questioning. A cow released a long, mournful moo. William almost missed what the man was saying.

'I shouldn't have been there.'

'It's fine. You didn't break into the house or cause any damage to the property.'

'No, not there. I shouldn't have been at the reservoir. It's illegal. I don't have a permit, you see? You won't put me in prison, will you?'

William sighed. 'No, of course not, Digger. What were you doing at the reservoir?'

'A spot of fishing.'

'Did you catch anything?'

'No. I got scared off and went back to the garage.'

'What scared you off?'

'Gunshot.'

William was floored for a moment, then adrenaline began to pump around his veins, making him feel younger than he had in a long time. 'Digger, tell me exactly what you saw and heard.'

'I was fishing when a car appeared from the direction of Rugeley. It went over the reservoir and turned off at the far side, down the lane. I didn't think anything of it. Sometimes folk, they go there for, you know . . . sex. Then I heard loud voices and a shot. Figured it was poachers. I skirted around the bank. I could see somebody walking up and down. Soon another car, a Land Rover, appeared from the opposite direction. It headed down the lane too. I saw somebody get out. They spoke to the person who was there, then got back in the Land Rover and drove towards Rugeley. They left the first person walking up and down again. After a few minutes, the Land Rover returned. Both of them put on coveralls with hoods. I saw them carry something large, like a deer, and put it into the back of the Land Rover. Afterwards, the Land Rover drove off, back towards Abbots Bromley. Then the other person put a bike into the back of the first car and followed it.'

'Could you see what make of car it was?'

'I know Land Rovers, but I don't know much about other cars. It was some sort of estate car.'

'Did you see either driver's face?'

'No. It was too dark. The Land Rover driver was a man, quite big and tall. The other was a woman, only a bit shorter than him and slim.'

'A woman? Are you sure?'

'Uh-huh. Before she put on the coveralls, she was half naked. She wasn't wearing a shirt or top, only . . . a bra.'

It might have been Gwen. She was slim and although shorter than her husband, she might have been wearing heels. Why she was wearing no top was a puzzle. 'Have you any idea who fired the shot?'

'No, sir.'

William's brain churned through the information. Bradley owned a Land Rover, John a Mercedes estate car. And the coveralls. Who would have access to such outfits other than a police or forensic officer, unless they'd been purchased specifically? Maybe Bradley and his wife had planned this and kept the suits at their daughter's old place. Where did the bike fit into it all?

'Digger, I'm going to need you to come to the station with me so we can write down everything you've just told me.'

The man took a step back. 'No, I've got these posts to do. I can't go.'

'You might be a witness to a murder. I'll explain to Mr Toller why you have to—'

'I can't be disappearing halfway through the job. He won't have me back again. I'll come to the station another day.'

'That won't be possible. The sooner we get this statement written, the sooner you can return and finish the fencing. It won't take long. I'll make sure you're brought back.'

Digger gave a reluctant nod. 'Okay. Let me finish with the post I was working on. It's almost in and then I need to take the rammer up to the barn to keep it safe. I'll meet you up at the farmhouse.'

William agreed, and headed off to explain to Mr Toller that Digger would be needed for a few hours at the station. Toller was accommodating and accompanied William outside to assure Digger that everything would be okay.

But there was no sign of the man. The steady *thunk* of a very heavy object slamming into a chestnut stake had ceased. William cast about for a sign of him.

'So, where is he?' asked Mr Toller.

'He said he'd meet me here.'

Toller gave a yellow-toothed smile. 'Oh, he did, did he? I'm afraid you've been had. You should have locked him in your car before you talked to me. Digger's a country lad, through and through. He hasn't visited a town in decades. That's why he lives as he does, odd jobbing for those of us happy to let him sleep in the sheds. He's a nomad with a pathological hatred of busy streets, towns and houses. He'll have sloped off somewhere.'

William rushed to the gate. There was no sign of Digger anywhere. He cursed loudly before marching back to the farmer. 'When he turns up again, ring me.'

'If I see him, I'll be sure to call you. Although, if I know him, he'll be steering clear of this place for a while.'

William marched back to his car, furious with himself for letting the slippery little sod out of his sight and for losing a potential witness to what sounded horribly like John's murder. As he climbed into the driver's seat, his thoughts turned to the mysterious woman Digger had mentioned. Who on earth could she be? Bradley Chapman's wife, Gwen? Bradley's daughter? It was a puzzle because, try as he might, he couldn't imagine either woman helping to dispose of a body.

◆ ◆ ◆

The tech team had sent Kate footage from the warehouse over-looking the towpath behind the kilns, and the team was having no difficulty in identifying the figure who strode along the path at around the time Gary Shardlow had been shot. With his muscular arms and a gold chain visible around his thick neck, they were certain they were looking at one of the three people traffickers: the man named Doncho.

'That's got to be him. Matches his description perfectly,' muttered Jamie.

'Someone else to track. We seem to be gathering quite a collection,' said Emma from her chair, where she'd been searching for information on Big Harry's whereabouts.

Morgan entered the office with, 'What an utter waste of time! I've been on a wild goose chase around Stoke. Pissed off doesn't even begin to describe how I feel.'

'Cheer up,' said Emma, getting to her feet. 'My tip-off is red hot. I've just found out where Harry is staying, *and* I have a location. You coming to help loosen his tongue?'

They shot off, Morgan's heavy footsteps thundering down the corridor. Jamie looked up. 'Can't wait to get back to proper active duty. I don't feel as involved behind the desk like this.'

Kate caught the wistful look he displayed. 'You're as vital to this operation as anyone. You'll soon be back tackling villains to the ground.'

Her words had the desired effect, lifting the corners of Jamie's mouth. Their conversation was interrupted by a call from Felicity. The head of the technical unit wanted to see her in person. She left Jamie and slipped downstairs.

As soon as she spotted Kate, Felicity escorted her into the office, shutting the door behind them and dropping her tone.

'I'll get straight to the point. I've been monitoring all the numbers of the unknown contacts we found in the burner phone. Only one has been active since Superintendent Dickson disappeared. The phone belonging to somebody known as Beta has made several attempts to contact the superintendent's burner. I managed to triangulate a signal and the first four attempts were made from within this vicinity.'

'Somebody at HQ?'

Felicity nodded. 'The penultimate call, however, appeared to be here.' She pointed to a small, circled area on a map. Kate's heart sank. It was right at Bradley Chapman's house. 'And the last time, it seemed to be here.'

Felicity pulled up a second map; the area in red was another Kate knew well. She'd visited William's home numerous times. She reined in emotions that threatened to destabilise her. Her husband had left documentation suggesting William was corrupt. If she could place him at Bradley's house when the phone was transmitting, she would have strong proof that he was Beta. She maintained what she hoped was a poker face and asked for a print-off with the details. Felicity pressed a button and paper spewed silently from a printer into a tray.

'I'll continue to monitor them,' said Felicity.

'Would you let me know if Beta's is used again?'

'Sure. Any idea who it might belong to?'

There was no way she was going to bring up William's name. To her knowledge, Felicity didn't know where he lived and wouldn't have leapt to the same conclusions as Kate. 'Not for the moment, but I'll work it out.' She gathered the papers and shuffled them into a small pile. 'Thanks again. This is really helpful.'

'I aim to please,' said Felicity. 'Talking of which, dinner's at 8 p.m. next Saturday, if that works for you.'

'Definitely. I'll let you know if I can't make it.'

Kate raced back upstairs, clutching the print-out to her chest. She wouldn't admit William was involved in any of this until she had definitive proof. Other than Tilly, William was the last person alive who cared about her. She couldn't bear to think he might be tied up in Dickson's business, that he too might be crooked.

'*Think you know somebody, then it turns out that you don't know them at all, eh, Kate?*'

'I'm not listening to you, you fucker. William's a . . . good, decent man. He wouldn't be involved with scum like you.'

'*Yet the evidence would suggest otherwise. And you know what a stickler you are for following facts. William is part of the syndicate. Face facts!*'

She took the stairs two at a time, desperate to speak to William and clear his name. She hesitated on the landing near his office, weighing up if she should tackle him now or wait until she'd checked her facts. As she did so, William's door opened and Harriet emerged and paced away without apparently noticing her. Without further thought and with Harriet walking away from her, Kate made for the door and knocked. There was no answer. Opening it, she realised William wasn't in. Why had Harriet entered when he clearly wasn't there? Was it to deposit a document? She made for his desk and rooted through the paperwork on it. There was nothing obvious that Harriet might have brought with her. She leafed through sheets of notes William had written and stopped at one that revealed the times Bradley Chapman's car had passed a camera; under it he'd written:

Bonfire – recent
Material John's coat?
Shit! William really was on to her.

◆ ◆ ◆

Emma directed Morgan down a winding country lane. The evening light shone across golden fields, the last of the hay baled and awaiting collection. The only dwellings were remote farms down narrow tracks. As they turned on to one Morgan commented, 'This really is the middle of nowhere.'

'I guess that's the idea. It would take some finding, which means it's a good place for Big Harry to hide out. He'd be able to see or hear somebody coming a mile off. Especially in this noisy old banger,' she added as the Jeep hit another rut in the track and bounced noisily.

'If we'd brought your car, it would have fallen to pieces by now.'

She looked across the fields, where animals seemed to be the only living creatures. The trees were beginning to exhibit their autumn colours and although it was beautiful, Emma couldn't imagine living in a place like this during the bleaker months, cut off from civilisation.

The lane forked. 'Where to now?' asked Morgan.

She enlarged the map on her phone. 'I think we head to the right.'

'Think?'

'It'd be less tricky if we had a phone signal, or your satnav, for this area. Look for a pair of disused barns.'

As they rounded a bend, the track straightened, and a pair of tumble-down barns came into view.

'This must be the place. Now we just need to find the wooden hut without frightening off Big Harry. Maybe we should pull over here and walk the rest of the way,' she said.

'My guess is it'll be in the woods, behind the barns.'

'Good call.'

The Jeep drew to a halt and Emma jumped out. A light breeze ruffled the long grass in the fields surrounding them, creating hypnotic wave patterns.

Morgan cocked his head. 'It's bloody quiet here. Big Harry must have heard the car arriving.'

'Then we'd better get a shift on before he scarpers.' Emma paced towards the first dilapidated barn with its imploded roof and rotten wood hanging from exposed timber frames. The second was in slightly better condition, and although there was nobody around, a dusty tarpaulin had been thrown over a large object, barely disguising its shape. Morgan lifted an end to expose the car numberplate. 'Harry's. He can't be too far away.'

Heading into the wood, they pushed quietly past branches until they reached a clearing and the cabin. Emma whispered, 'Give me a few minutes then knock at the door. I'm going to make sure there are no other exit points. And be careful. He could well have a weapon.'

'Ah, I knew you cared about me.'

'Of course I do, dummy.' She slunk towards the back of the cabin, a wooden structure with a front terrace and a pitched roof that reminded her of a chalet she and a martial-arts-loving boyfriend had rented in Wales. Thanks to torrential rain, they'd spent the full weekend hemmed inside, with one open-spaced room downstairs and a small bedroom and shower upstairs. After only twenty-four hours, they decided they weren't compatible and left.

The undergrowth here wasn't as thick and the small back garden overlooked fields. Rather than be spotted by Harry, she hunkered down and waited for Morgan to act. If Harry bolted, she was sure she could catch him. It was only a short sprint to the back door.

It wasn't long before she heard, 'Harry, it's DS Meredith. I need to talk to you.'

There was no reply.

'Harry. We're concerned about your safety. Could you come to the door, please?'

Emma spotted the back door opening and readied herself. Harry emerged, looked left then right before breaking free of the doorway and heading across the grass at a pace that took Emma by surprise.

Emma sprung after him. 'Police! Stop!'

Harry was surprisingly swift for such a bulky man. He didn't run in a straight line but swerved and weaved to confound his pursuers. Heavy steps nearby told Emma that Morgan had gained on them both. Within seconds he had overtaken her and floored the man.

Harry writhed and kicked, limbs flailing.

Emma grabbed his feet to stop them smashing into Morgan's face. He continued thrashing out, hitting Morgan in the jaw and kicking Emma in the stomach. Then he was off once more, staggering drunkenly towards the trees. Morgan recovered quickly and charged after him, hooking him around the waist and dragging him again to the ground.

Emma caught up with them, took hold of Harry's legs for a second time and hung on with all the force she could muster as he attempted to break free.

'We're police officers,' said Emma. 'Calm down!'

He grunted loudly, writhing from Morgan's grasp. His bulk and strength made it impossible to keep a grip on him. He'd soon be off again unless they could cuff him.

'Pepper spray,' shouted Morgan. 'Spray the fucker in the eyes!'

The thrashing eased. 'No! No spray. Don't.' Harry lay still.

'Get up,' said Morgan. 'And no funny tricks.'

He rose slowly, hands in the air.

'You carrying any weapons?'

'No.'

Morgan patted him down and, satisfied Harry was being truthful, said, 'Now, let's be civilised about this. We can cuff you and head for the station, or we can go back to your cabin and chat there. What is it to be?'

'Cabin.'

'Cabin it is.'

Emma gave him a look, which he acknowledged with a flicker of a smile. Pepper spray was classified as a Section 5 weapon by the UK government, usually used for crowd control, and neither of them were carrying any.

Harry was as tall as Morgan and much wider, but the younger man was strong and kept one hand tightly on him.

Harry gave him a sour look. 'This is pointless. I don't know anything.'

'We haven't told you why we want to talk to you.'

'If it's about Farai's death, I wasn't there and I know nothing.'

Morgan stared hard at him. 'Listen, mate. We're the good guys. I suggest you think hard while we walk because we're probably your best bet at staying alive, unless you want to spend the rest of your life hiding in that wooden shack.'

Light was beginning to fade as William reached the reservoir. A solitary swan drifted aimlessly, its head bowed as if studying its own reflection.

He'd made a rookie mistake in allowing Digger to vanish.

He shoved his hands deep into his pockets and stared across the indigo water. This was the side of the reservoir where Digger had been fishing, the same side as the Corbys' house. William tried to place himself here the evening John Dickson disappeared. It was around this time of day and already it was difficult to make out the far side of the reservoir and impossible to see what was happening there. Digger would have seen very little in the obscurity unless he'd been wearing night-vision goggles.

William traversed the causeway and drove down the narrow lane, parking up approximately opposite where Digger might have been. He got out and stared across the water again. It was too dark to make out anything on the far bank. Digger might have fabricated his story, yet there was no reason for him to do so, unless, thanks to drugs or alcohol, he'd imagined it. However, there was another possibility: Digger had witnessed everything, only not from where he claimed to have been sitting. To have been able to describe the strange events, he would have needed to have been a lot closer, and on the same side of the reservoir as the couple.

He lowered his head, searching for signs of a struggle, anything to substantiate Digger's story. The evening air cloaked William in an icy embrace as he walked along the shady bank. The hum of distant traffic was waning, leaving only bird calls as they settled in the woodlands surrounding the water. He studied tyre tracks in the dirt. Even the best forensic scientists would have difficulty determining the number of vehicles that had driven down and parked here. There was nothing that immediately stood out, and then he spotted a single bicycle tyre track. He followed it until it came to an end, deducing that somebody had ridden to this point, then dismounted. The tracks in themselves weren't unusual. The fact there were no return marks was.

He shone his torch on the ground. No drag marks. No dark patches that could be blood stains. The light fell on to a mound of earth, and he let it rest there.

This seemed fresher, somehow out of kilter with the other mixture of gravel, dust and track dirt. It was undisturbed by traffic and, if he looked carefully, it appeared to have been patted down.

Behind him was a hedgerow. He trudged along the track until he found a gap and squeezed through into the field behind. Here there were plenty of places for somebody to observe whatever was happening on the lane. If he were a betting man, he'd say Digger often hung out here. As the man had told him, couples came to this spot to have sex. It wouldn't surprise William to discover Digger had already positioned himself here in the hope of spotting such activity. He needed to find Digger again and quickly. The man clearly knew far more than he had said earlier.

CHAPTER TWENTY-THREE

DAY FOUR – NIGHT

Kate couldn't settle to any task. She was now consumed by the belief William could be one of Dickson's inner circle of corrupt officers.

Jamie.

Harriet.

Now William.

Who the hell could she trust?

She needed some air. Leaving Jamie alone in the office, she headed downstairs to the washroom. Opening the door, she surprised Harriet on a mobile. Seeing Kate, she cancelled the call.

'Didn't mean to interrupt,' said Kate.

'You didn't. They're not picking up.'

Kate made for one of the basins, where she doused her face in cold water. Harriet slid the phone into her bag and, placing it on the floor, joined Kate in front of the mirrors.

She unclipped her hair. 'Looks like somebody is having a bad day. Not making headway, eh?' She smoothed it down, so it was almost flat against her head, then replaced the grip.

Kate dried her face and said, 'Every investigation takes time and patience. It has its frustrating moments. Talking of which, I wasn't under the impression you'd cracked your case yet.'

'Hey, I wasn't mocking. I understand how it works. It was merely an observation. You look done in. Anyway, I understand there'll be some changes soon.' Harriet stooped to recover a butterfly from the back of one of the studs in her ear and replaced it, ensuring it was secure. She fixed eyes the same shade of ice blue as the earrings she wore on Kate. 'That more officers are being drafted in to help in the search for the superintendent's whereabouts. I agree with the chief constable on this matter. Being unable to track down one of our own reflects badly on all of us.'

She gave a tight smile and, picking up her bag, headed for a cubicle.

Kate fought the urge to snap a retort but instead pulled her phone from her pocket as it started to vibrate.

On the other end of the line, Felicity's voice was quiet. 'Don't speak. I just wanted to alert you. Iota's phone went live two minutes ago, somewhere in HQ. No call was made from it and it stopped transmitting a moment ago.'

Felicity hung up. It could be no coincidence Harriet had been on a mobile when Kate arrived and that she had put it away without connecting. She had probably turned it off while in the cubicle. And Iota had rung an unknown number the morning of the sting. Had the call been to the people traffickers to warn them? Could Harriet be Iota?

Harriet's voice rose from the toilet cubicle. 'I expect you'll be glad of the extra help.'

Kate walked out, allowing the door to slam behind her.

305

Emma and Morgan had returned to the cabin with Big Harry and were now in the open-plan kitchen-cum-sitting room. Harry had almost taken up all the space on the settee, so Emma moved a kitchen chair and settled in front of him.

Morgan stood by the kitchen door that overlooked a covered wooden veranda. Behind him the windowpanes only revealed the pitch black night sky.

'So, what can you tell us about these people traffickers who have a bunch of girls they're looking to move?' Emma said.

'They're after me.'

'Why? Why would they be searching for you?' said Morgan in a lazy tone.

'They killed Farai, didn't they? And that nonce, Gary Shardlow. They're tidying up loose ends, so unless you can offer me some protection, I'm saying nothing.'

'Okay, station it is,' said Morgan, stepping forwards and putting a hand on Harry's shoulder. 'I'm sure once word gets out you've been helping us with our inquiries, there'll be a queue waiting to take a shot at you. Can't say we didn't give you a chance to talk to us without rocking any boats. Up you get.'

'Fuck off!' Harry pushed Morgan's hand away. 'I didn't say I wouldn't help. I just can't tell you anything about them.'

Emma chipped in with, 'That's a bit of a contradiction, isn't it?'

'No. I don't know much about them. Farai was the one who did business with them. I didn't. I kept my nose out of it.'

Morgan snorted. 'I hardly think looking after Farai's girls and income while he's been in hiding is keeping your nose out of it.'

'I looked after the takings. Nothing more.'

Morgan bent down and spoke into the man's ear. 'I . . . don't . . . believe you. You know *something*. Now listen to me. It's late. I've had a very long day and I'm hungry, which means I'm in a foul mood, so you better start squealing before I decide to go rogue and hammer the living daylights out of you.'

'You wouldn't.'

'Try me. Nobody knows we're here. When eventually you did get found, we'd deny all knowledge. I have nothing to lose. You do. The choice is yours.'

Harry grunted. 'There's three of them. The main man is called Ognian.'

Morgan hissed, 'We already know their names and where they used to keep the girls. We know they're part of a larger gang.'

'No. You're wrong about that. They work alone. They've been operating in the area for about two years, bringing in girls from Eastern European countries and selling them to the likes of Farai. In the past, Farai has taken on a few of their girls, but he didn't want any more of them. Said they were more trouble than they were worth. Ognian's mob are trying to offload four more. Apparently, this time they're very young. Farai didn't want to know and broke off all dealings with them. I guess they weren't happy about that. That's why he got topped.'

'You know that for sure?'

'No, but who else would have shot him?'

Morgan resumed his place by the door, allowing Emma to take over. His heavy act had got them started.

'Farai was killed outside the Golden Moon pub. You arranged a meeting between DI Young and Farai there, didn't you?' she said.

'Uh-huh.'

'Did anyone other than you know he'd be at that meeting?'

'No one.'

'No one?' she repeated, eyes burrowing into his.

'Well, apart from a couple of Farai's girls. They didn't know he was meeting DI Young, though. I fixed up a meet for them too, half an hour before the one with DI Young.'

'Why did they want to meet with him?'

'One of them was stewed up about her little sister. Reckoned she was one of the girls that Ognian's lot was trying to offload. She came into the snooker hall and made a right scene, insisting she speak to Farai. I couldn't put up with all that carry on, so I sorted it for her.'

'What are these girls' names?'

'Can't help you there. I can't pronounce them. I call them Long Brown and Short Red. Based on their hair,' he added.

'Did you arrange any other meetings for Farai that evening?'

'No.'

'Not with Ognian or his mates?'

'No way! They're all nutjobs. Dangerous ones at that. I don't deal with blokes like them. I warned Farai he was taking a massive risk getting involved with them.'

'Was there anybody else who knew Farai would be at the Golden Moon?'

'Look, I didn't tell another soul. Somebody either followed him, or . . . maybe they overheard my conversation with Long Brown, okay? I swear I didn't tell anyone else. Speak to the girls.'

'We would if we knew where they were. Any ideas?' said Morgan.

Harry shook his head.

'What about Ognian's crew? Any idea where they might be hanging out?'

He looked away.

'Come on, Harry. You must hear all sorts of stuff at the snooker hall. Help us out. Where might we find them?' asked Emma.

He shrugged. 'No idea.'

Morgan strode across the room and bent down, grabbing a handful of the man's sweatshirt and hoisting him from the settee. 'Come on, Emma, we'll put him in the back of a police car and blaze up and down every street with lights and siren on to make sure he gets the attention he deserves. I'm sure that'll soon get back to his *friends* and they'll deal with him.'

Harry shook his head rapidly. 'Don't. I'll be dead meat.'

Morgan shoved his face in front of the man's. 'You know the alternative.'

'Dairy,' he said softly.

'What?'

'I don't know how true it is, but I heard they'd moved from the flats and were working out of a place called Dairy.'

'Is it a dairy farm? An old dairy?' Morgan asked.

'I dunno. Just Dairy. It's somewhere in or very close to Stoke-on-Trent. They haven't moved outside of the Stoke area. I also heard they have a buyer for their girls. They'll be disposing of them in the next forty-eight hours.' He lifted both hands. 'I swear on my life, that is everything I know.'

'No, it isn't. You must have an idea of who else was in the snooker hall when you spoke to those two girls. I want names,' said Emma, getting out her pocketbook. 'Now!'

'One of the goons, not the one with the ponytail, the one that looks like a weightlifter. I think he was there.'

'Think harder!' growled Morgan.

'Yes. He was definitely there.'

Kate twirled the pencil between her fingers, her mind on Harriet Khatri. The bitch wasn't to be trusted. Farai had claimed she was linked to the traffickers and Kate wouldn't have been surprised to learn that Harriet had been the person who'd warned them of their sting operation.

'Guv, I'm off.'

She glanced up. Jamie was wearing his coat. She checked the time, saw it was six thirty and waved him away. 'Sure. Night.'

With no news yet from Emma and Morgan and nothing from William since he'd gone in search of the drifter, she decided to check his office to see if he'd returned. She was in time to spot Harriet and Jamie talking at the far end of the corridor. Harriet handed a package to Jamie. Kate stepped back into the office before she was noticed.

◆ ◆ ◆

On his way back from the reservoir, William rang the farmer, Mr Toller, to see if Digger had reappeared, only to be told there'd been no sign of him since William's visit.

Instead of returning to the office, William ordered a takeaway and headed home to see his cats.

He hated to speculate, but in this situation, it was all he could do. Based on what Digger had told him, together with his own suspicions about Bradley's behaviour, a picture had formed of a woman killing John Dickson, then enlisting Bradley's assistance to dispose of the body. This theory explained not only Bradley's movements for the night, but the recent bonfire and attempt to burn material that possibly came from John's coat. The million-dollar question was, who would kill him and why? John was involved in nefarious activities, some of which William was party to and others he knew nothing about.

There was no way of finding the owner of the pay-as-you-go who'd rung John's phone to arrange the meeting, which William now assumed had taken place at the reservoir. Leaning on Bradley wouldn't yield any results because he wouldn't crack. The man was highly trained in interrogation techniques. He would remain silent unless William could come up with some novel way of persuading him. That required a lot more thought.

He pulled in at his favourite Chinese takeaway to grab his food, slamming the car door with extra force. The chief constable would be putting more officers on to this investigation in the morning, something William would rather didn't happen. In spite of Bradley, he was making progress and outside assistance might well hinder it. Also, he feared the greater the manhunt, the more likely it was that John's killer would simply disappear for good. At the moment, they were probably quietly confident that a small team wouldn't crack the case. However, they hadn't banked on William getting involved. And if nothing else, William was determined.

Fatigue stapled Kate's eyelids together as she sat in the office. They'd had two breakthroughs: not only could they place Doncho near Gary's flat at the time of his murder, but they also now knew he was at the snooker hall and had probably overheard the conversation between Harry and Stanka, which also made him a suspect for Farai's murder. Better still, they knew the girls were being held somewhere known as the Dairy. She cursed herself because Stanka had mentioned the men laughing about milking the girls in a dairy and she hadn't followed up on that information as she'd intended, having been sidetracked by other events.

To make amends, and partly to punish herself for her failing, she'd taken it upon herself to locate every property with that name. So far, she'd unearthed eleven dairies, a dairy produce shop, a housing estate called New Dairy House and another known as the Old Dairy House along with quite a few dairy farms. Morgan and Emma were currently out scouting several of them.

She forced her eyes open, blinked away the raw stinging, and got to her feet. She'd no option other than to join the search. Selecting a couple of dairy farms, she headed out into the night.

The wind slapped her in the face as she crossed the car park, noting Harriet's car was still parked up. The woman bothered her. What was of greater concern was Jamie. Whatever was going on between him and Harriet couldn't be good news for Kate.

Dickson's face seemed to materialise in the rear-view mirror. This time he said nothing. His smug expression said it all. She was in trouble.

CHAPTER TWENTY-FOUR

DAY FIVE – SATURDAY MORNING

Kate gripped the gun, felt the recoil as the cartridge flew from it. The arms that had grappled her for it loosened their grip and her victim slumped to the ground. Blood blossomed from the wound, as scarlet as poppies, yet when she looked at his face, it wasn't Dickson lying in a heap, but her husband, Chris.

His lips parted. 'Why?'

'Chris!' she screamed. 'No . . . no . . . It can't be you! It shouldn't be you. It should be Dickson.'

'You failed me, Kate. You didn't find any justice. All that time, all that effort, for what?'

She ripped off her T-shirt, rushed to his side and pressed it hard against the wound. 'Don't talk. I'll get you to a hospital. I'll fix this.'

'Too late, you're too—'

The words died on his lips.

As she clamoured, 'Chris! Chris, don't leave me!' his face began to elongate, his eyes narrowing until it was Dickson's face she held between her hands.

'Too late, Kate,' he said.

She leapt back, fear blocking all thoughts. Dickson was getting to his feet, casting aside the blood-soaked cloth as he did so.

'You can't get rid of me that easily.'

The alarm jerked her to consciousness. She lay in a tangled heap of bedclothes and perspiration. The nightmare had felt so real it had paralysed all sane thoughts. She pushed herself up into a sitting position, fear still circulating throughout her body. She'd been crazy to think she could cover up Dickson's death. She should have taken her chances, told the truth and hoped the courts believed her. A motorbike drove past her house, the engine whining loudly, stirring some sense back into her befuddled mind. No. She would have been charged with manslaughter. This had been the only route she could have taken, and she had to believe in Bradley to help her carry it off. No matter what William suspected, he could prove nothing.

That decided, she got ready for work. Their efforts overnight had come to nought; however, she remained undeterred, and on top of that, she had an additional mission today: to prove that Harriet Khatri was part of the syndicate and was as corrupt as Dickson.

Emma had slept in her own flat. Morgan had wanted her to go back to his place with him, but given how tired they were, it seemed more sensible to part company and grab much-needed rest. There were still other locations to visit – moreover, they had little time to flush out the traffickers before they sold the girls. For the first time in months, Emma hadn't been to the gym before heading to work and she felt bereft. Training was a huge part of her life, and she hoped her involvement with Morgan wasn't going to interfere with it. This whole relationship thing was a minefield with demands now on her free time. Was she really cut out for it? Had she grown so used to being a free agent she couldn't settle into being one half of a couple?

She harrumphed loudly as she grabbed her bag and keys from the hallway table. Obviously she was overtired and couldn't think straight. She should let things happen at their own pace. Morgan was, after all, a great guy – someone she trusted with her life. He knew better than to place too many demands on her.

She turned her attention back to today's tasks. It was imperative they found this elusive dairy where they believed the girls to be held captive, and she'd had a revelation while showering, one she wanted to pursue before heading for the office. Previously, the gang had rented accommodation and hotels to harbour their girls, so there was every reason to expect them to follow suit this time. A search on a few holiday websites had turned up several self-catering accommodations that were either converted dairies or named The Dairy.

She rang Morgan, whose voice was thick with sleep. 'Yo!'

'Yo? You turned into an American? Or have you been watching *Breaking Bad* again?'

'Nah. Can't speak. My tongue is too tired.'

'Well, give it a drink. I'm on my way over to you.'

'Bossy cow.'

'You know you love it.'

She made for her car. This hunch had better pay off. She couldn't bear the idea of any of the girls being abused any more than they already had been.

William washed out the takeaway cartons from the night before and emptied them into the recycling bin. He hadn't enjoyed a restful night and losing sleep always made him grouchy. His pets hadn't helped by clattering in and out of the cat flap all night, nor had the cats' present of a half-eaten mouse left on the rug to greet him when he'd finally got up.

Digger couldn't be too far away. The man moved from farm to farm and although somebody would give him up, it wouldn't be soon enough. William didn't know the man, yet he got the impression he was loyal and, to that end, would undoubtedly turn up again at Toller's farm. The man needed his assistance with the fence and Digger didn't strike William as somebody who would let down those who offered him food and shelter.

It was because of that he'd decided to return to the farm unannounced. It wouldn't surprise him if Mr Toller had kept the drifter's reappearance from him. The farming community was tight knit and William was an outsider.

He rolled down his sleeves, buttoned up the cuffs and picked up the blue silk tie he'd chosen for the day from the back of a chair and, standing in front of a small mirror, flicked it into position, tying the knot as he had done for decades, with ease. Appearances counted for a lot in his profession. People didn't look at his worn face, only the suit he wore and his identity card. To a stranger, he probably looked like a bank manager or an estate agent. Nobody could see into his empty soul. The job had drained him, physically and emotionally.

He really wished John hadn't disappeared. William had fully intended to slip away from everything and be left in peace to spend what days he was owed in his garden.

John had promised it would be over, that William had paid his dues and could retire without repercussions. Yet now he was left dealing with those who had looked up to John and wanted answers.

His mind flicked back to the reservoir the night John vanished. He'd thought about the bike during the long hours he was awake. As he understood it, a woman had brought a bicycle to the reservoir to meet John. For some unfathomable reason he could only think of Kate, who was a keen runner and cyclist. She hadn't turned up for his drinks party that night, offering the excuse about being tired and he'd believed her. All the same, he couldn't shake off the idea she was the woman Digger had spotted, especially as she and John had not got along. Nobody was more aware of their issues than William.

He shook his head to dispel the dark thoughts. No, Kate was one of a kind. She had the strongest moral compass of all of them. No matter how far she was pushed, he knew she would work within the law. Within the rules.

He should stick to facts, and for the time being the only person who could present those was a drifter who hated being cooped up inside.

As had been her intention, Kate was the first to arrive at the office. She'd had a rough night, Dickson's voice taunting her throughout, while she'd remonstrated with herself over her recent actions and tried to justify them by focussing on Harriet, who she was sure was part of the syndicate.

Where Dickson had used Operation Agouti purely to locate the two girls who could have implicated him in the murder of the boy at the Maddox Club, Harriet was manipulating Operation Moonbeam to suit her own ends. If Harriet was, as Farai had claimed, involved with people traffickers, the hotel tip-off could have come from her. She was using information uncovered during Operation Moonbeam to protect her own interests.

Prior to that morning, Kate reasoned, Harriet's team had been targeting restaurants and warehouses where illegals had been sent to work, not searching for sex-workers.

317

'Mere speculation,' said Dickson.

She grimaced. It might be speculation but if she added the fact that Emma and Morgan had told her that Ognian, Doncho and Grozdan worked alone, it made more sense. This trio weren't affiliated with any other major trafficking gang. Why, therefore, had Harriet suddenly decided to go after them?

'More assumptions. She probably acted on information she received from a source. You're reading too much into this.'

'I'm following my intuition on this so you can stop with all the counter-arguments. I'm sick of them and of you.'

'Tough, because you're stuck with me. I'm here to remind you that you've gone bad. That no matter how you justify your actions, you are no better than me!'

Although she knew in her heart that this was true, she hated hearing it. She had sunk to the same depths as Dickson and the others in the syndicate: lying, covering up crimes, manipulating people and events for her own ends, even if it was for some greater good. It was the latter thought that kept her from handing herself in. If her actions could result in some good, in exposing the syndicate, in saving Stanka and Maja and in helping many others, then the end would justify the means. Harriet was going to be the first of those members she would unmask.

Bearing that in mind, Kate had decided to test her theory by passing on information to Harriet. If Harriet was protecting the traffickers, she would act on it and warn them that the net was closing in. She'd already spoken to Felicity, who had agreed to monitor the phone she believed to belong to Harriet. The moment Iota's burner became active, Felicity would trace the call to what Kate hoped would be the traffickers' phone, from which they could pinpoint a location. Then she would swoop on them.

She peered out of the window that overlooked the car park. It was only seven thirty, but as she had expected, Harriet's Volvo rolled into the car park. Like her, Harriet rarely rested during an active investigation.

'*She'll see through your ruse straight away,*' said Dickson.

Kate really hoped he was wrong. Putting on her game face, she made for the stairs, where she intended to accidentally bump into the woman.

Harriet bounced up the stairs, meeting Kate on the landing.

'Oh, hi,' said Kate.

'Morning. You're in early.'

'Same could be said for you. Yes, we had a breakthrough late last night.'

The smile Harriet gave was frosty. 'Good for you. I hope it comes to something.'

'Actually, I've been thinking about our conversation yesterday. I was a bit . . . brusque with you.'

Harriet's eyes narrowed.

'*She isn't falling for this.*'

She couldn't let her resolve weaken. Ignoring the voice, she continued, 'We really should be cooperating with each other. It's not like we're on opposite sides or anything. When I was asked to lead the investigation into Superintendent Dickson's disappearance, I didn't expect to be chasing after traffickers. It makes much more sense if your team and mine are both involved in that part of the investigation.'

Harriet cocked her head. 'I don't disagree. What do you want in return? I take it we are bargaining here?'

'Erm, no. A source has given us valuable information and we've narrowed down possibilities to only a handful of remaining premises. Once we've established the location, I'll be happy to let you know, and you can come in on the raid. You want the traffickers. We want one of the girls. Should be a win-win for both of us.'

Harriet nodded thoughtfully. 'Okay.'

'I'll let you know.'

'Do you want us to get involved? It would speed things up,' said Harriet.

'Thanks, but we've got it covered.'

'Right, then. Let me know when you're ready.'

Kate bounded downstairs to the washroom. If she'd read the situation right, Harriet would contact the traffickers as soon as she could.

In the bathroom mirror, Kate caught sight of her sunken eyes that gave her a haunted air. Remorse that she had been carrying since that night swam in her pupils. She'd tried to ignore it; however, there was no denying that disposing of Dickson's corpse was horribly wrong. In covering her own back and ensuring she wouldn't face any charges, she'd committed an immoral act.

'You're going to have to keep up this pretence for a lot longer yet, maybe even for years. Be honest, you're not up to that. You can't cope with that amount of guilt, which will only keep building and building. It'll keep eating at you until you break. And eventually you will, Kate. You will.'

She groaned loudly and covered her ears. She had hated Dickson, true. He'd been evil and he'd been responsible for Chris's murder, but in covering up his death, she'd denied his relatives and his friends the opportunity of granting him a decent burial. Moreover, those people, especially Elaine, would be unable to get closure. She knew how painful that was. She'd spent over a year chasing the truth about Chris and yet here she was, committing the same crime as Dickson – pretending she knew nothing about what had happened.

She fought back tears that came out of the blue. She'd battled them every night when alone in bed, loathing herself for what she was putting Dickson's family through. The only way she could prevent herself from being eaten away by guilt was by reminding herself

Dickson had been despicable. Innocent people had been killed to hide his involvement in one boy's murder – Chris, Cooper and Rosa were dead because of him. In all likelihood, so was Heather Gaunt, and anyone else who had got in his way. He'd even treated her own father badly and was rotten to the core. Yes, his family would suffer, but no one else would fall in his wake.

She lifted her head, stared once more at herself. She had done wrong but for the right reasons. That was the difference between her and Dickson. And now she would make sure those she suspected to be part of his corrupt circle didn't replace him. William could wait, but Harriet was going down.

With no message from Felicity, she left the washroom. This was going to be a waiting game. It didn't matter. She was expert at those.

William tramped down a track towards the Tollers' farm, regretting his decision to leave his grey Toyota Corolla parked down the lane. He felt for the handcuffs in his pocket, the only insurance he had at present that he wouldn't lose his witness for a second time.

The repetitive thudding in the distance suggested Digger had resumed fencing. William headed directly for the field. He was in luck: Digger had his back to him and didn't see him approach. Only when William was upon him did the man give a startled, 'What the—?'

'Hello, Digger.'

Digger cast about for an escape route.

'Don't think about it. There are officers placed all around the farm. They're armed. For your own sake, put down that rammer and come with me.'

The steel implement fell to the ground. 'But Mr Toller—'

'Should have told me you were here. He'll understand why I'm taking you to the station and you can continue your work when you return. Now, are you going to come with me, or do I have to cuff you and call one of my officers over to escort you?' He dangled the cuffs in front of the man's face. Digger mumbled something William couldn't make out but took to be acquiescence and they crossed the fields together, William with one hand on the man's arm. There was no way he was going to be fooled a second time.

CHAPTER TWENTY-FIVE

DAY FIVE – AFTERNOON

Emma and Morgan still hadn't caught a break. They'd almost eliminated every place on Emma's list and, for both of them, frustration was mounting.

Emma passed the open packet of biscuits across to Morgan and checked her list for the next property.

Morgan wiped a crumb from his lips. 'I'm not the Ice Queen's biggest supporter, but I really feel her team should be doing the legwork on this, not us. It's turning out to be a massive ball ache.'

'You're unusually grouchy. What's up? Not enough sleep?'

'I'm sulking because my girlfriend wouldn't sleep with me last night,' he replied, shoving an entire chocolate-topped biscuit into his mouth and staring at her with accusing eyes as he chewed.

'Yeah, right. I know that's not the real reason.'

He didn't respond until he'd swallowed. 'Actually, I'm a bit brassed off with all this running around chasing shadows, that's all. If we find this girl, Maja, who's to say Girl X has any information to locate the superintendent? Plus, she and her friend were supposed to meet Farai before Kate did. They might even have shot him! Everything sounds . . . odd to me. It was already weird that we were assigned the case instead of Missing Persons, but since then, it's got a whole bunch weirder. I like things clear cut.'

Emma took a biscuit from the proffered packet. 'If my hunch pays off, it might give us what we need to find the super. The investigation is still about him. Once Girl X tells us what she knows, we'll steam ahead and find him. You wait and see.'

'Somebody must have eaten three *huge* Weetabix for breakfast and is feeling indestructible.'

'I'm a coffee-and-toast girl in the mornings. As you well know. Okay, tea break is over. Brush those crumbs from your shirt and let's go. The next place is called Old Dairy and it's only five minutes from here.'

'Old Dairy, New Dairy, The Dairy, Milk House, Ye Olde Milking Parlour. Who'd have thought there'd be so many milk-themed properties in one area?' He scratched at his neck before slotting his seatbelt into its latch. 'See. I'm itching. I'm beginning to develop a milk intolerance.'

They pulled away from the lay-by, Emma nibbling on a biscuit as they drove. To be fair, Morgan had a point. They were investing a huge number of man-hours into something that could turn out to be a ruse. Having said which, Kate believed Girl X, and if Kate believed in her, that was good enough for Emma. She finished the biscuit and checked the satnav. Part of her was quietly content to be in the same vehicle as Morgan. They didn't feel the need to fill a silence. They picked up on each other's emotions. In fact, they were damn good together. Maybe she would stay over at his place this evening.

They'd travelled to the edge of Stoke-on-Trent, to a village on the north-east fringe, away from the housing estates, built-up areas and retail parks. Here, bungalows and cottages edged one side of the road; opposite them were stone walls, fields and green hills. Warning traffic signs alerted motorists to horses and riders, and the road narrowed to become a meandering track, taking them past more golden fields, smallholdings and houses that to Emma seemed palatial.

She kept one eye on the moving dot on the screen. The houses were thinning out, acres separating them from their neighbours. Her blood fizzed in her veins. She'd checked out the area and it was ripe with rental accommodation – perfect for the trio of men who wished to maintain a low profile.

The road split, one way leading to Knypersley, three miles away, the other unmarked. They took the latter, and just when she thought they were going to run out of properties, she spotted a turning marked 'Old Dairy'.

'Here!' she said.

Morgan brought the Jeep to a stop, and she reached for the binoculars, held them to her eyes, then gave a triumphant, 'Yes!'

'What can you see?'

'A silver Merc belonging to Ognian!'

'No! Are you sure you've got the right one?'

'Defo. We'd better go. I don't want them to spot us.'

'Well done. You worked this out.'

'We can't celebrate too soon. His car's here, but it doesn't necessarily follow that the girls, or the other men, are. Head back down the lane and we'll let Kate know.'

William's attempts to draw Digger into conversation on the way to HQ had failed. The man had kept his head lowered and his mouth shut.

'I bet you know the area quite well, don't you?' said William. When no answer was forthcoming, he continued, 'And the people. I bet you know lots of locals. I've always lived in a town. I sometimes think it would be nice to move to somewhere more rural. I'm due to retire very soon. I quite fancy a bit of a smallholding. I've got bees. I'm sure they'd like it in the country.'

Digger shifted slightly on hearing this news. William continued, 'I wouldn't mind some chickens and a few sheep or goats either to keep the grass down. Have you always liked animals?'

Digger shrugged. 'S'pose so.'

'How long have you been drifting from farm to farm?'

'Dunno. Maybe fifteen years. Maybe more. I don't keep track.'

'Can I ask you something personal?'

Digger shrugged again.

'Why do you hate being indoors so much? Don't get me wrong, I would much rather be outside than in, too, but you actually hate it. Why is that?'

There was a huge silence and William thought he'd overstepped some line. Digger wasn't up for sharing with a stranger. Eventually, he spoke, his voice a half-whisper.

'My mum burned down our house when I was a kid.'

'I'm sorry to hear that.'

There was another long pause before he added, 'My older sister and brother both died. I don't talk about it.'

'Sure. I think I can understand now why you wouldn't want to sleep inside a house. You know, my dad was a firefighter. I wanted to join the fire brigade when I was younger. My mum was worried it was far too dangerous a job, so I went into the police force instead!' he said with a smile.

Digger just shook his head. 'The fire brigade couldn't save my family.'

William let it drop. He had enough information to understand the man; now he had to coax the other stuff he needed from him. 'We're almost there. I'll make sure we're on the ground floor in the largest interview room we have. It even has a window.'

Digger didn't meet his eye.

'You prefer cows or sheep?'

'Not bothered. I like pigs.'

'I read once that studies show they are more intelligent than dogs and even three-year-old children. Fancy that, eh?'

Digger turned sharp brown eyes on him. 'Is that so?'

'Uh-huh.'

'I always thought they were clever. They remember people. Whenever I go back to a pig farm, they come over to say hello. They let me scratch their heads too,' said Digger.

Back in safe territory, William managed to keep up the conversation about animals and farm life until they reached the station.

◆ ◆ ◆

By lunchtime, Kate still hadn't heard anything from Felicity regarding Iota's burner phone. She'd been out scoping properties and returned to the office in time for Emma's phone call to say she and Morgan had spotted Ognian's Mercedes outside a self-catering property.

'Have you any idea how many men are inside the property?' Kate asked.

'We're too far away to tell. I can't even be sure there's anyone at all. We didn't dare risk alerting them if they are, so we're further down the lane, a short distance from the house. There's a small caravan park at the end of the lane, but anyone coming or going from there, or the Old Dairy, will have to pass us.'

'I don't want you taking any unnecessary risks. It's likely the men have weapons. I'll request an armed unit to assist. Are you carrying an enforcer?' The battering ram would open any inward-opening doors with ease, especially in Morgan's hands, and could be concealed under a coat for covert operations.

'Yes.'

'I'll arrange a warrant in case these guys want to play hardball. Wait for my call.'

She raced to William's office only to find it empty. A fellow officer walking past said, 'If you're looking for DCI Chase, you might find him in one of the interview rooms. He brought somebody in a few minutes ago for questioning.'

'Cheers.'

She bounded down the stairs two at a time. The officer at reception told her that William was in interview room F. She knocked on the door and opened it with an apology.

'Sorry to disturb you.'

The man sitting opposite William had dark hair that curled over the collar of a waterproof green coat, open to expose blue overalls. He stared in surprise at her.

'What is it, DI Young?' said William.

'I really need to talk to you. It's urgent.'

He spoke to the man. 'Would you excuse me?'

The man didn't answer. His eyes remained fixed on Kate, who gave him a polite smile and withdrew.

'William, we think we've found the traffickers' hideaway. I require a warrant and manpower immediately.'

'Right! Yes. I'll arrange that. I need somebody to keep an eye on my visitor while I'm sorting that out. He has a knack of disappearing. Would you wait here, outside the room?'

'Sure.'

'Don't let him out of your sight. I'll send an officer to replace you.'

He opened the door and Kate heard the words 'Sorry about that, Digger—' before the door shut.

She wondered why William was questioning the vagrant at the station, but there wasn't much time to ponder before she caught sight of Harriet talking to Jamie again. Jamie nodded enthusiastically and then disappeared. Harriet didn't move; instead, she checked her phone then, looking up, spotted Kate. She turned away and headed back towards the stairs.

Thoughts squirmed in Kate's mind. Harriet and Jamie were up to something, maybe even discussing the traffickers and how to alert them. However, they were close to rescuing Maja, which took priority over these concerns. Once the girl was safe, William would expect Stanka to cough up information about Dickson – or even his whereabouts – and Kate needed to brief her on that subject.

CHAPTER TWENTY-SIX

DAY FIVE – MID-AFTERNOON

They'd eaten the entire packet of biscuits between them.

Emma drained a small carton of orange juice, scrunched it up and put it, along with the rest of the empty packaging, into a plastic bag.

Morgan watched her. 'I like a tidy house.'

'I've seen your place, and tidy it isn't.'

'But it will be, once you move in.'

'You're kidding! We've only just started seeing each other.'

'But you will, won't you? I know you will. Eventually.' He folded his arms and grinned to himself.

'Has anyone told you that you have too much self-confidence?'

'No such thing.'

She reached again for the binoculars. Morgan had moved the Jeep to a spot along the lane where there was a large enough gap in the hedgerow for her to keep an eye on the driveway leading to the Old Dairy. Suddenly she threw down the binoculars and began undoing her blouse.

'Oh . . . Right!' said Morgan.

She removed the garment, then shuffled towards him, lifting a leg over the armrest between them before manoeuvring into position, so she was sitting on his lap facing him.

'Erm . . . Emma!'

She pressed her body against his chest. 'They're on their way. Pretend we're making out.'

As the Mercedes appeared on the lane, he wrapped his arms around her, and she lowered her lips on to his. The car edged past their vehicle. She opened one eye slightly as she continued kissing Morgan. An unshaven man with heavy brows and black eyes glanced dispassionately in their direction. His fellow passengers made comment and laughed. She didn't move until she was certain they'd gone, then pulled away.

'Well, I've had less interesting stake-outs,' said Morgan.

She slid off his lap with a gymnastic movement that saw her back in the passenger seat in an instant. 'There were three goons in that car, which means if the girls are inside the house, they're probably alone. We've got a chance to rescue them.' She wriggled back into her blouse while Morgan rang Kate, who gave them permission to go ahead.

Out of the vehicle, they hugged the hedgerow to the turnoff, then jogged up the driveway. Decorative cartwheels stood against the white paintwork of the house. With its narrow windows, muddy brown painted frames and exposed brickwork under the edges, it was clear to see it had been sympathetically restored to resemble the old dairy it had once been. The long, narrow building had been extended by a new wooden-framed, covered porch, inside which stood two milk churns filled with spider plants. There was no front garden, only a patio area with a wooden bench and garden sculptures.

Emma peered through the first window. The rustic kitchen was empty.

Morgan looked through the windows on the other side of the porch, caught her eye and shook his head. He made for a wooden gate that was set in a wall to the side of the building, tried the latch without success.

'Probably bolted from the inside,' he said.

'We'll have to get in somehow. My money's on them being shut in a room inside. Most likely upstairs,' said Emma. 'I suggest a knock-and-enter approach.'

'Okay.'

The porch door was unlocked, and she stepped inside and hammered on the front door. 'This is the police. Open up!'

There wasn't a sound.

After the second attempt, Morgan produced the enforcer and with one swing the door opened wide.

'Police! Come out!'

Emma went first, checking the downstairs rooms, before mounting the stairs. 'Is there anybody here? It's the police.'

Nothing.

'Police!' shouted Morgan. 'Come out!'

They reached the landing and again, as a coordinated team, opened doors. Clothes were strewn across an unmade bed in the first room and blinds closed. It was much the same in every room.

'There's no one here, Emma.'

'They must be here! Harry said we had forty-eight hours. Time isn't up.' She clattered downstairs again and back into the kitchen. Items of unwashed crockery were piled high in the sink. She walked over to them. 'What do you see?'

'Dishes that need cleaning.'

'Seven mugs – that's three for the goons and four for the girls. They're here somewhere. Let's try outside,' she said.

'Emma, there's nobody here,' said Morgan. 'And, I hate to say it, but they could have moved the girls before we even arrived.'

'Well, I'm not giving up.' She chewed her lip for a moment, then began shouting, 'Maja! Maja! Your sister is looking for you.'

This time there was a faint tapping sound.

'Maja!' Emma shouted again.

She was rewarded with another *tap, tap, tap.* 'It's coming from downstairs. There must be a cellar.' She opened doors in the kitchen, calling the girl's name.

Morgan stepped out into the hall and shouted, 'Found it!'

The door was hidden behind a curtain and bolted from the outside. Morgan sprung the heavy black bolts and the door opened towards them. Soft whimpers rose to greet them.

'Maja. It's okay. We're police,' Emma said.

Morgan found a light switch on the wall outside and illuminated the room. Steep steps led to a small basement. Emma ducked her head and made her way towards the girls huddled together on mattresses. They stared with huge, terrified eyes. She held up her ID card.

'Hi. I'm Emma. I'm a police officer. Do any of you speak English?'

A small voice rose. 'I do.'

'We're here to save you.'

'I heard you calling my name. I hit that with my shoe.' She pointed to a pipe running along the ground.

'Are you Maja?'

'Yes.'

'Your sister told us about you.'

'Is she here?'

'No. We'll take you to her. All of you need to come with us now, before the men return. Can you tell them, Maja?'

Maja spoke to the others, who rose as one. As they filed in front of her, Emma gave them smiles and reassurances. She pointed to ·

Morgan, waiting upstairs. 'That's my colleague. He will help you. Maja, tell them he's a police officer come to rescue them.'

Maja translated and the girls climbed the stairs towards him.

Emma looked around the windowless room before leaving. There was nothing in here other than the mattresses, plastic bottles of water and a bucket, which was clearly used as a toilet. Although her priority was to get the girls away from this place, she wanted to be here when the men returned and were captured. She'd be very happy to ensure scum like them got their just deserts.

◆ ◆ ◆

Having sorted the requests for Kate's team, William had returned to the interview room to resume the interview with Digger, whose attitude had changed since he'd left. The hard work William had put in to relax the man appeared to have been eradicated during the ten minutes he had been gone.

He'd tried again, arranging for Digger to have a cup of tea and chatting about his life as a farm hand. This time he hadn't been willing to speak, forcing William to cut the chit-chat and get down to business. So far, it was like pulling teeth.

'Last time we spoke about the gunshot, you said you'd witnessed a woman and a man putting something you believed to be a dead deer into a car, from the bank opposite, where you'd been fishing.'

Digger stared at his milky tea.

'Listen, Digger, I've been back to the reservoir and,' he gave a small shrug, 'you and I both know that wasn't the case. I'm not saying you didn't see those people. Only that you couldn't possibly have done so from the far bank of the reservoir. So, no more beating about the bush. Do you want to tell me where you really were that evening?'

He sat back and lifted his own cup to his lips. Digger didn't move a muscle. With a gentle sigh, he set down his drink. 'Okay, how about I tell you what I think? You can simply nod if I'm right or shake your head if I'm wrong.'

Although Digger didn't move, a small muscle flexed in his jaw.

'Right, this is what I think happened. You were on the same bank of the reservoir as the people you saw.'

The muscle flexed again. Digger's eyes flicked towards him, momentarily afraid.

'There's no way you could have identified people or heard voices or established one of them was a woman unless you'd been closer. In fact, I think not only were you on the same bank as them, but right behind them, hiding in the bushes. I think that sometimes, you go to that spot to watch people making out in their cars. You told me people go there to have sex.'

Digger flushed and wouldn't meet his eyes.

'Listen, I don't care about why you were there. It's immaterial. What matters is what you saw while you were there. So, am I right? Were you hiding in the bushes?'

He waited for what felt like an eternity before Digger gave the tiniest of nods.

William placed his elbows on the table and leant forwards. 'Then, Digger, you must have known it was a person who was shot, not a deer.'

A small, frightened noise escaped from Digger.

'It's okay. I understand why you didn't want to come forward about it. You were scared. Not only would you have had to come to town, but you'd also have had to explain to an officer the real reason why you were at the reservoir at that time of night. Am I still right?'

Digger nodded again. 'Yes, I . . . was scared. I wanted to tell the police, but I thought you'd think I was making it up. They took the body away. I was worried the police would charge me or keep me in a cell. I . . . I can't do that. I'll go mad.'

'You won't be put in any cell. I promise. Have you told me everything you saw that night?'

'Yes.'

'Absolutely everything?'

'Yes.'

'Did you see the body?'

'No. I didn't. Honest. I didn't want them to find out I was there. They might have shot me too. I kept my head down and stayed still until after the woman drove off. I could only see some of what was happening through the bushes.'

'The man in the Land Rover arrived after the gunshot?'

Digger nodded.

'Did you see the vehicle's numberplate?'

'No.'

'If I showed you a photo of the man, would you recognise him?'

'No. I couldn't see his face.'

'And the woman.'

Digger rubbed his neck nervously.

'Digger, could you describe the woman in more detail to me?'

Digger got up in a quick movement, the chair falling backwards. 'I want to go.'

'You can. Very soon.'

'Now!' Digger began banging on the door.

William crossed over to him, placed a hand on his arm loosely. 'Okay. I'll drive you back to the farm. Come and finish your drink, then we'll leave.'

He didn't move.

'Come on. Finish your tea first,' he coaxed.

Eventually, the man turned around. William picked up the chair and set it straight. Digger sat again, lifted his cup and gulped the liquid. William watched him. Something had sparked the sudden panic. They'd been talking about the woman at the time. His drink finished, Digger stood once more. 'I want to go now.'

'Of course.' William rose too. Slowly, he lifted his coat from the back of the chair and began putting it on. 'You saw the woman's face, didn't you?'

Digger nodded.

William put his arm into his sleeve and said casually, 'Did you know her?'

Digger shook his head.

'Would you recognise her if you saw her again?'

Digger nodded. 'I have seen her.'

'Where?'

Digger tucked his hands under his arms, a look of distress crossing his features. 'I want to go.'

'Okay. Just tell me first. Where did you see her?'

'Here.'

'Here?'

'The woman who came in. She looked like her.'

On receiving the news that Emma and Morgan had rescued four girls, including Maja, Kate instructed the armed unit that was already on its way to wait for the traffickers to return. The girls were being transported to the station, where they'd be examined by a doctor and held there until they could give statements, before being passed over to the correct authorities. Kate texted Stanka to let her know that her sister was safe, asking her to ring as soon as she got the message.

So far, her plan to entrap Harriet hadn't worked. There'd been no activity on the burner phone and Harriet appeared to be going about her business as usual. Torn between doing her duty and establishing Harriet's trustworthiness, she found herself drawn to the latter. She had to catch her out, but the only way would jeopardise catching the traffickers. Risky or not, she was invested in exposing Harriet as Iota. She argued the point backwards and forwards, pausing several times along the corridor, before deciding it would be foolish to put something into play that could cost them their arrest. She would simply tell Harriet they had found the girls. If Harriet wanted in on catching the traffickers, then she could. After all, Kate had promised she would inform her once they'd located Ognian's men.

She passed through the large open-plan office where several of her old team were hard at work, and found Harriet in the back room, face lined with concentration.

'What is it? I'm up to my eyeballs here,' said Harriet.

'Just thought I'd let you know that the trafficked girls have been found.'

'What about the traffickers?'

'Ah, not yet. They weren't at the premises when my team stormed it, but we have surveillance in place. They'll be returning soon.'

'What makes you think that?'

'The girls were due to be moved today. They'll be back for them. There's an armed team in situ.'

'Your info was correct, then?'

'Yes. Do you want your team involved?'

'No, let the armed unit handle it.'

Kate nodded. 'Once the men have been arrested, we'll need to speak to them first over the not-so-small matter of murder, then they're all yours.'

'Thanks.' Harriet lowered her head back over the files.

'I'll leave you to your work.'

She returned to her office to find it empty. She rested her head in her hands and wondered if she had got it wrong about Harriet after all. There had been no calls from Iota. Harriet hadn't taken the bait earlier in the day and hadn't insisted on being involved in the arrest of the trio. In fact, she had seemed preoccupied with other work. Kate needed to ease up on her crusade. No sooner had she had the thought than her phone rang.

'Iota's phone has gone live. The signal is coming from HQ again,' said Felicity.

Kate raced from her office to Harriet's, only to be told by one of the officers there that she'd just left. *Damn!* She pounded downstairs, intending to search for Harriet in the washroom where she might be making the call, then ground to a halt when she spied her pacing in the car park, mobile pressed to her ear.

Kate made for the entrance to confront her. At the same time, Harriet ended the call and stalked towards her car. On a whim, and with no other reason than a feeling Harriet was on her way to warn the traffickers, Kate headed to her own car, where she waited for Harriet's Volvo to leave. Noting she had turned right, Kate set off in pursuit.

Digger had fallen silent again. William was no longer in the mood for casual conversation. What he'd discovered had turned everything on its head. He questioned Digger's reliability as a witness. It had been dark, and he'd been afraid of being discovered.

'Are you sure that was the same woman?' he asked as he drove.

Digger shrugged. 'I think so.'

'Think so or recognise her?'

'Think so,' he said after a while.

William gritted his teeth. He wanted to believe Digger had made a mistake in identifying Kate.

'What makes you think it was her?'

'She was thin and tall. She had the same sort of hair.'

William considered his words. There wasn't enough to prove it was Kate. All the same, part of him believed Digger. Even he had thought about Kate and her bicycle.

'Maybe it wasn't her,' said Digger eventually, nodding, his expression showing that he believed what he was saying.

Inside his head, William groaned with frustration. 'You must write a statement. I don't want any excuses.'

'I don't want to do it.'

'You don't *have* to, but here's the thing: unless you give me a full statement, you could become a suspect because you were at the reservoir that night.'

'But I didn't do anything.'

'*I* know you didn't, but investigating officers might think differently. You need to make a statement to officially clear your name. Do you understand?'

Digger nodded.

'So, think about what you saw tonight, and I'll come back tomorrow to collect you again and we'll write it all down in the interview room that we were in today. Okay?'

'Yes.'

'And, Digger, if you run off, I'll have to send police officers after you. It will look like you are guilty and so we'll probably arrest you. Clear?'

Digger swallowed hard. 'Yes.'

They'd reached the farm. Digger tumbled out of the Toyota Corolla without a goodbye, leaving William to drive back to the station, thinking hard about how he intended pursuing this latest information.

CHAPTER TWENTY-SEVEN

DAY FIVE – LATE AFTERNOON

Kate maintained a safe distance from the Volvo. She'd trailed cars before but, to do it properly, an entire surveillance team was required. This time, she was on her own, and fully aware that at any given moment Harriet might spot her. She was banking on the fact that Harriet had seemed agitated while on the phone. With any luck, her thoughts would be directed elsewhere rather than on checking whether she was being followed.

'You're quite mad, you know?' Dickson's supercilious voice rose from the passenger seat. *'Barking mad, in fact. Leaving your team to deal with illegals, off on a flight of fancy, with no evidence to support what you are doing. You've fallen a long way from your lofty, moral perch.'*

'Don't I know it.' Dickson's observation rankled her because she knew he was right. What she was doing *was* crazy and so out of character. Then again, hadn't she already proved she was no longer the person she'd once been? Eyes still on the black Volvo, she reminded herself that Farai's dying words had been a warning about Harriet and that somebody, most likely Harriet, had tipped off the traffickers at the hotel. Kate now firmly believed Harriet, unable to reach them by telephone, was on her way to warn the traffickers that the police were waiting at the Old Dairy for them. It was possible that Harriet knew the traffickers' location. It might be a place where she had met them before. Kate realised she was making a number of assumptions, yet they seemed logical ones and so she chose to follow her instinct.

Dickson snorted. *'Whatever! You'll come a cropper in due course, though. Mark my words.'*

They were entering the industrial area of Fenton and soon she noticed that, six cars ahead of her, Harriet's right indicator was flashing. By the time she had turned into the street, she could no longer see the Volvo. She slowed her speed as she passed the car parks outside buildings. There was no sign of the black vehicle in any of them.

Dickson's voice was quiet but smug. *'She's shaken you off. She knew all along you were tailing her.'*

'She's here somewhere. I can feel it.'

'Oh, well, if you feel it, then it must be right, because that's what proper policing is based on. Thank heavens for hunches and feelings.'

She turned towards Dickson, ready to bite back. The empty passenger seat brought her to her senses.

An enormous grey-coloured casting factory loomed into view. Slowing to a crawl and craning her neck, she checked the visitors' parking area without success. If Harriet had continued in this direction, and over the railway crossing, Kate would have difficulty locating her in the labyrinth of housing that lay beyond. Then, as hope was fading, she caught sight of a single-storey office block, windows barred and shuttered, ivy thick against the brickwork. Behind it stood a group of warehouses. The entrance gate was wide open, and Kate knew in a heartbeat that Harriet would be here. She left her car on some scrubland near other vehicles and jogged towards the place, slipping through the gate and hugging the wall as she made for the rear. She spied Harriet's car parked in front of one of the warehouses, a blue metal door to the building ajar. She sprinted towards it and slid inside.

It took a few moments for her eyes to grow accustomed to the gloom, during which she stood stock still, and hoped no one would see her.

A few weak shafts of light allowed her to determine she was in a cavernous space, empty apart from rows and rows of racking. She crept forwards, straining for any sound that would alert her to Harriet's location. There was nothing other than the sound of passing traffic in the distance and then a blast of a train's horn. She reached for a wall to steady her nerves, fingers rubbing against the rough surface. Striving for calm, she concentrated on quietening her thumping heart. The rushing of blood in her ears didn't abate. The whooshing obliterated everything else, including the soft tread of somebody approaching and, before she could react, the world went black.

William arrived at the station in time to see Morgan shepherding four young women through reception.

'Kate told me you found them,' he said. 'Well done.'

'Emma should take the credit. It was her idea to check out self-catering accommodation.'

William nodded. 'We'll get them processed and find a translator. Any of them speak English?'

'Only the one we've been looking for – Maja.' Morgan pointed out a pretty dark-haired girl with brown eyes.

William said, 'Okay, have them put together in the same room and find them something to eat and drink. They all look scared to death. Is Kate not here? I'd have thought she'd want to speak to Maja.'

'Her car's not outside. I tried ringing her earlier, but her phone is switched off.'

'Really?'

Morgan shrugged. 'She might be following up another lead or gone to fetch Girl X.'

'Yes.' William wasn't so convinced. Kate didn't usually turn off her phone during investigations. There were a few things about Kate that were beginning to perturb him.

'Or should I say, Stanka?' said Morgan.

'Sorry?'

'Girl X. Maja told me her sister's name is Stanka.'

'Stanka?'

'Yes.'

William digested this news. Kate had told him the girl who had slept with John Dickson had information about him. To his knowledge John hadn't slept with anyone called Stanka. He'd spent the night with Rosa. What on earth was Kate playing at?

Kate came to, wondering what the hell had happened to her. Pain swam through her head when she tried to move it. She couldn't open her eyes. She bobbed out of consciousness and drifted on a colourless sea. When she next came to, the throbbing was still present, but she was aware of sitting blindfolded on a chair, hands tied behind her. Harriet had set her up.

A hand shook her shoulder roughly and a deep voice spoke to her in a heavy Eastern European accent. 'You awake?'

She didn't reply.

Another voice said something she couldn't understand. Had Ognian and his goons taken her hostage?

'Wake up!' The first voice was louder. This time he shook her so hard, sharp darts pierced her skull.

'Are you going to kill me?'

A laugh. 'Yes.'

'Why haven't you?'

There was a pause. Then: 'We're waiting.'

'What for?'

'Never mind what for. Yes, we will kill you.'

'I'm a police officer. My colleagues will be looking for me.'

There was movement, another pair of feet coming towards her. She braced herself for whatever injury they might inflict on her: a slap, a beating. There was nothing, only heavy breathing, then somebody was by her ear. '*Nobody* is looking for you.'

'DI Khatri! Are you here?' she called.

The men chuckled.

'Is she here?'

'You ask too many questions. That is why you are going to die.'

'What do you mean?'

'Enough! You stay quiet and we wait.'

There was a harshness in the man's tone that silenced her. He was not to be provoked.

This had to be Harriet's doing. And having decided that it was, it was no great leap to then deduce Harriet would want Kate out of the picture for good. Dickson had disposed of anyone who was close to exposing him, therefore it followed Harriet would pursue a similar path. Basically, she was fucked. There would be no last-minute cavalry.

◆ ◆ ◆

William found Jamie in the briefing room now emptied of officers who had been drafted in to help in the hunt for John Dickson. 'How did it go?'

'The new guys are up to speed and on the case.'

'Thanks for stepping in at the last minute. I hope my notes were useful.'

'They were and thank you for having confidence in me to do the job.'

'You're a good officer, DC Webster. You are more than capable of handling something like this. Besides, you know the case well enough.'

'You made it easy for me. I only had to direct, as per your instructions.'

'I take it you've heard we recovered Maja and the others earlier?'

'Morgan told me. If we can get her sister to talk now, we might make significant headway in finding the super.'

'Hmm.'

'You sound unsure.'

William quickly shook off the frown he felt pulling his eyebrows together. 'No. I'm cautious, that's all. We'll have to see what comes of it.'

Harriet was passing the room and stopped to speak to them both.

'I hear congratulations are in order,' she said. 'You got the girls out.'

William nodded. 'The girls are safe, but we're still waiting on the traffickers.'

'About that. I understand an armed team was sent to watch the house in question.'

'Correct.'

'Shouldn't my team have been notified before that happened?'

'As I understood it, your team were, and still are, fully occupied.'

'But this is part of our investigation—'

'DI Khatri, not here.' He threw her a warning look. Jamie could overhear the entire conversation, which by his book was unprofessional. 'My office.'

Once behind closed doors, he let her vent until she'd said all she needed.

'I understand your grievance, but you can't spread yourself or your team too thinly. It made sense to send in extra officers and allow yours to continue pursuing leads and angles you've been amassing. It's an important operation, Harriet. You're not simply after three blokes trafficking a handful of young women every few months or so. You're looking at a much larger scale operation. Kate stumbled across these guys during the investigation into the superintendent's disappearance, and it was too messy to shunt it between you. And, to boot, she believes these men, or at least one of them, are responsible for two recent murders, which means she needs to interview them on that matter as well. The fact remains you will get to question these men once they're brought into custody and that should suffice.'

Harriet's jaw tightened.

'And, can I just say, I'm very surprised you've brought this up with me . . . and, moreover, in front of a member of staff. This behaviour is not what I have come to expect from you. Now, get back to your team.'

He dismissed her with a wave, and she left the room with her head high.

William couldn't understand what had got into her. She was notoriously calm and collected. She worked efficiently, and ordinarily would never have questioned his decisions, especially in a semi-aggressive way.

He dropped his head into his hands. Retirement seemed such a long way off now. And Kate? What the hell was he going to do about her? His phone buzzed. 'Dental appointment reminder' said the message.

It was a code used by the syndicate. One of them wanted to contact William via his second mobile. He reached for the burner and switched it on. It rang almost immediately.

'Gamma. Listen, she's become too big a problem to ignore. She was snooping again and followed Khatri. The guys have the situation in hand. I need to know what you want to do with her. Alpha still can't be reached. I know he was talking of sorting her.'

William didn't know Gamma's identity, only that they were Dickson's fixer and that the problem they were referring to was Kate.

He thought that she'd backed off from probing into John's business, but it appeared she hadn't. With John out of the frame, it now fell to William to make judgement calls. But he didn't have the same stomach for this work as John.

'Release her,' he said. 'Let her think she was taken by traffickers because she stumbled on to them.'

'You really think she'll fall for it?' Gamma's voice had taken on a wary note. 'I don't think she'll buy it.'

'Until the boss returns, I get to make the calls on this matter.'

'The boss will have different ideas.'

'He isn't available, and I say she gets released.'

'I'm not happy about that.'

'Tough. That's how I want to play it.'

'Then *you* better make the call to the guys.'

Gamma hung up. William tapped his phone against his chin. Of all the people to get embroiled in this, it would have to be Kate. The thought saddened him beyond belief.

Kate was sitting on a blanket, the sun on her face. She leant back to enjoy the warmth. Chris enveloped her with strong arms and whispered, 'I'm glad you've joined me. I've been waiting for you.'

She turned her head, her lips brushing against his. It felt so good to finally be home. She'd missed him more than she could put into words.

The ringing of a phone stirred her from her reverie. A man grunted 'Okay', then spewed a volley of angry words in a foreign language.

The other man responded in kind, voices rising as they batted sentences back and forth, frustration evident in their words. A chair was kicked across the room, landing noisily against metal which rang out. Footsteps marched towards her.

'You awake?'

'Fuck off,' she growled, in a final attempt to show she was no coward. She wasn't scared of them or of death. She would be well rid of this world.

He laughed. 'You are a funny woman.'

'And you are a pussy.'

He snarled. 'Bitch!'

The other man, in the background, mouthed off in his native tongue. Kate was under the impression he was telling the man to do something. Was her time up?

She heard the distinctive click of a switchblade opening close to her ear and stiffened in preparation for what was to come.

The man's breath warmed her neck. All the same, she didn't flinch, concentrating on the dream she'd just had. Chris was waiting for her. There was a tugging at her wrists and suddenly they broke free.

'Don't move! There is a gun pointed at your head.'

More tugging, this time at her feet, as the man cut through the binds.

'You leave on the blindfold. You count to one hundred, like in the game hide-and-seek, then you go back to the station and forget all about this. If you say anything, we'll find you and slit your throat. I shall look forward to that.'

Kate couldn't get her head around what was happening. 'Where are you going?'

'We had orders. Do not move until you have counted and do so very slowly. If I see you before we leave, I'll blow your head off.'

She couldn't hear them departing, and afraid that they might still be there and even watching her, she obeyed, counting silently, all the while listening for an engine or any sound to indicate they'd left. She waited beyond the full count then cautiously removed the blindfold.

Although it was dark in the aisle where she sat, she could make out shapes and racking. There were a few scattered plastic chairs – one on its back on the floor, another next to shelving. Her phone had been left on the shelf, the SIM card lying next to it. They'd either forgotten about it or decided to leave it with her. She fumbled to replace the card. The phone burst into life and she saw she had several missed calls and messages. Two stood out. Felicity had left a voicemail ten minutes earlier to say Gamma's mobile had made a call to Beta's phone. Both had been active around the HQ area. Felicity's second message had been left only a few minutes earlier and let Kate know that Beta's mobile had contacted another unknown pay-as-you-go number, which had been tracked to Fenton.

Kate felt her knees buckle and she dropped on to the chair.

William had been the person who had rung her kidnappers.

CHAPTER TWENTY-EIGHT

DAY FIVE – EVENING

William had gone home. His head throbbed and his back ached. He was still trying to process what he'd just learned about Kate. It didn't seem possible. Everything was getting out of hand.

Even with John out of the picture, there were others to consider – Gamma for one, desperate to take John's place. The syndicate consisted of only a handful of top-tier members, all police officers, but there were others – criminals, businessmen and even a politician – who'd been drawn in over the years. The syndicate was paramount in facilitating trafficking: guns, people and drugs. The scale of their operation was now significant, with those involved creaming large amounts of cash from transactions that they were making possible. Nobody would want Kate to spoil that by asking the wrong questions. There was an easy way of ensuring she didn't probe any further, but William couldn't quite bring himself to believe the word of a vagrant.

He would have happily taken out Bradley Chapman, but Kate was another matter altogether.

It had been challenging enough being her mentor and friend without this current situation. He couldn't be seen to favour her over others; however, she had proven her own worth. She'd shown courage and mettle, becoming the natural choice for many investigations and had John not got in the way, would have already been promoted to DCI by now. John's reasons for disliking Kate had stemmed from his dislike of her father, Mitch. He'd jumped on any excuse to have her sidelined, especially in the aftermath of Chris's murder. Even though William had felt aggrieved, he'd been in no position to challenge John. He was too tightly involved in his underhand activities to question anything John did, even when it came to Kate.

Therein lay the problem. Kate was the daughter he'd lost. After Mitch had died, he'd stepped into her father's shoes, and if he dared to admit it, he loved her as his own.

He hunted in the cabinet for some pain relief, wishing for the umpteenth time that he'd taken retirement a month earlier. Still, if he had, Kate would probably not be alive today.

Popping the pills from the blister pack, he glanced into his own reflection and made a decision: the subterfuge had to end. He owed it to Mitch. And to Kate. To tell her the truth about his involvement with Dickson and the syndicate.

He needed to divest himself of the guilt he'd been carrying for years. More importantly, he had to let Kate know what she was up against. Her life depended on it.

Kate blazed into the office and threw her bag on to the floor beside her desk. 'Hi. So sorry. I got delayed, following up on something,' she said.

'We were getting worried—'

Kate interrupted Emma with, 'I couldn't ring you. My phone died for no good reason. Turned out it was a dud battery. Had to buy a new one. Where's Maja?'

'Downstairs.'

'And the traffickers?'

'Surveillance is still in place.'

'No sign of them, then?'

'Not yet.'

'Shit! I hope they haven't got wind of what's happened. Has anyone seen DI Khatri?'

'I have,' said Jamie. 'About an hour ago. She had a go at DCI Chase. He wasn't best pleased because she blew up in front of me. Never seen her like that before. She wanted to know why her team hadn't been informed sooner.'

Kate was sure it had been a ruse. Both William and Jamie were now witnesses to her being at the station rather than in Fenton, which meant Kate would have difficulty proving she'd followed the woman to the warehouse. The crafty bitch was covering her back. Kate rubbed her head and winced. A large bump had formed.

'Everything alright?' asked Morgan.

'Yes. No. I had a bit of an accident. Hit my head. I'm okay, though.'

Emma's face registered concern. 'What happened?'

'It was stupid. I slipped and fell in a car park, of all places. It's nothing.'

'You should get it checked. You could have concussed yourself,' said Jamie.

'It's fine. Really.'

'Have you spoken to Stanka?' asked Morgan.

For a second, Kate was taken aback that he knew Stanka's name, then it struck her Maja would have told them.

Morgan continued, 'Maja's desperate to see her sister.'

Kate nodded. 'I'm sure she is. Tell her that Stanka knows she's safe. I'm waiting for her to contact me, and I'll get her to come in. She's understandably wary. Please don't bandy her name about. I'd still rather we kept her identity under wraps.'

Jamie looked directly at Kate. 'Why?'

Kate sighed. 'Because she is a terrified teenager who is harbouring something big about our superintendent – something she is only willing to divulge if we protect her. By that, I mean nobody outside this team can know about her until we have found out what that is. I know it's woolly and makes little sense, but all the same, go with me on this. I have no doubts that she'll soon be in contact. Listen, you've all had another long day. Get some rest. We'll pick this up tomorrow.'

Once alone, she typed a text message to Stanka, who she urgently needed to see. An idea had come to her as she was driving back to the station. There might yet be a way for Kate to extricate herself from the horrendous fix she was in. She shouldered her bag. Her day was not yet over. First, she had to pay William a visit.

Emma stood by Morgan's car. 'Well, that was weird,' he said.

'In what way?'

'Kate's been out of contact all afternoon, and then rolls up and sends us home without any real explanation or giving us a proper debrief. And as for slipping over, did you really buy that?'

Emma shrugged. 'Sort of.'

'Or the part about getting a new battery for her phone.'

'That's possible—'

'No, Emma. It's extremely unlikely. If something smells like bullshit and sounds like bullshit, then it probably is bullshit. I hate to say it, but I think the responsibility of finding the superintendent is proving too much for her. She's going off at all tangents. Between the high-rankers and the media, it's becoming increasingly important we find out what's happened to him, and I reckon the pressure has got to her.'

'Now that more officers are involved, we should make more progress.'

'And that's another thing. DCI Chase asked Jamie to brief those officers. Jamie, of all people!'

'He has been working with DCI Chase while we've been hunting for the traffickers. He's probably the most up to date of all of us on the progress being made.'

'But Jamie, for crying out loud. Why didn't the DCI take the briefing himself?'

'Don't let it bug you. We've successfully rescued four teenagers today.'

'And that doesn't make a great deal of sense either. We've been chasing our butts over finding Maja and for what? Stanka still hasn't come forward to tell us whatever this huge secret is. Normally, Kate would be on top of this and Stanka would be in an interview room by now. It really doesn't stack up.'

'It'll make sense in the end. Kate's never gone wrong before. She knows what she's doing.'

'Does she, though? I think taking on this investigation on the back of the bolt gun killer is too much for her.'

'Listen, can we drop this conversation? I don't want the whole work thing to become our lives. Some other good things came out of today.'

'Such as?'

'I got horny sitting astride you and would very much like to come back to your place.'

His face brightened. 'That's the best news I've heard all day. You want a lift?'

'No, I'll follow you in my car. I'm not ready for the gossipmongers to start up.'

He rattled his keys. 'Race you back?'

'No, you go on ahead. I need to stop off to buy some food. I lost the bet, remember? I owe you dinner.'

'You know how to cheer somebody up, big time.'

'I'm sure you'll be able to reciprocate. See you there.'

By the time she started her engine, Morgan had already left. As she cruised past the entrance, Kate exited the building, head lowered, lips moving. She pipped her horn and waved but Kate didn't look up. She pulled away feeling anxious. If Kate was beginning to crack, she might make poor decisions. In fact, she might already have done so, and the team would flounder for the foreseeable. She hoped Stanka would give them what they needed, or else Kate would lose face – not only with the hierarchy but her closest allies.

William opened his eyes to find one of his cats sitting on his lap, staring at him. 'Hello, beautiful. Is it dinner time?'

Wayan purred in response and leapt lightly on to the carpet. William hauled himself from his chair where he'd been dozing. His headache had dulled slightly. His back, however, twinged ominously as he bent to pick up the cats' bowls.

Both cats were now performing what William called the 'Dinner Ballet', weaving around his legs and purring harmoniously while he undid the food pouches, setting equal amounts in the bowls.

'Hmm! Mini chicken fillets in gravy. I fancy that myself, boys,' he said, placing the bowls on the floor. The cats darted forwards and began delicately pulling pieces of meat from the dishes.

'Ah, yes, dinner time. I suppose I ought to join you.'

He often talked to the cats. They were excellent company. 'What do you reckon? Minestrone or spicy parsnip?' He held up two cans of soup. Neither cat looked away from their dish.

'Okay, minestrone it is.'

He had just opened the tin when the doorbell rang. Kate was on the doorstep.

'Kate, I—'

'We need to talk.'

'Come in.'

He led her to the sitting room, sat back down. Kate took the chair opposite. Her face wore a familiar determined look. If she was going to tell him about being jumped at the warehouse, he was ready to act shocked. But he wondered if he should pounce first and ask her about the reservoir.

He had no time to decide before she began to speak. 'There's no easy way of saying this, so I'm going to come right out with it. I know. I know you're involved in something corrupt. A group of officers, led by the superintendent. I'm not sure exactly what you're all up to but it involves people trafficking.'

William tried to deflect her claims. 'That's ridiculous! Whatever makes you think—'

'Don't lie to me. You and the other members of your group have burner phones. You used yours to contact the people who were holding me prisoner this afternoon. I ought to thank you for making sure they didn't kill me but I'm sick to my soul to have found out that you, of all people, are tied up in this.'

'Kate, I—'

'No! You don't get to speak. You don't get to say a word until I've finished. I've trusted you my entire life. I've looked up to you, William. Other than Chris, you've been my one constant. *Nothing* you can say is going to make this better. The articles about the superintendent are true. I leaked that information to the press. You see, I found out about his corruption and his reach. I just didn't have you down as someone equally as immoral as him. Chris did. He left me a file with the names of those he suspected to be corrupt officers. Yours was among them. And you know what I did? I dismissed it. I thought he was wrong. I chose not to believe my own husband! Yet all this time, Chris was right: you've been in John Dickson's pocket. Why? Was it the money?'

William ran a hand around the back of his neck and pummelled the knots in his muscles in an attempt to fight off the headache that had flared again. 'It's not what it seems,' he said.

'Really? Then what is it?'

'You're right about John. I knew he was rotten. He was bent way back when your dad and I were sergeants. The thing is nobody could touch him. His influence was so far-reaching, nothing could stick to him. Teflon Dickson. That was his nickname. The only way to infiltrate the syndicate was to convince him I was as shady as him.'

Kate shook her head. 'No! I don't believe that. You're making excuses.'

'Kate, please listen to me. I've been doing exactly what you probably have been doing – gathering evidence to bring him down. Only I've been working from the inside. I've got almost everything I need apart from the identities of a couple of members of the syndicate – one known as Gamma, the other Iota.'

Kate gazed at William slack-jawed, unable to believe a word he spoke. 'You've been part of this . . . syndicate . . . for how long? A month? A year?'

'Two years.'

'Two years and you still don't know the names of all these members?'

'They're extremely cautious. They use codenames and burner phones and only John knows who they all are. His phone is missing. If we could find it, it will have names and numbers on it,' he said.

'I have it,' she replied flatly. 'It contains the code names. All the numbers are untraceable.'

'With the right technology, we'll be able to trace them.'

'This is bullshit, William. Is this all you have on them?'

He shifted uncomfortably in his chair. 'No. There's a lot more. You're right about the trafficking. The syndicate is involved in ensuring traffickers can move their wares without fear of being stopped. They get paid a percentage for each load that arrives successfully and extra for turning a blind eye and smoothing the passage for these gangs. It isn't only people they move, it's drugs, arms – anything that needs to come into this country.'

'Go on.'

'There's a document charting everything I've discovered: names, dates, times, information on various gang members and who their contacts are in the force.'

'Can I see it?'

'It's encrypted and in a safe place. I can't get to it immediately, but if that's what it takes to convince you that I'm only doing this to bring down John and end the corruption in our midst, then yes, I'll fetch it and show it to you.'

She studied his face. William had fooled her for two years. Even now, she couldn't be sure he was levelling with her.

'Kate, I swear I'm telling you the truth. I've had to work this alone. It's dangerous and I think others who have got too close to the truth have been . . . shall we say, dealt with. You sailed very close to the wind today. You're lucky John isn't around because he'd have ordered those men to kill you. You're very fortunate I've played such a convincing role that I've become accepted as one of them and that your fate was placed in my hands.'

'Really? Because the way I look at it, that decision would only be made by the second in command of this devious mob. Remind me of your codename, William.'

He raised both hands in supplication. 'Beta. But you already knew that.'

'And Alpha?'

'Alpha happens . . . happened . . . to be John's code name.'

'He was Alpha and you Beta. William, what the hell did you get yourself into?'

'You're wrong about me being second in command. While John Dickson was Alpha, the rest of us were assigned names based on the alphabetical order of our surnames, not our order within the syndicate. Chase apparently came first, hence I became Beta. Had my name been Smith or Watson, I would have been given a different code name.'

His body language suggested he was telling the truth. All the same, Kate didn't accept what he was saying. After all, Chase came before Dickson alphabetically. Why would Dickson choose to be Alpha, then distribute names alphabetically to the others?

William must have read her confused expression. 'I know it sounds peculiar but that's what John decided when he distributed the phones. Maybe he would have changed the code names in due course, or when other new members joined the syndicate.'

'When did you all receive these pay-as-you-go phones?' she asked.

'Eighteen months ago.' He steepled his hands together and cleared his throat. 'Okay, here's what I propose. I'll show you all the proof I have of what is going on and, between us, we'll work out how to bring down these people – in exchange for something.'

'I'm listening.'

'I want to know if you killed John Dickson.'

'Why would you think that?'

'Because I have a witness, Digger, the drifter Emma found in the Corbys' garage, who believes he saw you at the reservoir, offloading a body into the back of Bradley Chapman's car; because I believe Bradley Chapman helped you dispose of him; and because there are too many little things that indicate you were culpable. Kate, I've bared my soul to you. For the sake of our friendship, you *must* tell me the truth.'

She wanted so badly to trust William. Dammit! She'd known him for most of her life and she cared about him deeply. He was a second father figure to her. All the same, she didn't dare tell him the whole truth. If she confessed to covering up Dickson's murder, she could face consequences that would end her career.

Dickson's voice mocked her quietly in her head. *'It's over. You haven't got what it takes to cover this up. You are too weak-willed. You should confess everything to Uncle William and get it over with.'*

Dickson's voice became muffled – another drowning it out. Her heart soared at the sound of it. Chris was talking to her.

'Kate, listen to me. You can't let Dickson win. William has told you he will share his information about the syndicate. You have found an ally. Together you can accomplish something I couldn't: unmask these individuals. Do what is right for you. Do it.'

'Kate?' William had edged forward. 'Answer me.'

She blinked, and looked at him, distracted from reality by the realisation that Chris had returned! His voice had come back to help her at this pivotal moment.

'William,' she said, 'I had nothing to do with his death. For what it's worth, I believe he staged everything and has fled.'

'Were you at the reservoir the evening he disappeared?'

'No. I went home. I wasn't feeling great, probably because of the intensity of the investigation into the shootings. I went home and I fell asleep.'

William's chest deflated in front of her eyes as he released a lengthy sigh of relief. 'Thank you and I'm sorry I had to ask you.'

She gave a small smile and shrugged. 'Better to ask than not. Has Digger issued a statement accusing me of being there?'

'Not yet. I was going to collect him tomorrow and take him to the station to make it. To be honest, he didn't want to. He has a strong phobia about towns, buildings – anything that makes him feel trapped.'

He leant forward and held his head in his hands. 'I never wanted to become involved with Dickson. It was the only way I could get information. I became embroiled in a situation I hated. I despise myself for what I've had to do to win his confidence . . . to win *their* confidence. I truly do. I'm glad my time with the force is almost up. You know, Kate, I want a quiet life. I want to be left alone, here, in my home. I want to tend my garden, look after my cats and bees, and try to live with my conscience for whatever time I have left. If we can bring them down, it will help me get through the next few years without loathing myself.'

He rubbed his neck again. 'Look, I have a stinker of a headache and you've not had the easiest of days. Why don't we meet again here in the morning, after I've collected the information? I'll go through everything I've amassed with you then.'

Kate studied William's face. It had taken on a grey pallor. He wasn't faking his pain.

She hadn't intended staying long, anyway. Just long enough to confirm her suspicions. She had somebody else to talk to.

Stanka had responded to her text message earlier, and said she'd be waiting for Kate in Stafford.

'Okay.'

She got to her feet and found herself drawn in a hearty embrace. All the same, she found it difficult to react as enthusiastically, patting him gently on the back before pulling away.

'You haven't a clue how dreadfully concerned I've been about you today,' he said. 'I had no idea you were delving so deeply into the syndicate's business. I wish you'd confided in me. I could have saved you a lot of trouble.'

This was the man who had been her friend and guardian for over two decades. Yet, for all his words and impassioned pleas, she still couldn't fully trust him. Although she wanted things to go back to how they were before Chris died, she didn't for one second regret lying to him about what she had done.

He stepped back, tears in his eyes. 'You've no idea how much this has been weighing on me. Telling you has made me feel so much . . . lighter.'

'Then maybe you should have confided in me before now,' she said, wagging a finger at him.

He hugged her again. This time she returned the squeeze because, in spite of everything, William *was* her family.

After he released her, she noticed his cheeks were stained with tears. 'Off you go,' he said.

Both cats came outside with her, tails high as they paraded in front of the door like two small furry guards. She bent to stroke them, caressing their silken fur.

'Come on, you pair. I know you want to say goodbye to Kate, but you are fully aware you're not allowed out this way. It's too close to the road. You can play out back.'

The affectionate tone made her smile. This was the kind, fatherly man she knew. She turned to him. 'See you in the morning.'

'Make it around seven. I'll have coffee on the stove, and I even think I have some croissants in the freezer. I'll warm them and we can sort out all this mess.'

She wanted to believe what he had told her; nevertheless, suspicion held her back. After recent events, she'd arrived at the point where she trusted absolutely no one. It was hardening her, that much she knew. Where once she'd believed in good, now she was beginning to believe everyone was capable of bad – even her. Especially her.

She climbed into her Audi, her heart numb. Her old self would be astonished at the devious and deceitful person she had become. There was a way to reverse it, though, and if the meeting with Stanka went according to her plans, it would change the course of events.

CHAPTER TWENTY-NINE

DAY FIVE – LATE EVENING

All the tables at the cinema café, Oscar's Bar, were vacant. Kate had picked a time when there were enough screenings that they were unlikely to see anybody but the staff. She bought two colas and chose a seat furthest away from the counter.

She didn't have to wait long before Stanka arrived, her hooded top hiding her face. She crossed the brightly lit room purposefully and slid on to the chair opposite Kate's.

'I can see her?' Her first words were in earnest. When she pushed back her hood, Kate noticed dark circles under her eyes. Under the fluorescent glow, the girl's complexion looked unhealthy, red spots erupted on her chin and her hair was lank. She pushed the drink towards her.

'You don't need to worry about Maja.'

'She was not hurt by the men?'

'No, she says not. She and the others spent most of the time locked in a cellar.'

'I can see her?' she repeated.

'I'll arrange it. You understand, she'll be deported, sent back home?'

'Yes. It's better she is. But I must see her first. She's my baby sister.'

Kate nodded. She understood the bond between sisters. 'Will you return with her?'

'I . . . I don't think so.'

Kate grabbed the girl's cool hands between her own. 'This is no life for you. Farai is dead and it's dangerous on the streets. You have no protection.'

'I can't go back. You see, my mother . . . Maja, everybody . . . They think I am a model.' Her eyes glistened.

'They will understand. If you were my daughter, I would want you to be safe with me, not selling your body on the streets.'

'But I lied. My mother will be angry . . . disgusted. My friends, they will laugh at me. I will have no job there, and no boyfriend . . . ever. I will be called a slut. I will be alone. Here, I have friends. I won't go back.'

Kate squeezed her hands gently. 'At least think about it.'

She shook her head, chin jutting. 'No. I want to stay here. With Nevena. We are going to work in a bar. We have found a flat to share with other girls.'

'You have no visa, no passport.'

'We have jobs now! With the money I can buy a passport.' She pulled her hands away. 'When can I see Maja?'

'Tomorrow morning. I need you to come into the station to make a statement, tell us everything you know about Superintendent Dickson and Rosa.'

'You have the video.'

'That's safe and will be used as evidence but you must tell other officers what you told me, about Rosa, the female officer, Heather, and about being hunted by Superintendent Dickson.'

'Okay. I do this. I will speak to you, yes?'

'I'll be there, but you will need to speak to my officers, Emma and Morgan. They are the ones who rescued your sister.'

'They are good guys?'

Kate smiled. 'Yes, they're very good guys. The best.'

Stanka gave a quick nod. 'Okay.'

'Before you do that, I need your help. It's a very big thing I'm going to ask you. If you do it, we'll both be able to get on with our lives without fear of being hunted down.'

'You saved my sister so yes. What do you want me to do?'

Kate hesitated before speaking. She'd crossed so many lines she no longer knew who she was, yet this would be, she hoped, the final one. She checked nobody was in sight or earshot, leant across the table and explained.

Kate had no sooner left the cinema than her phone rang with news that Ognian, Doncho and Grozdan had been apprehended and were being escorted to the station.

'Anyone injured?' she asked.

'No, ma'am, although the suspects were all carrying firearms. We've bagged those and will have them dropped off at Forensics,' said the sergeant.

It was with relief she floored the accelerator. Despite her concerns, Harriet hadn't been able to warn them. If all went well, she should be able to charge at least one of the trio with murder before the night was out. She rang William, only to discover his phone was switched off, which was understandable given he had looked poorly and had claimed to have a bad headache. He could sit this one out. She and the team could handle the interviews.

Things were beginning to play out once more. Determination and optimism had returned. She would find out exactly what William had uncovered because, regardless of her concerns about his part in this, he was willing to confide in her. William could well have evidence that, once married with her own, would also bring down Harriet. The desire to help topple the remaining members of the syndicate fuelled her body.

'Careful what you wish for.'

She kept her eyes on the road as she spoke. 'Care to expand, Dickson?'

'William is probably going to successfully pull the wool over your eyes. What do you think he's been doing all this time? He's going to take you down.'

'Rubbish. If it weren't for his phone call to the warehouse, I wouldn't be here, so you know where you can shove that thought.'

'Do I detect a note of frustration? You know I'm right. William's a sentimental old fool. He couldn't allow you to be killed; however, he wouldn't think twice about ensuring you faced charges for my death. He has a witness. Regardless of what you may think, he'll use Digger to make a statement and he'll pursue Bradley Chapman until he gets a confession from him. He won't have believed you for a second. He's far too wily for that. I know what he's truly capable of. You don't!'

She drew into the car park at HQ for what felt like the twentieth time that day.

'Keep your opinions to yourself,' she hissed.

Until the men's lawyers turned up, there was little she could do other than ensure she was well prepared for the interview. That the men's weapons had been seized was a bonus, since they could be tested for a match to the cartridges recovered at the murder scenes. Gathering this evidence and checking DNA samples, however, would require time. Fortunately, they could hold the men on several charges, including trafficking.

Now was the time to throw everything they had at the suspects and for it to stick. She needed her team back at work.

Morgan finished the last of the tacos and sat back with a contented sigh. 'That was great. Although you definitely cheated. Takeaways do not count as cooking me a meal.'

'I have a confession. I'm a lousy cook.'

'Now you tell me!'

'I'm great at desserts, though,' she said.

'My favourite part of any meal. What's on offer tonight?'

Emma sat back in her chair and slowly undid the buttons on her blouse, one by one.

'I think I'm going to enjoy dessert,' he said.

'I know you are.'

The sound of her phone ringing shattered the mood. He groaned. 'Don't answer it.'

'It'll be work.'

'It's always bloody work.'

She checked the screen and grimaced. 'Yeah, it's Kate.'

He produced another lengthy groan. 'Not tonight!'

She took the brief call, then began doing up her buttons. 'We need to go back in and prepare for interviews. That trio have been caught and charged.'

Morgan slumped in his chair. 'Are we ever going to get any time together without being interrupted?'

'Maybe when we book some leave.'

He stood up and reached for her as she brushed past him and pulled her into an embrace. She withdrew eventually and stroked his cheek, fingers grazing his stubble. This relationship was going to be tougher than she imagined.

'I'll grab some water.'

'Right behind you,' he said. 'I'll need the toilet before we leave. I know what these marathon interviews can be like. No time for a break.'

As she delved in the fridge for some bottled water, she reflected on the situation. She was keen on Morgan. Really keen, which worried her. She had wanted to ignore the phone call as much as he had.

CHAPTER THIRTY

DAY SIX – SUNDAY, EARLY MORNING

It was just after midnight before Kate and Morgan were able to question the man who had been caught on CCTV near the bottle kilns – Doncho Petrov.

With his arms folded, his biceps looked like they might explode any minute. He stared at Morgan with something akin to hatred in his dark eyes. He'd refused a translator but had accepted a duty lawyer, a jaded man in his late forties, who wore mismatched socks.

'Mr Petrov, can you explain your presence on the towpath behind the bottle kilns on Thursday the twenty-second?' Kate asked for the third time.

'I was taking a walk.'

'Why there? You don't live there.'

He shrugged. 'I like it there.'

Doncho had been continually evasive throughout their questioning. Kate, however, wasn't flustered. At this juncture, it was no more than she expected. The other gang members had been equally slippery, with Grozdan grunting non-committal replies and Ognian offering 'no comment' to every question.

'We know you knew the deceased. Gary Shardlow visited you and the young women you held prisoner at the flats near the bottle kilns.'

He remained unfazed by the questions. 'I don't know any Gary.'

'He was the manager of the blocks of flats, two of which you rented.'

He shrugged.

'His wife is happy to testify that you stayed there on several occasions, and that her husband visited the flats for the purpose of having sex with the girls.'

'She's lying. She is a jealous woman.'

'So, you're saying you don't know Gary?'

'That's right.'

'That's strange because your friend Grozdan Draganov says otherwise. He clearly remembers Gary Shardlow visiting the flat. He also recalls the name of the girl Gary had sex with. In fact, he recalls watching him have sex. And do you know what else he remembers?' She smiled. 'He remembers you were standing next to him, drinking beer and cheering Gary on.'

Doncho looked away, jaw clenched.

'Does that episode ring any bells?'

His lawyer whispered in hushed tones.

'No comment,' said Doncho.

'And what about later that evening, outside the Golden Moon? I believe you shot and killed another man, known as Farai. You'd had dealings with him in the past – sold him some underage girls.'

'I don't know him.'

Kate turned to Morgan. 'Isn't it odd? Mr Petrov here has a terrible memory whereas Mr Draganov's is as clear as a bell.' She faced Doncho again. 'He told us about the girls you sold to Farai.

If the names Stanka, Rosa and Bisera mean nothing to you, they do to him, along with several others.'

Doncho shifted in his chair. The veins in his forearms stood out as he flexed his hands.

Kate continued, 'And do you know what else Mr Draganov told us?'

He stared at her with lizard eyes.

'That you shot Gary. He is willing to testify against you.'

Doncho glanced at his lawyer, who said nothing.

'He also told us that you killed Farai. I believe he is going through the exact details with one of my colleagues at this very moment.'

Doncho muttered something unintelligible under his breath and thumped the table with his fist.

She gave another smile. 'Says you were at the snooker hall when you found out that Farai was going to be at the Golden Moon that night for a meeting and that you headed there after you killed Gary.'

Doncho looked away, nostrils flaring as he breathed quickly.

Kate sent a prepared text message that simply said, 'Now' to Emma, as planned. Once received, Emma was to knock on the door and call Kate out into the corridor as if she wished to speak to her urgently.

The knock came moments later.

'DI Young, could I talk to you?'

Kate halted the recording and left the room, only to return a couple of minutes later and begin stacking her papers together. Morgan took his cue and stood up.

'Where are you going?' Doncho snapped.

'To see Mr Draganov again. It seems his lawyer is keen to cut a deal with us.'

Doncho turned to his lawyer. 'Stop them!'

Kate halted by the door. 'Do you have something you wish to add?'

'Will you deal with me if I tell you exactly what happened?'

'We can discuss that.'

He spoke to his lawyer. 'I want a deal for helping them.'

The lawyer opened his mouth to offer advice, but Doncho had already turned to Kate.

'Grozdan is lying.'

Kate feigned puzzlement. 'About what?'

'I didn't kill both men.'

She cocked her head. 'We haven't time to mess about. We'll be back later.'

'No! He's lying. *He* killed Farai. Grozdan killed Farai.'

His lawyer hissed at him, but Doncho waved away his concerns.

Kate returned to her seat. 'Go on.'

'Ognian gave instructions to have Farai killed.'

'Ognian?'

'Yes. He had orders from the top boss.'

'Who is this top boss?'

He shrugged. 'I don't know. We were ordered to kill them both. Yes, I heard Farai was going to be at the Golden Moon that night, but I passed that information on to Ognian, who arranged for Grozdan to make the hit.'

'And you?'

He shrugged.

'Did you kill Gary?'

He looked at his lawyer, who shook his head as a warning.

Doncho fell silent again.

Kate continued, 'And you both obey Ognian, without question?'

He didn't reply.

'Not to worry. I'm sure Grozdan will fill us in on those details.'

374

The mention of his friend's name worked again.

'There is no choice,' he said in a matter-of-fact tone.

'Mr Petrov, you are confessing to the murder of Gary Shardlow?'

The lawyer piped up, 'You don't have to answer that. DI Young, you are out of line here.'

She gave a curt nod. The wretched lawyer had woken up at last. It was time to go to work on the others. Now they'd got this much information, it shouldn't take long to squeeze them.

'I want a deal. I'll confess I shot him if you give me a deal.'

His lawyer spoke in low, urgent whispers. Doncho shook his head.

'I killed him because I had to. You understand that?'

'No, Mr Petrov, I don't. You had a choice.'

'No. I had *no* choice. None of us have.'

Kate stood again.

'So, will I get my deal?'

'I'll check with my superiors. Mr Petrov, you will remain in custody for the time being, while we continue our questioning. An officer will be along shortly to escort you to a cell.'

In the corridor, she leant against the wall with a satisfied sigh. 'That went much better than I expected. I didn't think our ploy would work so well.'

'How did you know all that stuff about the girls and Gary? We haven't yet spoken to Grozdan,' asked Morgan.

'Stanka told me what went on. You have no idea what they put her and the other girls through. We'll let him stew overnight and talk to him again in the morning before we turn them both over to DI Khatri's team.'

'I take it you're not going to deal with Doncho?' said Morgan.

'You're joking! I want him and the other pair to get exactly what they deserve. One down, two to go. With a bit of luck, we might even finish in time to grab some shut-eye.'

She marched down the corridor to the next interview room, where Emma, having played her part, was now waiting in the interview room with Grozdan. Kate slipped into the seat next to her. By first light, they'd probably have charged all three men, then she would visit William. Things were on the up. She gave Grozdan a smile.

'Hello, Mr Draganov. I've just been having an interesting chat with your friend, Mr Petrov . . .'

CHAPTER
THIRTY-ONE
DAY SIX – MORNING

Even after only two hours' sleep, Kate was ready for action, keen for Stanka's statement to be taken and to find out what William had uncovered during his time working with the syndicate.

Kate had always found William's house to be homely – a place that welcomed her back each time she visited. While there was only a low box hedge and small lawn to the front, the rear boasted a lengthy garden, usually awash with plants and blooms, all cared for by William.

She was about to ring the doorbell when she spied one of the cats hiding under the hedge, its ears flat to its head. She coaxed it out and scooped it into her arms, recognising it to be Wayan. The creature mewled pathetically. It was strange for the animal to be out here. William had placed a cat flap in the kitchen door to ensure they used the rear garden and had trained them to avoid the front and the road that passed by it.

'Are you hurt?' she asked, checking its paws and fur. There was no evidence of it having been in a fight, yet it was clearly upset. She stroked it as she spoke. 'We'll get you inside to your dad.' She rang the bell. William didn't answer. She heard the other cat miaowing inside.

'William!'

There was no reply. The door was locked. Holding on to Wayan, she reached for her phone and rang William's number. From where she stood, she could hear the ringtone, the music to a 70s police drama, *The Sweeney*. He didn't pick up.

She carried the cat to the gate that led into the back garden, where she tried the kitchen door. It too was locked. Alarm bells sounded in her head. William had been feeling ill. What if he'd had a stroke or a heart attack? She clung to the cat, more for reassurance for herself than for the animal. Animals could be incredibly sensitive and Wayan had been conveying that something was amiss. She knocked on the window and called out William's name. A sickening panic rose as she approached the French windows leading into the room where she had been sitting only the evening before. She tried the handle and, when the door opened, stepped cautiously inside. She lowered the cat to the carpet. It raced through the room and into the hall.

'William?'

The sense that something was wrong was all consuming. She had an idea of what to expect before she saw it but, even so, she was not mentally prepared for the sight of her dear friend lying on his back in a pool of blood.

Kate was utterly numb. She'd stared at the body for a good few minutes before checking for a pulse, a pointless task. William was cold. He'd been dead for hours. Although she called it in, she felt unable to ring Emma or Morgan. Talking to them, sharing their dismay, would make this feel real. For the time being, it didn't. She couldn't afford to break down. While she was running on adrenalin and lacking emotion, she should take advantage of the situation, secure the crime scene, make notes, film it.

She ensured the cats were shut in the kitchen, their bowls filled with milk, then grabbed her murder bag from the car. Suitably attired in a forensic suit, she began recording the scene.

'The windows appear to be unlocked. There is no evidence of a break-in. Victim . . .' She swallowed. 'The victim is in a supine position. There appears to be one shot to the head.' Why had he taken his life? Was it because he'd lied about his part in the syndicate and was up to his neck in corruption? Was it because she'd pushed him over the edge? Her heart spluttered like a dying flame. She took a moment to control it.

She crouched beside his body, noted the position of the gun and paused. The gun was in his right hand. The scene was all wrong. This was a set-up. William hadn't shot himself. He was left-handed. The revelation rocked her. She sat on her haunches. Somebody had murdered her friend.

She was about to stand up again when a glint caught her eye. She focussed on what she initially thought was a piece of glass, then, zooming her camera lens on to it, held her breath.

'There appears to be an item close to the body.' She zoomed closer still until it was clear what it was – a small silver butterfly clasp, used to hold earrings in position. An image of Harriet fiddling with her earrings in the washroom, ensuring they were secure, sprung to mind. Could it be possible? There was one way to find out. Kate knew something about William that others did not, and it would help her prove exactly who had killed him.

◆ ◆ ◆

With William's house teeming with forensic officers, and his pets temporarily housed at a cat sanctuary, Kate returned to the station. The chief constable had instructed an outside team to take over the investigation, but as far as Kate was concerned, it would be an open-and-shut case.

Although news of William's passing had got back to the station, nobody yet knew any details. She passed through the foyer, to be greeted by sombre faces. What had happened to William hadn't fully sunk in. She knew when it did, she would be bulldozed. For now, she had to work during this window of opportunity, while she was sane and raging inside.

She gathered her team in the office and shut the door.

'I don't know what to say,' Morgan began.

Kate lifted a hand towards him. 'Please don't say anything. I appreciate how you all are feeling, I honestly do, but we aren't doing this emotional stuff right now. Save it for when we have his killer in our cells. DCI Chase was murdered, and we're going to present a watertight case to those officers who will be taking charge of the investigation into it.

'I've ordered a rush job on the butterfly clip I found. There'll be DNA on it. Forensics are checking the crime scene for DNA and any evidence I may have missed, but regardless of that, this is what will determine the outcome.'

She held up William's phone. 'DCI Chase had a pet camera hidden in the bookcase. He used it to keep an eye on his cats while he was out. He bought the most expensive version so he could also play with his pets wherever he was, by shining a laser dot for them to chase after. It has night vision, but it also records 24/7. Can you link it up to your computer, Jamie, and download the information from last night?'

Jamie deftly attached the mobile and tapped at his keyboard. 'Do we know the code for the app?'

'It's WayanandMade,' said Kate, who remembered laughing when William had told her he used the same password for everything because he couldn't remember individual ones. It wasn't long before the screen flickered into life, and they could see into William's sitting room. The scene was unnerving – white-suited officers poring over every item in his room.

'Can you rewind, please?' she said. 'To when I was there.'

Jamie paused it to reveal Kate, in protective clothing, standing over his body.

Emma placed a hand on her shoulder. 'I'm so sorry, Kate.'

'I'd rather I found him than anybody else,' said Kate. 'Okay, Jamie, take it back now, to when he was shot.'

On screen, a speeded-up Kate exited the room, leaving William sprawled on the carpet. A cat, Made, wandered into the room and circled the body before retreating again. The room went dark, and the night-vision camera kicked in. The image didn't change until a dark figure in a hooded coat walked backwards into the room via the French doors. Jamie speeded the footage up so quickly no images could be discerned until he stopped it and allowed it to roll in real time. Nothing happened for a while, then the sitting-room door opened. William entered the room first, followed by his assailant. The person had their back to the camera but from William's expression it was clear they were arguing. He waved his hand, then his face changed. A look of horror replaced the anger. He lifted up palms, lips moving. His eyes grew large. The person stepped forwards and fired into the side of his head. He fell backwards. Emma let out a gasp and Kate clung to the desk. His assailant crouched down and placed the gun in William's hand. Kate noticed they were wearing black gloves. The killer stood back up and turned to face the camera.

Then Harriet Khatri pulled her hood over her head and departed via the French doors.

◆ ◆ ◆

The briefing room was packed with grim faces and red eyes. Both Kate's team and Harriet's had squashed in to listen to Kate.

'This has been an almighty shock for all of us. DCI Chase, well, I don't need to tell you how well respected he was. I know you want answers, and that you want to avenge his death. I know I do. Passionately. However, that can't happen. An external murder squad is on its way and will lead the investigation. Fresh eyes. No personal involvement. Whether you disagree or not is irrelevant. I, for one, think it is the right move. We can't have the investigation into his death clouded by emotions.

'DI Khatri has been arrested and suspended from all duties pending investigation. Operation Moonbeam, however, will continue under the guidance of DI Ali Rind, who has been brought in from Manchester HQ.' She pointed out the stocky man beside her. 'I know some of you have worked with him before. Welcome aboard, DI Rind.'

There were a few mumbled greetings, which he acknowledged with a nod and a small wave.

'The three traffickers currently being held are available for questioning. They have already been charged with several offences; however, don't let that stop you from having a field day. Having spoken to them myself, it is my belief they have knowledge that might lead to bigger fish, so, forgive the pun, but grill them well.'

She got some half-smiles from her audience.

'Our investigation into the disappearance of Superintendent Dickson will also continue, so I know it is with heavy hearts but it will be business as usual. I completely understand if any of you feel you aren't up to it.

'I've been informed that every one of us is to be offered counselling. A specialised team will be here within the hour, and I suggest we all speak to them. It's been a difficult time and losing a colleague, especially one as . . .' She cleared her throat. 'As well liked as DCI Chase, is rough. We haven't yet arranged a date for a memorial service, but you can rest assured there will be one and any donations you kindly make will be going to the cats' rescue home.' Her voice faltered again, so she dug her nails into her palms to prevent the emotion from overwhelming her.

'Remember, my door is *always* open. Thank you, everyone. Let's do DCI Chase proud and go catch some bad guys.'

Once Harriet's squad had departed, she gathered her own team around her. 'I meant what I said. If you need to take any time off, do it.'

Emma blew her nose. Even though her puffy face told a different story she said, 'I'm fine.'

'Yeah. Me too,' said Morgan. 'I can't believe it, you know? It's like we've dropped into some parallel universe.'

'Jamie, you're very quiet,' said Kate.

'No. I'm staying. I . . . I can't get my head around it either.'

'I don't understand how DI Khatri could possibly pull a gun on—' Emma faltered, dropping her head to hide runaway tears. Morgan rubbed her shoulders.

'Hey, it's okay.'

'No, it isn't. That fucking bitch. She shot him in cold blood! She wants stringing up!'

'She'll get what she deserves,' said Morgan.

'She better had.' Emma swiped at the tears. 'I'm okay. Sorry, Kate.'

Kate looked at each of them in turn. 'Nobody is feeling this pain more than me. I don't need to tell you what DCI Chase meant to me, but we must remain focussed on our current investigation, into Superintendent Dickson's disappearance. The way I look at it, we solve this, we do William proud. He tasked us with this because he believed in us. I want that faith to be justified, so Emma and Morgan, would you please take Stanka's statement? The duty officer informed me she's waiting at reception. Come on. We can do this. For William.'

Emma sniffed again, then nodded. The pair of them left. Kate noticed Morgan swing an arm around Emma and squeeze her. It was good they had each other. Colleagues who had your back were precious.

'Guv? What do you want me to do?' Jamie asked.

What she wanted to do was find out the truth about what had been going on between him and Harriet. Whether he was working with the syndicate. If he was a mole. What he knew about the other members.

Yet she was overcome with weariness. Why had this become her quest? She wasn't an avenging warrior, only a detective who had stumbled across something that was too much for one person. It had been too big for William as well, and cost him his life. Somewhere hidden among his possessions was vital information about the remaining syndicate members and there was nothing she could do about it. If she rattled cages, she would be in danger, and this time William wouldn't be there to save her hide.

'There's a stack of paperwork on your desk that I need sorting before this evening.'

'No problem.' He stood up, swallowed hard and extended his hand to shake hers. 'Guv, I'm truly sorry for your loss.'

After he'd gone, she remained frozen to the chair. Jamie's thoughtfulness had inched open the door to her emotions and she'd had to quickly jam it shut before they escaped. Her hands trembled. She mustn't think about William, or she would lose reason altogether and collapse in a sobbing heap. She scraped back her chair. There were a few questions she needed answering and hang the consequences.

Harriet was being held in one of the interview rooms. She jumped to her feet as soon as Kate walked in.

'What the fuck is going on?' she asked.

'You're under investigation for the murder of DCI William Chase.'

'You know this is all bullshit. Murder! That's madness. I meant, what is happening upstairs? Can I go home? I need to speak to my husband and get this sorted.'

'We're waiting for an outside team to arrive. They'll answer any questions you might have.'

'Any questions? For crying out loud, I already admitted to visiting William last evening to discuss Operation Moonbeam. I must have lost my butterfly then, but as for killing him, that's ludicrous.'

'Harriet, there's video evidence of you shooting him.'

'There can't be! I didn't! I didn't shoot him.'

For a split second, Kate almost believed her. However, the person in the hoodie had definitely been Harriet.

She shook her head. 'You'll have to talk to the team about that.'

'Kate, listen to me. I didn't kill him. The video is a fake. It's been tampered with.'

She couldn't listen to this crap any longer. 'I'm not heading the investigation!'

'Why are you being like this?'

'Like what?'

'Callous.'

'Can we stop the games?! Why did you go to a warehouse in Fenton yesterday afternoon?'

'I'm being accused of murder and you're here to quiz me about that?' She turned away. 'Fuck off, Kate. It's none of your business what I was doing there.'

'It is when I get jumped there, am tied up and have a gun pointed at my head. A gun that the kidnappers fully intended using until they were called off.'

'What? You're kidding me.' The expression of horror mingled with confusion was back on her face. Harriet was proving to be as expert at acting as Dickson.

'Do I look like I'm joking?'

'I don't understand,' said Harriet. 'Are you telling me you were attacked at the warehouse?'

'Yes. I followed you to the warehouse. When I went inside, somebody knocked me out then tied me up.'

'I've no idea what you're talking about. Why did you follow me?'

'You know why, Harriet. Stop pretending. You're a member of the syndicate, known as Iota, aren't you?'

'I don't understand a word you're saying. Has that bang to your head given you concussion?' Her eyes sparked. 'For your information, I received a text from one of my contacts asking for an urgent meeting. He lives near the abandoned warehouse. He always insists I park out of sight, behind the warehouses, and meet in an alleyway by the flats. That way, he's less likely to be pegged for a snitch. He said he had information for me, but he didn't turn up and he's not been answering his phone since. I collected my car and came back to the station.'

Kate wasn't buying her story. She'd had plenty of time to make up an excuse and had probably worked on it before setting Kate up.

'It's convenient that your source can't back up your story.'

Muscles worked in Harriet's jaw. 'You can't prove I'm lying.'

Kate saw red. The image of William lying on the floor filled her mind. She was certain Harriet had killed him either because he'd insisted Kate be freed, or to prevent him from spilling the beans to Kate about the syndicate.

'Tell me about the syndicate.'

'I don't know what the hell you're talking about.'

'I think you do.'

'Back the fuck off, Kate!' Harriet bared her teeth. The room was cloying with tension and rage. Kate shook off the anger, drew deep breaths. She lifted both hands in obeyance. Harriet gripped the back of a chair.

'I can't stay here. I have a family,' said Harriet. 'I want to speak to my husband. He's a lawyer. I'm entitled to a phone call.'

Kate shook her head. 'We can't do anything until the team arrives. Sorry.'

'No, you're not fucking sorry! You've had it in for me ever since I took over your old team. You're a jealous, half-crazed bitch. Don't think I haven't seen you spying on me, watching my every move. You're jealous because officers you once oversaw now respect me. I saw your face when I was speaking to Jamie in the foyer. You were green!'

'No. I wasn't jealous,' said Kate calmly.

'Sure you were. Were you frightened I'd convince him to join my unit?'

'What was in the package you gave him?'

Harriet strode to the far side of the room. 'Are you for real? I'm being investigated for murder! Not any murder, but of a senior colleague, and you're babbling on about a package I gave your officer.'

'Humour me,' said Kate.

'You know, I always thought you'd tipped over the edge after Chris died, now I'm convinced of it. You're raving! I gave Jamie a book.'

'What sort of book?'

'Oh, for . . . !' Harriet shoved the chair hard against the table. 'Does it matter?'

'What book?' Kate said firmly.

'It's for children who are expecting a new brother or sister. It's a sort of self-help book. My cousin wrote it. I gave him a copy because he told me his little boy was playing up. He and his wife thought it was because he was jealous of the new baby. Jealous. Like you! Now unless you're going to offer me some sort of support or let me ring my husband, get the fuck out of here.'

Kate didn't move. Had she really got it wrong about Jamie? A voice in her head spoke. *Don't believe anyone. Find the documents and all will become clear.* It wasn't Dickson or Chris she heard this time, but William.

Giving Harriet a tight smile, Kate left the room.

◆ ◆ ◆

Kate returned to the office, where Jamie was ploughing through the work as requested.

'Jamie, I just heard Zach's been having trouble getting used to the idea of having a new baby brother or sister. Sorry to hear that.'

'Oh, that's sorted. Actually, it was DI Khatri who helped me out with a book for kids going through the same thing as him. Sophie and I took turns to read it to him. He understands now that the baby isn't a threat, that he'll be able to play with it when it's older and help look after it. He's even put one of his old toys in the cot, ready for when the baby comes home.'

'What's the book called?'

'*It's My Baby Too.*'

Unless Harriet and Jamie had coordinated their stories beforehand, it appeared her explanation regarding the package was true.

'You can't trust a word she says, Kate. Look how long John managed to operate without suspicion.'

She listened to William's quiet voice in her head and set about her own paperwork. For now, she would set aside her quest into rooting out syndicate members. However, if all had gone as she and Stanka had agreed, she would soon be free to take up the challenge again. All she had to do was wait. Jamie was now on the office phone and called across, 'The chief constable wants to see you immediately.'

She rose again, wondering what it could be that he wanted to discuss with her. It couldn't be anything bad surely, could it?

◆ ◆ ◆

When she returned from her meeting, Morgan and Emma were waiting. Both seemed sideswiped by what they had discovered.

'Stanka has just told us the superintendent is dead. She also knows who killed him,' said Morgan.

Kate had been expecting this news. She and Stanka had talked in detail about the statement she would give, rehearsing until the girl was answer perfect. 'No! Who killed him?'

Morgan was aghast. 'Farai! Can you believe it? That sodding pimp was behind his murder.'

'I don't understand. Why? What possessed him to kill a police officer?' She marvelled at her ability to bluff, especially at this time of extreme stress and sadness. The decision to make Stanka complicit in her lies in order to deflect suspicion from her was not one she had made lightly, and she still wasn't sure how well it would sit with her over the coming weeks and months. It did, however, mean she would be free to take on the syndicate. William and Chris would be with her on that, and with them by her side, she would learn to cope with the duplicity.

Kate was now running on emotional fumes. William's death had not yet fully registered with her. She did not dare think about how she would feel when it did. For the time being, she was carrying out her duties as would be expected.

Emma stepped in. 'It leads back to the murder at the Maddox Club. The newspaper's been telling it straight. The information they've been printing came from Stanka. She wanted everyone to know how corrupt Superintendent Dickson was. And it's not simply hearsay. She has video evidence to support her claims. The super was complicit in covering up that boy's murder last year. Ever since, he has been on the hunt for those people who could bring him down: Farai, because he supplied the club with the sex-workers; Rosa and Stanka because they were witnesses to what happened. Stanka is positive Superintendent Dickson killed Rosa with an overdose of GHB. Certain that he and the girls would eventually be caught and murdered, Farai orchestrated a meeting at the reservoir supposedly to trade Stanka and the video for his life. It was all a set-up. He went along armed with the gun we found, shot the super, then disposed of his body at Grange Farm. He staged everything else to make it appear as if the superintendent had taken off.'

Kate shook her head in mock disbelief. 'Bloody hell! Why would he go to such extremes?'

'He was thorough. He didn't want anything to lead back to him,' said Emma.

'Were there any accomplices to his murder?'

'Not according to Stanka. Farai might have had help, but if he did, Stanka doesn't know of anyone else who might be involved.'

Kate let out a sigh. 'Incredible! Do we believe the girl?'

'No reason not to,' said Morgan. 'She's made a detailed statement without any hesitation. Seemed certain to me. What do you think, Emma?'

'She was sure about everything. And very calm. I believed her.'

'Then, we'll take her at her word. Her allegations will be thoroughly investigated in due course. We've done our part. We know where to find the super. Have you requested a team be sent to the farm?' asked Kate.

Emma nodded. 'Forensics are on their way. It's a pig farm so we're not holding out a great deal of hope of finding the superintendent.'

Kate screwed up her face. 'You mean—'

'I'm afraid so,' said Morgan. 'Farai fed the body to the animals.'

'Ugh!'

'We might still find evidence there to support Stanka's claim. By the way, she wants to know if she can have ten minutes with her sister.'

'Yes, I think we can arrange that,' said Kate.

Morgan blew out his cheeks. 'What an absolute fucker of a day! I can't believe we were working for somebody up to his neck in shit. What was wrong with him?'

'Sometimes power goes to people's heads,' said Kate.

Morgan let out a derisory snort. 'His fucking well exploded with it. It's a good thing DCI Chase didn't know about this. It would have broken him. They were friends.'

'It would have,' Kate said softly.

CHAPTER THIRTY-TWO

DAY SIX – AFTERNOON

Stanka hugged her sister for the final time, planting a kiss on her forehead. Kate observed them through the window, understanding the pain they were experiencing. Stanka, determined to remain in the UK, had struck a deal in exchange for the information she'd given. She had, however, been insistent that her sister be flown back to Bulgaria and Maja, along with the other girls who had made the journey together, would be deported within days.

The two held each other's hands, unable to say goodbye, yet knowing they had to part. Eventually, Stanka pulled away and stumbled to her feet. Without looking back, she made for the door and burst into the corridor, where she pressed her back to the wall, head down and sobbed. Kate placed an arm around her shoulders and soothed her.

'You'll see her again. When you get that passport, you will be able to go home and visit.'

The sobs turned to sniffs. 'Yes. Yes. I will.'

They walked along the corridor side by side. 'Thank you,' said Kate. 'For . . . you know what for.'

'You saved my sister. Dickson was a very bad man. Farai was already dead. I see no problem.'

'You will have to tell this version again in court.'

'I can do that. Don't worry. I will not change what I told Emma and Morgan. Farai shot Superintendent Dickson at the reservoir. Farai told me exactly what he planned on doing and told me to take my story and the video to the newspapers so everyone would learn what a corrupt man Superintendent Dickson was.'

Kate smiled at the girl's fierce determination.

'Is somebody coming to collect you, or do you need me to arrange transport for you?'

'Nevena is coming. We are going shopping.' She wiped tears from her cheeks.

'If there's anything I can do, ring me. You have my number.'

'Yes. And if you want a good meal, you come to the restaurant. And Bradley too.'

'I spoke to him earlier. He was happy to hear you're safe.'

'He is a good man.'

'Yes, he is,' Kate said, the memory of the brief meeting still clear in her mind . . .

Kate draws up next to the Land Rover. Bradley is standing by the garage, wearing a pair of old trousers and an olive jumper.

'I hope that's for gardening,' she asks, pointing at the spade in his hand.

'Yes. I'm tidying up for a viewing tomorrow. Hope it sells. I'm sick of the place. So, why the visit?'

'I just wanted to say thank you.'

'No need. We did what we had to do.'

'And update you.'

'Stanka's okay, then?'

'She's fine. She cut a deal, so she won't be deported and she's getting back on her feet.'

'She's a plucky kid. And what about you? How are you?'

'I'm okay too.'

'Well, you've got grit and determination as well.'

'I don't know if our paths will cross again,' she says.

'Without being rude, let's hope not, eh?'

She smiles. 'I appreciate what you did.'

'Me? Didn't do a thing,' he replies and winks. His phone rings. 'That'll be Gwen checking up on me. I'd better take it. Goodbye, Kate.'

'Bye, Bradley.'

◆ ◆ ◆

'And his wife too,' said Stanka. 'Maybe they can both come to the restaurant. You tell him.'

'I shall,' said Kate.

'I liked them.' Stanka aimed for a smile.

Kate returned it. They walked into the foyer, where Stanka gave up her visitor's pass. Kate spotted a young woman standing outside.

'I think Nevena is already here.'

'Yes, that's her.'

'Goodbye, Stanka.'

The girl faltered, then threw her arms around Kate, giving her a brief hug before withdrawing. 'Goodbye, Kate.'

Kate watched the girl head outside, where Nevena took hold of her hand and, hanging on to it, led her away.

Kate made for the washroom, where she rested her head against the large mirror. Seeing the sisters together had been the trigger for the swirling surge of emotions she'd been suppressing ever since she'd discovered William's body. She had no power to switch off the mountain of tears that leaked from her eyes, or the convulsing sobs that felled her until she became a curled-up ball, huddled against the wall. Pain speared her chest, making it impossible to breathe. Her father, Chris and now William were all gone. Without them, who was she? Nobody. A soulless, empty shell of a person. There was nothing left to live for.

The sobbing became uncontrollable, so loud and raw she was unaware of the door opening or Emma racing to her side. She did, however, feel arms surrounding her, a voice telling her it would be okay and to let it all out. She couldn't halt the tears, but Emma's presence was comforting, soothing, like a mother with a baby. Emma kept up a steady monologue, and she let herself be held until the sobs abated. Maybe she wasn't as alone as she believed.

EPILOGUE

Chief Constable Atwell jumped from his chair as soon as Kate entered his office and made sweeping gestures towards the seat opposite. 'Sit down. Please sit down.'

An auburn-haired woman, with striking features in a neatly pressed uniform, nodded in her direction.

'Kate, I'd like to introduce you to Superintendent Bree O'Sullivan, who will be replacing John Dickson.'

'Pleased to meet you,' said Kate.

'Lovely to meet you at last. I've been hearing grand things about you. How are you doing? I was terribly sorry to hear about DCI Chase.'

The voice was melodic, a soft Irish accent, and the smile genuine, producing crinkles around her sparkling emerald eyes.

Kate could do no more than mutter, 'I'm doing okay, thanks.' The hole in her soul couldn't be filled with platitudes, no matter how genuine they were.

'So, Kate,' boomed Atwell. 'As you can imagine, there's going to be a major shake-up here. In the wake of John Dickson's apparent misdemeanours, and the murder of DCI William Chase, we have a fight on our hands to win back the people's trust. There's a huge amount of controversy surrounding Harriet Khatri which isn't going to die down any time soon, especially not after the sensational spread in the *Gazette* last week, and the fact the case has made national news. Our media team is continuing to mitigate the ramifications of the articles and Bree here is part of the new charm offensive.' He gave a hearty smile in the woman's direction.

'She's agreed to give several interviews with a number of journalists, and I shall be holding another press conference later today to announce her position.' He double tapped the leather arms of his chair. 'Which brings me on to the reason for calling you in. William held you in very high regard, justifiably it would seem. We have all been incredibly impressed by you, Kate. Over the last few weeks, you have not only apprehended a serial killer but have worked investigations resulting in the arrest of a small gang of people traffickers and solved four associated murders.' He hesitated after the last statement, blinked and seemingly had to regather his thoughts.

'Erm, well, all of that is outstanding. We are not only impressed but very proud of you and your officers. To that end, I would like to offer you the temporary rank of DCI with the intention of making that a permanent position in the near future.'

Kate was lost for words.

'Congratulations, DCI Young,' said Bree, with a tilt of her head and a smile.

'Er, thank you, ma'am. Thank you, sir.'

'Once you've brought Bree up to speed and completed all that tedious paperwork that overburdens us all, I want you to take some proper leave.'

'I just took three days off.'

'Three days! After what happened, that's insufficient. See, Bree, I told you she was dedicated.' He gave Kate another smile. 'No, I know how very upsetting recent events have been. Especially for you. I understand you were very close to William. You need to take ten days at least, get away from here. Maybe travel abroad and grab some sunrays. You can't work yourself into the ground. I simply won't allow it.'

'Yes, sir.'

'As I mentioned, there are to be major changes and as we will be short of two DIs, I intend promoting DS Donaldson and DS Meredith to acting DIs. Should they agree, they will be expected to take the necessary examinations, but I see no reason why they wouldn't both pass those with flying colours. I'd also like to offer DC Webster the next step up to DS. I think that's a promotion long overdue, especially in light of his brave attempt to apprehend a suspect and save lives. Do you agree?'

'Yes. I agree wholeheartedly.'

'Excellent. Right, I'll let them all know in person, and if you could join Bree and me later today, for the press conference, I'll pass on the good news to the media. I think you are exactly what this force needs, Kate. The public looks to officers like you. Congratulations.'

He stood and held out his hand. She shook it.

Back outside, she waited for euphoria to wash over her, or at least a flicker of delight at the news. She was pleased for her team, but where there should have been some joy, there was nothing but a void.

The reason for this lack of enthusiasm was obvious to her: she'd only been promoted so Atwell could save face. She was to be his poster girl – brave Kate who followed in her father's footsteps, whose husband was brutally murdered, who recovered the body of her mentor and single-handedly found his killer and yet who continues to fight to make the community a safer place for all. Atwell would parade her and fresh-faced, wholesome Bree in front of the cameras, to dupe the public into believing he'd brought in new brooms, yet not much would change. She and her teams would keep fighting crime and, behind the scenes, the remaining members of the syndicate would regroup and find ways to continue their operations.

Morgan, Emma and Jamie had all been granted leave. They would be surprised and thrilled when they learned of their promotions. She had every confidence in two of her officers, the third less so. She'd seesawed between trusting and disbelieving Jamie. He was either the enthusiastic innocent he always portrayed or as good an actor as Dickson. His response about the book had been smoothly delivered, his explanations to why he'd been talking to Harriet plausible, and still a nagging voice warned her to watch her back while he was around.

'Find the document.'

William's voice in her head was that of an old friend, somebody she could always turn to. She knew all the imagined voices were simply her conscience coming alive, products of extreme emotions, and they no longer startled her or seemed odd. Chris's had been born out of a sorrow so profound it wounded her very soul, Dickson's out of guilt and William's out of loss. In the real world, Kate only had Tilly to turn to. In her mind, she had Chris and William.

Stanka hadn't wavered from her statement and stood by her story about Dickson. The GHB Kate had spied in his bathroom had been recovered, adding credence to the girl's allegations that her friend, Rosa, had been murdered by him. Forensics attended the pig farm and found microscopic remains containing DNA that matched Dickson's, supporting Stanka's claim that Farai had killed him. She wasn't concerned about Digger. He had no reason to make waves. More to the point, his phobia would keep him well away from HQ and police officers.

When the dust settled, she would return to William's house and hunt for the missing document. Once found, she might begin to dismantle what was left of the syndicate. Her phone lit up with a message from Tilly.

How's it going?

She replied.

Got some news for you.

Thought I'd tell it to you in person.

I'm coming over for a short break.

XX

With a gentle sigh, Kate acknowledged that this felt like a new beginning. One she should embrace. With her promotion would come fresh responsibilities and the opportunity to do a lot of good. The past shouldn't be swept away, but she would learn to live with it. It was the best possible outcome.

It felt strange to be in the office without the sound of keyboards tapping or calls being made or chit-chat among the others. This room would be reassigned, and she would probably move into William's old office, a thought that wasn't as unpleasant as she imagined. Being there, she would feel close to him. Her desk was festooned with paperwork. On the top of the pile lay a typewritten envelope, addressed to her. She opened it and pulled out some photographs.

The images of the reservoir had been taken at night, grainy black and white pictures, shot with a long lens.

In the first, a woman wearing cycling bottoms and a top was baring her teeth. She appeared to be swinging for a man. In the second, the pair were grappling. The man wore a look of surprise. The last photograph showed the man slumped on the ground, a dark stain on his chest, while the woman stood over him. The faces, in this last image especially, were clear. She was looking at photographs of her and Dickson.

The second hand on the wall clock turned, each movement accompanied by a soft click. Kate was trapped in time, unable to think or move. The photographs tumbled from her hands and floated to the ground.

Maybe this time, her luck had finally run out.

ACKNOWLEDGEMENTS

As ever, this book would not be in your hands if it wasn't for my agent Amy Tannenbaum, who has guided me over the entire DI Kate Young series.

The Thomas & Mercer team have been invaluable in kicking this novel into shape. I am particularly grateful to everyone who has played a role in bringing *A Truth for a Truth* to publication. Thanks to my sharp-eyed editors: Melissa Hyder and Ian Critchley. I marvel at your dedication and enthusiasm.

As always special thanks go to Victoria Haslam and Russel McLean. You are my dream developmental editing team.

Thanks also go to the amazing book bloggers and reviewers who always champion my efforts and boost my morale with their effusive praise. I honestly can't thank you enough.

Heartfelt thanks to you, my readers. I love interacting with you on social media and via email. Thank you for all your genuine support and kind messages.

And the greatest debt of gratitude is to Mr Grumpy, who continues to support my writing dreams and doesn't complain when I am so lost in the process that I forget all about cooking and housework.

ABOUT THE AUTHOR

Carol Wyer is a *USA Today* bestselling author and winner of the People's Book Prize Award. Her crime novels have sold over one million copies and have been translated into nine languages.

A move from humour to the 'dark side' in 2017, with the introduction of popular DI Robyn Carter in *Little Girl Lost*, proved that Carol had found her true niche.

February 2021 saw the release of the first in the much-anticipated new series featuring DI Kate Young. *An Eye for an Eye* was chosen as a Kindle First Reads and became the #1 bestselling book on Amazon UK and Amazon Australia.

Carol has had articles published in national magazines such as *Woman's Weekly*, and has been featured in *Take a Break, Choice, Yours* and *Woman's Own* and in *HuffPost*. She's also been interviewed on numerous radio shows, and on Sky and *BBC Breakfast* television.

She currently lives on a windy hill in rural Staffordshire with her husband, Mr Grumpy . . . who is very, very grumpy.

To learn more, go to www.carolwyer.co.uk, subscribe to her YouTube channel, or follow her on Twitter: https://twitter.com/carolewyer

Follow the Author on Amazon

If you enjoyed this book, follow Carol Wyer on Amazon to be notified when she releases a new book!

To do this, please follow these instructions:

Desktop:

1) Search for the author's name on Amazon or in the Amazon App.
2) Click on the author's name to arrive on their Amazon page.
3) Click the 'Follow' button.

Mobile and Tablet:

1) Search for the author's name on Amazon or in the Amazon App.
2) Click on one of the author's books.
3) Click on the author's name to arrive on their Amazon page.
4) Click the 'Follow' button.

Kindle eReader and Kindle App:

If you enjoyed this book on a Kindle eReader or in the Kindle App, you will find the author 'Follow' button after the last page.